The Wives' Tale

Alix Wilber

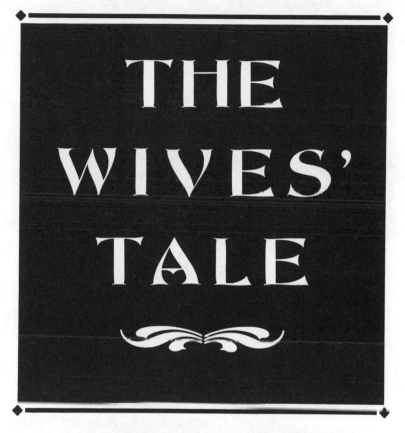

THE WIVES' TALE

W. W. NORTON & COMPANY
New York • London

Printed in the United States of America.

The text of this book is composed in Bembo,
with the display set in Abbott Old Style.
Composition and manufacturing by the Haddon Craftsmen, Inc.
Book design by Charlotte Staub.
First Edition.

Library of Congress Cataloging-in-Publication Data
Wilber, Alix.
The wives' tale / by Alix Wilber.
p.   cm.
I. Title.
PS3573.I3878W58 1991
813'.54—dc20   90-26720

ISBN 0-393-02975-1
W.W. Norton & Company, Inc.
500 Fifth Avenue, New York, N.Y. 10110
W.W. Norton & Company, Ltd.
10 Coptic Street, London WC1A 1PU
1 2 3 4 5 6 7 8 9 0

For
CAROL GALLAGHER
Who helped me put fiction
on the page where
it belongs.

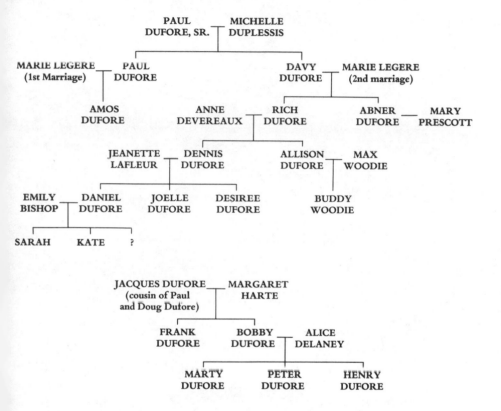

Prologue

The night before her great-grandson Daniel was to be buried, old Marie Dufore sat alone by the woodstove and kept him company on his last night among the living. She was over ninety, and felt closer to the dead these days, anyway.

It was dark in the living room; Gran Marie had turned off the lights hours ago. Now and then she opened the stove door to feed the fire; its warm, orange glow licked at her face, darted hungrily after shadowed corners, gobbled up as much of the dark as it could before she shut the door, plunging the room into blackness again.

Outside, February pressed cold against the windows, and even with the fire going strong she felt a chill. She'd been feeling it off and on for some years—even in the heat of summer it would creep up on her sometimes, freeze the blood in her veins, slow her beating heart. The chill of an open grave was how she thought of it, and it didn't frighten her; after all, she'd been born at the end of the nineteenth century, and now here she was, little more than a decade from the end of the twentieth. She looked at the coffin resting just a foot or two from her chair, felt a tiny surge of anger. Had it really been so unreasonable to expect the next grave dug for a Dufore would be hers?

Thief.

She reached out, and rapped her knuckles hard against the slick wood. The sound fell leaden into the silence.

There had been a lot of deaths over the last hundred years, not all but enough in her own family. She'd sat by enough coffins, kept vigil with enough of the dead—her brother, her son, her husband—to stop fearing her own death. She hadn't slept in nearly seventy years, and that in itself was a kind of dying, she thought.

This death was the hardest, though. The last of her line was sealed in his casket; tomorrow the Dufore name would be put in the ground for good.

Would it have come to this if Allie hadn't gone? She'd never know, of course, but it nagged her sometimes during the long nights when there wasn't much else to do except pull at loose threads in the fabric of her memory, and watch all the events of her life unravel while she tried to find some pattern in it all. She'd been doing it for years now, weaving and unweaving and reweaving the Dufore history, trying to remake it as it might have been. If Allie hadn't left; if Daniel hadn't gone to the quarry that day; if we hadn't left Davy alone . . .

It was an occupation of the old, she supposed; the young had no time for it and the middle-aged were too afraid to unravel the threads for fear of finding it had all been wrong from the start. No, only the old were suited for this game, and only when they were very old indeed.

She'd realized some years before the futility of playing. Like solitaire, you seldom won and on the rare occasion when there was a resolution to the problem, it was empty anyway. Still, it had become habit; monotonous, perhaps, but compulsive.

She sat alone in the dark beside her great-grandson's coffin, reviewing all the events in her life, in her family's, in the life of the community. Would I be here tonight, like this, she asked herself again, frustrated and bored even as she asked; would Daniel be here tonight, like this, if the juggler had never come?

Round and round she went, her mind casting far back over the years, as she waited out the long hours of the night before Daniel Dufore's funeral.

PART ONE

AB'S LEAP

Chapter

1

O n August 20, 1956, in the backseat of Jeanette La-
Fleur's father's Chevy, Dennis Dufore decided he
was in love.

It was not the first time he'd arrived at this decision, only
the latest. He wanted to marry her that very night, to have
permanent, legal custody over the one dark, heavy breast
that pressed against his lips and nose, and the other, pulsing
urgently under his hand. He was delirious with the smell
and feel and nearness of Jeanette LaFleur; he wanted her
forever.

In the dark, he could see the glint of her teeth, the reflected gleam of porch light glowing in her eyes. He shifted
closer, felt her legs open under him. There was nothing shy
about Jeanette—probably the thing he liked best about her,
since he was so shy himself. He didn't have to pretend he

loved her to have her, and she didn't expect him to make it up to her afterwards.

Naturally, he loved her to distraction and spent many miserable hours loathing himself for using her as he heard older men talk about using whores.

"Oh, Denny . . ."

She was pressing against him harder. He could feel her fingernails scraping along his backbone; he wondered how he would explain such marks to his parents. He felt himself sinking into her, deeper, deeper, until suddenly he heard the shotgun crackle of pheasants taking flight, felt bats' wings brush his cheeks as he was lifted out of his body, sucked up into the air even as Jeanette twined her legs over his back and sucked him even deeper into herself. He was being torn in two, struggling between earthbound and airborne. He wrapped her hair round his fingers, anchoring himself, and drove in deeper, planted himself more firmly inside her. Not the strength in his fingers or the strength in her legs could hold him, though. Higher and higher he flew.

Then, just when he thought he was marooned up there forever, doomed to fly forever, just when he got the first glimmer of how things might be, floating up there, weightless and unburdened forever, just when he'd begun to think flying was not so bad after all, he found himself on the ground again, panting against Jeanette's breast, her hair twined around his fingers. . . .

"Dennis? Dennis!"

Allie's voice floated thinly over the cornfield, woke him from the half-coma thoughts of Jeanette and the night before had put him in. If he kept silent now, she'd just keep walking in the direction of the house and miss him completely. Little foil envelopes of salt and pepper crinkled in his back pocket, reminding him he'd brought a packet of hard-boiled eggs out to the barn with him.

"Dennis!" Her voice was further away.

"Over here," he called.

She'd taken to wearing white lately. She said it made her feel graceful, light on her feet. She liked to feel the material whisper between her legs as she walked. Now, as he watched her float through rows of corn, he worried at the lightness of her step, the spring in it, as though any moment would find her launched into flight, her summer dress billowing out, wafting her up like a parachute.

"What ya doin'?" she asked, gliding from bright light into the dark of the barn. She flopped down beside him, her back against a hay bale.

"Nothin'. Just thinkin'."

"Oh yeah? Bet I know what you were thinkin' about."

"Bet you don't," Dennis said, though he suspected she knew right enough.

"I'll bet you were thinkin' 'bout Jeanette LaFleur."

When he said nothing, she began to chant in a whiny voice, "Jeanette LaFleur . . . Jeanette LaFlooooor . . ."

"Cut it out, Allie," he said, and when she wouldn't, he jabbed her in the stomach with his elbow, not too hard, but hard enough to make her shut up.

She managed to give his hair a good yank in return before her face turned serious and she suddenly curled into his side, leaned her cheek lightly against his shoulder, and whispered:

"Uncle Ab's done it again."

He noticed suddenly how still it was. No birds, no tractor-drone—nothing but the quickened stroke of blood hammering in his ears.

"Not dead, is he?" Dennis asked.

He felt her head shake against his shoulder.

"Just his foot, I think. Daddy's gone for the doctor."

"Then we probably oughta go back," he said.

She snuggled in closer against his arm, and slipped one hand into his.

"No," she said. "Let's just stay here. We'll pretend I couldn't find you."

Her hair smelled like sunshine and baby shampoo. It was easy to lean his cheek against the top of her head, let the noonday heat that still clung to her warm him wherever their bodies touched, let the smell and the feel of her take him back into his dreaming.

"How'd he do it?" Dennis asked after a long silence.

Allie's voice seemed to come from a very long distance away.

"Hunting rifle," she said.

He'd tried that once before, Dennis remembered, a few years back, and lost an ear. Afterwards, Aunt Mary had hired his cousins Jacques and Bobby Dufore to build a gun cabinet with a good strong lock on it; she kept every gun in the place, including Dennis's BB gun, in it, and the only key on a chain around her neck.

"Wonder how he got hold of it," he said out loud, but Allie didn't answer.

"Denny," Allie said, "why'd he do it this time, you think?"

"Dunno. Maybe for the same reason he tried last summer. Maybe somethin' different."

She curled in closer, then yelped in pain. She sat up and slipped one hand into his front pocket, extracting two sizable chunks of sandstone, which she tossed onto the ground next to him.

"Damned things near poked a hole in me," she muttered and curled back into his side.

Dennis's fingers folded around one of the pieces of sandstone as he closed his eyes. The rock in his hand felt good, heavy and substantial. Having that rock in his palm made the wind that whistled through the warped barn walls less threatening.

"Anyway," Allie said, "there sure does seem to be a lot of it in this family."

No need to answer; he'd known for years, ever since he'd started school and met other kids, that death from self-inflicted wounds, intentional drowning, self-incineration, and hanging was not common in other families as it was in his. He'd asked his dad about it once.

"Every family's got somethin' that gets passed down, son," his father had told him. "In some families, it's the sugar sickness, or a fondness for the bottle. . . ."

For the most part, life went on and Dufores behaved like other folk. Church, county fair, farmer's market filled Dufores' days and seasons the same as everyone else's. Occasional disruptions in the natural scheme of things by sudden, willful death were taken in stride by the Dufore generations in the same spirit with which they accepted birth, or drought, or a hard winter. Dennis had never before questioned his family's persistent propensity for self-destruction, but in recent months his mind had turned, more and more, to thoughts of marriage and children of his own.

He was aware that although the Dufores were one of the founding families of Esperance, Vermont, and well-valued members of the community, it was generally agreed among sensible folk that there was bad blood in the family, so for marrying purposes they were considered only in the direst circumstances, and as a last resort.

In the still of the barn, his cheek against his sister's silky hair, Dennis thought about all the times his uncle Ab had tried and failed, and about his own father's attempt many years before, and about his grandfather. . . .

He wondered how his mother had felt all the years she'd been married to a Dufore; he wondered about his Aunt

Mary, or Rachel Purcell, who had married his second cousin Burl only three months before he swallowed a whole bottle of rat poison and left her a widow. It was one thing to be born a Dufore, he decided, and quite another to marry one.

"We should get back," he murmured into Allie's shiny black hair.

On the way back to the house, Dennis took his sister's hand; she seemed to be springing higher than usual, and there was a sharp wind from the north.

Dinner that night was a bit subdued; Uncle Ab had tried to shoot himself in the head that afternoon, but only succeeded in blowing two toes off his left foot.

Now he sat at his customary place at the kitchen table, his maimed foot propped on an empty chair, his face a mix of embarrassment and despair. No one talked to him; Dennis's grandmother Marie, and Ab's wife, Mary, were both seriously annoyed with Ab, and nobody else had any desire to draw their fire. Pork chops, potatoes, peas, and squash made their silent rounds; conversation was hushed.

After dinner, Dennis's mother, Anne, said, "Dennis, you'll need to do Abner's milking tonight."

Anne never called anybody by a nickname. It was always Dennis, or Allison or Abner.

Uncle Ab looked up as Dennis passed, and their eyes met. There was something there in his uncle's expression, a pleading look, as though he wanted conversation or forgiveness, but could not speak in front of all these others. Then Aunt Mary said:

"Time you got to bed, Ab,"

and the connection was broken.

Dennis clambered down the back-porch steps, hesitated at the bottom, then quickly stooped to pick up an old red brick he kept hidden under the bottom step. The wind had picked up even more since sunset. It slapped at his back, tugged at his pantlegs as he crossed the wide yard to the barn. Sometimes it seemed the wind almost managed to insinuate itself between himself and solid earth, but Dennis's shoes were heavy, and he had some good weighty rocks in his pockets as well as the brick in his hand.

Still, it was a relief to reach the barn, and pull shut the door behind him. For a moment he stood in the pitch black and listened to the warm, snuffled breathing of the cows, to the floor creaking as they shifted their weight, and the occasional groan of old wood as they leaned into the walls of their stalls. He put his hand out, scraped it across the rough, splintered wall until he found the light switch.

In the millisecond it took for light to replace dark, he thought he saw the figure of a hanged man, dangling naked from the main rafter. In the space of a heartbeat he saw the brilliant tattoo of a winged woman that spread across the man's back, saw the body swing round, and the man's head come up, the eyes open, the mouth stretch into a wide grin.

Then a dim yellow glow flooded the barn and his vision cleared.

He saw the apparition often, whenever he turned on a light in a too-dark room, or opened his eyes too quickly after a dream. It used to frighten him, when he was a kid, but over time he'd gotten used to it. Sometimes, he wondered who the apparition was. A great-uncle of his had done himself in out here, half a century before, and he knew Uncle Ab had tried it, too, some years ago (only Gran Marie's unexpected arrival in search of the kitchen-garden rake had saved him), but as far as he knew, no one in his family had ever possessed a tattoo. He'd asked Gran Marie about it once some years back, but she'd got a queer look on her face and told him not to speak of such things to her again.

There were twelve cows; most nights he and Ab shared the milking, and the time went fast. Tonight, though, would take longer. He picked up a bucket and went into the first stall, positioned the bucket, and leaned his cheek against the cow's rough hide. She turned her massive head and blew hot, moist air down the back of his neck. His hands found the cow's teats, found their rhythm; he crouched there on the low stool with his hands working like slow pistons and the sound of the milk hissing against the side of the pail like rain on a tin roof, and let his thoughts drift away from the hanged man and from Ab, back to Jeanette.

Jeanette.

She was like a fever in his blood. In eighth grade he'd read all about the Panama Canal, how hundreds of workers had died of something called malaria, a fever that came on suddenly, racked you, then left you weak or dead. Lately, he'd been thinking of Jeanette in much the same terms. He could go for days, a week at a time even, without thinking of her especially; then he'd see her somewhere—at the general store, or gassing up her father's Chevy, or picking up the mail—and suddenly he'd want her so bad he'd break out in a sweat.

Just like malaria.

He wondered if she knew the effect she had on him and decided she did.

Other times, of course, he was sure she didn't.

Thoughts of her sustained him through the whole milking, and it was not until he was already back in the house and getting ready for bed that he realized he'd crossed from the barn to the house in a stiff wind without the brick to hold him steady. . . .

He was running along Pitt Road, near the schoolyard. His heartbeat throbbed in his ears. Far behind him, Allie was calling

for him to stop, warning him to slow down, but his legs had taken
on a life of their own and they carried him skimming over the
rutted tracks faster and faster until suddenly, his feet weren't
actually touching the ground anymore.

Up he swept, his arms and legs still pumping frantically,
because he knew that if he stopped, he'd fall. Below him, his
sister's upturned face was a pale blur against the mud-brown road,
then was lost as he was caught by a wave of air and tumbled up
another thousand feet. Somersaults, arabesques; his body tossed
and pitched out of control across the sky while he flapped his arms
and kicked his legs, imagined the green-brown earth coming up
lickety-split and smashing him like a bug on a windshield.

The sheets were sweat-drenched.

"Goddamned Christly dream," Dennis muttered, and
punched the pillow.

Saturday morning, the Dufores went to town.

Esperance life revolved around two main hubs: men con-
gregated in front of the firehouse or lounged by the gas
pumps at Ron Woodie's Texaco station; women generally
gathered at the post office. The church and the Esperance
General Store (P. Devereaux and Sons, Props.) were neutral
ground, where the sexes met and mingled.

Dennis and Allie rode in the back of the pickup while
their parents, Aunt Mary, and Uncle Ab, his foot wrapped
in white gauze and covered with one of Dennis's white
athletic socks, squashed into the cab. It was seven miles from
the farm to town, and Dennis dreaded the drive on windy
days. When Allie had been smaller, she'd liked to sit in his
lap with his arms wrapped tight around her. He'd enjoyed
the ride in those days; Allie was a steady anchor for him, and
he'd been careful never to relax his hold or his vigilance
against sudden gusts of wind. Now she was fifteen, and
insisted on perching perilously on the wheel well in her

billowing dresses and flimsy sandals; Dennis suffered agonies as the wind whipped her hair out around her head, set it lashing and snarling like a private warning to him of what it could really do if he ever dropped his guard.

"There's Jeannette!" Allie shouted, over the whine and rattle of the truck. Dennis didn't need to look where she was pointing; he could see Jeanette in his mind, her long dark braid lying demurely down the back of her red dress. Only he understood the electric energy in that tightly bound hair, how it could explode out of the ribbon, out of the plaits, tumbling over smooth golden skin.

He folded his hands over his lap and grimly considered the World Series prospects for the year.

The truck slowed down and pulled into the Texaco station. Allie got down first, careful to let her skirt hike up just enough for the Woodie boys to see her calf and knee as if by accident. In her thin cotton dress, the sheen of summer sun in her hair, she looked older and kind of "French" to Dennis, as though she might have been plucked out of some Provençal vineyard and dropped into Esperance. For the space of a heartbeat, he saw her as the Woodie boys did, and might have been seriously alarmed if the impression had lasted long enough for his brain to register. As it was, he was left feeling slightly annoyed that his sister didn't think to wear more practical clothing when riding in the back of a truck.

"Hi, Jack," Allie said, smiling a smile she'd been practicing for weeks in her mirror. She let it creep slowly across her lips, only lifting one corner of her mouth (the left side, where she almost had a dimple), and widened her eyes a little as she glanced sideways at the Woodies.

"Oh, hi, Max," she added indifferently.

The greeting had exactly the effect she'd intended: Jack swelled slightly, and darted a jeering glance at his younger brother, a glance which moved Max one step further towards abandoning all instincts for self-preservation and kissing Allie Dufore the first chance he got, no matter what.

Allie figured he'd get his chance Sunday, after church.

In the front cab, Ab was wondering if he could climb the big maple tree out behind the paper mill with only three toes on his left foot. The tree stood on a steep embankment overlooking Crockett's Brook, a location Ab found appealing, not only for its promising drop of seventy-five feet or so onto sharp rocks below, but also for its relative distance from more active parts of the village. A fellow bent on a little tree climbing was unlikely to be interrupted, no matter what he decided to do with himself once he reached the top.

"Dennis," Aunt Mary said, "get the crutches and help your uncle up."

No, Ab decided regretfully, he probably couldn't climb that maple. Of course, the tree wasn't strictly necessary; more of a safeguard, actually, to make sure you fell straight and didn't get slowed down or snarled up on the embankment. With a little luck, he could get it right even without the tree.

"You comin' to the general store, Ab?" his wife asked.

"Think I'll stay here and visit awhile."

He could use the crutches to push off with, he figured, adding a few inches to the trajectory.

"Suit yourself," she said, and started to walk up Main Street with Anne, towards the post office and the general store.

"Don't stay on that foot too long," she yelled back over her shoulder.

Ab didn't answer. His mind was on other matters.

Jeanette was talking to Becky Williams and Helen Prescott when Dennis got to the general store. He felt horribly self-conscious all of a sudden; as he approached the wide front stoop where she stood with her friends, he imagined every eye in town was fastened on his crotch.

"Hi," he muttered, brushing past her to enter the cool, shaded sanctuary of the general store.

The familiar, comforting smell of animal feed, leather, tobacco, and other men greeted him as he swung through the door. As a small boy, he'd come here with his father, sat on the huge feed sacks against the wall while the men talked and chewed tobacco, and secretly he'd craved his mother. Now, he accepted a cigarette from Bill Woodie, listened to one of Paul Devereaux's jokes, and laughed along with the rest of them, but all the time he was aware of Jeanette in her red dress, just a few feet away, separated by only a few splintered boards, and secretly he craved her.

He knew it when she came through the door, even though he was facing the back wall. The hair on the back of his neck just seemed to rise up and a weird prickle, reminding him sweetly of Jeanette's fingernails along his spine, ran down his back.

"Think I'll get a Coke," he said to no one in particular, and headed towards the front of the store.

She was standing at the counter with a soda in her hand.

"Oh, hi," Dennis said, as if he'd only just noticed she was there.

"Hi, Dennis."

Jeanette's smile was sweet and genuine. It told him she knew he was pretending, and she knew why, and that it was all right for him to pretend, since he was a man, though in general women didn't have to. His eyes dropped lower, to the spot where his head had rested a few nights before; her smile widened just a fraction.

"Wanna go for a walk?"

Why did he keep trying to sound so stupidly casual when he knew she knew, and probably all of Esperance knew, he would drop down dead for the sake of just one kiss?

"Okay."

He slapped some money down on the counter to cover both the Cokes, then wheeled around and started out a step or two ahead of her, cursing himself all the while for not having the courage to take her arm.

Not talking, not touching, they strolled down Main Street, toward the edge of town where Orchard Street branched off Main and ran along the bank of Crockett's Brook to the mill. There it crossed a narrow wooden bridge and continued on into rolling fields, ending, eventually, in a stand of woods. This was a favorite place to walk, for the road was quiet and not much traveled between shift changes at the mill.

At the top of Orchard, just past the Texaco station, Jeanette took Dennis's arm.

It had been easier than Ab thought to sneak away. Of course, if Mary'd been around, there would have been no chance. She was keeping a sharp eye on him these days, ever since he'd bollixed things up with the shotgun. But she'd allowed his injured foot to lull her into a false sense of security; she'd left him with the guys at the Texaco station, counting on that foot to keep him in one place.

He'd hung around visiting for a while, making more of a fuss about the pain in his foot than was actually called for. By the time he'd excused himself to use the men's room, no one was paying much attention to him at all. His niece, Allie, was busy with the Woodie boys, his wife and sister-in-law wouldn't be back for hours, and his brother, Rich, was lying stretched flat under a '53 DeSoto while Ron Woodie described the intricacies connected with patching its manifold. It had been easy to slip away.

Now here he was, under the maple at the edge of the

embankment, with no one around to fuss or bother him. Finally.

For many years—most of his life, really—Ab had lived with the knowledge that one day he would suddenly, unexpectedly burst into flames and die in horrible agony.

Usually, he managed to push that knowledge away, concentrating instead on family, chores, the ebb and tide of day to day. He even developed a kind of philosophical perspective on his fate as a combustible; all men had their individual crosses to bear, he knew, and suicide was a sin.

Sometimes, he even managed to halfway convince himself it was all in his mind.

But every once in a while, the constant stress of wondering when it would happen weighed him down, drained away any drop of comfort he'd wrung from the good things in his life. Those times, even eternal damnation seemed preferable to the constant, hovering threat of sudden incineration.

For sure he hadn't had much luck with guns; he'd tried drinking a bottle of perfume once, but only made himself dog-sick. Now, standing on the edge of the embankment over the brook, Ab was a little surprised at himself that he hadn't thought of this years before; what better way than to plunge into the cool green currents of the brook?

Now that he was actually here, he was in no particular hurry. he leaned his back against the gnarled trunk of the maple, shifting some of his weight off his upper arms, and squinted up into the clear sky. It seemed bluer to him now than it ever had before. The sun was warm on his face; the wind licked gently around the brim of his hat, almost playful as it tried to lift it from his head.

He pursed his lips and started to whistle, but soft, as though someone might be close enough to hear; he heaved himself back up to balance on the crutches and swung himself over closer to the edge of the embankment. He stood right at the edge with his gauze-wrapped foot hanging over and watched the water rushing far below, marked the deepest places and the sharpest rocks. He liked one in particular: large, half-submerged in the brook near midstream; an easy enough target, even for him, he thought, and decided to aim for it.

The sun was beating down on the back of his head now. Really, he thought, it was getting unpleasantly warm. His hands tightened slightly around the grips of the crutches. He stepped back and dug them into the earth at the edge of the embankment, prepared to swing out and push off. He couldn't feel the wind anymore, just the sun boring into his shoulders and the back of his head; below him, Crockett's Brook was calling.

On the other side of the brook, about fifty yards from the maple tree, there was a thick copse of bushes and high grass. Dennis had just tenderly slipped the last mother-of-pearl button out of its fragile loop, revealing the warm expanse of Jeanette's wheat colored skin rising in a gentle swell from the lace cups of her brassiere, and was about to bend his head to take her nipple, bra cup and all, into his mouth when the gunshot crackle of a pheasant breaking cover startled them both into sitting up.

They were just in time to see Uncle Ab launch himself up over the edge of the embankment in a perfect arc, then drop down to where he exploded against the rocks in Crockett's Brook and burst into flames.

Chapter

2

❧

When she was thirteen, Jeanette LaFleur seduced her older brother.

He was four years older than her. She'd left her bedroom door open one day while she was changing and Tommy had walked in when she had no shirt on. He'd looked kind of funny, sort of embarrassed and ashamed, but he hadn't hurried away. He had sat on the bed instead and watched her finish dressing.

From then on, Tommy always seemed to be just outside her door at bedtime or in the morning, or accidentally walking in on her when she was taking a bath. It didn't bother her; she'd been hearing things lately at school and was more than a little curious herself. She could vaguely remember taking baths with him when they'd been much younger, but at the time she'd been mainly impressed by how he could pee standing up. According to the girls in her gym class, though, pissing without taking your pants down was the least of what a man could do, and so she went out to the shed one evening after supper, where she knew he'd be working on the Chevy's crankshaft, and she asked him about it.

"Tommy?"

"Mm."

"You ever do it?"

That caught his attention.

"What're you talkin' about, Nettie?" he asked, straightening up all of a sudden, looking at her hard from under the shock of straight black hair that fell over his forehead.

"You know," she said, picking up a wrench and moving closer.

"You got a dirty mind, Jeanette," he said.

"How do you know what's on my mind?" she said. She came another step closer and stood beneath the window, stroking the wrench with the palm of her left hand.

"I been hearin' about it, Tommy," she said. "I been readin' *True Confessions* and *Real Love.* I know people'll do most anything to get it, but I just can't figure out why." She moved just a fraction closer. His breathing got heavy all of a sudden, and a little ragged. His eyes were fixed on the wrench in her hand.

"Why do you s'pose people get crazy over it, Tom?" she asked, tracing designs lightly down his arm with her fingers. "I mean, it's no different than dogs, is it?"

She was close enough now to feel his breath in her hair.

"Cut it out, Jeanette," he said roughly, but he didn't move from under her hand.

"I'll show you mine if you show me yours," she said, and pulled her shirt up to reveal a chest that was already pretty well developed for a girl her age.

Tommy licked his lips but didn't speak. She saw his hand twitch at his side, as though he'd started to reach out, then thought better of it.

"Wanna touch?" she asked.

His hand came up slowly, then; his thumb traced lightly over one tender nipple, started to drop back down again, then hesitated.

"Now you show yours," Jeanette said, and started to lower her shirt.

His hand still hovered over her breast; his eyes grew wider and wider, something a little like fear at the back of them; his mouth opened and shut but no sound came out.

Then he was pushing her down on the floor, all his weight on top of her, his mouth pressed against her throat so hard she could feel his teeth through his lips. He was kind of snuffling and rooting against her neck and shoulder, making queer, moaning sounds, like a puppy desperate to nurse. His hands were tugging at her clothes, rubbing her flesh too hard, then they were between her legs, forcing them apart so roughly her thighs scraped across the plank floor and she yelped as splinters dug into her. The whole time he made those funny puppy noises as he tugged at her legs and nuzzled her neck and armpits and breasts.

It hurt a little, but not much.

Afterwards, Tommy pulled on his pants in silence and wouldn't look at her. It was too dark to really see his face, but she imagined the same expression he'd had the time he'd helped slaughter pigs and had thrown up. In silence he picked up his toolbox and started back to the house without looking at her or speaking to her at all.

All in all, she decided, picking one or two splinters out of her backside and brushing the dirt from her skirt, she really couldn't see what all the fuss was about.

That furtive encounter with Tommy in the shed led to further experiments. He accosted her in the shed, out in the woods, behind the house. Once or twice, he crept into her own bed with her after everyone else was asleep. At first she didn't mind, but by the time she got to high school, she was getting tired of unexpected hands on her arms, breath on the back of her neck, followed by quick, bruising intercourse and sullen silence.

Then, in the summer of the year she turned fourteen, Jeanette rediscovered Dennis Dufore.

She'd known Dennis all her life, of course, and never paid him much attention. He was like most boys in Esperance: pimply, gawky, and indifferent to most girls. That summer, however, the summer of 1952, something happened to Dennis. His body filled out, the space between his chin and his Adam's apple became a well-defined jaw, and cheekbones emerged out of adolescent pudge. He shot up a couple of inches and started shaving, too. Jeanette found herself powerfully attracted, and Tommy's attentions became even less welcome.

It wasn't so much that Dennis was good-looking, Jeanette decided; after all, Esperance was full of dark-haired, dark-eyed young men, some of them (including her brother, Tom) taller, handsomer, and better-built than Dennis Dufore. What Jeanette liked best about Dennis was the air of gravity that clung to him; as though he bore a secret sorrow that made him more tender, gentler, than less-burdened folk. He made her feel older, wiser, and infinitely tender herself; she wanted to hold his head against her and stroke away the pain.

Although they went to the same school, belonged to the same church, and had regularly run into each other in town over the years, Jeanette found it suddenly impossible to speak to him.

Maude was in Dennis's class at school, so she spoke to her, instead.

"Dennis Dufore got a girlfriend?" she asked Saturday night as they were washing up after supper.

Maude looked at her open-mouthed for a minute, then said, "Don't tell me ole Cinderella's *finally* getting interested in something outside of a story book!"

"Does he?" Jeanette asked again.

"Him? He doesn't think of nothing 'cept cars and cows. He'll *never* get a girlfriend."

Jeanette rubbed the plate in her hand thoughtfully with the towel, then placed it carefully on the stack in the cupboard. She suspected her sister was more than a little interested in Dennis herself.

Maude relented; she had Bill Prescott interested in her, after all, which almost made up for her complete lack of success with Dennis Dufore.

"He's kind of cute, huh?" she said.

But "Mm" was all Jeanette said, and they didn't speak of him again.

On Sunday, Jeanette dressed with more care than usual. She brushed her hair one hundred strokes and let it hang loose down her back, a shiny cascade of black and blue-black silk, instead of its usual severe braid. She borrowed a wine-red dress from Maude that brought out the rich gold color in her skin and made her eyes and hair seem blacker. She rubbed a miniscule amount of Vaseline across her eyelids and finally was ready.

Her mother looked at her sharply, but said nothing; her father felt something was different and wished it would go away.

Tommy took one look at her and somehow knew the change had nothing to do with him; sickening jealousy washed over him, almost as bad as the trembling he felt in the pit of his stomach sometimes when he found her alone somewhere, almost as though he didn't know whether to shit or throw up.

Sometimes, when he was alone and thinking of her, he imagined his hands around her throat squeezing the life out of her before he somehow killed himself. When she was in front of him, though, his hands found themselves pushing her down on the ground and pulling aside her clothes, instead.

If she ever left him for someone else, though . . .

He knew he'd have the strength to kill her then.

All through mass, Jeanette kept up an unobtrusive observation of Dennis Dufore. He stood with his parents, sister, aunt, and uncle in the family pew, across the aisle, one row up from where the LaFleur family sat. She admired his profile through the sermon, then managed to get right behind him at communion, where she stared at the back of his head with fierce devotion.

After church, she slipped away from the rest of her family and followed him to the parking lot.

"Dennis Dufore!" she called after him.

He turned and looked a little surprised when he saw who it was. Slowly she walked over to him, stood just a hand's breadth away, and looked up gravely into his eyes. She saw his eyes change, as though a shutter had been opened for just a moment, then slammed shut. He shifted his weight, suddenly aware of how close she was to him, a little alarmed by it.

So she stood that close a second longer, till he drew one unsteady breath, then turned casually aside, as though examining the sky for signs of rain.

"You swim, right?" she asked.

"Yeah," he said, a little doubtfully.

"Will you teach me?" She didn't look at him as she spoke.

"How come you don't ask your brother?" Dennis asked.

She shrugged.

"Would you teach me?" she asked again, standing close but not looking at him.

"Jeez, Jeanette, I'm pretty busy . . ."

They stood in silence for a moment, eyes fixed on the singularly uninteresting line of trees in the distance. He didn't speak, but he didn't move away, either. Her skin was beginning to tingle and there was a funny glow starting in the pit of her stomach, a little like Christmas morning.

"Well, okay," he finally said. His voice cracked a little and he blushed.

"When?" she asked, this time looking directly into his eyes.

Once again, she felt like she was waiting for a window to open. She'd never realized there were so many shades of black. His eyes were matte and glossy, opaque as a coal smudge, transparent as the bit of smoked glass she'd watched a solar eclipse through, once.

"How about tomorrow afternoon," he said. "My folks won't mind so long as I get my work done in the morning."

"Mine neither," she lied; she'd lived her whole life in Esperance and had a pretty fair notion what her family would say to her keeping company with a Dufore. She had no intention of telling them where she was going the next day.

"I'll meet you at the quarry," she said.

"That one looks like a dragon."

"Nah . . . sorta like my uncle's coon dog."

They had climbed the steep cliff that rose up from the quarry basin and were lying on flat, sun-roasted boulders overlooking the water. They lay staring up at thick scudding clouds that reminded Jeanette of angel hair and Dennis of his mother's mashed potatoes, and tried making pictures in the sky to pass the time.

She'd felt shy, at first; she knew his heart had speeded up a bit, too, when he put his arms round her, helping her float. Pretty soon, though, the shyness had disappeared. Dennis was the one who had suggested climbing up to the overlook. Funny how quickly they had adjusted to one another; he didn't seem nervous with her anymore, acting like he took her presence there on the rock beside him for granted. Yet some newborn intuition told her that she was different, to him.

"There's a shark," he said.

"Where?"

"Over there, next to the one that looks like the state of Wyoming."

She followed his pointing finger, decided it looked like an anteater, to her.

"You ever read *The Three Musketeers*?" she asked, tracing the shape of an anteater in the dirt beside her.

"Nah," Dennis replied. "Don't read much."

"It's a real good book," Jeanette said. "Maybe I could read it to you."

"What for?" He made it sound like she'd suggested a trip to the dentist, or mucking out stalls, for fun.

"I dunno," she said. "One of the characters reminds me of you."

"Yeah?" There was some interest in his voice. "Which one?"

"Athos."

"What a pansy name!" he commented, obviously disappointed.

"It is *not!*" Jeanette fired up. "Well, maybe it is," she

conceded, "but *he's* not a pansy! He's . . . he's wonderful!"

Having said that, she was paralyzed with embarrassment and went back to studying the clouds. She knew he was looking at her; a slow flush came up over her neck and cheeks. Finally he looked away. Out of the corner of her eye she saw contentment, of a sort, on his face.

"That looks like a B-52 bomber," he said, pointing at one cloud that looked like the Eiffel Tower, to her.

Tommy was waiting for her when she got home.

"Where you been?" His voice was unnaturally high, and whiny, the way it got sometimes when he was real upset or angry about something.

"Swimming," she said, starting past him into the house.

"That's a lie!" he said, following her up the front stoop into the kitchen. "You don't know how!"

"Do now," she said.

The house felt dark and cool after an afternoon spent baking on granite slabs. It was like coming into a cave; there was still a hint of that morning's chill trapped in her mother's cramped rooms. She headed down the hallway to her bedroom, Tommy still on her heels.

"Who'd you go with?" he demanded.

"Just some kids," she replied.

"What kids?"

"What's it to you?" she asked. She opened her closet and pulled out a pair of dungarees. "I wanna get dressed, Tommy. Go away, will you?"

She wasn't entirely surprised when he suddenly gripped her shoulders and pulled her back against him. His lips ground against the side of her neck as he hissed her name in her ear.

She wasn't surprised, but she wasn't having any of it, either.

"Cut it out, Tom," she said and hung, limp and uninter-ested, in his grasp.

"I said knock it off!" she said when he kept it up; she jabbed an elbow into his rib cage and stepped out of the circle of his arms. He was panting a little and she could see a damp spot over the bulge in his chinos.

"Why don't you get a real girlfriend, Tom, and leave me alone?"

His eyes widened a bit, but he continued to stand and stare, the bulge in his pants gradually going down.

"You're not a bad-looking guy, Tommy. I bet there's lots of girls that'd like you."

Still no response.

"Well, I don't want you touchin' me again, Tom, or I'll tell Daddy."

"You started it," he croaked, and despised himself for the pleading tone he couldn't keep out of his voice. "He'll whale you good."

"I know," Jeanette said calmly, and Tommy knew that threats of physical violence would not sway her; she was the bravest person he knew.

"Jeanette," he began, stepping towards her, his hands spread wide, his fingers twitching to hold her.

"No more," she warned, then stood motionless, waiting for him to leave.

The door hadn't even shut behind him before he'd de-cided to kill her.

In a town the size of Esperance, keeping company with someone secretly was unheard of. Still, one of the peculiar codes of New England small-town life is to allow its citi-zens an illusion of privacy. If Jeanette LaFleur and Dennis Dufore wanted to pretend their daily meetings at the quarry were unknown to the rest of the populace, the people of Esperance were willing to oblige, never referring to it within earshot of either of the principals or any member of their respective families.

Anne and Rich Dufore knew, of course, but beyond a little worrying on Anne's part about rumors she'd heard of the LaFleur girls being uncommonly *fast,* they didn't think much about it.

Esperance was pretty well agreed, though, that the Dufores were not the ones who were in any rightful position to worry.

Andrew LaFleur, at the mill, knew about his daughter's carryings-on; it was just a matter of time before his wife found out too, and forbade Jeanette to ever have anything to do with the Dufore boy again. This made Andrew uncomfortable, because he knew Jeanette would not obey, and then he would be forced to go to extremes to make sure her disobedience did not come to his attention. His senses of hearing and sight would have to become extremely selective; he'd have to clear his throat loudly before entering outbuildings, and ignore hairpins in the back of his Chevy. It was going to be very inconvenient, and sooner or later Sally would discover it all anyway. Then he'd be expected to "Do Something About It."

He supposed he'd have to beat her then—something he was not, on general principles, averse to when he thought it would work—and threaten her with "worse" (though not even he, who frequently made the threat to his other children, had any idea what could be worse than a hiding with a leather strap). She'd probably run away after that, and marry the damned boy, he reflected glumly; Jeanette had never been a satisfactory child.

Sally LaFleur was already nursing unwelcome suspicions about her middle child's activities. She might even have

taken action if she hadn't started feeling uncommonly
queasy in the mornings. She seemed to lose interest then,
becoming more than a little preoccupied with an even more
unwelcome suspicion that popped into her mind more and
more frequently as the month wore on.

Maude knew, but was more interested in her own love
life.

Angel and Maryellen knew, but thought Dennis probably had cooties.

Tommy was planning on shooting them both.

He'd followed her out to the quarry one day, and seen the
two of them out on the rocks: her lying on her stomach,
reading aloud from one of her books, him close beside her,
on his back with his face turned towards her, not touching,
just listening. Something about the way they lay there together, comfortable and friendly, made Tommy's throat
tighten with tears of rage.

He spied on them lots after that. It became a compulsion;
he had to know where they were. He crept down dirt roads
after them, dodging from tree to tree, even lying flat on his
belly in the ditch to keep out of their sight. He hovered in
the shadow of the cliffs out by the quarry, straining his ears
for scraps of conversation the wind might blow his way.
Each time he saw them together, his rage grew, making him
feel almost as good as being with Jeanette had. In fact, with
time it felt even better; there was nothing in the pure white
heat of anger to make him feel dirty or ashamed of himself.

He started imagining her lying naked on the sun-washed
quarry rocks, underneath Dennis Dufore. It was the same
daydream he'd had for years, only this time he wasn't in it.
Then he imagined himself pushing a huge boulder over the
edge and squashing them both like bugs.

He spent two hours at the quarry one evening, trying to
loosen one of the big rocks at the top of the overlook with a

lever. Eventually, he had to admit there was no guaranteeing that when Dennis Dufore finally got around to screwing Jeanette it would happen in the exact spot where the boulder would hit.

That was when he decided to shoot them instead.

"How come you read so much, Jeanette?"

The were sitting in the shade of some maple trees, about a mile downstream from the mill, tossing pebbles over the embankment into the brook below. Jeanette had just finished reading aloud from *The Three Musketeers*.

"Dunno," she said, dropping a rotten chunk of bark over the edge. "Always have."

"You sure do make it real," he commented. "Not like at school."

He struggled for a moment with a thought too big for him.

"Bet you could make 'em up good as books, too," was what he finally said.

"Maybe." Jeanette shrugged. She wasn't interested in literature at the moment. Dennis's skin had tanned nut-brown; his blue-black hair smelled warm and clean and vaguely of hay. She wanted to bury her nose in that hair and breathe deep.

"My mom's pregnant again," she said.

"Isn't she kind of old?"

"Yeah. . . . I don't think she's too happy about it."

"What'd your dad say?"

"Not much. Just got a six-pack out of the icebox when she told him and started drinking. It's 'cause of this baby my folks aren't fussing 'bout me going around with you, Dennis."

He flushed a little at that. He knew very well how Dufores were regarded in Esperance, one reason (or so he told himself) he'd never had a girl before Jeanette.

"Dennis, you like me, don't you?"

"Wouldn't be here if I didn't," he muttered, and squirmed a little. he felt uncomfortable all of a sudden, and couldn't tell if he was scared to death or just terribly excited.

"A lot?" She moved a little closer; he could smell peppermint Life Saver on her breath and see the fine beads of sweat gathered in the little crease of flesh right at her dress's bustline. His mouth felt dry; he couldn't have spoken if his life depended on it. He stared into her eyes, paralyzed like a rabbit caught in the glare of a car's headlights.

"Dennis," she said, and put his hand on her breast.

Only moments after Dennis Dufore lost his virginity, two things happened almost simultaneously. Jeanette, moving rapidly beneath him, suddenly arched her back, widened her eyes, and began to moan on a long, throbbing note that frightened him very much, since he thought he was killing her. He tried to scramble up on his knees, but her legs were locked around him, her arms holding tightly as vises. Then, just when her cries had reached a peak, there was the loud report of a gunshot and the bullet from a .22 rifle buried itself in the dirt about three inches from Dennis's hand.

"Jesus Christ!" Jeanette swore. "Hand me my clothes!"

Another shot slapped into the trunk of the maple as Dennis and Jeanette, their clothes in their hands, slipped over the side of the embankment, slithered and bounced down over jagged rocks and protruding tree roots in a fog of dust and pebbles, and fetched up in a bleeding, cursing heap, in about eighteen inches of water, at the bottom.

"Your dad?" Dennis whispered, then yelped as he put his foot down on a piece of glass.

"Shhh!" Jeanette hissed. "Daddy wouldn't try to *shoot* me, no matter how mad he got!"

They were struggling into their clothes now, their one

thought being if they were going to be murdered by some madman, they'd rather have the dignity of dying in at least their underwear.

"You got another boyfriend?" Dennis asked.

"No," she said, but a glimmer of understanding began to peek through the terror of the previous few minutes.

"We can follow the brook up to the bridge and get out there," Dennis said.

"That's what he'd expect us to do," she argued.

"Well, we can't just sit here in this puddle and wait for him to come pick us off from the cliff. Come on."

He took her hand and they started picking their way along the brook bed. It was rough going, for they were bruised, barefoot, and in mortal terror of their lives. It took them forty-five minutes to where the bank was low enough to make climbing up possible.

Dennis had just got his head and shoulders over the top of the bank when another bullet ricocheted off a chunk of quartz and skimmed across the back of his hand.

"Ouch!" he yelped, falling backwards over Jeanette, back down into the brook.

"Dennis!" she shrieked, and scrambled down after him.

"He shot me," Dennis whispered. "The son of a bitch actually shot me."

Enough was enough.

Faster than she would have thought possible, Jeanette was back up the embankment and over the edge. Madder than she would have thought possible, she was stalking towards the copse of trees and bushes (the same ones from which she would witness Ab Dufore's amazing leap, four years later) screaming:

"Tommy LaFleur, you drop that *goddamned* gun *this minute*. Do you *hear* me?"

She was so consumed with rage she wasn't even aware

Dennis had shot up the bank after her and was trying to put himself between her and the assassin in the copse. Angrily, she shoved him aside and advanced on the trees.

"Come out of there *right now,* Tommy."

There was a dead silence, followed by rustling and crackling of branches. First a gun barrel, then Tom LaFleur emerged from the brush.

"What the hell . . ." Dennis began, starting forward, then stopping abruptly when he found the gun pointing at him.

"You been screwing my sister." Tommy's voice was a little unsteady, almost as if he were trying to keep from crying. "I saw you . . . you were kissin' her and touchin' her, and . . . I saw you."

His shoulders began shaking and the gun wobbled crazily.

"Have you been spying on me?" his sister demanded.

"You goddamned motherfucker!" Tommy screamed at Dennis as he waved the gun around wildly, "You shoulda kept your hands off my sister! I'm gonna goddam kill *both* of you!"

He raised the .22.

"You son of a bitch," Jeanette said, in a low growl. "You've been *spying* on me!"

And she tackled him low, slugging him in the groin, as hard as she could.

He pitched forward onto his knees and face, lay there for a moment feebly clutching his crotch, and made wet, mewing sounds in the dirt.

"Don't you *ever* follow me again, Tommy," Jeanette said, picking up the gun.

Dennis, only beginning to take in the fact he was not going to die as a consequence of sinning with Jeanette, decided this was probably the most unforgettable day of his life, and wondered if this sort of thing was likely to happen frequently if he kept on seeing her.

"Come on, Dennis," Jeanette said. She shifted the rifle to her right shoulder and took his hand in hers. Dennis looked doubtfully at Tommy, still groveling in the dust, his face streaked with dirt and blubber. He wasn't crying anymore; he just lay there, kind of limp, as though someone had pulled the backbone right out of him.

"You just gonna leave him there?" Dennis whispered.

"He'll be all right," she replied, a little impatiently. "Let's go."

Dennis looked back once as they trudged down the hill, but Tommy hadn't moved.

They skirted the mill, where Jeanette's father had been enjoying a cigarette by the window till he saw them coming and quickly shifted his attention to a flyblown production chart on the wall, and parted with a swift, secretive kiss at the bottom of the road that led eventually to the Dufore farm.

Dennis climbed on his bicycle and pedaled home, thinking of sin, gunfire, and the paradise he'd experienced with Jeanette that day.

Jeanette walked home in a mixed state of irritation and tenderness. As she bathed her bruises and cuts she decided Dennis Dufore was undoubtedly the man she would marry. She also decided she would give Tommy a big piece of her mind when he got home.

But Tom didn't come home that night, or the next, or the night after that. In fact, he didn't come home at all.

It wasn't until six months later the Dupres received a postcard from Korea, telling them he'd decided to join the Army.

Chapter

3

O n that hot August afternoon in 1952, just hours after
Tommy LaFleur shot Dennis in the hand and almost four years to the day before Ab would make
his fatal leap into Crockett's Brook, Ab and Rich Dufore
stood side by side at the back door of the farmhouse and
watched Dennis pedal his bicycle up the driveway. The boy
was looking bruised, tired, and a little dazed.

"Been fightin'?" his father asked.

Dennis shook his head, leaned the bicycle up against the
side of the house, and passed through into the kitchen. The
two men stood silently for a moment, then Rich scratched
his head and commented, "LaFleur girl, most likely."

"Must rut like a bobcat to leave him lookin' like that,"
Ab rejoined.

Rich transferred his hand from the back of his head to the

tip of his nose and started rubbing at it absently. There was sadness in his eyes as he stared out over the farmyard towards a distant line of trees that marked the north boundary of his property. If Jeanette had been there right then, she might have seen how Dennis would look in thirty years: no longer grave, or sensitive, merely sad, instead, displaying sorrow nakedly in his eyes.

"Suppose I oughta say something to him?" Rich asked his brother.

Ab shrugged. "Nobody listens to advice 'less it's what they want to hear. You gonna tell him what he wants to hear?"

The two men stood side by side, caught in a shaft of afternoon light—the last light of that day, if they only knew it—that sent sun-coated motes of red-and-gold dust whirling around their heads, threading through their thick black hair like licks of flame—the image came immediately to Ab's mind when he glanced over at his brother. Is that how I'll look when it happens? he wondered.

For a moment, Ab thought about the LaFleur girl— Jeanine, her name was, he thought, or maybe Janet. She was attractive in a dark, voluptuous way; sort of reminded him of Dorothy Lamour, or Jane Russell. He could remember back when he'd been younger, and Mary Prescott had looked just like Marlene Dietrich to him.

He wondered if Jeanine (or was it Janet?) would make his nephew happy; if she'd be enough to make whatever cross he bore worth the weight. He thought about his sister-in-law, Anne, how she'd seen his brother through two bouts with a razor and a rope. He thought about his own wife, how she'd look in just a few short hours, curled up beside him, her head half buried in the pillow and her breathing deep and regular, and then, as happened more and more as he grew older, the memory of another late afternoon in another August, thirty years before, came into his mind.

On that day, Ab and his brother, Rich, were down by the pond on the other side of the cornfield, just messing around as boys do. They were trying to knock a bird's nest out of a tree with a long, rotted birch limb. Ab was hopping up and down on one bare foot, his hair standing straight up, stiff from dirt and boy-sweat, one skinny arm brandishing the branch in ineffective swipes at the nest, while Rich bounced and jiggled on the other side of the trunk, shouting encouragement.

He didn't notice how hot he was becoming; it was, after all, a warm day and he was an active boy. The heat just seemed to build up gradually, making his face shiny and red while his skin puffed up from his bones, becoming tauter, plumper, like dough rising.

He didn't really notice anything, except he was suddenly awfully hot, but Rich stopped jiggling suddenly and whispered:

"Jesus, Ab, you got *smoke* comin' outta your head!"

Ab only heard his brother taking the Savior's name in vain. He pointed a jeering finger in his brother's face; a threat to tell their parents rose to his lips; then he noticed smoke spiraling up from under his fingernails. The flesh on his hands was puffed, beginning to rise and undulate like scalded milk. He froze, hands stuck straight out in front of him, puffing up more and more, smoke pouring out from the fingertips, streaming up from the top of his head.

He opened his mouth to scream, and a little lick of fire darted out from the tip of his tongue.

At which point Rich shoved him headfirst into the pond.

Later, when Ab felt safe enough to leave the water, Rich, looking at him furtively out of one corner of his eye for a minute or two, finally commented:

"That was weird, huh."

And they never spoke of it again.

Ab hadn't forgotten, though.

Several times, in later years, his niece or nephew found him wallowing in an animal trough by the barn, or emerging from an irrigation ditch; he knew it looked kind of funny. True, he had never actually burst into flames, or even come close, since that day with Rich at the pond, and in all the years he'd worried, waited, and taken precautions, he'd never spoken about it to a living soul. At first, he was too horrified; then, as time went on, he began wondering if Rich remembered what had happened, or if he was inclined to think it had all been make-believe. Sometimes Ab even half believed he'd made it up.

Only once had he felt an urge to confess.

He'd turned to Dennis one afternoon while the two of them were heaving bales of hay into the barn loft and said, "I nearly burst into flames when I was just a few years younger than you for no reason at all."

Dennis, who was fourteen at the time, was not paying much attention to his uncle; a sharp wind had suddenly picked up and he was worried, feeling more than ordinarily light on his feet. He looked at Ab with an uncomprehending expression Ab interpreted as disbelief.

"I could feel it happening," he explained earnestly. "I could feel myself just getting hotter and hotter . . ."

Ab's voice trailed off as Dennis, who had picked up only the last part of the conversation and was desperately trying to figure out what his uncle was talking about, nodded solemnly and went back to worrying about the wind.

Ab always slept naked, window open, even in the dead of winter. This was a habit his wife, Mary Dufore (formerly Prescott), never got used to, but eventually stopped trying to change. In thirty years, he never owned a winter coat, or wore gloves, or a hat or scarf.

He married late in life. He was over thirty before Mary Prescott, whose first husband, Hal, had died in a logging accident three years before, broke down his resistance. If she hadn't already been a widow, experienced in burying one husband, Ab might not have married her. But he figured that since she'd lost one, the possibility of losing a second wouldn't hit her so hard.

Besides, he was lonely. . . .

Still was, he realized now, as he stood watching the flaming light flicker and fade from his brother's face as the sun sank finally below the horizon. He understood the sad look in Rich's eyes, though he did not realize the same look was in his own, as well: no woman could make the weight worth bearing.

Jeanette came to the house a few days later, looking for Dennis.

There was a tiny cut on her lip and the skin around her left eye looked as though it had not yet decided whether to turn black or not.

Her dad's found out, Anne thought, as she stood at the top of the back stoop looking down at the girl in the red dress.

Out loud she said, "He isn't here right now."

She could remember a time, sixteen years before, when she had stood at the bottom of this step, three months pregnant, with a bloody nose her father had given her. It had been Rich's grandmother who'd met her then. Old Michelle Dufore hadn't said a word, just brought her into the kitchen and cleaned her up, then sent Ab out to the field to tell Rich she was here. She'd made tea for both of them as chill November sun spilled over the oak table, splashing her bruised face and Michelle's lined one with stark light.

She could remember holding the steaming mug between

cold, quivering hands and looking out over Michelle's shoulder, to see Rich, framed in the window, running towards the house, and her.

"Fool of a girl," old Michelle had sighed softly, her voice gentle, her eyes sad.

"You want to come in and wait?" Anne asked the La-Fleur girl. "He probably won't be much longer."

In the kitchen Anne moved quietly to the icebox and took out a chunk of ice. She wrapped it in a linen napkin and offered it to Jeanette.

"You walk into a door?" she joked.

Jeanette pressed the napkin to her eye.

For a moment, they looked at one another, then Anne put water on to boil. She and the LaFleur girl maintained a neutral silence until the kettle had started to shrill.

"You take honey or sugar in your tea?" Anne asked.

"Maple syrup, if you got it."

"Why'd your daddy hit you?" Anne asked as she pulled the jug of syrup out of the cupboard and plunked it down on the table in front of Jeanette.

Jeanette shot her a quick glance sideways, but said nothing.

"You in trouble?" Anne asked her bluntly.

"No."

"You like my boy a lot, don't you?"

Jeanette nodded, a quick jerk of her head, the vehemence of it telling Anne more than words could have.

"Then you're in trouble," Anne remarked, a little wryly. Boots thudded on the back step; an instant later, Dennis came through the door, bringing the smell of sunshine and alfalfa with him. He stopped when he saw his mother seated across the table from his girlfriend, who was looking a little more the worse for wear than he remembered seeing her the night before.

Anne stood up and crossed to the back door.

"I need some radishes," she said, as she brushed past her son. "Why don't you invite Jeanette to stay for supper?"

As she closed the door behind her, she heard Dennis ask, "What happened?" in a tight, unhappy voice.

They were gone when Anne came back in, but Gran Marie was standing in the kitchen, arms plunged up to her elbows in a sinkful of leafy greens: acid-green radish stalks, deep glossy green spinach, cool, green-yellow leaf lettuce caught jeweled droplets in their veins as rivulets of water streamed across their leaves. The vegetables were ready to cook, but there wasn't much sense in starting them until everyone was home.

"Dennis come in yet?"

"Mmm," her daughter-in-law replied, walking through to the porch off the kitchen. She started to haul in the clothesline. Sheets, shirts, jeans, underwear jerked and flapped their way across the yard, to the loud complaints of unoiled pulleys. Anne pulled in the first sheet as it came fluttering over the porch rail, folded it, then dropped it into the basket. She threw the pins into a little sack that looked like a doll's dress and hung from the line.

"Somethin's happened to him," she said.

She continued to fold laundry while Gran Marie washed vegetables. After a few minutes, Anne said, "I told his father. I told him, 'Sooner or later, somethin's goin' to happen to him.' I told him he ought to say something."

Gran Marie put down the vegetable brush and joined her daughter-in-law on the porch. Silently, they pulled in clean, wind-dried bedclothes and nightclothes, everyday and Sunday-best clothes. Out beyond the barn, the sky slowly opened fists of gold, releasing pale pink and mauve streamers into the deeper smoke-gray that was unrolling itself across the horizon like a carpet.

"What if she gets pregnant?" Anne demanded, taking it for granted Gran Marie understood her conversation.

"Then there'll be another Dufore wife around here," Gran Marie said.

Anne folded the last sheet into quarters, then eighths, then punched it flat as she held it against her chest.

"Poor girl," she said, and dropped the sheet into the basket.

Later that night, she and Gran Marie were washing up together. Dennis had borrowed the pickup to take Jeanette home; Anne suspected it would likely have a breakdown somewhere along the road that would take considerable time to fix.

"The LaFleur girl pregnant?" Gran Marie asked her as she ran a cloth expertly over the serving platter.

"Not yet," Anne answered. "You know, I almost told that girl she should listen to her daddy. I almost told her that."

She sighed and stared out the window at the reflection of her face and Gran Marie's, framed against the velvet-black night like pearls in a jeweler's case.

"But what would have been the use?"

The dishwater had turned lukewarm, gray, the soap bubbles long used up. She swished the water across the face of a dinner plate, thinking all the while of her son, Dennis, and the LaFleur girl out there somewhere in the dark. A slick of grease floated on top of the water, ringing her two arms like bracelets, and she thought of Rich running across the fields to her those many years before, of the feel of his body against hers in the still dark of their room. She thought of the time a year or two before their marriage when she'd found him lying in a pile of wood with a wrenched ankle and a frayed rope around his neck. She'd thought she'd understood, then, for his best friend had recently been killed in a freak accident and Rich had been depressed, but there was no understanding the afternoon some years later when she'd found him bleeding into a tub full of tepid water.

Dennis had been six at the time, and Allie had just turned three.

The night before, Rich and Anne had gone to the movies in Bennington. They'd seen something with Bette Davis and Paul Henreid, and the next day Anne had gone into Bennington again, to have her hair done the same as Bette Davis's.

Gran Marie was in the kitchen when she got home, feeding Allie her midday meal, while Dennis scraped around in the dirt just outside the back door, playing with sticks and tormenting a beetle.

"Rich feeling poorly?" Marie asked her when she came in.

"Not that I know of," Anne answered.

"Seemed a bit quiet at breakfast this morning. He come in just a while ago wanting to take a bath! Fancy takin' a bath in the middle of the day!" Marie snorted.

"He had a restless night," Anne said. "Maybe I'll just go up and make sure he's feeling all right."

At the top of the stairs she was assailed by the familiar stink from the room her father-in-law, Davy Dufore, shared with Gran Marie. Though nothing was ever said, it was commonly known the man was almost completely rotten through and through; it had been more years than anyone could remember since he'd left the room where he now crouched in a wheelchair by the window, a stinking, bloated bag of living decay.

Anne could hear the sound of water running in the bathroom. For a moment she hesitated and almost went back downstairs. Then she noticed the trickle of water seeping out from under the door, soaking in between the wide pine boards.

"Rich!" she called out, and wrenched open the door.

He was lying half on the floor, half draped against the tub, his arms hanging over the edge, corpse-white in pink-tinged water that poured out of the tub and across the floor.

"Jesus Christ!" she cried, as she hauled him back over the soaking tiles and out into the hallway.

"Mother!" she screamed. "Call the doctor!"

Frantically she ripped the scarf she was wearing from around her neck and tied it tightly around one of his upper arms. Then she grabbed his handkerchief out of his pants pocket and tied it around the other arm. She felt for a pulse in the throat and found one, faint but pumping.

There in the hall, her wet husband lying half in her lap and half in a pool of pinkish bathwater, she wondered if she had found him in time, hoped Dennis would not climb the stairs in search of her, wondered how she would explain this to the doctor, if he'd say Rich would have to go to the State Hospital at Waterbury. Mostly she hoped no one would ask her why Rich had done such a thing, because she would not know how to answer.

The doctor came and took Rich away to the hospital in Bennington. He was stitched up, antiseptic white bandages were wrapped around both wrists, and he received a blood transfusion. Anne went to see him every day, but Rich never said anything about the suicide, never said a word about the straight-edge razor Anne had found at the bottom of the bathtub.

"You act like you're in here for an appendix operation!" she shouted at him once, tears of frustration in her voice and eyes. "I can barely hold my head up in town."

But he only said, "You wouldn't understand, Annie. Please just take me home."

"So you can try it again?" she spat.

He didn't answer her, just rolled over on his side with his face to the wall.

He stayed in the hospital for three weeks. Every day a psychiatrist came and asked him if he was unhappy, if he ever thought about sleeping with other men, why he'd tried to kill himself, but Rich just rolled over and stared at the wall.

For a while, they tried giving him pills, but he flushed them down the toilet when nobody was looking.

Finally the hospital told Anne there was no point in keeping him there any longer, so she brought him home, and he didn't even seemed surprised to hear his father had died when he got there.

He seemed all right, but each evening, as the clock wound round towards bedtime, Anne felt a tightness wrap around her heart. When she finally climbed the stairs to the room she shared with Rich, her face was drawn and tired.

He seemed all right, but things were different between them. She wished he'd betrayed her with another woman, lied to her or stolen from her—those were things she could understand; she could forgive almost anything she could understand. But this! Even when he finally told her about the dreams, the terrible dreams of death and destruction that tormented him because inevitably they came true, even when he told her of how he'd dreamed his best friend dead, his father dead, she was furious—disbelieving and furious—that mere dreams, shadowy fears that might never come true (or even if they did), could drive him to take himself out of her life forever.

During the day, she could push the anger away; sometimes she even thought she was done with it. It always came as a shock when she found herself lying wide awake and angry in the bed beside him. Nighttime was the hardest because there was nothing to do but lie there in the dark, listening to him breathe and wondering if or when he might try it again.

Years had passed, but still nighttime was the hardest.

Anne rinsed the last plate and met her mother-in-law's eyes in the reflecting glass window.

"What would've been the use?" she asked again, and handed the plate to Marie.

Nearly eleven o'clock, and Dennis wasn't home yet.

She pulled the plug and watched the water whirlpool down the drain. She thought about the first time Ab had tried to do himself in, but only succeeded in blowing off an ear, and of the times after that. Mary swore she hadn't slept a whole night through in years. She thought about her father-in-law, Davy Dufore, and how he'd somehow managed to get himself to the top of the back stairs that night when they'd all been at the hospital with Rich and throw himself down, leaving a fine mess for Gran Marie to find when she got home.

"What the hell's the matter with these crazy Dufores?" she asked out loud. "What the hell they keep doing it for?"

Gran Marie said nothing. She'd married two Dufore men and lost them both. Of the three sons she'd borne, one was gone and the other two seemed hell-bent on going. She'd given up trying to understand years ago.

"Maybe they just can't help themselves," Anne sighed. "I remember once, when I was just a girl, my daddy took me to Montpelier in his Ford. For about six or five miles along the highway there was just thousands of dead frogs, all squished in the middle of the road.

"I asked my daddy why all those frogs were squished

dead, and he said every once in a while, they get this crazy urge to find water on the *other* side of the highway. It's just instinct, he told me, but instinct's a real powerful thing. It's hard to fight."

She folded the damp dishtowel in half and draped it over the back of the stove, then turned on the porch light for Dennis and turned off the kitchen light. On the way upstairs, Anne said:

"I think that's how it is with the Dufores, too. Just instinct."

Four years later, just moments after Ab Dufore launched himself off the embankment behind the mill that day in 1956, Dennis and Jeanette rushed breathless and half hysterical into the parking lot of the Texaco station, yelling something about Ab, the brook, and fire. At first no one was able to make head nor tail out of what they were trying to say. Dennis had fallen against one of the pumps, hanging there limp while he sobbed out nonsense in ragged gasps of breath. Jeanette had stopped a few feet behind him, her chest heaving, her hair all awry, and, to the Woodie boys' great interest, her dress misbuttoned to show a glimpse of cleavage.

Finally, one of the men said, "I think he's saying Ab Dufore jumped off the cliff into Crockett's Brook."

So they went and had a look.

There wasn't much left, just some charred bones and black, oily lumps where flesh had been.

People in Esperance weren't too surprised, though it did seem a bit extreme, setting fire to oneself in addition to jumping off the embankment into the brook.

"Oh well," Gran Marie said when they broke the news to her. "Like as not it's better so; if he'd kept on with the rifle, there wouldn't have been much left of him 'fore long, anyway."

Chapter

4

❧❧❧

In the half-light Allie turned, turned, and her white full-
skirted cotton dress swirled round her legs as she turned,
whispered against her calves.

"Tony," she murmured, her eyes closed tight, the better
to see him. Slowly they waltzed across stripes of light that
stretched down from between the warped board walls to the
floor, and her face felt warm, then cool, then warm again as
she passed from light to shade, turning, turning. . . .

Sometimes he said: *I love you,* and held her so hard against
the wall she could feel ridges of old pine pressing into her
shoulders. *I love you,* he'd say, and drop his lips down on
hers, his kiss as light and inevitable as a snowflake falling
while he held her there, his hips pressing hard against her,
pushing the small of her back into the rough boards.

Sometimes she said goodbye, and sent him away, though

it half broke her heart to do it, to see the pain and longing in his hound-dog eyes.

"You're a star and I'm just a nobody," she'd say, her voice just barely catching. "I couldn't let you sacrifice your career for me."

He argued, of course, but still she sent him away, eyes stinging, the sense of her own nobility soaring in her heart.

Other times she tried his name on hers, rolled *Mrs. Curtis, Allie Curtis, Mrs. Tony Curtis* across her tongue, the words sweet as hard candy in her mouth.

Turning, turning now in the circle of his arms, she saw palm trees silhouetted against the orange screen of her eyelids, saw the wide curve of the driveway leading up to a Spanish-style villa in the Hollywood hills, saw herself swept up that drive in a long gleaming limousine that slipped through zebra stripes of light under the palms.

. . . This week we're visiting the home of two of Hollywood's most popular stars

(Sometimes she was the interviewer)

who also happen to be one of its most happily married and glamorous couples—

(and sometimes not)

—Tony Curtis and Allie Dufore. . . .

Now she was resting against his chest, gathered in against him with her one free hand raised to stroke his face. His cheek was warm from the light that slanted in through the venetian blinds in their fully modernized kitchen (in and of itself as big as the whole first floor of the Dufore farmhouse), and rough. They'd stayed in bed so late he hadn't had time to shave, and she hugged that secret to her, hugged him to her while the interviewer talked on and on and the photographers' flashes exploded against her closed eyes and Tony's lips moved soft as a moth's wing across her hair.

Darling, he said. *My darling.*

"Not in front of the photographers," she sighed. . . .
"You got somebody in here, Allie?"

Dennis was standing in the doorway of the barn.

All around him the white light of a cloudless afternoon crowded through to drown the shadows, and send palm trees and pink stucco Spanish villas flying. In the square of light where he stood she could see the roof of the farmhouse behind him and the line of pines that marked the course of the East-West Road beyond it.

"Of course not," she said, disengaging herself from the splintered post she'd been embracing just moments before.

"Could've sworn I heard you talking to someone," he said.

"Who would I be talking to in here?" she asked, picking a splinter out of her lip. "You must be imagining things, Dennis Dufore."

"Maybe so," he said, and shrugged. "Gotta set some posts. You seen the shovel anywhere round here?"

"Over there."

She stayed leaning against the post while he searched out just the one he wanted from the collection of various shovels that hung, along with rakes, hoes, and gardening equipment, against the far wall. It took him nearly forever to do it, and all the while she leaned there with her eyes fixed on the tough brown grass that fringed the perimeter of the barn-yard, then stretched all the way down the hill to the house. She tried squinting her eyes, but even with the scenery blurred all brownish green, no palm tree would superimpose itself there.

"This place must be about as far away from Hollywood as you can get," she murmured, and tried to imagine the staid white farmhouse pink or pale lavender.

"Maine's further," Dennis said, scraping the shovel with

the side of his boot to loosen the clumps of dirt and dried
manure that clung to it.

It was no use; she couldn't keep squinting forever. With a
sigh she let her face relax, and the dull, familiar world
snapped back into focus. The sight of that brown grass depressed her, though. She shut her eyes completely.

"You ever think about goin' west, Denny?" She asked.

"Nah, what for?"

"Dunno," she said, "but it sure would be different out
there. No snow, everything warm and green all year long
... you can have strawberries in December, Denny, just step
right outside your back door and pick 'em, and there's palm
trees and orange trees and big houses and everybody driving
big shiny cars, havin' parties . . ."

Dennis just said: "You read too many movie magazines."

But in her head she could see those cars coming up the
long curve of the drive, women in sparkly tight dresses and
white furs, men in tuxedoes getting out and walking up the
front steps and into the house, where somewhere music was
beginning to play. . . . She moved her hips to the beat of it,
felt just the tiniest pressure against her buttocks as they
brushed back and forth against the post. If she squeezed her
eyes tight shut and concentrated hard, she could hear the
clink of ice cubes, a hum that might be conversation.

The floor trembled slightly under her feet as Dennis
walked to the door.

"You coming?" Dennis asked as he brushed by her out
into the yard.

In her head she could see Tony dancing with some
blonde, the two of them revolving slowly in a bright circle
of light, like a spotlight, but his eyes stared out straight over
his partner's gleaming head, searching for *her*.

"In a minute," she said. "Shut the door, will ya?"

Dennis pulled the door shut behind him; as it closed the spotlight dwindled, the blonde disappeared, and she found herself in *his* arms once again. The music played, and Tony bent his head to whisper in her ear

I thought he'd never leave.

Chapter
5

Jeanette wondered why Dennis always kept rocks in his pockets.

Lots of them.

Not small, round pebbles, the kind boys might pick up unthinking as they hunted for birds' nests or daydreamed under trees; not flat skimmers for skipping across the surface of the quarry or chunks of granite or sandstone to lob into fields as they walked along country roads.

No, these were not like the ones that had filled her brother Tommy's jacket pockets. There was nothing unpremeditated about the collection of small boulders that bulged on either side of Dennis's denim jacket, or dragged down the hems of his winter coat.

"I like 'em," he'd said, when she'd asked about it, and that had been that.

He often gave her rocks as some boys might have given her wildflowers, collecting them as they walked together across fields, through woods, or down roads. She'd thought, at first, he was nervous with her, and trying to hide it, so she'd accepted the rocks he handed to her, pitching them in ditches, where they often made a satisfying plunk in the run-off, or back into the road to kick along in front of her for a while. Sometimes she sent them spinning in a high, wide arc, far out into a bordering field.

He seemed hurt by that, though, so she took to putting them in her pockets, as he did, and dumping them later, when she got home.

She noticed as time went on and they spent more time together that the rocks seemed to get bigger and heavier, and he gave her more of them, more often.

So she'd started keeping some of his rocks on the table next to her bed.

The summer of 1956, the summer Ab made his leap from the cliff into Crockett's Brook, Jeanette turned eighteen.

She woke up the morning of her birthday and lay quietly in bed, waiting for something to happen. She didn't know what she expected; she just didn't think she'd feel so exactly the same that morning as she had the day before.

She got out of bed and went to look at herself in the mirror. Same face, still unlined. She examined her upper body in the mirror but detected no change there, either. When she thought back to sixteen, she knew she was different now; how long would it take before she'd see a difference between seventeen and eighteen? What was the point of birthdays anyway, if you didn't have anything to show for them?

"Jeanette!" her mother shrilled from the bottom of the

steps. "You gotta take the trash to the dump. Your daddy
don't have time!"

"In a minute," Jeanette yelled down from her room, then
shut the door.

"My true love has wandered far over the sea . . ." she
hummed, pulling the ribbon from the heavy plait that hung
down her back, then shook her hair loose and started to
braid it again.

"All over creation, he wanders for me,

"To Asia and Persia and lands far and wide," she sang, her
eyes on the latest collection of Dennis's offerings.

"And always my pebbles are by his bedside . . ."

Down in the kitchen, she found her mother on hands and
knees, scrubbing the linoleum floor they'd put down new
only two years before.

"Look at it," her mother muttered. "Not even two years
old, and already yellowed."

She looked up as her daughter appeared in the doorway.
"Take big steps," she said.

Jeanette snatched an apple out of the bowl on the counter
near the sink.

"There's three big barrels out back that gotta go. Maybe
you oughta ask Wally Martine to help you load 'em up."

"Don't need Wally," Jeanette said with her mouth full of
apple. "I'm strong enough."

For as long as she could remember, Maurice LaStrange
had worked the gate at the dump. He was there now as she
drove up, slouched in a chair inside the little green shack at
the entrance. Behind him, mountains of garbage rose in
glory, country cousins to the greater ranges of the Rockies
or the Himalayas. Beyond the piles of refuse, a thick funnel
of smoke gusted up from the burning pit. There were no
trees to diffuse the light that beat mercilessly down on the

rusted car frames, broken bedsteads, twisted hunks of metal that had once been farm tools or integral parts of some necessary machine. Worn leather harnesses, dead batteries, the front seats and back seats of automobiles, smashed radios, scrap lumber, furniture splintered beyond repair blanketed the earth in all directions, save for one chaste corner reserved for the everyday contents of family trashcans.

Over this private kingdom Maurice LaStrange held sway, a product of his environment. His fox-colored hair, cut in the same bristly crew cut he'd worn for twenty years, had taken on a patina like the bloom on old chocolate. His clothes were culled from the heaps of refuse behind him, as was the chair he sat on, the boards the shack was built of; he looked as if he'd been thrown away himself.

What stood out most about Maurice (Maury, as his family called him) was the tattoos. Ugly blue tattoos, coarse and crudely done, crawled up one arm and down the other in thick, sinewy lines. From earliest childhood Jeanette had been fascinated by those tattoos.

There was one, especially: a squat, buxom woman, completely naked, posed with her legs coyly crossed, a ball and chain trailing from one thick ankle. She stretched from his biceps almost to his elbow; Jeanette could never come to the dump without sneaking a look at her.

Maury looked up as she pulled in and threw the Chevy into neutral. His practiced eye scanned the contents of the backseat.

"Seven'five cents," he said.

Jeanette dug into the back pocket of her dungarees and snaked a limp, crumpled dollar bill up from the bottom. When she reached it out through the window, she caught Maury's eyes looking straight down the open neck of her shirt; it occurred to her he couldn't be much more than thirty-five or forty.

"I'll come down 'n' help you unload," he offered unexpectedly. Maury seldom left the gate.

He came around to the passenger side of the car and slid in beside her, bringing with him a faint odor of must, old metal, and mildew. Jeanette thought he smelled a little like a cellar (she liked the smell of cellars) and wondered if his skin felt cool and damp.

"So, how old're you now?" he asked as they bumped slowly down the dirt track that wound down to the dump.

"Eighteen," she said.

"You were sure an ugly kid," he remarked, leaning back against the seat. "You've improved."

They pulled up in front of a soaring heap of rubbish. Jeanette got out, opened the back of the Chevy, and leaned in to grab one of the trash barrels by its handle. She heard Maury LaStrange's feet crunching over gravel and garbage as he came round to her side, then felt him pressing against her as he edged in and reached in for the other handle. His free hand wandered lightly across her bottom, resting briefly on her right buttock.

"Cut it out," she told him.

"Just trying' to help," he said as they wrestled the barrel out of the backseat.

"I see you goin' up the Ridge Road a lot," he said.

Jeanette didn't answer. She dove back into the car and hauled out the second barrel. Maury made no move to help her this time. He stood with his buttocks resting lightly against the first barrel, arms crossed so the striking snake on his right arm seemed about to sink its fangs into the monstrous bosoms of the naked woman on his left arm.

"You got a nice ass, Jeanette," he commented after watching her drag the last barrel out of the car and dump it onto the heap.

"You're a pig, you know that, Maury LaStrange?" she said.

He just laughed a strange, silent laugh. All the LaStranges laughed like that; even the children hugged laughter to themselves, like misers.

She loaded the empty barrels back into the car.

"You're sitting on my barrel," she told him.

He stayed where he was long enough to get under her skin, then moved a step or two, so she had to push by him to get it. Her bare shoulder brushed against the tattoo lady's breasts.

She grabbed the last barrel, heaved it in on top of the others, and got into the front seat of the Chevy.

"Next time you go up to visit Dennis Dufore, stop by," Maury said as she pulled away.

She looked back at him once, in the rearview mirror. He was standing where she'd left him; the way he smiled told her he'd known she'd look back.

The LaStrange family had been in Esperance as long as the Dufores. The bones of the two families were mingled in the graveyard, and names of long-dead LaStranges marched down lists of births, marriages, deaths and property transfers side by side with Dufore ancestors, while the living representatives of each generation continued to live in close proximity on the banks of Crockett's Brook.

The first LaStrange was a trapper who came to Esperance at the end of the eighteenth century, accompanied by an Indian squaw and several half-breed children. He built first a lean-to, then later a cabin on a knoll above the brook; two hundred years later, LaStranges still lived on the same spot.

Unlike other founding families in Esperance, the La-Stranges were neither farmers nor merchants. Each generation of LaStranges made their living as men-of-all-work.

They sugared in sugaring season and hayed in haying season. They trapped when they could and hired themselves out when it was necessary. Aside from the land where their house stood, they owned no property until the summer of 1912, when Pierre LaStrange, who would drown in a flash flood three years later during the worst mud season in forty years, acquired several acres of barren, rocky ground with a notion of raising goats on them.

Pierre was the only member of the family who had any real enthusiasm for the goat scheme; when he died, the herd was neglected until complaints from various people who found starving goats raiding their gardens, compost heaps, and trashcans, or were attacked by the ornery ram who seemed to regard the road running past LaStrange land as his own property forced Pierre's sons Bertrand and Christian to do something about it. They brought two of the goats home to help keep the grass around the house under control and sold the rest of the herd to farmers around Esperance. The ram they shot and ate through most of the autumn.

The land lay neglected for several more years until Pierre's sharp-witted daughter Hannah noticed townsfolk were using it to dump their unwanted rubbish and suggested the family should turn this happy circumstance to good account.

Jeanette's birthday fell, that year, on the first Friday in August, the night of the regular monthly dance at the town meeting hall. Bob Munson's band played, mostly contras and waltzes. That night, Jeanette stood against one wall with Becky Williams and Annie Martine and waited for Dennis. Though the windows and doors were open, the air was close and heavy with the sweet smell of home-baked cakes, human sweat, cheap cologne, and new-mown grass. A lot of people were there that night; Jeanette found herself looking again and again at Maury LaStrange as he danced, first with his wife, then with his sister, then with Paula Delagarde.

She was surprised to see he danced well, making even Paula, a notoriously bad dancer, look good. Perhaps the fact he was wearing a long-sleeved shirt that covered the tattoos allowed Jeanette to see him as a dancer, not a garbage man.

"What're you looking at?" Annie asked.

"Nothin' special," Jeanette said, as the music wound down and Maury LaStrange led Paula Delagarde off the floor.

He was standing near her when the next song began.

"Wanna dance?" he asked her.

She had never danced with Maury or any other LaStrange before; her father called them "white trash," a term that seemed to depend more on what a man left on his lawn than on what he did. But she'd been eighteen, a legal adult, for almost a whole day, and this was the first unusual thing that had happened to her, so she nodded and walked out on the floor with him.

The band was playing a waltz. She felt Maury La-Strange's arm snake around her waist holding her close, but not too close. She could feel his hand settle firmly into the hollow between her rib cage and the swell of her hip as though it had every right to be there, as though it had always rested there, and belonged there. Just a slight pressure from that hand guided her around the floor as easily as following a map, and he never once stepped on her feet, as Dennis often did. His shirt was open at the neck; she could see tracks where sweat had slid down his throat to nestle in beaded clusters among the fine, curly mat of fox-colored hair on his chest. He smelled wholly human tonight; no trace of rubbish clung to him.

They circled round and round, like Ginger Rogers and

Fred Astaire. Jeanette began to think she might be feeling different: grown-up and graceful, more like a woman and less like a schoolgirl.

When the dance ended, Maury said, "You've got two left feet, Jeanette LaFleur."

Dennis showed up almost an hour later.

"Happy birthday," he said, ducking his head as though he might have kissed her, then changed his mind. They'd been going together for three years, but he still found it almost impossible to touch her in public.

"I got somethin' for you. Come outside."

They walked out across the dirt parking lot, beyond the glow of meetinghouse lights into the blackness of the trees at the far end of the lot. Under the trees, Dennis slipped an arm around her, his hand resting on the spot where Maury LaStrange had so recently laid his.

"I'm not going to be able to *see* what you got me out here," Jeanette complained. "It's too dark."

"Wait till your eyes get used to it," he said, and stopped walking to kiss her full on the mouth.

They walked through the belt of trees and emerged in an open meadow where a million fireflies pierced the darkness like candlelight shining through lace curtains.

When they had settled themselves on a fallen tree in the middle of the field, he handed her a small box.

"Here," he said.

She fumbled to unwrap the paper.

"I can't see," she said.

Dennis fished in his pocket, dug out a lighter, then cupped his hand around the fragile flame and held it close as she tore away the wrapping. She opened the box and gently folded back the fluffy cotton that nestled inside. She lifted out a thin gold necklace with a gold heart-shaped pendant dangling from it.

"It's real gold," Dennis told her.

"Oh Denny," Jeanette breathed. "It's beautiful! It's the best present I ever got!"

She held it up to her neck and turned away from him.

"Help me fasten it," she told him.

He took the thin chain between awkward fingers and fumbled the clasp in the dark. He wished he could see the gold against the nape of her neck; when he'd seen it in the store in Bennington, it had reminded him of Jeanette's skin.

He managed to slip the hook through the eye and bent his head to kiss the back of her neck.

"Dennis, you're so sweet to me," Jeanette murmured as his lips wandered across the back of her neck, down the side of her throat to the hollow of her collarbone. One hand slipped the sleeve of her blouse and her bra strap down, leaving her shoulder bare, while the other squeezed and kneeded gently at her waist. She could hear his breathing become slower, deeper, as his mouth trailed along her bare shoulder and his hand moved up to cup her breast, but she didn't turn around.

Jeanette was thinking: This feels nice, but it's just the same . . .

She felt so sad, thinking like that, she thought she might start crying.

Dennis wrapped both arms around her and began kissing her neck and shoulders, so she didn't cry. Instead, she wriggled around in his arms to face him, and began removing the rocks from all his pockets.

Ab's demise at the end of August created a deal of heated discussion between Father Dozier, the priest of St. Claude's, and the Dufore family.

The church took the position that Ab could not be buried in sanctified ground, since he'd died by his own hand.

The Dufores clung buckle and thong to the mendacious
story he'd simply taken a fancy to climb the tree out behind
the mill, and had slipped. When Father Dozier demanded
why Ab had apparently seen fit to douse himself with some
flammable substance if suicide had not been his intent, the
Dufores answered with perfect sincerity that he had done no
such thing; if anything, Ab had been a victim of an Act of
God.

The argument might have gone on interminably if the
undertaker, Raoul DuMont, had not pointed out that high
summer was not the time of year to be dragging out a burial.

"There's not much left of Ab," he told Father Dozier,
"but what there is ain't gettin' any sweeter, don't you
know."

Still, Father Dozier was a man of principle. He might not
have surrendered if he hadn't already buried a number of
Dufores who had died in circumstances nothing short of
miraculous. Ab was eventually buried in the Catholic graveyard.

A week after the funeral, Jeanette rode her bicycle up to
the Dufore farm. She'd baked three loaves of bread in the
morning, and when they were ready, she wrapped them
carefully in a towel and put them in the basket on the
handlebars.

There were two ways of getting to the Dufore farm. The
first was to go seven miles up Clark Hill Road, past the turn
off for the East-West Road, then turn left onto Piggery
Road, which crossed the East-West Road a mile above the
long drive leading to the Dufore house. The second way was
to turn directly onto the East-West Road and follow it as it
wound along beside Crockett's Brook.

The first route was preferred during mud season, because
Clark Hill Road was paved, while the dirt East-West Road
was narrow, rutted, and often treacherous. During the dry

months, however, the East-West Road was shorter, and that was the route Jeanette chose. She was within a mile of the Dufore farm when her front tire burst.

A few hundred yards further on, a small dirt road forked sharply away from the main road, crossed the creek by way of a wooden bridge, then climbed steeply up the back of a ridge of pines. It was called the Ridge Road and led to an old cabin that sat at the edge of the Dufore property line. For many years Dennis's grandmother Marie had lived there, first with Dennis's grandfather, Paul, then after his disappearance with her second husband, Paul's younger brother, Davy.

When Michelle Dufore, Dennis's great-grandmother, finally died, Gran Marie and Davy had brought their sons to live in the main farmhouse. The cabin stood empty for several years until Ab married and brought his wife to live with him there.

Now Ab was dead, Mary would probably move down to the main house with Gran Marie, Rich, and Anne, and the cabin would be empty again. It occurred to Jeanette as she wheeled her bicycle past the turnoff that she might possibly be the next woman to live in the cabin on the ridge.

The LaStrange house was almost directly opposite the Ridge Road. It had grown, over the years, from a ramshackle cabin into a full-blown ramshackle house that leaned crazily in all directions, yet remained erect in stubborn defiance of gravity. Jeanette had passed it many times on her way to and from Dennis's house, never paying much attention except to wonder, now and then, at the way garbage seemed to follow the LaStranges around. Piles of junk rose all over the front yard in pale imitation of their more impressive brethren at the dump, and a promising collection of automobile parts gathered in a heap at the side of the road. LaStrange children cluttered the yard in clothes that were either too big or too small and had obviously never belonged to them. Even the dog, a fat, wheezing, brindle-colored beast, and the chickens roosting on the front porch looked as though they'd been pulled out of a trashcan.

There was a '49 DeSoto up on blocks in the front yard, and Maury LaStrange was just emerging from underneath it. He was naked from the waist up, covered with grease. There was a boy with him, a stringy, gangling, fox-haired kid of maybe fifteen or sixteen; Jeanette had seen him at the dump now and then.

"Get me a beer, Mike," Maury said to the boy.

The kid slouched towards the house and disappeared through the torn screen door.

"Hey, Jeanette," Maury said as she passed. "Goin' up to Dufores'?"

"Yes."

"Flat tire?" he asked.

"My goodness, you *are* a genius," she answered.

"Want a beer?"

"No thank you."

"Want a ride?" he offered.

"I can walk," she said.

"Want a screw?" he called after her.

"You're a *pig!*" she yelled at him.

He grinned. The boy appeared in the doorway of the house.

"We're outta beer, Pop!" he called.

"Well, go get some more, for Chrissake!" Maury told him.

"See ya later, Jeanette!" he yelled up the road after her.

She met him on a mountaintop. She had climbed up the face of a steep cliff that crumbled and shifted with every step she took. She had hauled herself up that mountain on her hands and knees, knife-sharp rocks biting into her fingers, slashing her legs until she bled. She had crawled up the side of that mountain, her hair tumbled down her back in crazy knots, her breath coming in deep, sobbing gasps.

He was waiting for her on the mountaintop, naked from the waist up. His hair was the same color as the rocks she'd climbed over.

"I knew you'd stop by sometime," he said. His arms reached for her; his hands slid under her arms and held her waist. She was falling towards him, falling against him. She was lying on the mountaintop and he was running his tongue down the hollow between her breasts.

One hand on each of her shoulders, he held her firmly, slid himself between her legs, then paused a moment before he began lowering himself.

Only then did she realize they were making love on a mountain of rubbish.

"Shit!" Jeanette swore, when she woke up and found herself naked in bed, clutching the pillow to her breasts, her nightgown wound tightly around her knees. It was the third time in one week she'd dreamed of Maury LaStrange.

Jeanette was on her way to the quarry two days later when the DeSoto pulled over a little ahead of her and Maury leaned across the passenger seat and opened the door.

"Want a ride?" he asked.

She kept walking. The DeSoto crawled along, keeping pace with her.

"Where you goin'?" he asked. "Cat got your tongue, Jeanette? You feelin' a little shy around old Maury?"

He stopped the car and sat behind the wheel, watching her.

She looked at him consideringly for a moment, then retraced her steps and slid in beside him.

"Where you goin'?" he asked again as he pulled back out into the road.

"The quarry," she said.

"Kind of cool to be swimming," he remarked. "Why don't you come to Bennington with me? I'll take you to a picture show."

"You've got to be kidding," she said.

He shrugged and said nothing more until they reached the narrow track that led from the road to the quarry. Then he put the car in neutral and twisted to face her, his arm lying across the back of the seat, his fingers brushing the back of her hair; Jeanette knew a crazy impulse to lean back and let that hand cradle her head.

"Thanks for the ride," she said as she opened the door.

"Be seein' you," he said.

That night, as she lay in bed, Jeanette admitted to herself that for some unexplainable reason, she was powerfully drawn to Maury LaStrange. All in all, he was a pretty poor excuse for a human being; his very presence set all her nerves on end in sheer aggravation. He annoyed the hell out of her, but that didn't seem to alter the fact she wanted to trace the contours of his atrocious tattoos with her tongue, feel his dirt-encrusted fingernails scrape the length of her spine.

She loved Dennis, but what she wanted from Maury had nothing to do with love. In fact, until she got this Maury bug out of her system, things between her and Dennis could never be quite the same.

So she went to the dump early the next day. He was there, as usual, the chair tipped back on two legs, his head resting against the chipped boards of the shack. He didn't say anything as she wheeled her bicycle slowly up the drive, but when she leaned it against an oil drum just outside the gate and came to stand in front of him, he tipped the chair back down and sat up straight.

Jeanette leaned over with her hands on his knees, her face level with his. He looked straight down her shirt and saw her breasts wobbling out the sides of her bra. He pulled her shirt up out of her jeans and thrust one hand up under it, squeezed her breasts, first one, then the other, ungently. She didn't move, but he could see her chest begin to rise and fall a little faster. She lowered her head and pressed her mouth against his; he could feel her lips open and he rammed his tongue deep into her mouth. She still supported herself with one hand against his knee, but the other came up to cradle the back of his head, pressing his kiss even harder against her mouth. His hands began kneading her breasts; when she suddenly ran her other hand up his thigh and grabbed the swell in his groin, he moaned, wrapped both arms around her back, and pulled her down onto her knees, between his legs.

Her hands fumbled at the belt of his pants. She thrust one hand into his fly, pulled out his penis, took it into her mouth. He could feel her trace around its head, then down to the root. He leaned back in the chair, closed his eyes, and put one hand on each side of her head to hold her steady.

Just when he was about to forget who he was, that he even existed, she stopped and pulled her head away. He whimpered and made a grab for her hair, but she scrambled up from her knees and backed away from him until she was standing with her back against the opposite wall.

He stood up, his penis still thrusting through the opening of his fly, pointing ramrod-straight, like an accusing finger, at Jeanette.

"What the—" he began, then shut up as she unzipped the fly of her own jeans and started to slide them down over her hips.

He yanked her pants down around her knees and slammed her hard against the wall, rapping her head sharply.

His hands tore at the underwear her mother had given her for her birthday; she could hear the fabric rip in his fingers. Then he pushed himself into her as they stood braced against the wall. Deeper and deeper he thrust, until he had filled her with himself. His lips ground against hers; his tongue, tasting of tobacco and whiskey, darted between her teeth.

She screamed a long, throbbing wail as he grunted obscenities in her ear and kept pumping against her until he finally fell out of her.

Afterwards she said, "Good thing nobody came by."

This is what Jeanette thought about Maury LaStrange:

His mouth tasted stale, and he pushed his tongue too far down her throat.

He played with her breasts as though he were trying to unscrew a jar.

He didn't bathe half as often as he should; his groin smelled of sweat and three-day-old underwear.

He wasn't good-looking, he didn't screw very well, and she thought he was a pretty poor specimen of a human being.

Nevertheless, she knew she'd go back

Chapter

6

❧❧

She became well acquainted with Maury's tattoos over the course of the next few weeks.

In addition to the naked woman, there was a snake entwined around a crude, flabby sword, a heart with the name Amelia in it (Maury never explained who Amelia was; his wife's name was Elyse), a cross, and, high up on his left shoulder, a skull and crossbones. His back and chest were unmarked.

"I did the snake myself," he told her one evening as they lay in the backseat of a junked Ford at the dump. Her head was on his chest and she was practically eye-level with the tattoo in question.

"My brother Jock did this one," he said, jerking his chin towards the woman. "The body, I mean. I had a guy in Bennington add the ball and chain, later."

"Why?" she asked, running her tongue experimentally over the tattoo lady's blue breasts.

"I was gonna go to Hollywood once. Was gonna start a business out there, maybe even get famous."

He laughed. "Got married, instead."

Maury rolled over so she was pinned beneath him, half falling off the torn black car seat. Dirty batting spilled through rents in the upholstery, and pointed, coiled springs poked through a dozen different places.

"Ow!" she yelped as one of these caught her in the small of her back. She tried to squirm out from under his arm, but he started kissing her neck and rubbing his hand up and down between her thighs; she forgot about the spring.

After the third time with Maury (a rough encounter in the swampy ravine down the road from his house, a place easily seen from the East-West Road; Maury had had to put his hand over her mouth and bury his own in her neck to keep back cries that could have been heard all over Esperance), Dennis suddenly asked her one night,

"Have you been kissing someone else?"

"Who else would I be kissing?" she asked, innocence in her eyes.

"Dunno," he said. "But somethin's different."

He was noticing other differences, as well. Nothing he could put a finger on, nothing he could give a name to; *Attitude* was what it came down to, he thought.

Dennis was pretty sensitive to attitude these days. For as long as Dennis could remember, his mother, Aunt Mary, and Gran Marie had spent a lot of time together in the kitchen, or evenings after supper on the veranda, sipping tea and talking about whatever women talked about. That hadn't changed, but Dennis sensed some difference in the way those three were getting along since Ab's death, almost as if they'd reached some mutual realization and shared like opinions about it, almost as if underneath idle talk, everyday chores, the occasional laughter, the women were waiting, listening, for the other shoe to drop.

That was *Attitude,* too. He couldn't put it into words; it would come out sounding dumb and crazy; but he knew it was there as sure as he was alive, and he sensed *Attitude* in Jeanette, too.

That was how he thought about the trace of tobacco smell that clung to Jeanette's hair sometimes, the slight taste of unfiltered cigarettes in her kiss. There was something else, too, some indefinable odor or flavor that was new and disturbing; it settled like mist, sometimes, into the hollows of her body, stirred in the air between them every time she moved. It gnawed at one corner of his brain, demanding to be named, but he pushed it away until the morning he walked with her down the East-West Road past the LaStrange house.

Maury was sitting on the stoop as they passed, with his wife, Elyse, and the ever-present tribe of LaStrange progeny who hurled themselves around the yard in frenzied play.

He nodded to them as they ambled past and took a pull off his beer. Dennis nodded back; Jeanette didn't even turn her head to look. The wind changed then, blew a tiny puff of air that tickled Dennis's nostrils with a familiar, elusive scent and was gone, but suddenly, he knew.

It was the odor off the LaStrange house he'd smelled on Jeanette's skin. Tobacco, beer, sweat, and sun-roasted rubbish; a smell he'd lived with most of his life, not unpleasant, really, but noticable whenever a LaStrange was in the vicinity. An inherited odor, passed down along with fox-colored hair and timber-wolf eyes.

He felt funny for a minute, kind of light-headed, as though he were looking at things through the bottom of a glass. There was Maury, tiny and distorted, on his faraway porch; Dennis could hear the screen door slam shut with a sharp crack as Mike LaStrange came through it with a beer for his mother and one for himself. There were Maury's nameless, numberless progeny scutting across the lawn like dried leaves. Here was Jeanette close beside him but far away, too, on the other side of the glass bottom. There was no sound except a high-pitched humming in his ears, and he was mildly surprised to find his feet were still moving, that he was still strolling sedately down the East-West Road beside Jeanette.

Then they were past the LaStrange house and he could see and hear properly again. Behind him he could hear the creak of the rusty swing set in Maury's front yard, the endlessly squabbling children. Jeanette turned to say something to him; her eyes were so clear, so free of guile, he found himself wondering if he was the only one who realized the whole world had stopped, briefly, just a moment before.

He might have talked himself out of what he was thinking, then, if the smell of Him on Jeanette's skin hadn't still been in his nostrils long after he'd taken her home.

He couldn't get that smell out of his nose, try as he would. At first, it was only Jeanette, who wore it like perfume, but sometimes, if the wind was in the right quarter, blowing down from the LaStrange house, he'd catch a whiff of it in the air. Gradually, it seemed to gather and grow stronger, permeating other things, until Dennis felt he lived under a permanent LaStrange-scented cloud.

He detected it in his food, so he stopped eating. Even Gran Marie's pie with sharp cheese melted over it could not tempt him; with the fork held to his mouth, chunks of cinnamon-browned apple swimming in lemon and cornstarch-thickened juice dripping from between thick, flaky crusts, the smell of Maury LaStrange rose up to strike him a blow in the face, and he pushed the pie away, untasted.

The smell was in the barn when he did the milking, in the fields as he helped harvest the corn. He could smell it in his clothes, and began insisting they be washed every day.

"D'you smell something funny?" he asked Allie one Saturday as they rode into town in the back of the pickup.

"Just the mill," she said, but Dennis shook his head. That stink was familiar, almost welcome.

The smell of LaStrange hung in his nostrils more acrid and sulfuric than the mill could ever be.

He began to imagine the air he breathed was swarming with fine specks of LaStrange dirt: all the dandruff, flakes of dead skin, sweat, and dirt scraped up by ragged fingernails and cemented into tiny clots by LaStrange spit riding the wind after every LaStrange sneeze or cough.

He imagined the stuff clogging his nose, coating his lungs and throat in an ever-thickening blanket, until one day he would be so choked with LaStrange pollution there would be no room for clean air.

"Disgusting!" Allie commented when he examined the goo in his handkerchief after sneezing. He didn't hear her, though; he was too intent on spotting any signs of LaStrange there.

The smell assailed his dreams as well. In nightly flights he found himself scooped up and tumbled end over end on a wind that stank of stale beer, unfiltered cigarettes, the feral scents of semen and garbage. In these dreams he did not drop suddenly a thousand feet to splatter against clean, brown earth; rather, he strangled slowly in the hot wind, suffocated like a flea rolled between the wind's forefinger and thumb, air leaking from his lungs until they were collapsed and only the stink remained, thick and unbreathable as pond water.

Over the course of a few weeks, he stopped eating, sleeping, or talking; the smell was everywhere, robbing his life of every small pleasure. He tried to stop breathing, too, but only succeeded in taking fewer, shallower breaths, which required remaining absolutely still.

So he stopped moving.

He lay as motionless as he could on his bed, counting the heartbeats between each breath.

Anne Dufore called the doctor, but after the first visit, when he opened the door with such cheerful force that new LaStrange air poured into the room, gushing into Dennis's mouth and lungs, Dennis kept the door locked and refused to open it to anyone, not even Jeanette.

Especially not to Jeanette. The day she stood outside his room, the smell was so strong he thought it had to be seeping in through the very wood.

"Go away!" he croaked and felt the extra breath he'd expended in speaking to her barred him from getting up and stuffing a towel under the door, though the smell was getting in that way.

"Dennis, what's the *matter?*" she asked. "Are you sick? *Please* open the door!"

She pleaded with him like that for quite a while, but he lay obstinately still, holding his breath completely, until, at last, she went away.

After she'd gone, Dennis lay on the bed, waiting as long as possible before inhaling the filthy air Jeanette had left behind. He could imagine the way she'd looked on the other side of the door: black hair hanging in thick, heavy plaits over her breasts, skirt and sweater hiding the curve of her belly and her smooth, wheat-colored thighs.

Imagining her like that, he knew he still loved her. For as long as Maury's stench clung to her, though, in her hair, on her skin and breath, he couldn't bear to be near her.

His lungs were burning. He hadn't taken a breath in nearly two minutes.

He knows, Jeanette thought as she started home. She guessed it was stupid to think he'd never find out.

Well, it was fine while it lasted, she thought.

Maury was out in front of Ron Woodie's gas station when Jeanette got into town. He was leaning out the window of the old black DeSoto talking to Ron, who was pumping gas. Maury's oldest boy, Mike, was barely visible in the seat beside him, hunched way down, his feet propped up on the dashboard.

She strolled over to the Coke machine outside the double garage doors, dropped a nickel in, then stood puzzling over Coke or Royal Palm Grape. She opened the machine door and pulled out a bottle of Coke just as Maury came up beside her and put his own nickel in.

"I gotta talk to you," she said.

He gave her a little sideways grin and nodded, then pulled out a root beer and stroked the beaded condensation from its neck suggestively.

"At the dump, tonight," he said.

They stood on either side of the soda machine and finished their drinks. When he was done, Maury dropped the bottle into a wire rack on the ground and sauntered back to his car.

"Get yer goddamned feet offa the dashboard," she heard him say to his son as he put the DeSoto in gear.

The smell was growing stronger.

Dennis pushed through the undergrowth along the banks of the brook, blowing a little from the exertion; he hadn't been off his bed in nearly two weeks. He was at a narrow part, where the water was barely a trickle between marshy banks of grass; the mud squelched under his shoes, sucked at his ankles as though it had divined his intent and were trying to anchor him in one place, far from the LaStrange house.

Dennis paused for a moment, to calm himself and get his bearings. He shifted the can he carried from one hand to the other, swore softly as some of the gasoline he'd siphoned from the Ford sloshed up and out of the open neck.

He hadn't dared bring a light, and the moon was just a nail paring in the sky. He'd waited until well after midnight before starting out, and still he worried some errant La-Strange might be up and about.

The odor that had plagued him for so many weeks was tickling his nostrils as he plunged back into the brook, making his way towards the wooden bridge and the knoll where the LaStrange house perched. The stench didn't seem quite so bad to him now; the gasoline cut it, and for the first time in weeks he could smell the sweet night air beneath it. Soon he would be rid of it forever. He was breathing normally again; since he'd made up his mind that afternoon to do something about it, the sharp, unwelcome scent no longer caught at his throat, making him gag.

He could just make out the silhouette of the house now, a black patch flush against an even denser black. The brook had widened, grown deeper and faster-moving; he sensed rather than saw he'd reached the bridge. He clambered up onto the bank and stood for a moment, eyes and ears straining for signs of movement in the still night.

There was nothing but the rustle of wind through the trees and water lapping gently against the bridge supports. He could hear frogs singing somewhere behind him, and a cricket was throwing its voice so it sounded almost as though it were just behind his left ear; his hand crept up to brush his neck.

The air vibrated with sounds and tiny movements, but there was nothing human in it, except for Dennis himself.

A gust of wind scudded down the hill from the LaStrange house and eddied around his head in giddy spirals, breaking the night's hold on him.

Not much longer, he thought, swallowing hard against the burning in his throat. Slowly, he started up the knoll toward the house, gasoline slapping softly against the sides of the can with his every step.

On her way to the dump that evening, Jeanette imagined telling Maury that it was finished. Sometimes he just shrugged and grinned. Sometimes he argued. Once they made love a final time; most often, though, she just told him quickly, then rode away on her bicycle.

The gate was closed when she got there, but the padlock had been left off, so she knew he was there. She pushed the gate open just enough to slide her body through; any wider and it screeched something terrible. The only light she had was the lamp on her bicycle. It was a black night out here away from the lights of houses and streetlamps. She leaned her back against the gate and waited for her eyes to adjust. Overhead, the moon hung just over the horizon and stars swarmed across the sky with a brightness that illuminated heaven but cast no light on earth.

"Maury?" She spoke softly; something about the dark, and the stillness, and her own intentions, made her want to speak softly.

There was no answer. After a minute, she went into the shed and fumbled under the counter, looking for a flashlight. She found two that didn't work at all before she found a third without batteries. Hunkered down there near the doorway, she took the batteries out of the first two flash-

lights and put them in the empty one. She was rewarded by
a pale trickle of light that picked out objects directly in front
of her and nothing more. Still, it was enough to keep her
from stumbling by accident into the burning pit or the
barbed wire that stretched around the perimeters of the
dump.

Since he wasn't waiting for her in the shack, Jeanette
thought the most likely place to look for him was in the
junk heap, where they had often made love in the backseats
of abandoned cars.

She stumbled between twisted, rusting chassis, skirted a
mountain of tires, played her light over the cab of a wrecked
pickup, all the while calling his name. The wrecked cars
ended and she found herself wandering around heaps of
broken furniture, rusted tools, punctured milk cans. She
began to wonder if he was there at all.

She finally found him sprawled at the bottom of a garbage heap. The flashlight was growing dimmer now, but she
could tell from the sound of his breathing that he was deeply
asleep, mouth open. She came a step or two closer and
caught the strong liquor smell on him. She played the light
over his unconscious body; he'd fallen dead drunk into a pile
of kitchen refuse with his head resting comfortably on old
cabbage leaves.

Jeanette turned to make her way back to the main gate. It
was not the first time she'd come late and found him like
that. She'd just have to come back in the morning and tell
him then.

The flashlight died when she was still some distance from
the gate, but it was lighter now. There seemed to be a faint
orange glow in the east that cast a soft sheen across the night
sky, enough for her to see the outline of the shack ahead.
The gate lay just beyond.

It wasn't until she was outside, wheeling her bicycle

down the rough dirt track back to the main road, that it occurred to her it was still too early for dawn to be lighting the sky.

Smoke and crackle followed Dennis as he walked down the East-West Road towards town. Behind him fire shot like a geyser a hundred yards in the air; over the roar of the burning came faint screams and babbling; barking, and gobbling from the house on the knoll.

The wind had picked up a bit, was gusting around him, plucking at his shirt and jabbing at the backs of his knees as though it were trying to kick his feet out from under him. It was an old trick of the wind's, that one, but Dennis was hardly aware of it. He ambled down the middle of the East-West Road, through flame-shot darkness, breathing in the purifying odors of smoke and burning wood. Far off he could hear the wail of Esperance's fire alarm; he supposed some neighbor, perhaps even Gran Marie, had seen the blaze and phoned Gladys Broussard, the operator.

The crazy old house had lit easy as kindling; he reckoned there wouldn't be much left to save once the volunteer fire department got there.

He felt light-headed, a little giddy, walking down that road in the dark. He knew he was clearly visible to anyone coming up toward the LaStrange place, but he didn't care. The air smelled so sweet and sharp; he drank it in with huge, greedy gulps, laughed out loud with the sheer, crazy joy of breathing and moving and living again.

Suddenly, he was ravenously hungry. He couldn't remember the last time he'd eaten. Saliva squirted up from under his tongue as his brain flooded with the look and taste and smell of his mother's pot roast; of Thanksgiving and Christmas turkeys, of Easter ham, mashed potatoes and boiled sweet potatoes glazed with brown sugar, slabs of butter melting into a mountain of fresh green peas, and Gran Marie's chocolate mayonnaise cake washed down with sweet black coffee.

His stomach muscles contracted painfully under the barrage of memory; he wanted desperately to eat, to stuff himself with good, plain fare, then find Jeanette, unbraid her hair, undo her blouse button by button, and run his tongue over every inch of her.

The wind was blowing steadily now. It gave him little shoves in the small of his back, tried to wrestle the rocks out of his windbreaker pocket, but he was drunk on clean air and memories and didn't care. The wind swallowed the sound of the fire truck; when it came suddenly around a sharp bend in the road, its glaring headlights caught him in the middle. For a moment he froze, blinded by the light, too firmly in the grip of his hungers to move, pinned to the spot by the glare of lights and the howling siren.

At the last moment, he lurched crazily to one side and felt the fender brush his trouser leg as the truck rushed by.

He thought it was terribly funny he'd nearly been killed by the fire truck on its way to salvage the LaStrange house. There had to be some kind of justice in that, he thought. It was terribly, terribly funny; he thought he was laughing, then became aware of the tears pouring down his face. He was weeping like a girl.

The siren stopped in mid-wail; the truck had arrived, and Dennis wondered if there was anything left to save.

The hunger was gone, sudden as it had come; so was his desire for Jeanette. Now all he wanted was to go back and look at the LaStrange place, see the result of his night's work and assure himself he was indeed free forever of Maury LaStrange. There would be time enough for food later. There would be time enough to find Jeanette, get off to a fresh start.

There was quite a crowd when Dennis arrived at the house.

The fire was subdued, no longer threatening the surrounding trees. He could still see the outline of the house through smoke and licks of flame; it seemed completely whole, untouched by the fire. Then he realized it was nothing more than a shell of charred ash standing though the frame was gone.

Light leapt weirdly, illuminating little groups of people who stood watching the fire department hose down the wreckage. He spotted his father and sister near the bridge, their near neighbors, the Shores, nearby. Numerous raggedy, barefoot children huddled in a forlorn clump at the bottom of the driveway leading up to the LaStrange place; around them skulked various dogs and cats, chickens, goats, and ducks. The sight of them was like a cold douche; he began to feel as though the whole night were a dream. He saw Elyse and her oldest boy, Mike, talking to the sheriff; it occurred to him he had broken the law. Arson was a serious offense, he knew; it could get you sent to the state prison for he didn't know how long.

Dennis Dufore, criminal. His earlier drunken, joyous feeling was dissipating rapidly.

". . . ain't been home all evening," he heard Elyse say to the sheriff. "Don't know what he'll say when he sees this mess."

Maury hadn't been there.

Dennis had burned down a house. He had broken the law.

And it was all for nothing, because Maury hadn't even been there.

He stood in the road, just outside the glare of firelight and hurricane lanterns, his hands shoved deep into the pockets of his windbreaker, and felt something die inside him. His left hand curved around a chunk of granite, and slowly he pulled it out of his pocket.

He started to walk along the road, back the way he'd come, shaking the rock gently inside his closed fist, like a die.

He thought about Maury, wondered where he was. He thought about Jeanette, wondered if she was with Maury.

He dropped the rock he was carrying, fished in his pocket for another one, drew it out, and started to toss it from one hand to the other as he walked. The wind was really quite strong now.

So much for fresh starts, he thought. He dropped the second rock and reached into his pocket for another.

He imagined Jeanette and Maury together and wished he'd crushed LaStrange's head with a sledgehammer.

"Screw you, LaStrange!" he shouted into the wind, smashing the third rock into the ground.

He tried to imagine killing Jeanette too, but realized sadly he couldn't harm a hair on her head, even in his mind.

"God *damn* you, Jeanette," he whispered, but it came out sounding like a caress. He pulled another rock out of his pocket, let it fall to the ground.

The wind was beginning to bully him, pushing, slapping, as he continued down the road, rocks trailing after him like salt pouring from a torn sack.

In liquor-soaked dreams, Maury LaStrange thought he heard multitudes cheering; thought he saw searchlights sweeping the sky; thought he felt the burning heat of spotlights on his skin; thought the sky was glowing orange from a thousand electric lights and realized it must be Hollywood.

In a liquor-soaked coma, he rolled over heavily onto his

face and quite accidentally asphyxiated himself in a pile of cooked cabbage leaves.

It was nearly dawn before the Esperance volunteer fire department finally managed to douse the fire at the La-Strange place. There was no doubt in either the fire chief's or the sheriff's mind that it was arson; they'd found an empty gasoline can down by the brook. The driver of the fire truck remembered nearly driving over someone in the road, though he hadn't got a good look at the face, it had all happened so quickly.

It was nearly noon before Brent Gouger found Maury LaStrange's body sprawled across a heap of garbage. He'd come out to the dump, found the gate closed but not locked. He'd heard about the fire, of course, and assumed Maury had opened up, then gone back home to help clean up the mess. So Brent had opened the gate, left fifty cents on the counter in the shack, and driven his flatbed into the dump, where he'd found Maury, dead as a doornail.

It was a little after two o'clock when a group of men from the paper mill found Dennis lying in a heap under a huge catalpa tree. He was unconscious, lying like a dropped doll, his arm at a weird angle to his body, his collarbone poking through the skin. They figured he had to have been there all night, but nobody could understand why he'd been climbing trees in the first place.

Just before Thanksgiving, Jeanette rode her bicycle up the East-West Road, past the LaStrange place, and on up the steep, rutted driveway leading to the Dufore farmhouse. As she came up over the top, she could see old Marie Dufore just coming down the back steps from the kitchen with a pan of chicken feed in her hand. The old woman stopped when she saw Jeanette, stood waiting while she dismounted from the bicycle and wheeled it slowly, slowly, across the yard.

"Morning, Jeanette," Gran Marie said. "It's been a while."

Actually, this was the first time she'd been to the house since the day of the fire.

"Dennis in?" Jeanette asked.

"Aye," Gran Marie said. "He don't go out much these days."

They stood, the wheel of Jeanette's bicycle just grazing the hem of Gran Marie's long black skirt. Then Marie said:

"I'll tell him you're here."

She turned and went back up the steps, disappeared through the porch door. Jeanette heard the kitchen door click shut behind her. She leaned the bike up against the side of the stairs and stood there at the bottom hugging herself against the chill. Snow was in the air. Her breath blew out of her mouth in white gusts that ballooned across her face and then disappeared. Cold crept up through the soles of her sneakers, and she stamped in a little circle at the bottom of the steps to keep the blood circulating.

She hadn't seen Dennis in almost two months, not since the afternoon of the night Maury's house burned down. That he'd burned it down she had no doubt; that he'd done it because of her she was certain. So she'd stayed away, because she didn't know what to say to him, and he'd made no effort to contact her.

September became October, and then it was November, now almost December, almost a new year, and still not a word from him.

She'd dreamed the night before that he was making love to her, and woke that morning with the touch of his lips still on her own. Almost as soon as her eyes opened she was out of bed and getting dressed. She still didn't know what she would say to him, but figured something would come to her when it was time. Now here she was and still nothing had come into her head. She jammed her hands deep into the pockets of her winter jacket; her left hand grazed something hard and rough, and she curled her fingers around a solid chunk of granite. A gift from Dennis that had lain there, forgotten, since last winter.

She pulled the rock out, and was inspecting its speckled grayness when she heard the kitchen door creak open behind her and felt Dennis's presence on the porch.

He was standing just outside the door, looking like he might whisk himself back through it at any moment, so tentative was the way he stood. His arm was in a sling and his hair was too long. He'd lost weight, and his eyes looked too big and too black for his white, narrow face. She opened her mouth to say something tender, something wise, to say something that would make things right between them once more, but found she could only say his name.

"Dennis," she said, and became wordless.

Slowly he advanced to the top step and stopped there while his eyes searched her face as if he were trying to remember her name.

She looked the same as always to him; he hadn't let himself realize, until this very moment, that he'd missed her. He hadn't wanted to come out here, hadn't wanted to see her again, until he saw her; now he didn't want to look away.

"Dennis," she'd said, and stood looking up at him as if he were her one desire.

So he'd come to the top of the stairs, not knowing what he would say or do next, not knowing what she would say or do, just knowing that here, at the top of these steps, his life, his future, hung perfectly balanced in the distance between them.

When she put her foot on the bottom step, he caught his

breath, but didn't realize he'd stopped breathing until she was on the fourth step. Her foot came up, found the fifth step, and slowly, deliberately, he let all the air out of his lungs, then breathed in deep as she climbed to the seventh. Only two steps between them, and the air blowing up through her hair was clean, chill, pure in his nostrils.

She stopped on the step just below him, put her right hand up on his good shoulder, brought her left hand up, and slowly uncurled her fist to reveal a heavy, jagged rock.

"Dennis," she breathed, so soft he might have imagined it, and gently pushed the piece of granite into the pocket of the coat he'd slung over his shoulders as she drew herself up onto the porch with him.

It was a small rock, but the weight of it seemed to pull him forward so that his good arm was around Jeanette's shoulder and his forehead was resting against the crown of her head. He took another breath, deeper this time, and felt the weight in his pocket shift a little, pulling him even closer to her, anchoring him there, in her arms, forever.

PART TWO

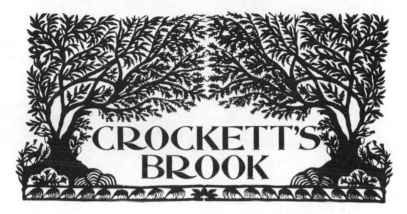

CROCKETT'S BROOK

Just about everybody in Esperance has at least a drop of Dufore blood in his veins.

It is widely held that the Delagardes might just as well consider themselves Dufores and have done with it, there's been so much marrying and carrying on over the generations between the two families; and when Marie Legere found her younger brother Peter crumpled up out behind the sugar house, his head like a smashed pumpkin, a rifle lying nearby, folks recalled their great-grandmother Christine had been a full-blooded Dufore married to a second cousin whose mother had also been a Dufore.

Marie Dufore, nee Legere, was fifteen when her brother died, and sixty-one when her son Ab leapt off the cliff behind the paper mill. Her first husband, Paul, had disappeared some forty years before, and taken her first child with him; some people speculated he'd gone mad and was locked up at the hospital in Waterbury, others that he'd run off to join an evangelical sect.

Most folks assumed he was dead—most probably by his own hand.

Marie knew the truth, of course, though she never spoke of it, even to her other children. If they suspected, they never said anything to her.

"You got a brother who's a fish," she'd crooned to Abner as he lay sleeping in his crib the afternoon he was christened. The baby had stirred a little when she spoke; perhaps her words conjured cooling visions in his fevered brain of a secure infinity spent under refracted-green currents.

Certainly the last thought that passed through Ab's mind,

forty years later, a millisecond before he dashed his brains out on the boulders in Crockett's Brook, was a hope he wouldn't crush any fish. . . .

But Ab was the only person Marie ever told, and he'd been too young to remember, anyway.

She was a vigorous woman, in spite of her age. Sometimes she walked down to the bridge that spanned the brook at its widest point and watched shadowy trout flit across the water. Natural partiality made her want to believe he was the particularly large and cunning brown trout that had eluded fishermen for several seasons.

Chapter
7

❧

G ran Marie was always awake, Dennis thought, no matter what time of day or night.

Moonlight through the window had wakened him; as he lay stiff, one arm in a cast, his mending collarbone aching dully, he could hear the faint creak of floorboards in the hall and the pad, pad, pad of bare feet on wood. Down the hall, he heard his sister's door open, then shut again.

Gran Marie, making her nightly rounds.

It had to be close to three, he figured, as the hour, the darkness, and the comforting nearness of his grandmother conspired to drag his eyelids down again. How hard it must be, he thought, as he pulled the blanket up over his shoulder and hunched down deeper into the bed, staying awake when the rest of the world sleeps. He couldn't imagine how she'd done it these forty years and more.

"Doesn't Gran *ever* sleep?" Dennis had asked his father once.

He'd been six, going on seven; for his whole short life Gran was always up, always dressed, no matter when he happened to come across her.

She was in the sitting room, reading, when he got up to go to the bathroom in the small hours of the night.

She was making herself a cup of tea in the kitchen when he crept outside at dawn to go hunting for birds' nests.

Sometimes he heard her patrolling the hallways, opening doors just a crack to check the sleeping occupants. She often came into his room to rearrange the blankets, cover him up more warmly.

Her bedclothes were never rumpled.

Dennis wondered if she ever changed her sheets.

"Nope," his father replied. "She hasn't slept in more 'n thirty years, don't you know."

"But *why?*" Dennis asked. "How can she *do* that? How does she stay *awake?*"

His father shrugged. "Dunno," he said. "Best ask her."

Marie Legere married Paul Dufore when he was twenty-three, and she was seventeen and almost three months pregnant. The marriage was greeted with less opposition and more resignation than might have been the case had the Legeres not already owned to several close connections with the Dufore family. Still, for a wedding it was a pretty morose affair, both families doing their assigned parts without enthusiasm.

Even the bride and groom seemed subdued. Marie walked down the aisle feeling bloated and a little like she might throw up on her father's shoes.

Paul waited at the altar, hands clasped behind his back, morbidly conscious of the small, angry pimple that had bloomed that very morning in the center of his forehead.

One night, brought on by heat, corn liquor, and too much dancing at the town hall, one night, and now he was committed for life to the girl who floated towards him in a long white dress. She *was* pretty, he decided; that night had not been a terrible experience by any means. If a wedding gave him rights to more of that, he could grow reconciled.

Marie arrived at the altar, felt her father's dutiful kiss on her cheek when he gave her away, glanced up into Paul's face at the red spot on his forehead. She wondered what she could have been thinking of that night. It had been dark then; she had felt flushed, giddy; his hands might have been anyone's. She had traced a winged woman across his naked back, almost believing she'd imprinted flames in his flesh with the heat from her own.

The priest was speaking; Marie looked up at the altar, up at Father Lambert, and imagined for a moment it was the tattooed juggler who stood in his place.

It was the tattoo that had attracted her.

It spread across the juggler's back, a winged woman rising from flames, in orange, red, and yellow; the fire seemed to lick along her body as the juggler's muscles worked beneath his skin.

It was the most beautiful thing Marie had ever seen. Then and there she decided to leave Esperance, join a carnival, and get a tattoo of her own.

The carnival had come to Esperance almost by accident, it seemed, as though it had lost its way between Montpelier and the New York border and had sat down in the town common to rest awhile and rethink things.

There was a medicine show, freaks, including a most awe-inspiring fat lady, a human fetus in a bottle, a seal-boy, and a dog-faced girl. There was a sword swallower, a fire-eater, and a strongman, who nightly lifted up two chairs, a grown woman sitting in each one, over his head. There was also a world-famous (the marquee said) pugilist who offered to fight all comers for a modest purse three times nightly. There was a bearded woman, a dwarf, some trained dogs, and, of course, the juggler.

The carnival was in Esperance for a week, and Marie went every night.

When it left, she went with it, stowed snugly away in a wagon filled with tarpaulins.

Her father caught up with her just before they crossed over the border into Hoosick Falls, New York. He hauled her down off the wagon and stood stiffly at the side of the road, his fingers digging into the soft flesh of her upper arm until the carnival troop was out of sight.

Then he beat her soundly and took her home.

For a while, she thought the juggler would come back for her. She took to walking along the road that led through town, towards Bennington, half believing each time she did that he would one day appear over the horizon.

For maybe a month she waited—almost twice as long as it took for the bruises her father gave her to heal; even after she stopped walking towards Bennington she still dreamed of him sometimes. In time, the juggler's features became fuzzier and fuzzier until eventually she dreamed only of the winged woman.

When she turned eighteen, she decided, she would leave Esperance and find the juggler again, no matter how long it took, or where she had to go to do it.

She only wished she'd thought to ask his name. . . .

"Marie? Marie!"

Paul's voice tracked her to the washhouse, where it worried and pulled at the back of her mind until it finally succeeded in tearing her away from her private thoughts, forcing her to deal with it.

"What!" she hollered in the direction of the back door. After a moment, he appeared in the doorway, blurred by the screen, looking in the brown, hazy light of late afternoon as though he'd stepped out of the sepia wedding photograph adorning the mantelpiece in the sitting room.

"I'm starving!" he bawled through the screen. "What's for supper?"

She straightened up from the sinkful of sheets she was blanching and groaned as the bones in her spine cracked. She ran her wet, chapped hands along the sides of her swollen belly to dry them, brushed the sweat out of her eyes. The very thought of food made her stomach heave.

She lumbered painfully up the back steps, using her belly as a battering ram to move him out of the way. There was no tattoo, no flames, no romance; only Paul, the laundry, and a baby on the way.

She took the lid off the pot simmering on the stove and felt her flesh creep as the savory steam from beef stew rose up to hit her full in the face.

"Hand me your bowl," she said, swallowing hard.

The stew looked so ordinary she wanted to lie down and cry for the shame of it. She stood with a ladle in one hand, Paul's bowl in the other, shaking from the effort to swallow sudden panic. What if I die? she thought; what if I drop down dead this very minute, a bowl of stew in my hand and nothing to show for my life except a sinkful of half-blanched sheets and Paul Dufore's unborn child?

"You feelin' okay, Marie?"

She'd had the belly for almost all their short married life; sometimes Paul forgot she was pregnant until she would suddenly come over queer. Then he'd realize, with a creeping feeling, that there was another, complete human being floating inside her. Clumsily he pulled up a kitchen chair and pushed her into it, removed the bowl from her hand, and stood staring down at her, concerned, a little exasperated, completely befuddled.

Her lips were moving, but he couldn't catch her words.

"What's that?" He hunkered down beside the chair and put his arm around her shoulder, as much to steady himself as to comfort her; they seldom touched outside of bed. "What d'ya say, Marie?"

"What if I die, Paul?"

She looked very young to him all of a sudden; he didn't know what to say. Tendrils of her hair lay plastered to the nape of her neck with sweat; he could smell the bleach on her hands and a musky woman-odor wafting up from the bodice of her dress. Something that might have been love stirred in him.

"Women have babies every day, Marie," he muttered, patting her thin shoulders with one calloused hand. "You'll be just fine."

He continued to squat beside her. The blood drained slowly out of his legs, and pins and needles in his feet tormented him. It seemed right, somehow, to suffer like that for her, as though in some way he were atoning for the pain and fear he'd caused her to endure.

Marie said nothing, just sat unmoving in the chair, barely aware of his hand on her shoulder. She had no fears about childbirth; she'd been through it with her own mother often enough, knew exactly how much blood and pain and cursing she was in for.

Death in childbed was the least of her worries.

But was it possible, she wondered, to die of nothing to show?

"Marie—" Paul began, then stopped. At the front of the house they could hear the sound of footsteps coming up the wooden stoop, the bang of the screen door.

"Davy's here," Paul said, dropping his arm from her shoulders and straightening up. "Guess we'd better get to work on finishing up the roof."

He sounded relieved.

"Best set another place for supper," he said.

Paul Dufore's younger brother, Davy, started hanging around shortly after the wedding.

Their house had been built hastily; started hardly more than two weeks before the wedding, and completed soon after. It wasn't much more than a cabin, really, one floor with two rooms and a kitchen; a washhouse and a privy had been installed out back. It was built on the ridge just out of sight of the main house, and Marie had moved herself and Paul into it before there were even doors on it, or a proper roof; one night in her mother-in-law's house had been enough.

Davy had helped move them in; afterwards he came by every day to help hang doors and nail shingles. He was fourteen at the time, and no one thought much about him being at his brother's house practically from first light until bedtime.

If Marie ever thought of him, it was as a person younger than herself, who provided companionship as she moved through the dull routine of getting from one day to the next. She gave him little more thought or attention than she might give a dog. Paul never seemed to notice him at all, except to tell him to do something, or get out of the way.

He was a quiet boy; no one, least of all his brother or his new sister-in-law, could have guessed the feelings he had for

Marie, bending over the washtub with her hair tumbled down her back, or stretching to hang laundry, the wind lifting her skirt slightly, permitting him a glimpse of her calves; they could not have imagined the agony such glimpses caused him when he imagined the paradise his brother had nightly access to: Marie's ankles and knees, her thighs even.

He loved her dumbly, with the full, unquestioning devotion of a dog. Like a dog, he eventually won himself a place at their fireside; by the time Marie's child was born, Davy was practically living with them. There never seemed a time when he was not a part of their household.

"There it goes again. . . . Quick, Davy, put your hand right there. Feel him?"

They were in the kitchen, Marie with a chopping knife in one hand, the other pressed against the side of her stomach. Davy stooped before her with his head inclined towards her belly as though he thought the child would speak to him, both palms caught beneath his sister-in-law's hand.

"Feel him?" she asked again.

He nodded, too full of awe at this brush with life, at actually touching Marie, to speak.

"Ooh! You devil! You're gonna be a handful, you little devil!" She laughed.

She smelled wonderful: onions, flour, and sweat mixed with a mysterious, womanly smell that seemed to rise from her thighs. To stand up slowly, put his arms around her shoulders, and draw her close as her belly would allow seemed the only sane response to so heady an odor. So he stood up and put his arms around her, though she hardly seemed to notice.

"I love you, Marie," he said, so low he was half afraid that she hadn't heard him, even more afraid she had.

CROCKETT'S BROOK ◆

She laughed and gave him a tiny shove that dislodged his arms from her shoulders and set her free.

"You're a card," she said. "If you wanna stay for supper, then how 'bout helpin' set the table."

He went to get the silverware out of the drawer, choking on humiliation and despair; he hadn't really expected a response to his declaration, but she'd never have asked him to set the table if she considered him a man grown.

Hadn't she even noticed he was shaving at least three times a week now?

As Marie's belly swelled, Paul found himself alternately attracted and repelled by her. The greatest benefit of marriage, as far as he was concerned, was regular, legal access to a woman's body. Even the increasingly frightening sight of her naked, swollen, could not overcome the stirring in his groin one glimpse of her now pendulous breasts could cause.

The first time he ever felt the child move, he was inside her, thrusting, grinding, fever mounting in his brain, his breath coming in deep gasps. He was about to explode out of his own body into hers when he felt a stirring beneath his hands and the impact of a tiny foot against his palm.

His heart seemed to stop, his breath seemed to stop, his penis, engorged, overflowing, shriveled and slipped right out of her.

Marie's eyes were closed, her breathing light and regular; as usual at such times, her mind had been on other things. She did not immediately realize that Paul was no longer thrusting and jerking beneath her.

Gradually she became aware of the stillness of the body under her.

"Paul?"

She bent over slightly as she whispered his name, and her

breasts hung in his face. One nipple brushed his nose, and he thought he could smell the sweet odor of milk on her.

Suddenly, he was scared, terrified of the power in her: the power to stir him, have him sucking at her breast like a helpless newborn, whimpering and rooting, blindly thrusting himself as far back into her womb as he could possibly go. The power to make new men inside her body, and emasculate grown men with that selfsame power. He could feel himself shrinking smaller and smaller until he was sure he had all but disappeared. Try as he would to make it grow again, to retake her body with a power of his own, he knew only she, with her hands, her lips, the pressure of her breasts against his chest or her legs around his hips, could restore that power to him.

"Paul?" she said again, but though she whispered in his ear, her voice seemed to come from far away, from miles underwater.

"Get off," he muttered, and pushed at her big belly so that she toppled sideways onto her side of the bed. Just as she started to go over, he felt a blow against his palm again—the child striking back.

"What's the matter with you?" Marie asked.

But he just rolled onto his side and pulled the sheet up over his shoulder.

Marie shifted onto her side and propped herself on her elbow.

"Paul?" she said a third time. "You okay? you sick or something?"

No answer. She could hear by his breathing that he was awake, and his body was stiff as a bale of wire.

After a minute or two, she realized she was holding her breath, so she exhaled and flopped down onto her back, her hands folded across her stomach. Inside, it felt like the baby was doing slow somersaults.

Half a mile or so down the ridge from the cabin the track narrows, then splinters off, one thin arm of it running down the steep flank of the ridge while the main path continues along its spine, down to the East-West Road. In August, when the heat hung over the land, stifling as a wool blanket, Marie made her way down the narrower path to where it fed into a small meadow. The grass there was tall, lush, and cool at its roots, and there was a pond, half in the shade of ancient maple trees.

It was very, very hot. She lay dozing at the edge of the pond, just her feet in the water, while bees droned among the milkweed not too far away, and small creatures went about their business, rustling and creaking through the sweet-smelling grass.

She felt drugged by sunlight, seduced by the hum of insects. Something tickled her cheek, the side of her throat; she raised one languid hand to brush away some errant insect, but it had moved further down her body, was running lightly across her breastbone and down between her breasts.

She lay perfectly still, hardly breathing, the sun fizzing against her lids, and waited.

There it was again, fluttering against her mouth like the wings of a dragonfly; she opened her lips slightly and let it in, where it buzzed and beat its wings against the roof of her mouth, then darted out, then in, then out again, while a thousand more dragonfly wings beat a delicate tattoo against her arms and breast.

She knew if she opened her eyes, she would find herself enveloped in a gossamer cloud of brightly colored dragonflies. She knew if she opened her eyes, she would have to brush them away, slap them down, shake them from her clothing and hair. They felt good, though, fluttering tenderly across her skin, insinuating themselves beneath her clothing, touching her most private places.

So, she didn't open her eyes.

She lay dozing at the edge of the pond and completely gave herself up to the pleasure of the dragonflies.

"Marie?"

Reluctant, she opened her eyes; for a minute she thought she saw the juggler's face suspended just a few inches from her own.

"You okay?" he asked. "The heat getting to you, Marie?"

It was Davy bending over her; he looked worried.

She shook her head. There was a slight stubble on his chin and across his cheeks; funny she'd never noticed it before. Though his hair was dark, the stubble on his chin was reddish gold; motes of sunlight were trapped in its sparse net.

"Hey, Marie, you feelin' okay?" There was just the faintest tremor in his voice, as though it would have cracked but for the iron will he exerted over it. "You want me to get Paul?"

Paul. He hadn't come near her, had barely spoken to her in weeks.

She shook her head again. The dragonflies were gone. Had she dreamed them or had Davy frightened them away? It didn't matter; she could still feel the flutter of their wings against her thighs, throat, and lips. She felt such gratitude there were dragonflies in the world; she felt such overwhelming tenderness towards a world that harbored dragonflies she just had to share it with someone.

Still she didn't speak; she brushed her palms across Davy's cheeks, drew his head down to cover his face with dragonfly kisses.

"Marie—" he began, but she put her hand over his mouth quickly, before he could break the magic.

She didn't say a word, didn't even open her eyes as she pulled him down beside her, and felt the dry rough of his sunwarm cheek against her breast, then, a moment later, his lips, moist, a little tentative, dragonfly-tender, tracing across the nipple.

The baby weighed almost eight pounds when it was born. They named him Amos. As she held him to her breast that first time, and felt the greedy, insistent tug of his toothless gums against her swollen nipple, Marie thought she would die of love.

Chapter
8

The winter of 1914–15 was a harsh one, and all of Esperance greeted the beginning of mud season with relief. Though it promised to be one of the worst in forty years, at least it was a different kind of bad.

The earth froze deep that winter, and the thaw came suddenly, fiercely, at the end of March; temperatures soared into the sixties and low seventies.

Then there was the rain, torrents of it, almost every day.

The result was mud, sometimes four or five feet deep in places. Back roads became impassable by horse or wagon. The main street of Esperance was a mire. The few motor vehicles Esperance could lay claim to in those days remained safely stowed in outbuildings. Streams overran their banks, and there was bad flooding in many areas.

Flash floods claimed four lives that year: Lainy Marcus

and her brother Cal, ages twelve and ten, who were playing where they shouldn't have; Pierre LaStrange, who had foolishly tried taking his wagon into town for supplies, gotten mired down in a sinkhole, and was still trying to pile rocks and deadwood under the wheels for traction when the flood got him; finally, there was Pierre LaStrange's horse, Sugarfoot.

For almost two weeks, Marie and Paul were cut off from almost everyone except Davy, who managed to slog up the ridge from the main house at least every other day. Sometimes he brought baked goods from his mother as an excuse for his visits; most times he had no excuse at all.

The weather didn't allow for much outdoor activity. For most of those two weeks the three of them sat in the tiny parlor, Davy and Marie playing cards sometimes, or tickling the baby, torturing themselves with the very nearness of the other and no possible way to relieve the tension. Occasionally, while dealing cards for another round of gin, their hands brushed. Even that casual contact, Paul just a few feet away, was enough to bring a flush to Marie's face and throat.

Any other time Paul would have sensed the atmosphere in his sitting room, might even have finally recognized it for what it was; he was, after all, a farm boy and had spent enough time around animals in rut to know when he saw it in humans. He might have done something about it, too; might have whipped his brother and beaten his wife, or killed them both, or maybe only Marie, since killing Davy would be repeating the sin of Cain, something the Bible seemed to regard as infinitely worse than wife-slaughter.

He would have done something about it, though, if he'd seen it a few weeks earlier, or if mud season hadn't been so bad that year.

But Paul had other things on his mind during those days he, his wife, and his brother were so closely confined in the cabin. The harshness of winter, combined with the deaths of the Marcus children, Pierre LaStrange, and his horse had started something nagging at the back of Paul's brain, and eventually he'd turned to the Bible.

He was reading Genesis and cogitating fiercely during those mud-bound days in the cabin. As he read, he felt as if he were poised on the edge of some great realization, as though he possessed some sure piece of knowledge that lay just beyond the boundaries of his memory or understanding. All his life it had lain buried, waiting for some event to jog it loose.

Mud season and the four deaths had done that. For several nights after he'd heard about LaStrange, the Marcus kids, and the horse, Paul lay awake in his bed, Marie curled in a cocoon of blankets beside him, and struggled to capture that thing he knew he'd always known as it dodged about at the edge of consciousness, worrying at the corners of his mind. Sometimes as he awakened from exhausted sleep he'd feel it front and center in his memory for a few seconds. But even as he reached out to grasp it firmly, carry it with him into waking, it would slip over the edge of awareness and disappear once again into the swampy depths of his dreams.

He finally turned to the Bible because it was the only remaining source of comfort and knowledge Paul knew of. If Father Lambert was right, it was the repository of all the answers to all the questions a man could ask about the universe and his place in it. Paul decided to begin at the beginning and read to the end; if by then he had not satisfied the thing that nagged and worried him, waking and sleeping, he would find a way to cut it out of him.

He found the answer in Genesis.

With the book open on his knee, Paul thoughtfully reviewed the evidence.

A Great War in Europe had recently begun—a war,

from what he could tell, of tremendous destruction and suffering, caused by weaponry that could only have been inspired by the devil.

Something new was afoot in Russia: "Bolshevism," which Father Lambert described as being anti-Christian, almost satanic in its scope.

Pierre LaStrange had been a notorious bootlegger and womanizer.

Everybody in Esperance knew Guy Marcus wasn't really married to the woman he'd brought back from Montpelier with him one spring fifteen years before; it was widely rumored she had a husband, still living, somewhere in Canada. That made the children illegitimate.

He couldn't explain the horse, except to say that often and often the Innocent had the bad luck to be in the vicinity when the Wicked finally got what was coming to them.

It all fell into place at last. Wickedness was loose in the land, and the end of the world was at hand once more. This mud season was just a warning of worse things to come. Sooner or later, he thought, there'd be another flood and only the fish would survive.

He didn't have much time if he was going to learn how to live underwater.

When the mud finally began to dry up and the roads became passable again, Paul took to spending long hours down by the banks of Crockett's Brook, observing the water life there. He watched how the fish moved and ate; he tracked the water beetles skittering across the surface of the water; he spied on every frog and tadpole.

At first he watched from a distance, gradually moving closer until he could sit at the very edge of the water while the fish, frogs, and insects lolled in his shadow. One day he even put his face in the brook and stayed that way, baby trout and salamanders tickling at his nose and chin, the hair rising from his forehead and fanning out like a halo, until he thought his lungs would burst.

Then, black stars exploding before his eyes, he finally erupted up out of the water, oxygen-starved, sobbing, heaving, gasping for air, coughing up little streams of brook water.

Those were the black days for Paul. The days when he thought he'd never find the way. Days when he could see a new world opening up before him, could reach out and touch it but seemed forever barred by his own weakness from entering it.

For his sixteenth birthday, Marie gave Davy a baby.

She hadn't meant to, of course, but she was ignorant of most things concerning sex except how to have it, and had not yet reached the age or the requisite number of children for older women to think to initiate her in the ways of preventing conception or of undoing it.

"Jesus, Marie," was all Davy could say when she told him. "Jesus!"

He imagined all the men in his family lined up with sticks, belts, and horse whips. His brother Paul, his father, his three uncles; he thought even his grandfather, who was so ill and infirm he spent most of his days in bed, might summon the strength to rise up and join the others when he heard his youngest grandson had *not only* slept with his brother's wife, but had planted *his own seed* in that forbidden womb, as well.

"You sure it's mine?"

She nodded. Her sexual life with Paul had been perfunctory at best, since Amos was born; since mud season, Paul seemed to have lost all interest whatsoever.

"Paul's gonna kill us both," Davy stated emphatically.

"No, he won't," Marie said. "He'll never know. I'll just have to sleep with him, that's all."

"Jesus," Davy swore, again. He was feeling pretty terrible, as if his bowels would loosen any minute and shame him in front of Marie. He had been content to love her from a distance until she'd pulled him to her that day by the pond; he wished he could go back to old times.

"We can't ever do this again, Marie," he told her, despising himself when his voice broke and her name came out high and ridiculous.

"It's a little late now, don't you think?"

"Maybe so, but just 'cause we've been doin' it up to now is no reason to keep on. It's *wrong*, Marie."

She didn't say anything, just looked at him, then came up close so he was inhaling her breath.

"Chickenshit little bastard," she said, very calmly, and slugged him hard in the stomach.

When she told Paul a few weeks later she thought she might be pregnant again, he hardly said anything at all.

They'd had relations once, a sad, passionless little episode that left them both depressed afterwards and was nearly forgotten by the next day. Since mud season, Paul's mind had been engaged almost exclusively by the problems posed by living underwater; there was a new diet to adapt to; a whole new way of hearing, seeing, and sensing the world; he still had to solve breathing underwater. With problems like those worrying at his brain, he'd had little thought for his wife or the pleasures, such as they were, of the marriage bed.

Still, when Marie put her hand around his penis and started pulling at it, a little too vigorously and businesslike to be strictly comfortable, his body responded almost in spite of his feelings. Throughout the brief interlude he felt he and Marie were conducting a transaction of some kind;

afterwards he wondered which one of them had been bought, or sold. He wasn't sure why she had bothered to arouse him in the first place.

Now she was pregnant again. He supposed she'd wanted another child from him, that was all. He couldn't really feel much about it, one way or the other. He was the head of his household, responsible for the well-being of his family; one more child, an infant at that, was complicating an already impossible situation. He had tried to talk to Marie about the coming disaster once, but she'd laughed and refused to listen. Eventually, he'd accepted that Marie probably couldn't be saved and turned his energy towards other problems.

Paul took to disappearing for long hours while the fields lay neglected and work cried out to be done.

Davy started avoiding the cabin on the ridge.

Marie spent her days walking beside the pond, searching for dragonflies.

People were starting to talk, so one day Marie's mother-in-law, Michelle Dufore, made her way up the steep path to the cabin for only the third time since the wedding and Marie's declaration that she would not move into the farmhouse with her in-laws.

She came stiff with disapproval, bristling with suspicion. One of her boys, rumor had it, spent most of his days with his head in the brook; the other moped around the house and jumped like a shot deer whenever Marie's name was mentioned. Michelle Dufore wanted to know just what her daughter-in-law thought she was up to.

Partly to avoid more visits from her in-law, partly out of loneliness and boredom, Marie took to visiting her own family more than usual. It was a three-mile walk to her parents' house; in the beginning, she took Amos with her, but as the weather grew hotter and her belly larger, it became too difficult to carry the boy when his legs tired. She stayed at home for two weeks straight, then, and might have gone completely out of her mind if Paul hadn't unexpectedly offered to watch the baby for a few hours while she went into town.

Marie might have thought twice about leaving her son with his father if she'd been privy to the same stories her mother-in-law had been hearing, but she led a pretty isolated life up on the ridge. Besides, people in Esperance tended to believe other people's madness was their own business. If Marie Dufore had no notion her husband divided his time between haranguing folks in the general store about a second great flood and lying with his head and shoulders submerged in Crockett's Brook till he was half drowned, then it was not their business to tell her.

This is what the jungle must be like, Marie thought as she trudged back from her parents' house in town, along the narrow, rutted road that ran beside the brook, then crossed it, winding its way up the ridge to disappear into the woods beyond. The part that followed the brook was a legitimate road and people had used it, lived along it, for many years, but where it ran up the spine of the ridge it was an old logging road that got longer every year as loggers penetrated deeper into the treeline. The cabin was built a quarter of a mile further up from where the logging road now ended, connected by a narrow footpath that also ran down the north face of the ridge into the Dufore fields.

There had been rain for the better part of the week, a warm steady torrent that slicked the roads with an inch or so of mud and dropped a more or less permanent cloak of mist over the lowlands. It had begun to break that morning; as the day lengthened into afternoon, watery sunlight shouldered back the few remaining black thunderheads, strained itself through the gathered gloom, and merged with moisture suspended in the air, creating a diffused, humid, steaming glare. Every leaf and blade of grass seemed coated with moist light as they drooped, aggressively lush, beneath the beaded weight of water. The air was thick and hazy; Marie could almost see steam rising from the earth.

She had almost reached where the Ridge Road forked off from the East-West Road and crossed the brook; on the left was the crazy tar-paper shack that housed countless generations of LaStranges. It was a structure that defied gravity as it tilted precariously on its cinder-block foundation, all the walls seeming to fall outward from the center in four different directions, but halted in midair by God only knew what miracle of engineering. As usual, the yard was filled with rusted farm equipment, bales of wire, chickens, dogs, and children as crazy and tumble-down as the house. As usual, they were whooping and hollering: children, animals, and inanimate objects alike swept into a maelstrom of make-believe that came to a temporary halt as Marie drew abreast of the house. They froze in mid-whoop and waited in preternatural stillness until she passed, only the eyes in their heads moving.

It was a funny thing, Marie mused, how the LaStrange children never seemed to grow any older; there just seemed to be *more* of them every year.

She could see the bridge up ahead, which heartened her; only the ridge remained between her and home. The climb was a steep one, but the longest part was behind her.

Something was lying on the bank of the brook, a few yards below the bridge. It looked like a bundle of clothes; Marie wondered if one of the LaStrange women had brought it down to wash, then unaccountably left it. As she drew closer, she saw it was not one bundle, but two, then that they were not bundles at all, but two human bodies, one large and one small.

Another fifty feet, and she recognized clothing she'd washed earlier that week, and realized her husband and son were lying side by side on the bank of Crockett's Brook.

She gathered her mud-soaked skirts in her hands and started to run.

They both had their heads under the water. Paul's hand was on the back of Amos's head, holding him down.

"Jesus—" Marie shrieked, dropping to her knees and dragging her baby son up the bank by his heels.

"—Christ!" she screamed, turning his head to the side and kneading his back frantically to pump the water out of him.

"Oh God, oh *God,*" she panted over and over between the deep breaths she blew into his mouth and nose, one hand moving back and forth across his plump chest in a desperate search for a heartbeat.

It seemed like a hundred years before Amos finally coughed up a considerable amount of water and started breathing on his own. She hadn't even noticed Paul had left the water and was standing over her and Amos.

"He was learning," Paul began. "He was doing just fine—"

"You *crazy bastard!*" Marie screamed, and launched herself at him over Amos's trembling body, pounding at his chest, ripping at his face with fists and nails. *"You nearly drowned my baby!"*

"I wasn't *drownin'* him," Paul shouted over her screams. "I was *teachin'* him! I was teachin' him to *survive!*"

His words didn't make much of an impression on her, for she continued to kick and strike at him, murder in her crazy face.

"Cut it *out,* Marie!" he yelled, knocking her fists away from his face. When she wouldn't stop, he slapped her once, but not very hard, because she was, after all, pregnant.

"He was learning to breathe underwater, Marie," he said

once her crying and swearing had died down. "I was teaching him how. I'll teach you, too, if you want me to."

Painfully, she climbed to her feet, one hand pressed to the spot where he had slapped her, the other wrapped fiercely around Amos's upper arm. She was still breathing heavily, but she was calm, now.

"You are one crazy son of a bitch," she told her husband, "and I don't want you *ever* to come near me or my son again. You got that?"

She grunted a little when she swung Amos up to straddle the swell of her belly, his legs dangling along each flank. The jungle greenery swallowed her and the boy almost as soon as they crossed the bridge and started up the Ridge Road, but Paul could still hear her labored breathing long after she was out of sight.

She brought the baby into bed with her, and took to locking the door at night.

Every evening, she made up a bed for Paul in the sitting room, and every morning she found it untouched; she suspected he spent his nights at the brook. She was seized with the fear that some night while she slept, he would creep through the window, snatch Amos right out of the bed, take him down to the brook, and drown him there.

So she managed to stay awake for almost thirty-six hours before finally succumbing to the deep, dreamless sleep of exhaustion.

"C'mere, son," Paul whispered from the window.

The moon was full behind him, the night alive with the hum of insects, the rustle of concealed animals in the woods; beneath his feet a whole other unseen world teamed with life in the rich, dark earth. He reached his arms through the window he'd jimmied open with a pocketknife and spread them wide to the little boy who lay peering at him from the tousled bed.

"Come to Daddy," Paul said.

Amos came, was lifted out of the musk-scented warmth of his mother's room, out into the chill night air, out into his father's arms.

"Don't worry about him, Marie," Paul whispered tenderly to the unmoving form of his sleeping wife. "I'll be with him."

Then he turned away from the window and started down the path that led to the Ridge Road and Crockett's Brook.

When he reached the bridge, he set Amos down and removed his clothing, carefully folding each piece and laying them in a neat pile on the bank. Marie would probably need them for the new baby, he thought. Then he did the same with his own clothes. For a moment they stood naked, side by side, father and son holding hands on the banks of Crockett's Brook. Paul concentrated on the feel of wind across his exposed flesh, the sweet, pungent odor of pine trees tickling his nose. A mosquito whined in his ear, and his mind snatched at that, too. He concentrated on the last sounds and sensations he would ever know of his old life, until he was as certain as he could ever be that he would remember them.

"Remember what I taught you, Amos," he said as they waded into the brook at its widest, deepest, most slow-moving point.

The water closed over their heads. They were never seen in Esperance again.

Everyone agreed that everything connected with Marie Dufore was touch and go for several weeks after Paul and Amos's mysterious disappearance. She wouldn't eat, she barely slept, she refused all comfort or counsel from her family.

She spent most of her days down where they'd found the

two little piles of clothes, staring into the slow-moving brown water. Donald Woodie came across her one day, standing knee-deep in the brook, smacking the surface of the water with the palms of both her hands and screaming.

"Marie Dufore's goin' out of her mind," he reported to his wife later that evening. "I saw her shoutin' at the trout down in Crockett's Brook."

"Poor thing," his wife answered. "It's hard, losing a husband and a son all at once."

"Like as not it's better so," Donald said brutally. "Paul Dufore was touched, that was plain to see. All that talk 'bout floods and learning to live like the fish. Prob'ly the boy would've took it from him, as well."

His wife clicked her tongue, but acknowledged the truth of what he said. "Still," she said. "I feel sorry for the poor girl, her expectin' another, and all."

There was a search for the bodies, of course. A group of men combed the banks of the brook as far down as ten miles. When they found no sign of either father or son, they figured the bodies had got hooked on an underwater obstruction, or swept into a backwater somewhere. "They may still turn up," folk told one another, but everyone hoped not; a couple of weeks in the water didn't contribute much towards the dignity of the corpse, or the comfort of the relatives.

Marie knew they weren't dead. For weeks she wandered up and down the brook, searching, pleading, cursing on its banks; one day she attacked Christian LaStrange as he sat fishing from the bridge near his house.

"Murderer! Murderer!" she shrieked, and launched herself at him, scratching his face and biting him on the shoulder.

He hadn't even heard her coming down the Ridge Road behind and wouldn't have thought anything of it if he had;

Christian had fished from this bridge for years. Marie was not a large woman; under other circumstances he could have easily subdued her; but he had a sane man's healthy regard for the unstable, rightly putting nothing past her in her present state. He dropped the fishing pole, wriggled out of her grasping, scratching hands, and ran.

When he was gone, Marie broke his pole into three pieces over her knee and flung them into the brook, after carefully removing the hook from the line.

"Bring him back, Paul," she pleaded from the bridge. "He's just a baby."

The shadow of a large brown trout detached itself from the deeper shadows under the bridge and swam in wide, lazy circles below her.

"Is that you, Paul?" she whispered.

The trout didn't appear to notice her, just continued to swim in wider and wider spirals.

"Goddamn son of a bitch!" she screamed. *"Bring him back!"*

The trout stopped circling, hung suspended in the water for a moment with just his fins backstroking gently. Then with tremendous speed he darted suddenly back into the concealing gloom of the bridge and was gone.

Maybe she really would have gone crazy, ending her days on the banks of the brook (or, more likely, in it) searching for her stolen child, if it hadn't been for the baby growing inside her. An instinct stronger than her grief for Amos pulled her back from the crazy edge she teetered on, gradually forcing her to take up the business of living once again.

Her parents suggested she come back to them, and Michelle Dufore tendered a stiff invitation to move into the farmhouse, but Marie refused both offers. She stayed by herself in the cabin on the ridge. For a while, she kept alive the hope Amos would come back, and she was afraid to leave the house for fear he'd think she had abandoned him.

As the months dragged on, from summer into autumn and towards another winter, that hope faded. She stopped going down to the brook entirely; on the rare occasions she went into town, she took to scrambling down the narrow footpath leading down the face of the ridge to the Dufore farm, and the East-West Road, thus avoiding the bridge, and the brook, completely.

In those early days, when the pain was still new and raw, and people left her alone because grief is a private thing, indecent to intrude upon, Davy started going up the ridge again.

His mother sent him with food, blankets, and whatever else she thought a lone woman in a family way might need. At first, he left the stuff on the front step, unless the weather was inclement; then he would open the door just wide enough to shove his offering through before hurrying away. He could hear her moving around inside, sometimes.

After a while, he started noticing things that had been left undone around the place. The kitchen garden was neglected, choked with weeds. No wood had been chopped or stacked for the winter. The caulking around the windows looked patchy in places. He often stayed on after he'd dropped off supplies, tending to things.

He thought he caught glimpses of her from time to time as he worked around the yard, but the door remained firmly shut to him. It got so he often forgot Marie even lived there, so abandoned was the feel of the place.

At the beginning of November, the front door suddenly opened and Davy saw Marie close up for the first time since Paul and Amos had disappeared. She looked much as she had when he'd first come to love her: big-bellied, round-faced, cumbersome.

"Thank you for taking care of things around here, Davy," she said, formally. "Would you care to come in?"

He hadn't been this close to her in months.

They sat across from one another at the kitchen table, drinking coffee in near-silence, neither companionable nor bitter. When the coffee was gone, he stood up and she escorted him to the front door.

"I'll be up tomorrow, to finish stacking that wood," he told her.

She nodded.

"Tell your mother I thank her for all she's done," she said.

And so they were reconciled.

Rich was born in early January.

The birth was remarkable only for the fact he came feet first and was born with a caul.

When she saw it after taking the baby from Marie's body, the midwife, Aimee Bouchard, made a sign behind her back before she removed the caul from his head.

"He'll have the second sight," Aimee said, laying the baby in the bed next to Marie.

When Aimee went away, she took the caul with her.

About the time the soft spot in Rich's head became tougher and less pronounced, Davy began noticing a slight softening in his own skull.

It was a small spot at first, hardly bigger than a dime. It felt punky, tender, and he thought for a while that a horsefly had got him. After some days passed, however, it was still there and seemed, if anything, bigger and softer.

He poked it hard, once, with his finger and was sure he'd felt his brain move underneath.

Damned if he didn't seem to be going rotten, just like a piece of unpicked fruit.

"Right there ... there! C'n ya feel it?"

He was standing by the woodpile, the ax dangling negligently from one hand, his head bent while Marie ran her hands over his crown. He was seventeen; he and Marie had married six months after Rich was born.

"Don't feel soft to me, Davy," she said doubtfully. "Well, maybe a *little,* but some people just got softer heads than others."

"I'm tellin' you, Marie, my whole head's just gettin softer an' softer! Where's it gonna end?"

She stepped back and looked up into his worried face. She didn't know what to say; she was beginning to find this Dufore tendency towards crazy obsessions wearing.

"When you finish with the wood, I'll have some tea and a nice piece of pound cake waiting for you," she said, patting his arm before she stumped back to the cabin.

He sighed and started to split wood again. There didn't seem to be anybody who took him seriously. His ma scoffed when he put her hand on his head and asked if she couldn't feel his brain beneath the skull.

"*All* Dufores are soft in the head!" she told him.

Marie had been kinder, but he could see she didn't really believe him either. He wished his father were easier to talk to, but the man hadn't so much as opened his mouth for fifteen years, not since the time at the Bixby auction when he'd opened his mouth to make a bid, and locusts had flown out. Fat, humming locusts almost as big as a man's thumb. It had been an embarrassment; inconvenient as well.

Paul Dufore, Sr., had no idea how the locusts had got into his stomach, but he thought he must have millions of them inside him; he could feel them swarming around and around inside, their wings beating against the walls of his stomach, and he knew if he so much as sneezed, such a swarm would be released as would destroy every crop between the New Hampshire seaboard and the Mississippi River.

So he'd shut his mouth—even going so far as to tie a sling

around his jaw to prevent snoring at night—and never opened it again.

Davy knew *something* was happening to him, something he didn't understand and probably wasn't going to like; it was beginning to prey on his mind more than was comfortable.

Chapter

9

〜〜

Sometimes, Dennis thought about his grandfather
Davy.

There'd been an old, white-haired gentleman
when Dennis was just a baby. He hadn't done much; mostly
just sat in a chair in the upstairs back bedroom he shared
with Gran Marie and looked out the window facing the
ridge where the old cabin still stood.

The room smelled strong: odors reminiscent of meat left
out too long in summer, of milk that had turned, of the
bloated, maggoty body of a dog Dennis found down by the
brook one summer and went back to, day after day, watching it decompose with childish wonder.

The room smelled like all those things, overlaid by a
strong minty scent, and children were not encouraged to
enter it. What little Dennis ever knew of his grandfather

Davy, and the even less he remembered of him, was snatched in passing from the hallway.

Once, when he was six, something happened to his father.

First the doctor came; he and Mama put Daddy in a car and drove away. Later, Gran Marie put him in his bed and threatened him with fearful consequences if he left it. Then she and Ab got into the pickup and went away, too.

He lay in bed for hours and hours; maybe even as long as a week went by. He was getting tired of being alone in the house, in the dark; he thought maybe he'd just go and make sure Allie, who was just a baby, wasn't scared or anything. He got up, started down the hallway, scaring himself with the sound of himself on tiptoe being swallowed up in the great silence of the farmhouse.

So he put his feet down deliberately, instead; a bold Thud, Thud that echoed instead of disappearing. He began to feel a little braver.

"Yer grandma tol' you to stay in bed."

Dennis's heart sky-rocketed right up his throat, slammed into the roof of his mouth, then dropped, bruised and pounding, back into its rightful place. He'd forgotten his grandfather was in the house.

The old man was in the doorway; Dennis noticed for the first time his chair had wheels on it. The table lamp on the dresser by the window was on. Dim yellow light followed his grandfather out the door and now lay draped around his shoulders, picking out the shock of still-thick white hair but leaving his face in darkness.

Along with the light, that peculiar, unpleasant smell had followed Grandfather into the hallway.

"C'mere," his grandfather Davy commanded.

Dennis moved a little closer, then stopped. Grandfather Davy said nothing; after a moment Dennis came to stand unwillingly within a foot of the chair. He'd never been this close to the old man before; he'd never been spoken to by him, either. Up close, the stench of rotting meat and peppermint was sickening.

"Sickening, isn't it?" his grandfather commented.

Dennis nodded in complete agreement; it was nothing less than the truth, and besides, he had been taught never to contradict his elders.

"I've been this way for more'n twenty years," the old man said. "Don't know why that woman keeps me alive. Revenge, maybe."

He coughed, and it seemed like his whole body rippled and sloshed from the force of the explosion. His breath was hot, reeking; Dennis thought if the old man coughed again, he, Dennis, would most likely throw up.

"How old do you think I am?" the old man asked. "Eighty? One hundred?"

Dennis hesitated, nodded.

"Hah!" Again his whole body seemed to ripple. "Not even fifty! Still a young man, for all the good it does me."

"Sickening, isn't it?" his grandfather said again.

"She don't sleep, you know." He leaned forward a little, his voice dropping into a cozy, confidential pitch. Dennis stared at him the same way he'd studied the dead dog by the brook.

"She don't sleep, and she don't hardly leave me alone for a minute."

Dennis could see the old man's features better now. His face seemed caved in, as if there were no bones underneath to support the weight of the skin; his nose and eyes were sunk deep into the flesh. His forehead and chin were concave, pulpy, too, and his cheeks were pitted with deep, coarse pores, like a muskmelon left too long on the vine. His eyes were bright, however, clear reflectors of an unclouded mind.

"She hasn't closed her eyes in years," Grandfather Davy whispered, leaning back again in his chair. "Not since she caught me down by the tracks. Look what's come of it."

Dennis was becoming restless standing by this smelly old man's chair, listening to him maunder on about Gran Marie's sleeping habits. He started to yawn and shift his weight from foot to foot.

His grandfather leaned forward again suddenly; the motion released another cloud of noxious odor. Dennis's stomach heaved, and he took a step back.

"Yer daddy cut himself tonight," Grandfather Davy hissed, and Dennis saw he had no teeth. "*That*'s what's come of it."

He sounded almost satisfied.

Dennis's mind was occupied with trying to figure out how and where his father had cut himself. His finger? His toe? Dennis had cut himself plenty of times, but his mama had never called the doctor, just kissed the hurt and put a plaster on it.

"How come Mama called the doctor?" he asked his grandfather.

Grandfather Davy ignored the question.

"This is the first time she's left me alone in twenty years," he said. "If this had happened fifteen years ago, I might have got outside, to the barn." He sounded fretful and whiny, the way Allie was when she wanted something she couldn't have, Dennis thought.

"You a strong boy?" his grandfather asked him suddenly.

"Sure," Dennis said, and made a muscle to prove it.

His grandfather laughed. He sounded so normal, so human, that for a moment Dennis almost forgot the horrible smell clinging to hair and clothing that was beginning to attach itself to Dennis, as well.

"Good boy!" he chuckled. "Think you're strong enough

to push me an' this chair over to the steps?"

Dennis nodded, puzzled by his grandfather's request. Surely Grandfather Davy didn't think he'd be able to get himself down those steps once Dennis had rolled him over there.

"You want somethin' from the kitchen, Grandpa?" Dennis asked him. "I c'n make cocoa, if you want some."

"Yer a good kid, Dennis," his grandfather said; Dennis hadn't been sure he even knew his name. "Just see if you can push me over there."

Dennis got behind the chair and pushed with all his strength. It was hard going, for he was a small boy and Davy was heavy with corruption, bloated with gas and liquefied bone and flesh. Eventually, however, the chair stood poised at the top of the narrow back stairs. The front steps, leading down to the parlor, were closer, but Davy had insisted on the back ones.

"No carpet," he explained cryptically. "Don't want to make more of a mess than we have to." The back of the wheelchair was high, too broad for Dennis to come around its side and stand by his grandfather. He could only hear his voice, and smell him through the caned back.

"What d'ya want me to do now, Grandpa?" Dennis asked, after keeping a respectful silence behind the chair for some minutes.

"Go to bed, boy."

"How ya gonna get back to your room, Grandpa?"

Dennis had a pretty good idea of what would be said— and done—to him if Gran Marie returned to find her husband stranded in his chair at the top of the back steps.

"You let me worry about that," his grandfather answered snappishly. "Go to bed!"

Dennis hung around a bit anyway, in case his grandfather changed his mind; after a while, though, when no talk or movement seemed forthcoming from the chair, Dennis started back to his room.

His grandfather's voice stopped him at the doorway.

"You won't forget tonight, will you, Dennis?" he called in a stage-whisper bellow.

"No sir."

"There's a lesson to be learned here," his grandfather said.

"Yessir."

"You know what that lesson is, Dennis?"

"No sir."

"You will, someday. This is what comes of not doing it clean, when you still have the chance."

"Yessir."

Dennis lingered in the doorway, in case his grandfather had anything else to say. His feet were chilled through and through; the sight of his bed, just a few feet away, tortured him.

"Dennis!"

"Yessir?"

"She's a good woman, your grandmother," Davy said. "She's a good woman, in spite of everything. You remember that."

"Yessir."

"Good night, now."

"Good night, sir."

Perhaps at some point during that long night, Dennis was disturbed by some unaccustomed sound. Perhaps he came briefly awake for a second or two, troubled by some sound or movement he could almost recognize, before slipping back into sleep. Perhaps the sound he'd heard, the wet impact of something heavy and semisolid against stone, insinuated itself into his brain, for he dreamed all night of apples, brown and bruised with rot, dropping from their trees and splattering against the earth.

Davy was lying at the bottom of the back stairs when Gran Marie got home from the hospital, the night Rich slit his wrists.

The smell hit her the minute she opened the door, and she knew, right then, what had happened.

Ab was behind her; instinctively she stepped back, half turned toward him so her body was between him and the kitchen.

"Jesus, Mama!" Ab exclaimed as the horrible odor came rolling through the doorway in waves. It was so bad his eyes watered, his breath caught in his throat and doubled back on him. "What the—"

Marie didn't answer him, just straightened and took a deep, shuddering breath before turning back to the kitchen and going in through the door.

Davy's features were no longer recognizable; indeed, his affinity with human beings was hard to see. He had launched himself headfirst out of his wheelchair and burst his head on the third step, leaving a thick, viscous trail of bodily fluids down the rest of the staircase until he had finally struck the flagstone landing and split clean down the middle like an overripe tomato.

There he lay, an oozing gelatinous mess bubbling out from beneath the frayed edges of his terry-cloth bathrobe, congealing in the toes of his slippers.

Ab took one look at his father and started to retch.

"Get the hell outside!" his mother shrieked. "Don't you *dare* throw up on your daddy!"

She cuffed him hard across his ear, chased him towards the back door with pushes and blows between the shoulder blades. Hot, bitter bile rose in Ab's throat as he stumbled down the back steps and practically fell in a sobbing, retching heap by the cellar door. He swallowed hard, and the acid burned even worse going back down.

It wasn't until he'd calmed down a bit himself that he realized his mother was sitting on the back steps twenty feet away, with her head between her knees.

"Jesus, Mama," he whispered. "What are we gonna do? Should we call a doctor, or something?"

"Or something!" She snorted. "Fat lot of good a doctor'll do him now. Oh, *Davy!*"

Her voice rose on his name; in grief, or anger, Ab couldn't tell.

"What're we goin' to do?" he asked again.

She was silent for so long he thought perhaps she hadn't heard him. He stood up slowly and went to stand in front of her at the bottom of the steps. The stench was everywhere; he could almost see a cloud of stink hovering over the house.

"We can't leave him like that," Gran Marie said finally. "It isn't respectful."

Ab found an old door leaning up against the back wall of the barn and brought it back to the house. It was made of oak, and heavy; he seriously doubted just the two of them would be able to lift it, even if they got Davy onto it. When he had got it as far as the back steps, he suggested stopping down to the LaStrange place for some help.

"Nobody's goin' to see him like this," Marie told him firmly. "We'll manage ourselves."

So he brought the door into the kitchen and laid it next to the unspeakable contents of the terry-cloth bathrobe. He'd grown accustomed, as much as was humanly possible, to the smell. The whole evening, commencing as it had with Rich's suicide attempt and ending with his father splashed all down the back steps and across the kitchen floor, had become dreamlike to Ab; he found himself staring down at Davy's remains as though they were nothing more than a knotty problem that needed solving.

He didn't feel much, not grief, disgust, or horror at the

sight. He studied his father with queer, hungry eyes; at last, after years of furtive glances and an unspoken agreement to disregard the obvious, he was free to look his fill and see the truth.

Davy had no bones, as far as Ab could tell. He had landed on his back, the flesh splitting in a jagged tear, almost two feet long, from mid-chest to groin. Where the edges of the bathrobe had fallen away, Ab could see his father's in-nards—pulpy, congealed, stinking to high heaven; nothing solid like bone, or any recognizable organ floating in the mess.

He glanced surreptitiously at his mother, then prodded the body once with the toe of his boot. The flesh wrinkled slightly where his foot touched, then began to split, spilling more of Davy Dufore out onto the flagstones. He stepped back hurriedly, scraped his toe against the heel of his other boot.

"What're you just standin' there for, you fool!" his mother scolded. "Help me get him onto the board."

Till the day he died, Ab would never forget the strange, sickening sensation of laying hands on his father's body: like reaching for an orange that seemed firm and fresh until your thumb poked unexpectedly through the peel to sink into black, rotten pulp at the center.

After nearly an hour, they were still no closer to getting Davy on the board and out of the kitchen than when they started.

There is not one solid place to get a grip on, Ab thought, as he and Marie took up positions on one side of Davy's body, she at his hips, he at his shoulders. They hunkered down, balancing on their haunches, their hands under the body so that between the two of them, he was supported at the shoulder, midback, buttocks, and knee. The board lay with its edge slid just under Davy's side. On the count of three, they planned to roll him right onto it.

"One, two, three!" Ab panted. They both began to lean into the weight and lift.

"Shit! He's coming apart at the ribs!" Ab swore, and they dropped him back down to the floor.

This was maybe the tenth attempt they'd made to get Davy off the kitchen floor; with every try, his flesh ripped a little more, and more of the thick, evil-smelling corruption inside spilled out. The bathrobe was stained almost black; both Ab and Marie were liberally coated with Davy's remains, and the body itself was now almost in three distinct pieces.

"Mama, it'll have to be the tub," Ab said.

They'd discussed it before, when the full implications of Davy's advanced state of decomposition had first become clear, but Marie had refused to consider it. It wasn't "respectful," she'd said.

Now she sat dejectedly on the floor near her husband and thought nothing could be more obscene than the continued subdivision of his body.

"Go 'n get it," she told her son.

Ab came back with a large zinc tub they used in the winter to water the horses. He ran the hose over it once or twice to get the dirt and cobwebs out of it, then put as much of it as would fit on the back stoop, so the lip of the tub was almost level with the kitchen floor. He put cinder blocks under the part that still hung over the stoop for support, then scrambled up over the tub and back into the kitchen.

"Here, Mama, you take this," he said, handing her a wide, stiff-bristled broom.

He stooped over, took the bottom hem of his father's bathrobe in his two hands, then began sliding the body across the floor towards the back stoop. Marie followed in his wake, pushing whatever got left behind with the broom.

He went slow, to avoid rips and tears as much as possible; at the end of ten minutes, Davy was half-dragged, half-mopped into the zinc tub on the back steps. Once there, his body seemed to expand into the boundaries of its new container, becoming almost round.

The tub was too heavy for just the two of them to lift, so Ab covered it securely with a tarpaulin, and there it sat until morning.

Chapter
10

O ne day almost three years after Ab leaped to his death out behind the mill, Dennis met his cousin Bobby outside the post office. Dennis had straddled the motorcycle he'd bought the year before and was about to kick it into gear when Bobby Dufore came round the corner, a toolbox dangling from his left hand. Dennis liked the look of the toolbox—there was something heavy and substantial about it.

"Hey, Bobby," Dennis said. "Got a job?"

"Mm," Bobby assented, nodding towards the other end of the street. "Miller place. New sills."

Bobby Dufore lived with his wife, Alice, and their three children in a house on the edge of town. Bobby's father, a first cousin of Davy Dufore, had built the place back in the early thirties. He'd run a woodworking business out of there for almost fifteen years before suddenly blowing his brains out one evening in the lumber room.

Bobby and Alice were living in a trailer when Jacques Dufore died; they moved in with Bobby's mother the next month. Now, almost eleven years later, they were still there; Bobby and Alice, Marty, Peter, and Henry, and Bobby's mother, Margaret. Bobby had put an addition on the back of the house, so they managed to rub along tolerably well together; Margaret and Alice hardly ever got in each other's way anymore.

Like his father, Bobby made his living as a man-of-all-work, and was able to keep his family pretty well. In addition to carpentry, Bobby helped with sugaring in the winter, harvesting in the fall. He could cane chairs and put in storm windows and was a pretty fair picture framer. No job was too big or too small for Bobby.

"Jeanette well?" Bobby inquired politely. He was several years older than Dennis—almost old enough to have fathered him, in fact—and had never felt comfortable around Jeanette. There was something dark and disturbing about her, he thought; she had the uncomfortable effect of always making him feel like he was about to get an erection.

"Fine," Dennis said.

"And the boy?"

Their first child, Daniel, had been born in their first year of marriage.

"Growing like a weed," Dennis said.

"I saw Marty hangin' around the mill the other day," he told Bobby. "He thinkin' of gettin' a job there?"

"First time I've heard of it," Bobby said, not unpleased by the information. "Mightn't be a bad idea. My boy's not much for schoolwork."

"You 'n' Alice comin' by for the barbecue?" Dennis

asked. "Ma and Gran Marie will be pleased to see you."

"We'll be there," Bobby said, standing back to give Dennis room to start up the bike. "You oughta get saddlebags for that bike," he remarked as the engine kicked over. "Then you wouldn't have to wear that backpack."

Dennis, who had thirty-five pounds of sand in the pack, merely smiled as he pulled out into the road and roared back up towards the Clark Hill Road.

Alice was boiling eggs when Bobby got home.

Alice Dufore had been pretty, once, the way very blond women often are: a fragile, pastel prettiness that didn't last through her twenties. China-blue eyes had become watery; flaxen hair was darker now, more like dried straw, and her skin, once delicate, was creased. Her personality seemed to fade along with her looks, though most people in Esperance would probably agree she'd never had much character to begin with.

She was the last woman anyone would have expected to marry a Dufore. In fact, when the engagement was announced, there had been heavy betting on whether the wedding would take place; a few people, most notably Earl Hammond and Michael Duplessis, made a considerable sum backing the dark horse Bobby. There was some bad feeling when Earl and Michael claimed their winnings. Popular opinion held that since Earl's daughter and Michael's cousin had both married Dufore men, they should've disqualified themselves on the grounds of inside information. Earl and Michael countered that Dufore men had succeeded in marrying women from the best families for over two hundred years. If other folk in Esperance didn't have sense enough to apply the law of averages, that was not their problem.

When the wedding went through on schedule, most people assumed there'd be a seven-month child before long. It

CROCKETT'S BROOK ◆

was almost two years before Bobby and Alice's first child was born, though, so it appeared to have been a love match, after all.

"Somethin' smells good," Bobby commented as he came through the door and scraped his feet on the rag rug.

"Shepherd's pie," Alice told him. "You see the boys around?"

Bobby sauntered over to the sink, opened both taps wide, and thrust his grimy hands and forearms under the gush of water. He grunted a negative to his wife, picked up a nail brush, and attacked the filth under his fingernails.

"Can't you do that in the bathroom?" Alice said in the same voice she'd been using to make that request for fifteen years.

"Where's Mama?" Bobby asked.

"Out back, in the herb garden."

"How long till supper?" he asked.

"'Bout twenty minutes," she said.

He nodded and started down the hallway towards the back of the house. At the end of the hall was a small room, hardly bigger than a closet. Old Jacques Dufore once had had grandiose plans to make a downstairs master bedroom with an adjoining dressing room. His wife seemed to like the idea, but what with one thing and another, they never actually got around to moving their bed downstairs. The room had filled up with mending, ironing, and account books while the smaller room adjoining it had become Bobby's private territory.

As a child, Bobby had used the room as a fort, then later as a place to stash birds' nests and comic books. Lately, he'd turned it into an observatory, of sorts. Sticking out the lone window was a large telescope, its body supported by a sturdy homemade tripod. There was a small three-legged stool positioned in front of the telescope, its height carefully adjusted so Bobby could sit comfortably and look through the glass without stretching or stooping.

Now he sauntered over as he did every night and adjusted the stool just a mite, then settled himself into the comfortable groove his buttocks had made in the round cushion adorning it. With a sigh he put his face up to the eyepiece and looked up through the telescope. Its lens magnified the pale moon, the width of a nailparing, that hung in a still-blue sky. He swiveled the telescope on its tripod in an arc across the sky, tracing the sun's path from nadir to zenith and back. Of course, it was still too light to see much of anything—unless, of course, there was something unexpected and uncommonly close in the sky.

A meteor, for example.

The telescope swept back, its arc lower this time, then back again. Still nothing up there.

From the front of the house, he could hear Alice calling the boys for dinner. He unbent himself from the telescope and pushed up off the stool. He suddenly felt very hungry for some of Alice's shepherd's pie.

He'd come back and check the sky again, in an hour or two.

The night was alight with fire and falling bodies.

Huge, pitted boulders streaming flames and molten lava screamed across the starry sky and crashed into the house where his children and wife and mother lay sleeping.

Afterwards, there was just a crater where the house had stood.

With a start, Bobby woke to find his wife bending over him, her hand, cool and slightly damp, resting lightly on his shoulder.

"Wha—what is it?" he muttered, struggling to sit up.

The vague, terrifying knowledge that something had happened took possession of him; his one thought was to get to the telescope.

"Hush now," his wife whispered, settling back into the comfort of the blankets, her hand slipping companionably down from his shoulder, her arm wrapping itself like a bandage across his chest.

"You been dreamin' again," she murmured in his ear and molded herself against the curve of his back and legs until he felt himself cushioned, pinioned by the warm musky body of his wife; drowsily he wondered how he had endured the thousands of nights before she'd come.

He managed to raise one clumsy hand and grasp her fingers in his fist before he slept again.

On Fourth of July weekend, there was a barbecue at the Dufore farm, and most of the Dufore family attended.

It had been on that weekend, forty years before, that Davy, fingering a soft spot in his head, had lain down on the railroad tracks for the first time and only been saved from a quick and gruesome death by a cow who had apparently had the same intention some seventy-five yards up the track and had stopped the train before it ever reached him.

It had been on that weekend twenty-six years before that Rich Dufore had tried hanging himself from a rotten beam in the old sugarhouse. The beam had broken under his weight, and he'd fallen against the woodpile and wrenched his ankle; it still pained him in damp weather.

As a young bride, Bette Dufore Delagarde had jumped out an attic window on the Fourth of July, almost eighty-seven years before, belly-flopped onto the sunporch roof, then slid off and landed on top of the cowman who happened to be standing at the bottom of the steps going over the milking schedule with her husband.

Most people in Esperance considered the Fourth of July weekend an unlucky time for the Dufore family. The Dufores, however, pointed out that no one who had attempted suicide on that weekend ever actually succeeded; from their perspective, there was every reason to celebrate the holiday.

In fact, that weekend had seen only one fatality amongst the Dufores, and that the result of a freak accident, almost thirty years before.

A few days before the Fourth of July, 1933, Rich Dufore dreamed his cousin Frank, blew up. Frank and Rich were best friends—had been since they were both babies in the cradle; naturally he found the dream upsetting. He couldn't remember much about it when he woke up; only an image of Frank, hair fanned out around his head in streaming flames, hands stretched out in supplication, mouth open in a silent scream, came into Rich's mind from time to time in the days following the dream.

It wasn't until the annual Fourth of July picnic at the Dufore farm that Rich understood the import of his dream. He was eating grilled chicken at the time, standing with his napkin held up close under his chin to catch rivulets of grease and barbecue sauce that ran down from the corners of his mouth, when he heard Frank say to his younger brother, Bobby,

"You wanna go see some fireworks?"

Rich glanced up and saw Frank beside the grill. Ripples of heat rising up off the coals seemed to make Frank ripple, too; the dream-vision of Frank Dufore on fire erupted behind Rich's eyes.

The picnic became riddled with hidden dangers. Coals that had glowed so cozily beneath charcoal-blackened chicken breasts and wieners seemed sinister all of a sudden, while the pop and hiss of grease dripping down from the grate onto the fire whispered threats in his straining ears. He saw Frank wince, then swear and laugh as hot grease spattered across his arm.

Dusk was settling in, and the night promised to be a fine one: clear and cool, moonless, a perfect night for fireworks. There'd be a fine display in Bennington, put on by some fellows from Albany, New York. Rich loved fireworks. He loved firecrackers and sparklers, the scream of rockets and the burst of blinding color when the Roman candles exploded. He'd been looking forward to going down to Bennington in the back of his dad's truck with his cousins Frank and Bobby, who was just a kid but not bad if he stayed in line, Doug Peterson, and Fred Delagarde. Ab did not appreciate fireworks, and never went. It was twelve miles to Bennington, but most of Esperance went there for the fireworks on the Fourth. Anne Devereaux would be there, he was sure; the last time he'd seen her, he'd managed to get one of the hooks on her brassiere undone.

Yes, he'd had hopes for this Fourth of July.

For a moment he dwelled on a fantasy image of Anne in her underwear, the straps of her brassiere slipping gently down over her shoulders, one white breast almost falling out. Unbidden, a picture of Frank wearing a halo of fire superimposed itself.

"Great night for fireworks," Frank said as he took Bobby's hand and started across the yard towards where a group of people no longer interested in eating or drinking had gathered around the Dufores' pickup truck, waiting for a ride into town.

"Step on it, Rich," Frank said.

"Step on it, Rich," Bobby repeated.

Rich, who had been straggling ten feet behind, suddenly came to a halt in the middle of the drive.

"Let's not go," he said.

Frank turned to look at him.

"You're kidding," he said.

"No," Rich said. "I mean, it's the same thing every year. Let's do something different."

"I wanna see *firecrackers!*" Bobby wailed.

"Shuttup," Frank told his little brother.

"What about the girls?" he asked Rich. "I bet Annie Devereaux's gonna be looking for you."

"So what?" Rich shrugged. "She's not so great."

Bobby was beginning to cry hard. Frank jerked his head in his brother's direction.

"Look at him," he said. "I been promising him firecrackers for two weeks now."

"We got some sparklers and stuff here," Rich offered. "Or he could go with someone else."

"What's the *matter* with you?" Frank demanded. "There's gonna be beer an' girls an' everything! You sick or something?"

"I just feel like doin' something different. That's all."

"Yeah? Well, I don't feel like hangin' around here all by myself in the dark. You sure got a weird idea of having fun, Rich." He started back towards the pickup truck.

"You comin'?" he called back over his shoulder. Rich stood looking after him, rockets going up behind his eyes.

"Shit!" he swore, and started after them.

Bobby was seven years old that Fourth of July. He could remember the trip into Bennington in the back of the crowded pickup truck, wrapped in his brother Frank's jacket and curled into a corner of the truck between his cousin Rich's legs.

He could remember crowds of people on the common,

the outline of a tent at the far end set up to shelter the rockets in case of rain. There was a pale glow from the torches they kept down there to light the rockets.

He could remember a sound like the dull thump of a fist against flesh that was the rockets igniting, then explosions high above his head, and fireworks flowering, blooming, dropping their dying petals in a few seconds' imitation of life.

He could remember standing between his big brother and his cousin, wanting to hold their hands when the explosions were loud but keeping his hands in his pockets instead, because he was seven now, and too old for that.

And he could remember the meteor.

Rich felt sick to his stomach. He prayed for the display to be over, Frank still beside him, still in one piece. There was a sizable crowd gathered on the green; refreshment stands dotted the perimeter of the field, along with booths selling cheap American flags and straw hats with red-white-and-blue bands. Off to the left a group of people huddled around a tattooed juggler; once, Rich thought the man had winked at him.

"Bet you're glad you came *now,*" Frank said. "I thought I saw Julie Wright and Anne Devereaux over by the cider stand."

"Yeah? Let's go," Rich said. Anything to be away from the fireworks display.

Frank laughed. "I thought Annie Devereaux wasn't so hot."

The way to the refreshment stand skirted dangerously close to where the rockets were launched.

"Wait a minute," Rich said. "You gotta do something with the squirt here."

"I wanna go with you," Bobby said.

"Too bad," his brother said. "I'm gonna take you back to the truck. You can go to sleep in the cab.

"I'll bring you some cider," he added, when it looked like Bobby was going to start crying.

"Be back in a minute," Frank told Rich. He took Bobby by the hand and started walking towards where the truck was parked. Rich breathed freely, watching them go; by the time Frank got back from the parking lot, the display would be over.

Frank and Bobby were still only about halfway across the field when there was a dull thump. A streak of flame suddenly jetted through the night sky about thirty feet above the ground. The last rocket, Rich thought. But instead of rising a hundred feet into the air and bursting there, it veered sharply earthward and exploded barely six feet above Frank Dufore's head.

The explosion lifted Frank right off his feet and carried him straight up into flames that reached like a lover's arms to embrace him. It seemed like he hung there forever, burning embers of gunpowder burrowing into his clothing, licks of fire wreathing themselves through his hair like ribbons. Then he was on the ground again, howling with fear and pain.

Rich stood mesmerized, frozen by shock as his cousin turned towards him, his blackened arms stretched out in supplication.

His hair and clothes were streaming flames as he ran screaming towards Rich, those horrible black arms stretched out in front of him.

It wasn't until he'd almost reached him that Rich realized there were no hands on the end of Frank's arms.

Bobby had been knocked unconscious by the force of the explosion. The last thing he remembered was something like a star exploding right over his brother's head.

People told him his brother Frank had been killed by a Roman candle, but in his heart of hearts, Bobby knew better. It would take something a hell of a lot bigger and more dangerous than a piddly old firecracker to kill his brother Frank.

In fifth grade, when they studied the solar system, he finally discovered the only answer that made any sense: huge celestial bodies hurled themselves through space with incredible force, he learned, sometimes colliding with planets. Imagine if you had the bad luck to be standing right where one of those falling bodies hit!

It made sense, now, what had happened to Frank; how anybody could mistake a meteor for a Roman candle, he'd never understand!

Now, on the Fourth of July, 1959, Rich Dufore sidled up to his cousin Bobby and whispered, "Bob, I had a dream last night."

Bobby nearly dropped his hamburger.

"Shit," he said. Rich, as everybody knew, had second sight. It was well known his prophetic dreams just about always came true, though often not in the manner expected. He looked at the burger in his hand and felt his appetite die within him.

"Whaddja dream?" he asked.

"Fire," Rich said. "Explosions. Death. Same as usual."

"Me this time?" Bobby asked, though he knew Rich wouldn't be telling him about this dream if it hadn't concerned him.

Rich nodded miserably, patted Bobby awkwardly on the shoulder.

Meteors, Bobby thought. A meteor had got his brother Frank and now one was after him, too. Gloomily he wondered how long he had before it caught up with him.

Bobby was subdued when he, Alice, and the boys got back from the barbecue that evening. He wandered from room to room through the house, picking up various objects, then putting them down, clearly distracted. The boys were overexcited and acting up, sated as they were on hot dogs, hamburgers, ginger beer, and the company of all their Dufore cousins. They whooped and hollered through the house, sliding across the linoleum floors, sending throw rugs skuttering into corners. Bobby hardly seemed to notice; he simply walked into the room where he kept his telescope and closed the door behind him.

The sky was a deep velvet black, perfectly encircled in the lens of his telescope. Within those perimeters, pinpoints of light pricked through the dark; he could see nothing unusual or menacing up there, nothing to cause the profound uneasiness that plagued him. He was unnerved by his cousin Rich's warning, but he'd felt unhappy and ill at ease long before that. He swung the telescope in a wide arc across the sky, across the Big Dipper and the constellations Leo and Virgo, hovering high in the sky, searching for something a little out of the ordinary, but finding nothing. Not yet, anyway.

He sighed and sat back from the telescope.

Fire. Death. Explosions. The usual, Rich had said. What could he do against all that? It was then that the memory of Rory Miller popped unbidden into his brain.

Rory Miller had built a bomb shelter shortly after the United States dropped a bomb on Hiroshima. Although Rory was only an elderly Vermont farmer, illiterate at that, he was famous for common sense; as he was fond of telling anyone who would listen, it didn't take a college graduate to figure out what Americans could do, Commies could too.

One day he came to Jacques Dufore asking if he and

Bobby would build an underground bunker in the Millers' backyard. Jacques and Bobby worked on it for most of that summer and into the first part of the autumn. Rory had firm ideas about what that bunker should be like. He had no concept of radiation, but he did know if he and his family were planning on surviving several months (up to a year, he figured) underground, there'd have to be enough space and enough diversions to keep them from getting in one another's hair. So he got Jacques and Bobby to build him a bunker big as a cellar, and he'd kept his wife and daughter-in-law busy canning for most of the summer while he and his three sons built beds, chairs, and cabinets specially designed for the space.

For a month or two after it was finished, Rory insisted the family sleep in the bunker, to accustom them to it; he even made them live for an entire weekend underground. At the end of three days in the cellar, his wife made it clear she would take her chances with the A-bomb rather than spend another hour cooped up in a musty basement with six other people and a chemical toilet. To humor Rory, she agreed to occasional surprise bomb drills, but by Christmas the bomb shelter had been pretty much forgotten by everyone except Rory's grandchildren, who used it for a secret fort.

Bobby could still remember helping his father build the shelter, and he could remember the jokes townsfolk made about Mad Rory; he'd made a few himself. But now Bobby began to think differently about the bunker. Everyone knew it would be useless if the Russians ever really did attack; it had not been constructed to keep radiation out. But it was deep enough and sturdy enough to withstand the impact of a pretty strong explosion. Maybe even a direct hit on the house, Bobby thought; maybe even the impact from a meteor.

Tomorrow I start digging, Bobby thought.

When the hole appeared in Bob Dufore's backyard, people began to talk. In the beginning, he tried to pretend he was digging another root cellar, but it soon became clear the hole was far bigger than what a root cellar required.

"Crikey!" Thom Spinney, Bobby's closest neighbor, said. "Damned if he ain't digging some kind of bomb shelter, like old Rory Miller!"

Once he had begun, Bobby felt an unbearable pressure to be done with the project quickly—as though some unseen presence were standing at his shoulder as he dug, urging him to hurry, before it was too late. Nevertheless, he planned carefully. For nearly three days he went without sleep as he drew plans of the underground shelter. He spent most of one afternoon when he should have been finishing up the new sills at the Miller house at the library, the *Encyclopedia Britannica* open to the section on meteors. He was trying to figure out how far from the house the shelter would have to be to withstand the aftershocks from the impact of a celestial body. When he finally got to the Miller place, it was only to examine Rory's bomb shelter more closely. He enjoyed the digging. In the beginning it had been difficult; he had only a standard gardening shovel to work with, which seemed woefully inadequate when measured against the image in his head of the finished shelter. He'd started, though, and that was the important thing. As time went on, he began to enjoy the rhythmic motion of his arms stabbing the earth with the point of the shovel, his foot jamming it further in, followed by the one-two lifting and heaving of heavy brown earth up out of the hole, over his shoulder, onto a pile that grew higher as the day wore on.

He stopped only occasionally that first day, was nearly paralyzed the next. The muscles in his arms, shoulders, and neck seized up on him; he could barely roll himself out of bed to get to the toilet. Alice came up when he was trying to pull a shirt over his head, and immediately bullied him back into bed. He spent the rest of the day there, his body smelling powerfully of the ointment Alice had rubbed into his muscles.

He was still sore the next morning, but after digging for an hour or so, the aches went off and he was able to move almost as fluidly as before.

"I told you," Alice's mother said sadly one afternoon, about a week after Bobby had started to dig. "I told you sooner or later that crazy Dufore blood would act up. Didn't I tell you?"

"Shut up, Mama," Alice said. Her mother had been saying the same thing for fifteen years. Alice was beginning to wonder, however, if maybe this time she might be right. For a week now, Bobby had refused all offers of work in order to stay home and dig. Worse, he'd pulled Marty out of the mill two days before and got him down in that hole, helping. He got up every morning before sunrise and continued digging until well after dark. Then he disappeared into his back room and remained practically glued to the telescope until God only knew when. The first couple of nights, Alice tried waiting up for him but had fallen asleep long before he finally came to bed.

Alice decided to go visit old Marie Dufore.

Marie was one of those women who seemed to reach middle age, then stop there for a while. At forty, her hair had been as black as when she was twenty, the lines in her face stamped there by grief, not age. At fifty, she'd appeared much the same, and again at sixty. Ab's death, however, had brought about a change; overnight, it seemed, she became an old woman. When she'd followed his coffin to the grave three days after his leap, her hair was white and she walked as though she were eighty.

She had worn nothing but black since the funeral, refusing to put it off even after the period of mourning had passed. She had taken off her blacks six months after Paul and Amos's disappearance, six months after Davy's death, but it seemed as though Marie saw no point anymore in putting her mourning clothes up carefully in mothballs when she would almost certainly have to bring them out again before long.

She was shelling peas in the kitchen when Alice arrived. The whole time Alice talked, Marie listened in silence, popping open one fat, green pod after another and running the ball of her thumb along the inside spines, peas spilling into a colander in her lap.

"He don't talk about it, Gran," Alice said. "He's not eating right, and I don't even know if he's sleeping."

She had gripped a hank of her skirt in her hands, twisting, twisting the material in a tight wad in her lap as she spoke.

"Now he's got the boys out there, helpin' him. Marty got took on part-time at the mill, but he's gonna lose that job if Bobby don't let him go."

Marie reached her hand into the sack next to her chair and pulled out another fistful of peas.

"Mama says . . ." Alice's voice trailed off.

"He's never done nothin' like this before . . ." she finished, lamely.

Marie continued shelling peas. After a moment, she looked up into Alice's worried, watery eyes.

"What do you want from me?" she asked. "There's nothin' I can tell you."

She waved her free hand down the length of her black dress, speaking as though she blamed Alice for the two husbands that had destroyed themselves, the two sons she had lost.

Of course, Alice thought as she trudged homeward, Gran Marie was more than half Dufore herself, and had not slept in forty years. Lack of sleep alone would account for the old woman's crotchets. Alice considered various members of the Dufore family and sighed; if the taint caused Bobby to do nothing worse than dig a bomb shelter in the backyard, she supposed she should be grateful.

By the end of August, the bomb shelter was almost complete.

He had reinforced its walls with concrete and covered it with a six-foot shield of earth, so there was a swell in the backyard resembling an Indian burial mound.

Bobby had managed to do most of the digging himself, with some help from Marty. When it came time to pour the concrete, however, he had gone to his cousin Rich for help. Rich and Dennis both had come over and stood for a while at the lip of the deep cellar he'd dug, looking down at the pattern of two-by-fours he'd laid out on the dirt floor to mark the room divisions he planned to make.

"Nice 'n' roomy," Rich commented after a while.

He'd been worrying ever since he told Bobby about the dream; though he foresaw tragedy unerringly, he never seemed able to avert it. The bomb shelter gave him some hope, though. He had no clear idea just what it was menacing his cousin; he supposed it would probably be some ordinary thing: a car crash, a lightning bolt. This hole, however, looked reassuringly deep, sturdy, and far removed from things that could explode or burn.

"Looks pretty airtight," Dennis said. He was admiring how solidly entrenched the shelter was, irrevocably earthbound and safe from prying drafts and bullying winds.

By the end of the afternoon, they had put in a concrete floor. By week's end, the main walls were reinforced, and they set about putting in the roof. Now Bobby's urgency to finish the shelter increased even more. Even after Rich and

Dennis left at the end of each day he continued working. For almost four days Alice barely saw him. He came out of the shelter only to use the bathroom; the rest of the time, she took his meals out to him, climbing backwards down the wooden ladder with a tray balanced precariously in the crook of one arm.

"You listen to me," Rory Miller's widow, Emma, said to Alice when they met one afternoon at the general store. "Sleepin' underground ain't no way for people to live. You tell that man of yours to stop his foolishness, now, or you'll regret it!"

"I told you what would come of marrying a Dufore," Alice's mother said. "Don't expect me to come visit you when you're living in a hole in the ground."

"Everybody is laughing at us, Bobby!" Alice said one evening as she laid the tray on a cable spool Bobby was using as a table and poured soup from a thermos into a bowl.

"Marty's lost his place at the mill—Andy LaFleur can't rightly justify keepin' him on if he misses three days a week to help you. . . ."

She took the packet of ham-and-cheese sandwiches out of the napkin she'd wrapped them in and set them on the spool next to the bowl.

"No money's come in for more 'n a month. Money for a new roof is gone. Money for the boys' fall shoes is gone. Pretty soon, money for food'll be gone into this damned hole!"

She took the waxed paper off the square of brown Betty, folded it carefully, neatly, into a smaller square, and slipped it into her pocket with the napkin.

"Bobby," she said gently, coming up behind him and putting her hand lightly on the back of his neck, on just the spot where her kisses made him shudder. He turned when she touched him; she could barely see his face in the light of the hurricane lanterns he used for illumination.

"Alice," he began, then stopped.

He had explained it to her before, all about Rich's dream and the meteor. She'd listened, but he knew she hadn't believed a word of it. Though she didn't say so, he knew Alice believed, along with most other folks, that Frank had been killed in a freak fireworks accident. It hurt a little, his own wife doubting him, but he cheered himself with the knowledge that soon the shelter would be completed, his family safe underground. Then it would be only a matter of time before events proved to Alice and everyone else he was not crazy at all.

In the meantime, there wasn't anything more he could say to reassure her. They stood close together and silent for several moments before Alice gave a tiny sigh and dropped her hand from the back of his neck.

"Come eat your supper before the soup gets cold," she said.

Chapter

II

Someone was setting off firecrackers. The air vibrated with their shotgun explosions every two or three minutes; the Dufores, who had been waking up and going to sleep with the sound of them in their ears for nearly two weeks, were barely aware of the noise anymore.

It was the LaStranges, of course. They had started eleven days before the Fourth this year; their firecrackers went off with mechanical regularity, a minute or two apart, from sunup until well past dusk. After the first day or two, people who lived within earshot grew accustomed to the sound; by the time the Fourth of July finally rolled around, the explosions had become as much a part of the LaStrange commotion as the frequent screams, curses, and arguments that emanated from that house year-round.

When Allie was a child, she had imagined the brood of

LaStrange children took turns lighting the firecrackers. She pictured them lined up across their lawn in neat rows, bending, one after the other, to a sack of fireworks, choosing a firecracker, straightening up, lighting it, throwing it in synchronized movements, like so many wind-up toys. Once, when she was eight, she'd walked down the road to the LaStrange place but found only the usual number of LaStrange children cluttering the lawn; the pop-*pop* of firecrackers came from somewhere behind the house.

Ron Woodie's younger son, Max, was at the celebration, Allie's "official" beau. They'd been going together for almost two years; she supposed the next step was marriage.

She swallowed a yawn.

Originally, she'd fallen for Max because he looked a little like Tony Curtis. He had the same thick dark hair, the same build and coloring, and he could look sad and innocent, just like Tony, when he wanted to. Having a real live man who looked a little like her idol was sure better than playing to a wooden post that held no resemblance whatsoever.

Then, a few months before, she'd gone to a re-release of *East of Eden* and discovered James Dean. It didn't matter that he was dead; there were times now when Max's touch, the sound of his voice, or the way he smiled at her set her teeth on edge and made her want to slap him.

She sat on the lowest stoop of the back porch, a glass of lemonade in one hand, a half-eaten wiener in the other, and allowed the discontent to well up in her.

From the back step Dufore land rolled down in gentle dips and swells across fifty acres or so of tillable fields until it disappeared into a stand of apple trees. Beyond the orchard, the ridge rose sharply, a protective fence of pine and maple, running from east to west for as far as the eye could see. Allie looked out over rows of young corn thrusting up against a cloudless blue sky; she breathed in the pure sweet air and watched a hawk circle lazily in ever-widening spirals, high over the ridge. She felt as though that towering wall of trees were collapsing right on top of her.

Pop.

Pop.

Pop.

The LaStranges never seemed to tire of setting off their little explosions. Allie tried to remember whether they went all night, too. Suddenly, she wanted to walk down to the LaStrange place, skirt the collection of children on the lawn, go around *in back* and discover for herself, once and for all, just how those people managed. Were there an equal number of children *behind* the house? Did the ones on the front lawn alternate with those in back? Was there someone back there with a stopwatch regulating the time between explosions?

She stood up, shook out her dress, then started down the drive to the East-West Road.

She simply had to know.

For the first couple of months after the fire and Maury LaStrange's death, the LaStrange family had lived in tents and makeshift lean-tos made out of tar paper, blankets, the rusted shells of old cars, and surviving pieces of the original house. To be sure, there wasn't much left. The crazy old building had gone up like a torch, but even so the LaStranges had managed to turn the heap of smoking rubble to good account. A board from the front porch, part of a crossbeam, six or seven bricks from the foundation—all were incorporated into the flimsy structures poking out from the skeletal remains of the house.

The fire had happened at the end of September. By the end of November, people in Esperance were beginning to worry about the LaStranges, who continued living out of tar-paper-and-blanket tents despite several frosts and one or two light snowfalls that had arrived before Thanksgiving.

"We'll have the whole kit 'n' kaboodle of 'em living in the root cellar before long!" Anne grumbled to her mother-in-law one morning as they drove past the LaStrange place on their way to Esperance. "I just know I won't be able to set back and watch all those children freeze to death."

"Something's got to be done about them," Sally LaFleur said to her daughter Jeanette one morning in the general store, jerking her head in the direction of Elyse LaStrange, who was making a sizable purchase at the candy counter.

"D'you suppose those kids *live* on licorice?" she whispered.

She waited until Elyse had paid for the bag of candy and left the store. Then she said, "Somebody oughta do something, now Maury's gone. They can't sit out there on that hill all winter in them little tents!"

On the 1st of December, 1956, there was a change in the normal yap and squabble from the LaStrange place: there was added excitement to the hubbub; curses were uttered more in anticipation than anger, punctuated by a snarl of large machinery.

Dennis, who had religiously avoided going anywhere near the LaStrange place since the fire, found himself compelled against his will to leave the house and walk down the road towards the bridge. The excited yells of the LaStrange children, the growls of machinery, were like a siren's call to him. He found himself pulled down the road and around the bend just in time to see Maury's oldest boy, Mike, perched atop a backhoe, bulldoze the remains of the house, the tents, and the tar-paper constructions over the edge of the ravine that ran along behind the knoll. There was a deafening rumble as several tons of rubble slid down the embankment, collapsing in on itself at the bottom. A plume of dust rose up over the naked hill. There was a moment's silence, then all the LaStranges started talking, screaming, and cursing at once. The backhoe reversed itself, rolled down into the road, and disappeared back the way it had come, towards town.

Word spread quickly along the East-West Road. For the rest of the day, one neighbor or another found some good reason or other to be passing the LaStrange place. The knoll looked strange without the house on it, like a bald head.

That evening another crescendo of shouts and curses broke the quiet of the night, accompanied this time by the grind of tractor treads. For perhaps an hour the sound of pounding hammers, brick scraping against brick, and metal scraping against brick floated down the East-West Road. Then, silence.

The next morning, balanced precariously on a haphazard foundation of cinder blocks and salvaged wooden planks, gleaming in the bright winter sunlight for all the world like a gigantic, burnished milk can, was a bullet-shaped silver trailer.

Mike LaStrange was sitting on the front stoop when Allie came down the road from the Dufore farm. The family had salvaged cinder blocks from the original foundation and stacked them in a crude flight of steps leading up to the aluminum door of the trailer. Like the makeshift foundation the trailer rested on, the steps were narrow and rickety but functional.

Regular, sharp explosions sounded from behind the trailer, but Allie didn't like to circle round back with Mike LaStrange sitting right in front of her, almost like a guard. He seemed completely preoccupied by some operation he was performing on his upper left arm; from where she stood, Allie could see him carefully drawing a design over his biceps with a pen.

Pop.

Pop.

The firecrackers continued going off at regular intervals.

Mike LaStrange looked up. He had the same fox-colored hair and eyebrows as his father, the same eerie eyes, so pale a blue as to appear almost transparent. In the past six months or so, his body had begun to shift and harden into the same spare, well-muscled frame that graced all the LaStrange men.

It occurred to Allie, all of a sudden, that he looked like a fox-colored James Dean, and her heart lurched a little in her chest.

He looked at her without any expression on his face. Allie felt foolish, standing in the road before him; her earlier curiosity about the firecrackers struck her as childish. She wished she hadn't come. She remembered she and Mike LaStrange had been in the same grade in grammar school, but she'd never spoken to him, in school or out. He'd stopped coming after fifth grade; thereafter, Allie had seen him sometimes at the dump, where he occasionally helped his father, or in front of the LaStrange house, interminably tinkering with broken cars. She searched her memory, trying to remember where he had sat in school; somewhere in the back of the room, she thought.

"Hey," she said, the first time she had ever greeted him.

He just continued looking at her.

"Who's shooting off them firecrackers?" she asked.

He didn't answer.

"They're more regular 'n clockwork," she said. "I was just wonderin' who was doin' it."

He looked back down at his left arm.

"Well," she said, not certain how to bring her faltering one-sided conversation to a close.

"You know how to draw?" he asked. His voice was deep, too big for his spare body.

"Not really," Allie replied.

"Think you could draw a skull and crossbones?" Mike LaStrange asked.

"Dunno," she answered cautiously. "I never tried."

"C'mere," Mike LaStrange said.

She hesitated for a moment in the middle of the road. If he'd looked at her right then out of those pale, feral eyes, she might have turned round and gone home. But he didn't look at her; he kept his eyes on his upper arm, seemed to expect she would come, so she did. She picked her way through twisted frames of junk automobiles, heaps of chicken wire and broken furniture, abandoned toys and piles of refuse that dotted the knoll until she stood at the foot of the makeshift front stoop.

"I'm making a tattoo," Mike LaStrange explained. She saw that in addition to the pen, he had a bottle of ink and a straight-edge razor sitting on the cinder block beside him.

"I just can't see to draw it good," he said.

He picked up the pen and handed it to her.

"You do it," he said. "I want a skull and crossbones."

She looked doubtfully down at his biceps and saw he'd already made several crude attempts to trace the design on his skin. The bones were curved, the skull oddly foreshortened. She took the pen and carefully drew over the best of his attempts, lengthening the jaws of the skull, broadening its cranium. She made the bones thicker and straighter, reworked the eye sockets so they were the same size. When she had finished, Mike held up a small round mirror and surveyed her work.

"Not bad," he said. "You might as well finish it."

He jerked his head at the bottle of ink and the razor.

Allie put the pen down and stood up.

"No thanks!" she said.

He shrugged.

"Suit yourself," he said, and picked up the razor. He twisted his arm around as far as he could and traced along the line of the bone she had drawn. She watched the black line of ink split under the edge of the razor and disappear under a thick line of red as blood welled up to fill the cut.

"Why are you doin' that?" she asked.

He shrugged and began cutting along the other side of the bone, leaving the more difficult curved endings for last.

"You'll probably get blood poisoning," Allie told him. "I bet you didn't even sterilize that blade."

"Lit a match under it," he said. He was trying to cut around the heart-shaped ends she'd drawn on the bones, like the ones on halloween skeletons. His hand slipped a little, and one of the endings became pointed.

"Here," Allie said, sitting down beside him. She put her hand out for the razor. "You're making a mess of yourself. Let me."

He handed her the knife.

"When you finish with that bone, we got to put some ink in it before it closes up again," he told her.

She pressed the blade to the place on his arm where he had stopped cutting and started following the line she'd drawn. She was surprised at how easily the blade moved through his flesh, like slicing a ripe peach with a sharp knife.

"Don't it hurt?" she asked as she finished up the first bone.

He picked up the bottle of ink and an eyedropper.

"Nah," he said. "Put this in it."

She filled the eyedropper with the ink and began tracing along the wound. He followed with a grubby piece of cotton, rubbing the ink into the cuts and wiping the excess away. When they'd finished with the first bone, Allie took the razor up again and started on the second.

When they were done, Allie put down the razor and looked at the black, smeary design on Mike LaStrange's arm. Blackened blood had formed a crusty ridge along the cuts in his flesh, while smudges of the dried ink and blood disfigured the drawing.

Mike looked down at it with satisfaction.

"Soon as the scabs heal, it'll look somethin' fine," he told her.

Allie stood up.

"It's getting late," she said. "Better get home."

She was a little piqued he made no effort to keep her, tendered no invitation to come back. She turned and walked quickly down the knoll, past the piles of junk to the road. It seemed only neighborly, however, when she got there to make some kind of farewell gesture, but he wasn't even looking when she turned to wave goodbye. He was examining the tattoo in the mirror; her presence there had been forgotten.

It was almost three weeks before Allie saw Mike LaStrange again. She had passed the trailer on the knoll once or twice but there had only been the usual collection of stray children out front. She even volunteered to take a load of trash down to the dump one Saturday, but only saw Mike's uncle Phil LaStrange at the entrance gate. If Mike was there, she hadn't seen him.

Then one day he appeared suddenly on the road in front of her as she was bicycling back from the post office. She wondered if he had been waiting in the bushes for her.

"Hey," she said, coasting to a halt a few feet away.

"It's all healed," he told her. "Wanna see?"

He hiked up the arm of his T-shirt and displayed the design on his biceps. The lines were wobbly and uneven, thicker in some places than in others. The ink had run slightly from one of the eye sockets, so tears seemed to well from one glaring eye. Still, the design was recognizable.

"Nice," Allie commented. "It turned out pretty good, huh?"

He was craning his neck, admiring the design.

"Soon as I get some money, I'm goin' into Bennington an' get a professional tattoo," he told her. "Maybe a snake, or a tiger."

He raised his pale, pale blue eyes to her face suddenly.

"Maybe a dancing girl," he said.

"You look a lot like James Dean," Allie said.

"Yeah? Who's he?"

"A movie star. If your hair was blond instead of red, you'd look just like him."

"Huh." Mike seemed unimpressed.

"See ya," he said, and disappeared into the bushes.

Two days later, she found him leaning over the railing of the brook bridge, almost as if he'd known she'd pass there on her way to Betsy LaRue's house; almost as if he'd been waiting for her.

"I asked my sister 'bout that guy," he said, straightening from his slouch and turning to lean his back against the rail.

"That Dean guy," he added when she looked at him blankly.

"She showed me a picture of him in some movie magazine."

"Oh," Allie said, and wondered which member of that whirling vortex of LaStrange progeny ever stood still long enough to look through a magazine.

"He looks okay," Mike said.

He appeared to have said what he'd come to say, yet he continued leaning there against the rail in the middle of the bridge, not obstructing her path, but standing so she would have to brush close by in order to pass.

"Yeah, well . . ." she said after a moment, and started to move forward, a little uncertainly.

"You wanna go to Bennington with me?" Mike La-Strange asked her. "I got the DeSoto working."

Allie's jaw dropped. In her whole life, she had never for one minute imagined Mike LaStrange would ask her for a date. For that matter, she had never imagined exchanging more than two words with him. She had a good idea what her friends would say if they knew; she knew what she'd say, herself. Besides, Dennis had taken an unaccountable dislike to all things concerning the LaStrange family, to the point where he generally took the long way to town, adding three miles onto the trip in order to avoid passing the trailer.

"Gee, Mike," she said after a moment, "I got a boyfriend, you know, so I don't think I can. Thanks anyway."

She smiled brightly and started across the bridge, turning slightly to squeeze past where he stood leaning against the rail. He straightened up to let her go by; for a moment they were practically breast to breast before he stepped back. She had thought he was taller, before; now she realized they were almost the same height; she only had to tilt her head back slightly to look into his eyes.

"See ya," she said, and walked briskly down the road towards town.

She saw him again a week later in Bennington. It was Sunday and she'd hitched a ride in for the matinee showing of *Rebel Without a Cause* at the Prince. She was forty-five minutes early, and was killing time looking in shop windows along Main Street when his reflection loomed up behind her in the Woolworth's display window.

"Hey," he said. "Where's your boyfriend?"

"It's his turn to work at the station," Allie said. "What are you doin' here?"

"I got some money," Mike said. "Came for another tattoo, like I told you."

"Oh yeah? What'd you get?" she asked.

"Ain't got it yet. Wanna go to the movie with me?"

"I thought you were getting a tattoo," Allie said.

"Later. After the movie. Wanna come?"

She didn't know what to say. She didn't want to be rude and turn him down when she was going there anyway; what if he saw her in the theater? But she didn't want him getting any ideas about this being a date, either. She decided to compromise.

"I was goin' there myself," she said. "I guess we can sit together if you want."

He nodded and fell into step beside her as she started across the street to the theater.

As she watched the movie, Allie wondered time and again how she could have ever wasted her time and affections on Tony when there was a man like James! The flesh-and-blood Mike LaStrange in the seat next to her was completely forgotten.

So it was a shock when, three quarters of the way through, she felt herself suddenly gripped between his hands, turned away from the screen, her lips pried apart by Mike LaStrange's tongue.

For a moment, she thought it was James who was kissing her so deeply and thoroughly. Her hands went up to bury themselves in his hair and pull him closer.

His lips were full and soft, yet firm. His tongue in her mouth circled gently over her palate and tongue, probing, pressing, thrusting slightly, then pulling back teasingly, suggestively, as though he could afford to take his time to know her thoroughly.

His hand slid down over her neck, her shoulders, brushed briefly across her breast, then continued down to her thigh.

She could feel his fingers squeeze her knee, then slide up under her dress. She wondered if anyone else in the theater was close enough to see what was happening; then his hand slid surely up between her legs, his fingers began imitating the rhythm and action of his tongue, and she found she didn't much care if people could see, or how the movie turned out, or that it was Mike LaStrange doing these things.

When the house lights came up at the end of the movie, she and Mike walked out of the theater like strangers. After the dimness of the theater, the sunlit street seemed garishly bright. They stood in front of the ticket booth, squinting at each other and shielding their eyes from the glare.

"You want a ride home?" Mike asked. His voice and expression seemed so normal that Allie wondered if she had somehow imagined the episode in the theater. The tingle in her cheeks where his stubble had scratched her and her bruised lips reassured her.

"If it wouldn't be too much trouble," she said.

They drove most of the way without speaking. It was a funny kind of silence, Allie thought; not precisely uncomfortable, not really friendly. It was a kind of waiting silence, like when you think you hear someone calling from a distance, so you stop moving, stop breathing, just stand waiting till you hear it again.

"You can drop me here," she said as they rumbled around the bend in the road just before the LaStrange place. He stopped the truck at the bottom of the driveway leading up to the trailer and she opened the door and jumped down.

"I thought you were going to get a tattoo after the movie," she said as she started to shut the door.

"Some other time," he said, slamming the truck into gear.

She stood back and watched him go snarling up the steep incline, then turned to walk the quarter mile to her house.

Without a doubt, Mike LaStrange was the oddest person she'd ever met. By the time she reached home, she'd just about decided she didn't like him at all.

Yet, for the rest of the day, she continued to feel his full, firm mouth against hers.

"C'mon, Allie . . . you know I love you."

Max had managed to get his hands up under her shirt and gotten two of the three hooks on her bra strap undone. One hook away from paradise, Allie had gone stiff in his arms and twisted away from him. He practically had to bite his tongue to keep from swearing; the mass in his groin was so engorged it ached. He dropped his lips to the hollow of her throat, felt her soften momentarily back into his grasp.

He forced his hands to drop down from her breasts to her waist, and grazed gently across her neck and shoulder until he was sure she had relaxed completely again. He could hear her breath coming in shallow gasps next to his ear. He knew from the way she was pushing up against him she wanted it as bad as he did. So why did she always stop him?

Sometimes she let him get the third hook undone and suckle at her breast; once she'd even let him kiss her all the way down her stomach to the waistband of her skirt. He'd gotten his hand partway up her skirt a few times, but she always stopped him before he really got anywhere. When he was really hurting, she took him in her hand and relieved some of the pressure that way, but mostly they just kissed and petted until they were both half crazy with wanting it.

"Allie, please . . . let me do it just this once," he panted, wondering glumly how far she would let him go tonight. "You know I love you. . . ."

They were parked on the road at the bottom of the drive leading up to the Dufore farm. He had promised to have her back by midnight and already it was quarter to; the sinking feeling in his stomach was almost proportionate to the rising tension in his groin. Only fifteen minutes and he wasn't past first base.

"Stop it, Max," Allie panted as he made a sudden grab at her left breast. "It wouldn't be right."

They'd gone to the movies in Bennington. It was the third time she'd seen *Rebel Without a Cause,* though she hadn't told Max that. Now, sitting in the dark grappling with Max Woodie, Allie closed her eyes and imagined James Dean in the car with her. It was easy in the dark to pretend; the fact that James sometimes had blond hair, sometimes fox-red, only made it more exciting. So overcome with her fantasy was she, she almost gave in to Max. She had been ready to fall back against the leather seats, pull him on top of her and into her; then he'd thrust his tongue down her throat and she'd come back to reality with a jolt. He kissed like a dog, she thought, sloppy and wet. She hated the way he bit her tongue whenever she put it in his mouth.

When she pulled away, he started nibbling on her neck. That was better; quite nice, in fact. She was feeling very fond of Max by the time he grabbed at her breast and gave it a squeeze.

"It wouldn't be right," she told him.

He didn't answer her. Instead, his lips trailed lightly across her cheek and throat, down her collarbone, brushing the top of her breast, cobweb-gentle. She sighed deeply and imagined James Dean with red hair and pale eyes brushing her breasts with his lips. The hand inching up under her skirt retraced the path another hand had forged earlier; when his fingers slipped beneath the elastic band of her panties, she moaned softly and let her legs drop open, a little. She felt him pressing her shoulders back against the seat leather, felt her blouse slip down over her arms, felt his sudden weight press down upon her as he wriggled in between her thighs.

As Max fumbled frantically with his belt buckle, finally managing to slide his jeans down far enough to free himself, Allie imagined James Dean with red hair and pale, pale blue eyes looming above her. She'd been waiting for him ever since that afternoon in the movie theater.

Allie was up early the morning of her wedding day; not even Gran Marie had beat her downstairs to the kitchen on her last morning living in the Dufore house.

Someone was moving around upstairs; she heard the muffled slap of bare feet against bare wood, then the click of the bathroom door shutting. She didn't feel like facing anyone yet; later she would be the focus of everybody's attention, but this morning she wanted to be left alone. She rifled through her father's jacket for the pack of cigarettes he kept there and took two, plus a box of matches. She'd started smoking the year before and her parents still hadn't found out; at least after the wedding she'd be able to smoke in public if she felt like it.

On the back porch she paused long enough to light one of the cigarettes, then wandered down the driveway onto the road. Although it was the last week of October, the days were unexpectedly mild, with temperatures in the fifties and clear, sunlit days. A perfect morning for a wedding, she guessed.

Back in September, when she'd first begun to suspect the consequences of her single night with Max, she walked down to the cliff where Uncle Ab had jumped into the brook and considered her future. She was not afraid of her family beating or disowning her; this sort of thing happened too often for people to get mightily upset. No, her parents would get together with Max's folks and pretty soon Max would show up on her doorstep with a ring and a proposal. A couple of weeks later, Father Dozier would join them together as man and wife and that would be that.

Eventually, she'd turned around and gone back home, and three weeks later, when she'd been sure, she'd told her mother. From that point on, things turned out pretty much as she'd expected.

"Hey."

Mike LaStrange was standing twenty feet in front of her, as though he'd known she'd come this way; as though he'd been waiting for her.

"Hi," she said.

The stood facing one another, the same strange waiting silence stretched like taut wire between them.

"Today's the day, huh?" he asked.

She nodded, fumbling in her coat pocket for the other cigarette she'd snitched. Before she could dig out the matches, he was in front of her with one already lit. She inhaled deeply on the cigarette, felt the smoke slide smoothly down her throat. Wordless, they turned and started across the bridge over the brook, stopping exactly in the middle to lean against the rail and stare down into the rushing water below.

They stood close together; even through her jacket she could feel the warmth of his skin where his upper arm pressed lightly against hers.

"You ever get that other tattoo?" she asked him suddenly.

"Yeah," he said. "Couple of months ago. I was waitin' to show it to you, but you never did come by."

"Show it to me now," she said, turning to lean sideways against the rail so she faced him. She was close enough to see the red-gold shadow of a beard on his cheeks.

"Nah, not now," he said. He turned his head, looking at her with grave, unsmiling eyes. "Some other time."

He reached over, took the cigarette out of her hand, put it between his lips, and inhaled deeply. Then he placed it gently between her lips, holding it there while she breathed in the smoke. The gesture was intimate as a kiss; she felt her stomach turn over, and a flush of warmth creep up over her chest and throat and face.

When the cigarette was finished, he threw the butt into the brook and straightened up.

"Be seein' you," he said, and walked quickly across the bridge back towards the LaStrange trailer.

PART THREE

GONE WEST

D aniel's last thoughts before he pulled the trigger were of pigs squealing the morning his father and grandfather loaded them into the back of a borrowed half-ton truck and took them down to Piggery Road to be slaughtered.

He'd been fond of the pigs, and sorry to see them go each year on their final trip to Piggery Road, but was too young to understand what awaited them there. He cried when they went, then forgot them, knowing in the spring there'd be new litters of piglets to feed and care for.

The year he turned six, however, his father and grandfather decided to get out of pig farming entirely. New regulations requiring garbage to be boiled before it could be fed to the pigs made the whole proposition too costly. More and more, the Dufores were turning to their apple orchards and maple trees for their livelihood. Once the decision was made, there seemed little point in keeping any of the pigs around.

Even on the last day of his life, many years later, Daniel was able to summon up a clear recollection of the day the last pigs were taken away. It was a cold, crisp morning, the last hurrah of a glorious autumn, before winter set in. He remembered standing in the driveway between the barn and his grandparents' house watching the men tie ropes round the pigs' hind legs and drag them up the rough wooden plank into the truck. The pigs were screaming, the men swearing, and the scene was forever seared in Daniel's memory.

When Lillian and Wally were dragged last into the truck,

Daniel understood for the first time that this was the End of an Era; they were the first pigs, bought when he was still a tiny baby, the founders of a pig dynasty, permanent fixtures in his narrow world of cabin on the ridge, farmhouse kitchen and barn, and they were going. He came up close to the truck after the men had jumped down and taken the plank away. He was too small to be able to look in—his head barely reached the floor of the truck bed—but he could see several snouts poking out between the slatted sides. He reached a hand up, just managing to brush one of them with his fingertips.

Then the truck started and he was scooped up, up off of the ground, swung onto his father's shoulders, from where he watched the truck bump its way down the steep drive to the East-West Road and on, out of sight.

He never knew which pig he had touched, and it bothered him forever after.

Chapter

12

Emily brought Daniel's body back to Esperance on the train. It was about a five-hour trip from Boston; she'd bought a magazine in the station, which she rolled and unrolled between her hands as she stared out the window into rapidly gathering gloom. February was a hell of a month to die in, she reflected. She thought briefly about the casket riding in the unheated baggage car and wondered what kind of conveyance the Dufores had arranged to have meet them at the station.

Them. She still thought of herself and Daniel that way. They were still a couple, at least until this last journey together ended in Esperance. She pictured every foot of the way from the train station in Brattleboro to the Dufore farmhouse, imagined bumping down the East-West Road, treacherous and rutted after the January thaw and subsequent snowfall. She'd met Daniel for the first time on that road, back when they were twelve. Death had introduced them there, one summer; a dead dog had brought them together. Death and his cousin Buddy and a dozen or so LaStranges had all been there the day they met.

Emily laughed. In hindsight, it was perfect.

It was the LaStrange turkeys that were responsible.

They were a strange flock: half a dozen dirty, stringy birds, feathers missing from their tails where children had pulled them out, scars on their necks and breasts where dogs or cats had savaged them. The cock was missing an eye and so shuttled crablike on a diagonal to where he wanted to go.

Maury's widow, Elyse, had bought half a dozen turkey eggs at the beginning of mud season and kept them in an incubator her brother-in-law Pete had salvaged from the dump and repaired, after a fashion. She'd had some idea of starting a turkey farm; then the incubator broke down after the first eggs hatched and she lost interest in it. The turkeys grew wild and neglected; for reasons best known to themselves, they adopted the nameless mongrel that slept beneath the LaStrange porch and defended the LaStrange property when it suited him as their mother. They followed him everywhere. The dog resisted parenthood at first, snapping at them when they tried to crowd under the porch with him at night, snarling if they approached too close to his food. Eventually, however, they wore him down; by the end of spring it was common to see the old dog loping down the East-West Road, his brood trotting behind him.

One day, Ren Fortesque was coming up the East-West Road with a load of firewood in the back of his pickup when he heard what sounded like a pack of dogs just beyond the bend in the road. As he came round in sight of the LaStrange house, he saw the turkey cock and five hens charging down the driveway in full cry. They chased his truck for fifty or sixty feet, flapping their wings and yelping like terriers before finally losing interest and turning back.

"You'll never believe what I jes' saw, out LaStrange way," he said to his wife and brother-in-law when he got home.

Word spread quickly. For a week or two, most people found some reason to drive by the LaStrange house at least once to see the phenomenon for themselves. Pete LaStrange down at the dump became quite boastful, even talked about writing to the Ed Sullivan show a few times, until Paul Devereaux pointed out how difficult it would be to demonstrate car-chasing on a New York City stage.

The turkeys, meanwhile, continued chasing cars and barking at passersby; the turkey cock lost his eye when he chased a cat up a tree, then unwisely tried to pursue his advantage further. People began complaining when the birds started knocking over trash cans and dragging garbage around people's backyards, but soon enough they only created a sensation among unwary strangers.

That summer Daniel built a wagon for his cousin Buddy. Buddy was an idiot, people said; it was true he couldn't do much for himself, not feed or dress himself, or even sit up without support, though there was no physical reason why not. He was almost nine that year, too big for a baby stroller, too heavy for Daniel to carry and too old for him to drag, as he'd done when they were both much younger. Daniel built the wagon with a back on it; with one of Dennis's belts encircling both the back and Buddy's chest, he could go everywhere Daniel did without flopping like a ragdoll.

There'd been a lot of whispering about Buddy, back when he'd first been born, then again after Max and Allie Woodie's *trouble*. People found Daniel's attachment to his witless cousin peculiar, but in time the pair became an accepted sight, much like the LaStrange turkeys or Bobby Dufore's bomb shelter, and no more was said about it.

They were on their way down the East-West Road one day near the end of June, Daniel alternately pulling the wagon behind him and pushing it in front, Buddy staring at nothing out of his smoke-blue eyes, when they came upon the dead dog.

It was the nameless mongrel—like the generations of children inhabiting the LaStrange house, this dog looked much like dogs of previous eras. No one was certain whether it was the same immortal dog, or else a descendant of some animal possessed of such powerful genes that it could replicate itself exactly for generations. No one in living memory could recall ever seeing it as a puppy, nor had any other dog even remotely resembling it ever been sighted. In any event, its allegiance to the LaStranges was legendary in Esperance.

So it came as a bit of a shock to Daniel to find the dog lying dead in the road, a group composed of half a dozen LaStranges of varying ages, three strangers, and six hysterical turkeys standing around it. There was a car with New York plates pulled over to the side of the road, and the dog's head was badly dented.

"Dog's dead," old Jules LaStrange was saying to no one in particular as Daniel came closer. "You killed the dog."

Daniel looked at the strangers with interest; not many flatlanders came to Esperance, so even a minor event like one of them running over a stray dog was invested with a little glamour. There was a woman and two children, one a girl about his age, the other a toddler of indeterminate sex. The woman looked soft and pleasantly untidy; wisps of hair escaped from the bandanna she had tied around her head, and the back of her blouse pulled out from the waistband of her jeans. Of all of them, she seemed the most distraught.

"It just ran right out in front of me," she said, sounding like she was about to cry. "Shouldn't we call a vet?"

"Dog's dead," Jules said. "You killed the dog."

Jules's wife, Claire-Bette, said, "I thought you hit one o' the birds. Coulda sworn it was one o' the birds, but it's Scratch, all right."

"Is there a phone we could use to call the vet?" the woman asked again.

"Yep, it's Scratch, all right," said Claire-Bette as she stood looking down at the corpse in the road. "I coulda sworn it was one o' them birds."

"Please," the woman said. She sounded upset, and a little frightened as well. "We have to call a vet, or somebody! We can't just leave it here."

"Dog's dead," Jules said. "You killed the dog."

"She run over Scratch," his wife affirmed. "I coulda sworn it was one o' them birds, but it's Scratch, all right."

No one, except the woman from the New York and the turkeys, who kept trying to break through the circle of legs surrounding the dog's body, seemed upset by the death. Even the woman's daughter stood looking down at it with detached, clinical interest, an expression on her face that might have been embarrassment at the way her mother was carrying on. She looked up suddenly and caught Daniel staring at her.

"There's a phone inside you can use," Elyse LaStrange said to the woman. "Don't s'pose there's much point to it, though."

Daniel stood in the road watching them trudge up the slope to the LaStrange trailer. Twenty feet away, the dog lay forlornly sprawled on the shoulder of the road with only the turkeys to mourn him.

The girl's back was straight and bony. Her hair, the color

of his mother's copper-bottomed pots, hung down to the middle of it.

"Dog's dead," he heard Jules say as the screen door swung shut behind them. "You killed the dog."

Daniel saw the flatlander girl again a few days later, in a field behind the schoolhouse.

Buddy was with him, of course; a basketball, a pad of paper, and a pencil were wedged between Buddy's body and the side of the wagon. It was still early, not much past eight o'clock, when the cousins reached the intersection of the East-West Road and Clark Hill Road. There had been a heavy rain the day before; steam rose from drenched fields, and the smell of damp earth was so rich that Daniel hunkered down, scooped up a handful of it, breathed in deeply, his stomach trembling with elation.

In the cart, Buddy chuckled.

They continued on their way to the schoolyard, where a lone basketball hoop nailed to a telephone pole was available to all comers. It would have been easier to pull the cart along the road, but they cut across the field instead, bumping over clumps of coarse hay, rocking over gullies cut in the ground by run-off. The grass was almost as high as Daniel's waist; it would be well over his head by the end of summer, when Paul Devereaux would eventually come with his mower and hay the field. A million invisible insects whined in their ears and unseen things scuttled through the tangle at their feet. The air was still cool from the night before, but clammy.

"Hey!"

The redheaded girl popped out of the grass on Daniel's left.

"I'm playing prehistoric valley," she said. "I'm Kayla, and I live in a cave over there."

She waved her arm in the direction of Mort Bennet's tool shed, which teetered on the edge of the field fronting his property.

She was wearing a pair of shorts, a T-shirt, and sandals. Her hair was braided, and he could see her eyes were pea-soup green. Bewildered, he fastened onto the one thing she'd said that made sense.

"Your name is Kayla?"

"Mm. Who are you?"

"Daniel," he told her. "This is Buddy."

The girl looked Buddy over critically.

"He retarded or something?" she asked.

Daniel shrugged.

"What happened to the dog?" he asked.

"Oh, one of those men put it in a plastic bag an' took it somewhere."

She was still looking at Buddy in the wagon.

"He sure looks weird," she said after a while. "You wanna shoot some hoops?"

Daniel shrugged again, and the three of them continued on towards the school.

"My mom's renting a place up here for the summer," she told him after she'd sunk three baskets in a row.

Daniel wondered why anyone would come to Esperance to spend the summer.

She shot another three baskets, from half court, from offside, from directly under the hoop, then passed the ball to him so suddenly it caught him hard in the stomach and knocked the breath out of him a little.

"Gotta go," she said, and left him standing in the middle of the court, the ball still clutched to his chest.

She paused at the wagon, where Buddy sat strapped into an upright position. A tiny stream of spittle ran down from one corner of his loose, wet mouth; he looked more like a monstrous infant than a nine-year-old boy. The girl bent down, her hands braced against her knees, and brought her face within inches of his.

"You sure are weird!" she said.

A few days later, Daniel was passing by the general store as Emily was coming down the steps, a quart bottle of milk in her hand.

"Hey, Kayla," Daniel said.

She looked at him and said: "Today I'm Sarnell, from the Andromeda Galaxy."

She came up to Buddy's wagon and bent down so she was looking straight into his blank, staring eyes.

"Is that your brother?" she asked.

"Nope. My cousin."

"How come you take him around with you so much?"

"Dunno."

"You wanna play Star Trek?" Emily asked.

He shrugged, but fell in with her and walked back to the house her mother was renting.

There was at least another hour before the train reached Brattleboro. It was completely dark outside. The glaring bulb over her head rendered the window opaque, reflective; she saw herself outlined against the blackness in a muted version of what she really was.

Her hair fanned out around her head like a halo of flame, its redness heightened by the electric light behind her. Her eyes seemed huge, hollow, emptied of any thought or feeling; she wondered if it was a trick of the glass, or an accurate portrait of how she appeared to other people. Would a stranger looking at her instantly deduce her husband had committed suicide two days before?

She reached for the tote bag on the seat beside her and rummaged inside it for the pack of cigarettes she'd bought in

Boston. She lit one, reflecting that twenty-nine was an odd age to start smoking. She decided she would not give in to societal pressure; having started, she would never quit.

The tote bag was heavy. Daniel's last, unfinished manuscript was still in it. She wasn't sure why she'd packed it. She wasn't sure Daniel's family even read his books. She thought maybe she'd give it to Buddy; Daniel would probably like that, since he'd dedicated every one of the books he'd written to his cousin. Maybe someday, someone will read it to him, she thought. Maybe I will, myself.

It was a little before nine o'clock when the train pulled into the station in Brattleboro. Dennis and Jeanette were waiting on the platform. They didn't move when Emily got down; they didn't wave or shout to draw attention to themselves. They stood rooted where they were and waited.

There didn't seem to be anything to say, under the circumstances, so they stood in a little huddle while the wind ripped and clutched at their clothing and one or two more people got down from the train. When they saw the door to the baggage car being slid open, Dennis said:

"I'll bring the truck around."

The drive back to the farm was a silent one. It had snowed the night before, and the roads were still slick with ice; snow lay like a pelt across the back of Searsburg Mountain, and more was beginning to fall. Dennis stopped the truck once, a quarter of the way up, to put chains on the tires. Along the side of the road other vehicles had spattered mud and rock salt across the shoulder; the snow looked pocked there, dirty and diseased. The sky, alight with snow, was the color of weak tea and milk; against the horizon, bare branches of trees wove an intricate pattern, black on beige.

As the truck shuddered up the mountain, Emily rolled down the window and let the wind slap at her face. She could hear the coffin shifting slightly in the flatbed behind her. When she finally pulled her head back into the cab and closed the window, her cheeks and lips were white and bloodless.

The truck rolled into Esperance, fishtailed a bit down Main Street. Past the post office. Past the Texaco station. There, pushed off to the back, almost hidden behind a row of battered vehicles waiting to be fixed up and sold, was the house where Daniel's aunt had lived. Emily squinted through smeary glass at the shuttered windows and unwelcoming storm door.

She'd never met Buddy's mother. The *trouble,* as people in Esperance referred to Allie's disappearance, had happened three years before Emily first came to Esperance for the summer. People didn't speak of her much, and once when she'd asked Daniel about her, he'd just shrugged and mumbled:

"Dead, most likely."

She'd thought about her, though, from time to time— had tried, once, to jimmy the lock on that little house out behind the Texaco station just because she'd wanted to see where Buddy had lived and what kind of house his mother had kept.

"You would've liked Allie," Gran Marie had told her, the summer she married Daniel. "You're something like."

They were sitting on the front porch in the late evening, she and Daniel's great-grandmother, just the two of them alone watching the fireflies swarm so thick along the side of the hill they made a carpet of light that stretched up to the crest and on into the night sky, where it was lost among the stars. Daniel was getting Buddy to bed, Rich and Anne had gone up an hour before, and Jeanette and Dennis had gone back to the cabin shortly after dinner. It was a week before the wedding; Emily and Daniel were staying at the main house.

"How'd she die?" Emily asked.

"Who told you she was dead?"

"Daniel. He said that's why Buddy lives here now." Emily said.

Gran Marie shrugged.

"There's no proof of that," she said. "They found him, and the motorcycle, but they never found Allie."

"But she has to be dead!" Emily said, leaning forward to try and see the old woman's eyes in the dark. "Otherwise you'd have heard by now."

Gran Marie smiled and reached for Emily's hand. Her skin was dry and creased with age—hadn't Daniel said she was over eighty? Her grip was not gentle; she squeezed Emily's hand in her own crabbed fingers until the bones scraped together. She brought her face up close to Emily's.

"They found him, and the motorcycle," she repeated, "but they never found her."

She dropped Emily's hand and leaned back in her chair, swallowed up by the darkness. Emily could only see the ghostly lines of her dress, the faint halo of white hair and nothing where her face should have been.

No fireflies, now. There in the blind, cold night, Emily sighed and watched her fogged breath spread across the glass, obliterating her own reflection.

The house behind the Texaco station—the whole town—was shut down; dead. She glanced at the profiles of her mother- and father-in-law. There was something bruised about Dennis, she thought; as though, in spite of his calm, he were hemorrhaging just below the surface. Jeanette, though, looked chilly as a statue. Emily rubbed her frozen hands and wondered if there was any warmth left in the world.

Chapter

13

⚜

T here were ghosts in Buddy's room.

He lay in the parlor of the main farmhouse, the coffin of his cousin Daniel just beyond the door, the ghosts and voices of the dead and the not yet born crowding into the room with him. A man missing an ear, his foot wrapped in white gauze, stared mournfully from the window; a boy with flames streaming from the place where his hands should be hovered near the bed.

Buddy blinked.

A man missing an ear, a boy with blackened stumps where his hands should be; Buddy smiled. There was a baby dressed in a christening robe lying across the foot of his bed; its chest gaped open, exposing an empty cavity.

"I'm cold," it wept. "I'm cold."

Buddy blinked.

A man missing an ear, a boy with blackened stumps, a baby in a white robe. There was a man with seaweed in his hair floating above the bed. In the doorway, another man stood, wearing a khaki jacket; in his eyes was the reflection of a little girl sitting in dust.

Buddy blinked.

A little girl in a yellow sundress, sitting near water.

Buddy blinked.

Sitting near water, a pile of smooth, round marbles in front of her. Creamy blue, yellow; some clear glass and others enameled.

Buddy blinked.

Mirrored in the man's eyes he saw a little girl in a yellow sundress sitting near water, a pile of smooth, round marbles in front of her. Creamy blue, yellow, some clear glass and some enameled.

Buddy blinked.

Daniel grew to love Buddy while staying with his Aunt Allie and Uncle Max during the time his twin sisters were born and one died. It was the year he turned six, the same year they took the pigs away, the year he started carrying around paper and a pencil everywhere he went.

Every afternoon for the ten days he spent in the little house behind the Texaco station, Daniel sat down in his Aunt Allie's living room with his cousin Buddy wedged between his knees, and watched *Hope for Tomorrow,* followed by *Search for Love,* then *Young Dr. Malone,* and finally *Another Day.* Afterwards, he would half-carry, half-drag Buddy into the kitchen, where he sat at the table, Buddy lying between his feet, while Aunt Allie got dinner ready and discussed that afternoon's episodes.

After dinner, he played for a while, then sat on the edge of the cot Uncle Max had set up in Buddy's room and watched while Allie got his cousin ready for bed. He liked sharing the room with Buddy; it made him less afraid when, starting the second night he was there, he began waking up, night after night, to the sound of voices crowding into the narrow bed with him.

Squawking, quacking, cooing, burbling, the sounds, punctuated by screams of laughter or pain, came and went, sometimes shouting suddenly in his ear, other times whispering too softly for him to catch what they were saying. When he closed his eyes he could hear their footsteps coming; faces, shapes, flashed across his eyelids while the squawking and babbling rang in his ears. Some nights he lay awake until dawn, stiff in his bed, ears and brain straining to understand. Those mornings, he appeared in the kitchenette looking more tired and worn than a six-year-old had a right to be.

He often wondered if Buddy could hear the voices, too. From time to time he'd glance at his little cousin, see the moonlight reflected in his empty eyes; Buddy gave no sign that anything disturbed him. Daniel found his cousin's serenity comforting, and when the voices became too strident, too demanding, he took to crawling into the crib with Buddy, curling his body around his cousin's so his legs and stomach fit into the curve of Buddy's knees and back, tight as spoons in a drawer. With his mouth resting against Buddy's ear, Daniel told his cousin stories he made up about the voices he heard in an attempt to drown out the babbling in his head with his own soft whisper. It seemed to work; for a while the voices would be silent and sometimes he could sleep through the night.

And then it was time for Daniel to go home. His father came for him in the pickup truck, rode him slow up the Clark Hill Road, cuddled him gently in the curve of his big arm.

"Got a new sister, Dan," his father told him.

Daniel nodded. He'd known that the morning Gran Marie had taken him from his bed and brought him down to Aunt Allie and Uncle Max's. He curled deep into his father's side and thought about the other stuff he knew, too; stuff he'd heard from his aunt and uncle, from people at the Texaco station when he'd go there for a Royal Palm grape soda, from the ladies at the post office when Allie took him to fetch the mail.

The cabin on the ridge looked strange when they drove up over the crest of the bumpy drive and rumbled to a stop. He'd been gone so long. He went through the screen door, breathed in the familiar odors of furniture polish and cooking oil, moved gingerly around the kitchen as though he expected things to be out of place.

"Come see your mama, Dan," his father said.

They went through to the back room and found his mother sitting in a chair by the window, her hand just barely rocking the same oak cradle she'd told him he'd slept in once.

"Danny," she whispered, and rose up out of the chair, bringing herself up, scooping him up in her arms, carrying them both up up towards the ceiling in one fluid motion. His arms were wound tight around her neck; her arms were satisfyingly tight across his back. He'd been gone so long he'd forgotten how it felt. He buried his head in her shoulder, breathed in a new half-strange, half-familiar odor that wafted up from her body.

"Wanna see the baby?" she asked.

He nodded and she carried him over, set him down on his feet by the cradle.

"This is Joelle," she said.

He looked down at the tiny mewing thing and was reminded of a spotted piglet he'd been fond of in Lillian's last litter; this new baby had the same mottled pink-and-white flesh.

"Can I touch her?" he asked his mother.

"Sure. Just don't wake her," Jeanette said.

Her skin felt soft as a horse's nose; he enjoyed stroking her wrist and arm with his finger. She lay on her back; he could see the scar poking up from under the collar of the T-shirt she wore. He wanted to touch that, too, trace it all the way to its other end with his thumb, but he knew his mother wouldn't like it.

"When can I play with her?" he asked.

"When she's a little older," Jeanette said.

Maybe when she's as big as Buddy, Daniel thought. Buddy was almost three, but he lay much as Joelle did now. Still, Allie didn't seem to mind Daniel dragging Buddy across the floor with him, rolling him round like a rag doll. He wished Buddy were lying in this crib instead of the baby. A sister didn't seem very useful, somehow; besides, she made him uncomfortable.

Nobody'd said anything to him, of course, but Daniel knew just the same that there'd been two babies, once. He hadn't gone to the funeral, but he knew the other baby was buried in the graveyard near the church. He'd worried about that baby a lot while he'd been staying at Aunt Allie's. What if she wakes up in a little box, in the dark? Wouldn't she be scared? How could she breathe down there? Sometimes he'd pulled the blankets up over his head and tried to imagine being buried. Soon the air became fetid and thick; he'd felt he was choking and terrified himself by imagining he was unable to move his arms or roll onto his side.

Now that he'd seen this baby, a new and troublesome worry preyed on his mind: what if they had buried the wrong baby? What if there'd been a mix-up at the grave-

yard and they put the wrong baby in the ground? He wished
he could ask his mother how she could be certain this was
really Joelle, but he didn't want to worry her, too.

"Careful you don't wake her up, Danny," Jeanette said,
and kissed the baby lightly on her cheek.

Daniel lay in bed that night, muffled laughter and sounds
that had the rhythm of speech in his ears. He thought he'd
left the voices at Buddy's house, but they'd found him here,
as well. Flashes of bright color burst behind his eyes; shapes
suddenly materialized and hung in his mind, or appeared
and disappeared instantly, leaving behind the impression of
something tantalizingly familiar. It was even worse when he
closed his eyes; then the colors and shapes seemed to pour
into his head. Only fixing his gaze on something real and
solid offered any peace; he spent most of one night staring at
his dresser, another night, at his closet door.

He wished Buddy were there with him. . . .

Buddy lay in his crib in the back room staring up at the
mobile that hung over his bed. The shapes of fish, ducks, and
cats suspended on thin wires circled above his head, swayed
by the merest breath of air, perpetually twisting just above
his head.

When Buddy looked at the mobile, he loved it passion-
ately. He loved the brightness of the colors, the way the
light from the moon or the naked bulb in the hallway reflected off the metal, making the shapes ripple and change.

Buddy closed his eyes for a moment. When he opened
them again, he was delighted; there was a beautiful mobile
suspended above his head, alive with dancing shapes. How
lovely it was! Even as he thought to raise an arm and reach
for one of the spinning shapes, his muscles forgot how and
his hand remained motionless on the blanket.

He closed his eyes again; when he looked up again, a

smile spread across his face, for there, just above his head, was a beautiful mobile. He wished he could touch it, but he hadn't learned how, yet.

Buddy lay in his crib, perfectly content. From second to second, life was a perpetual surprise.

"This is a fish, and this is a duck," Daniel explained to his mother the next morning while she sat in the baby's room holding Joelle to her breast.

He had recognized the shapes as soon as he'd drawn them; once committed to paper, they faded gracefully from his mind, leaving his vision clear.

"This is a cat," he pointed out.

He'd drawn them carefully in crayon, trying to stay inside the lines when he colored them. From now on, he thought, he'd keep the crayons right next to his bed, just in case.

"I'm gonna give this picture to Buddy," he said.

For the first six months of his life, Buddy Woodie was known as a "good" baby, because he did not fuss. In fact, he didn't cry at all: not when he was hungry, wet, or cold. He lay quietly in his crib, smoke-blue eyes fixed on some invisible horizon, only occasionally making tiny cooing sounds like the call of a pigeon, or a dove.

By the time he was eight months old, people began to wonder about a baby that made no sound, showed no interest in his surroundings, and seemed completely indifferent to food or comfort or his mother's presence. He showed no inclination to crawl, remaining instead wherever he was put. Little by little, talk started up: people reminded each other there was bad blood in the Dufore family. Old stories were resurrected and circulated afresh around Esperance; people speculated again about Paul Dufore's mysterious disappearance nearly half a century before and Ab's more recent leap. New whispers went around about Bobby Dufore, who'd taken his family down into the hole he'd dug the year before and not been seen since. Bred in the bone, people told each other, glancing sidelong at Allie when she took Buddy out in the stroller.

It was Max who finally took Buddy to the doctor in Bennington. He'd begun wondering about his son some little time before; he'd seen the way his parents and brother looked at the boy. Allie didn't seem at all worried, it was true, but then, Allie didn't seem much of anything these days; she went through the days and nights of their life together, performing tasks marriage and motherhood had assigned her competently enough, but without any real feel for it. The only time she seemed really involved in anything was when she listened to the radio in the afternoons.

She turned it on when she got up in the morning, and it was still playing when he came home from the station at night. She listened, in particular, to the serials: *Young Dr. Malone, Search for Love, Hope for Tomorrow;* little by little, the plots and characters of the radio dramas entered her conversation.

"Roberta and Mark are getting a divorce," she told him one evening as he came through the door.

"Who?" he asked.

"Hope for Tomorrow," she said, as if that explained everything, and went back to melting the cheese sauce for the macaroni.

"Roberta has discovered Mark only has three months to live," Allie reported a few nights later, "so she's not going to divorce him after all."

"Who?" he asked, his forkful of pot roast halfway to his mouth.

"Of course, he doesn't know she knows," Allie said. "Want some more beans?"

He found her in tears a few weeks after that, and thought at first something had happened to Buddy. Heart in mouth, he tore into the little room he'd built on the back of the house, but his son was the same as always, lying quietly with his eyes fixed on nothing in particular, making that queer, cooing sound.

"What the hell is the matter with you, Allie?" he demanded when he came back into the kitchen.

"Mark's *dead!*" she wailed, and was unable to fix anything for supper that night, so he had to subsist on peanut butter sandwiches and milk.

The doctor in Bennington couldn't put a name to what was wrong with Buddy. For a name, they'd have to go to Boston or New York; that would cost more money than they could afford, so they did without.

There was nothing physically wrong with the boy, the doctor told Max. He was healthy and big for his age; his hearing and eyesight were fine; there was no physical reason why the boy wasn't talking or crawling. The doctor stopped there, but Max was not deceived; his son was an idiot.

For a while after the trip to Bennington, Max spent a lot of time with Buddy, talking to him, waving toys in his face, manipulating his arms and legs in simulation of crawling. Eventually, though, he gave up, turning his energies towards trying to convince Allie to have another baby.

"I don't want another baby," Allie told him, "but I wouldn't mind gettin' a TV set."

About the time Jeanette's twins were born, Mike La-Strange joined the Army and got sent to Vietnam. He went quietly enough; barely anyone in Esperance knew he'd enlisted until after he was gone and sending postcards to his mother from boot camp in North Carolina.

Babe Prescott was sorting mail at the post office one morning when Allie Woodie stopped in to pick up a catalog.

"One of them LaStrange boys has gone and joined up," Babe said, holding up a postcard. "North Carolina. Next stop'll prob'ly be Vietnam."

She dropped the card into the LaStrange post office box and said: "Who'd have figured Mike LaStrange'd do his patriotic duty!"

So that's where he's gone to, Allie thought, starting back across the street to the little house behind the Texaco station. She hadn't seen Mike LaStrange since the morning of her wedding. In a community the size of Esperance, that was a little unusual; suddenly, Allie was amazed all that time had gone by and she'd never even wondered about Mike La-Strange.

She thought about him constantly until *Hope for a Better Life* came on at one o'clock, then didn't think about him again.

That night, Allie Woodie couldn't sleep.

She'd gone to bed at ten o'clock, the same as always, and fallen almost instantly into a deep sleep, only to awaken suddenly an hour later. The room was absolutely dark; a thin ribbon of moonlight slipped through a crack in the curtains and trickled across Max's side of the bed, highlighting his cheek and nose, sinking the rest of his features in even deeper gloom. As her eyes adjusted to the dark, his face came into relief against the white pillow case and she could see the outline of his brows, his mouth and eyes, gray on gray. Asleep, he looked like Buddy: blank and empty. She lay quietly, listening to the sounds of his breathing, the crickets outside, the wind sighing through the catalpa trees out front.

She studied Max's sleeping face and felt a rush of tender-

ness come over her. That happened sometimes, with Max or
Buddy. She'd look at them, usually when they were sleeping, and feel all the things a wife and mother was supposed
to feel all the time. She didn't feel it all the time, though; not
even most of the time. It only seemed to happen now and
then and usually when they weren't in a position to appreciate it. She felt bad about that, but there it was.

She drew one hand out from under the sheet and touched
his cheek lightly, drew just the tip of her finger down from
his temple to his chin, light as moth wings. Tenderness was
in the pit of her stomach, fluttering against her insides; she
imagined rays of love-heat shooting out from that spot,
tracing up and down her arms and legs, melting whatever it
was that kept her dissatisfied and discontent with the way
things were, forever. She was so filled with tenderness her
body trembled from the burden of containing it and she
wanted to cry.

She thought about Buddy, lying in the next room, and
the warmth shot out of her body, out through her fingertips,
piercing the wall that separated his room from hers; she
imagined the force of her love carried right through the
wall on beams of light, bathing her son in a wash of affec-
tion.

For a while she lay gripped by a perfect ecstasy of love,
then it was gone as quick as it had come, leaving her even
emptier than she had felt before.

She rolled onto her side and shut her ears to the sound of
Max's breathing behind her.

In March of 1966, Allie got a postcard from Vietnam. It
said: "Six months," and was unsigned.

"Allie, how can you think of staying in this loveless
marriage? Come away with me! I love you!"

"Oh, Rodney . . ."

She pulled her hands out of his manly grasp and turned to stare blindly out the window. She could see the back of the Texaco station, big green oil drums lining the concrete wall, an air pump between the bathroom door and the water spigot. She felt his hands on her shoulders, running possessively down her arms, where they suddenly gripped her elbows and pulled her back against his hard body.

"Allie, Allie, I've waited for you all my life," he whispered urgently in her ear. "Come away with me, now."

The back door opened, then slammed shut. The refrigerator door opened, then shut. Max Woodie came into the living room, a beer in his hand, to find Allie in the rocking chair near the TV, where she always was at that time.

"Lunch ready yet?" Max asked.

"Ssh!"

She didn't blink when she watched TV, Max noticed; she hardly seemed to breathe. On screen, some guy with greased-back blond hair was wrestling some woman on an overstuffed couch.

"Oh, Rodney . . ." the woman moaned.

"Hey, Allie, how 'bout lunch?" Max asked again.

She didn't answer. Max wasn't sure she even knew he was there. He sighed. Peanut butter again. As he turned back to the kitchen the guy on TV was saying: "Come away with me. . . ."

There were no other postcards.

Babe Prescott would surely have noticed if there had been, and from Babe's mouth to the town's ear was a short trip indeed.

Allie knew who it was from, of course, and she understood the message completely, accepted it completely. With the arrival of Mike's card, her whole past and future became absolutely clear; everything she had done up till then had been in preparation for the moment, six months in the future, when he would come back.

She kept the card in her underwear drawer, buried under a soft stack of cotton panties and nylon slips. It was a plain white card with only her name and address written on one side and two words on the other. No picture to attract the eye, no words to reveal the secret. No reason to throw it away, or to keep it, either.

But she did keep it. Sometimes, when she was alone in the house, she took it out of the drawer and pressed it between her palms as if she could somehow draw the living warmth and strength of the hand that wrote those words out of the ink itself. The writing was sturdy, but crude; she remembered Mike LaStrange had sat at the back of the classroom.

"Six months," she whispered.

In six months, he would come back. Quietly, she set about making preparations.

That summer, Daniel was nine. Almost every morning he rode his bike into town, stopping first at the Texaco station to say hello to Uncle Max (and maybe get a soft drink from the machine for free, if he was lucky), then to the little house tucked behind to get Buddy.

When he came to pick up Buddy in the morning, Aunt Allie had the game shows on. When he brought him home in the afternoon, she was watching the serials. Daytime dramas were a bond between them; they both remembered watching them together, back when Joelle had been born.

"Alistair sure has it in for Kip Simpson," Allie reported one afternoon as Daniel labored to lift Buddy out of his stroller and drag him up onto the back porch of the cottage.

Daniel nodded. He knew all about Alistair on *Young Dr. Malone*. Sometimes he thought Alistair's was one of the voices he heard nights. Just in case, he'd started including him in the stories he wrote down when the chaos in his mind became so bad he had to spill it out onto paper or else risk his head exploding.

It was like that, he thought, as he followed Allie into the kitchen. Like blowing a balloon up bigger and bigger until the rubber stretched so tight you could begin to see it come apart even before it actually popped. That's how his head felt sometimes when the voices and the pictures in his mind started piling in too fast, filling his brain till he felt sure his skull must be expanding to hold them.

Writing it down, or drawing it, made the chaos go away, he'd found. Sometimes for just an hour or two, sometimes for days altogether. Recently it had seemed the quiet time lasted longest when he read or showed his stories and pictures to Buddy.

Daniel trailed into the living room and dropped onto the floor in his accustomed place, leaning back against the side of his aunt's favorite chair. Buddy lay, as usual, flat on his back between his mother's feet, his head on a pillow. Daniel hooked him under the arms and dragged him over between his legs so Buddy half lay, half leaned against his cousin's chest. His head lolled onto his left shoulder and a thread of saliva spun down from his lower lip to Daniel's arm, encircling his chest.

In perfect communion, the three watched *Young Dr. Malone.*

Chapter
14

❧❧

Daniel was at Aunt Allie's house the day the strange
man came.

It was the middle of September. School had
started two weeks before; Daniel's hair was still springy
from the Labor Day weekend trip to the barber; scuffs and
dirt had not yet scarred the black of his new sneakers; there
was still a crease in the sleeves of the plaid shirt his mother
had bought especially for the first day.

A motorcycle was pulled up to the back door of Allie's
house when he got there. It was big, shiny, and black, with
out-of-state plates.

Aunt Allie was at the screen door when he started up the
steps. Behind her, he could see Buddy already strapped into
his stroller, and beyond him, in the doorway of the kitchen,
was a man.

"Buddy's waiting for you, Danny," Aunt Allie said when he'd reached the top step. "You'll take him out for a while, won't you?"

She made no move to open the door for him, just stood, her hand resting on the latch, her body blocking the entrance. Excitement crackled in the air between them; if he took the outside latch in his hand, an electric current might flow through it from her to him, strong enough to stun him. Though she stood in the doorway, absolutely still, he felt she might explode into action at any moment.

The stranger in the living room hadn't moved, either, but his stillness was a different kind. A waiting kind of stillness; the patient stillness you feel in the air just before a thunderstorm.

"He's right here, waiting for you, Danny."

Allie turned then, grabbed the stroller by its handle, and wheeled it through the door. She helped Daniel lift it down the three shallow steps to the ground. Her eyes were electric with excitement; never in all of Daniel's life had he ever seen this much life in her.

It occurred to him then that *Young Dr. Malone* was on at this time, but he hadn't heard the television playing in the living room.

"Is everything okay, Aunt Allie?" he asked.

She laughed, hugging him hard; a trace of perfume tickled his nostrils. She'd never hugged him before.

"You take Buddy for a good walk," she said. "Take him for a nice, long walk."

Her hair was clean and shiny, brushed back and up from her face and held by a comb. She wore a sleeveless dress of thin white cotton; with the sun behind her, Daniel could see the silouette of her legs through the full skirt. She looked dressed for church, or for shopping in Bennington.

"You going out, Aunt Allie?"

She laughed again, and it sounded different from her usual laugh.

"You watch out for your cousin," she told him. "Now get along with you."

The screen door banged behind her.

When they reached the general store at the end of Main Street, Daniel stopped. He thought he heard the sound of a motorcycle starting up.

Allie wasn't surprised at all when Mike LaStrange showed up at the door. He looked different, of course: leaner, older; his hair was shorter and he was in uniform, but she'd known him immediately.

She opened the door and let him in just as if he came calling any day of the week, as if their last meeting on the bridge had been the day before. He walked in as though he belonged there, filling the room and, in a few short moments, making it his own as Max had not in six years. He sat down in the BarcaLounger and swept the Army cap from his fox-colored head, holding it between his hands while he looked up at her out of those pale wolf eyes.

He said: "I come to show you that tattoo."

She nodded, as though it were the most reasonable explanation for his postcard, for her secret preparations, for his presence right then in her living room—as, indeed, it was. He'd waited six years to show her the tattoo he'd got after that one time in Bennington. She'd waited six years and six months to see it. She came closer while he removed the leather jacket and the blouse of his Army uniform.

He unbuttoned his shirt, one button at a time; one by one in a steady, rhythmic motion. Pop. Pop. Pop.

The shirt was open. He stripped it off his shoulders, slid it down his arms, and let it drop in a heap in the BarcaLounger behind him. He sat there in only his T-shirt and Allie saw for the first time the tattoo decorating his left biceps:

ALLIE

it said on a banner wreathed around a plump red heart.

"Wanna see it beat?" he asked. When she nodded he flexed his biceps slightly and sure enough, the heart seemed to pump while the banner with her name on it rippled gently.

She wasn't surprised at all; she looked at that beating heart and wondered at herself for not knowing, always, it was there. When he stood up and pulled her to him she knew she'd been waiting for this moment ever since he'd kissed her in the movie house six years before.

He kissed her, and time rolled back on itself. She knew his mouth instantly, remembered every contour of his shoulders and back, recognized the shape of his hands on her waist.

They dropped to the living-room floor and finished what they had started in Bennington that day.

Afterwards, they didn't speak. No need to—they both knew what was coming next.

"Anything you wanna bring?" he asked her as he pulled his shirt back on, adjusted the bar of colored ribbons on the left breast pocket.

She looked around, shook her head. There was nothing; she hadn't even bothered to pack a bag.

He led her down the shallow wooden steps to the gleaming black motorcycle pulled up to the porch and helped her throw one leg over the back, showed her where to put her feet. Then he kicked the bike to life, let the throttle out so it roared loud enough for half of Esperance to hear, and turned it away from the little house behind the Texaco station. The motorcycle nosed its way across the grassy tract of backyard out to the narrow lane that led to the main road. Once there, it gathered speed all at once and tore up the highway, away from Esperance.

Wind in her hair.

Wind slapping her face and ripping at the fabric of her dress. She wanted to stand up on the back of the motorcycle, arms spread, head back, and scream with the sheer joy of flight.

They were out of Esperance now, on the road to Bennington, where they would join Route 9 and follow it till they came to the interstate just outside of Brattleboro. South to New York—Allie wanted to see New York—then they were heading west. Going to California.

Going to Hollywood.

Somehow she'd known, the minute she woke up, it would be today. Somehow she'd known he would come, today.

She wrapped her arms tighter around his chest, laid her cheek against the cold leather jacket, and let the joy wash over her, through her, lap around her in wave upon wave. She felt his shoulders twist slightly as he turned his head to yell back at her:

"Okay?"

The wind snatched his words, carried them away down the road behind them, back to Esperance.

(Back in Esperance, trudging up the Clark Hill Road, puffing with the exertion of hauling Buddy, who weighed almost as much as he did, Daniel heard someone shout "Okay?" but when he looked around, no one was there.)

"Okay!" she screamed into the leather jacket, laughing like a crazy thing.

(Max Woodie looked up from under the hood of the '64 Dodge he was working on. He thought for a moment he'd heard Allie laugh.)

The roar of the motorcycle was deafening. He nodded and leaned into the first, sharp turn as the road climbed up towards Bennington.

When they reached Bennington, Mike slowed the bike down and took them decorously along Main Street, past the movie theater, past the Woolworth's, up the hill leading to Historic Bennington, past the church, past the entrance to Bennington College. Then they were on Route 9 again and she felt him lean over the bars while the motorcycle picked up speed. Then she was clinging again like a monkey on his back while the wind screamed in her ears and the road swept them up the side of Searsburg Mountain.

They stopped in Wilmington for a sandwich and coffee, though neither of them was hungry. It was really just an excuse to kiss in the parking lot before they got back on the motorcycle and continued the journey. Allie wondered if Max had found her note yet, and what he would do about it when he did, but it wasn't really important; she was going west. Tony Curtis, James Dean, Rodney . . . they were waiting for her there, she knew. They'd been waiting all her life. Suddenly she couldn't wait to get there.

"Let's go!" she said, grabbing the collar of Mike's leather jacket between her hands, pulling him close while she kissed him. His mouth was still warm from the coffee he'd drunk; she could taste bologna and mustard on his tongue.

Back on the motorcycle, and out of Wilmington, heading east to where the road narrowed, winding more tightly than ever up and around Hogback Mountain, then sweeping down again in a series of loops and curves into Brattleboro.

They took the curves at tremendous speed, leaning so deeply into them at times they were practically parallel to the ground and Allie felt almost as though her shoulder would touch asphalt. The shadows lengthened on the ground as the sun followed its arc towards the western horizon. The September day was aglow with the light that ignites treetops and mountaintops for a few fleeting moments before sunset, permeating the air with liquid gold. The motorcycle roared up the final ascent to Hogback, the light weaving itself through Mike LaStrange's hair so he seemed to wear a crown of gold. Allie laughed and reached one hand out, palm open, fingers spread so golden light streamed through them, pure and cold as the water in Crockett's Brook.

Max closed the garage early that day in September and walked across the asphalt parking lot towards the house, an unreasoning feeling of panic squeezing his chest.

The house looked the same as always, but he knew something was different the minute he opened the door. He knew without going any further than just inside the front door the house was empty and would remain so, from now on.

In the kitchen, he found a note propped up against the sugar bowl. It said:

"Gone west."

He stood for a moment, the note clutched in his hand, his thumb planted squarely over the strong, sloping "A" with which she'd signed it, and thought deeply. Time seemed to suspend itself just for him; he had all the time in the world to think about what she'd written, to measure the weight of all the years they'd been together against this sudden betrayal, and to come to some kind of resolution about it. He thought slowly, methodically; when he'd worked through to the end, he folded the note carefully into quarters, making sure the edges met evenly, and placed it in the pocket that had his name embroidered across it. Then he took the keys to the Ford from the nail where they hung next to the back door and went out, shutting the screen door gently behind him.

He drove up the Clark Hill Road, well within the speed

limit, then down the East-West Road, careful of his car's shock absorbers and front-end alignment. There was nothing in the way he negotiated the narrow, twisting logging road to his brother-in-law's cabin to suggest this was anything other than a social call. When he got there, he found Jeanette cutting Joelle's baby hair in the kitchen, Daniel sprawled across the linoleum with a piece of paper and a box of crayons, and his son, Buddy, staring without really seeing, from the stroller.

"Where's Dennis?" he asked.

"Upstairs."

He went up the stairs slowly, for time was on his side, he knew. Dennis was in the attic, putting the finishing touches on a partition that would divide the room in two.

"Hey, Max," he said when his brother-in-law's head appeared over the landing. "Mind handing me up that screwdriver?"

Max reached it up and said, "Allie's gone."

"Gone where?" Dennis asked through the screws he gripped between his lips.

"West, her note says."

Dennis stopped then, screwdriver raised above his head, and looked down over his shoulder at Max. The screws dropped from his mouth to the floor, rolling between the wide pine planks. Max extracted the note from his pocket and handed it up to him.

" 'Gone west,' " Dennis read.

"I'm going after her," Max said. "I'd be grateful if you could keep Buddy till I get back."

Dennis nodded, and climbed slowly down the rungs of the ladder.

They went downstairs together and out to the car in silence.

Max slid in and put the key in the ignition while Dennis

stood with his hand on the handle of the car door.

"Don't know how long I'll be," Max said, starting the engine. "Could take a while to find her."

Dennis nodded.

"Don't worry about anything here," he said. "Good luck."

Max put in the clutch and shifted into first gear, then sat for a moment while the engine idled and time continued to stand still, just for him.

"Reckon it'll be mighty warm out there, this time of year," he said. "Allie always preferred the warm weather, don't you know."

Dennis stood at the top of the drive and watched the Ford bump its leisurely way down the dirt logging track. When it finally disappeared around the first bend, he sighed deeply and turned back to the house.

In the kitchen, Jeanette was sweeping up the fine latticework of baby hair that coated the floor. He stepped over the shining black heap, crossed straight over to the stroller, and squatted down in front of his nephew, searching in vain for some flicker of recognition or even animal intelligence.

"Buddy'll be staying with us for a while," he said without taking his eyes from the idiot moon-face.

Behind him Jeanette stopped sweeping and Daniel jerked up suddenly into a sitting position. Even Joelle stopped fussing in her high chair for a moment. Only Buddy showed no reaction.

"Why?" Jeanette asked after a silence that threatened to stretch into the rest of the afternoon. "What's happened?"

"Allie's gone west," Dennis said.

At the very top of Hogback Mountain, the road curves sharply past an overlook called the Hundred Mile View. From there the valley stretches from the mountain's foot thousands of feet below to where the borders of Vermont, New York, and Massachusetts join, and beyond to a distant range of mountains. There is a telescope there, and a tourist stand where travelers can buy Vermont maple syrup, maple candy, and mugs that say "Souvenir of Vermont" and have the state map traced in enamel on their sides.

That day, just as Allie and Mike LaStrange were leaving Wilmington, beginning the climb towards Hogback, a car with New York plates stopped at the overlook. A man in an Air Force uniform got out and opened the door for his wife and nine-year-old daughter. They stood admiring the view, first without benefit of the telescope, then with it.

"Buy me a cup, Daddy," the girl said, so her father gave a dollar to the man behind the counter of the stand.

"Look at his back!" the girl whispered to her mother as the man turned to make change; the head and wing tips of a glorious winged woman was just visible around the neck and armholes of his T-shirt.

Then they got back in the car and pulled out onto the road heading west, back to Elmira, New York, to the last few days of leave before he shipped out to Vietnam. They passed the motorcycle on the final curve where the road straightens for fifty yards or so before the hairpin turn at the crest of the mountain.

Emily doesn't remember, of course, her only sight of Allie Dufore Woodie. A brief glimpse of a laughing woman, hand stretched out to grasp the afternoon light between her fingers, was not enough to capture a nine-year-old girl's attention. The motorcycle flashed into view, then past. The Hundred Mile View was hidden by a turn in the road; even if Emily had thought to look back, she would not have seen the motorcycle take that final turn too fast and lose control as the front wheel skidded on a patch of gravel.

She wouldn't have seen how, just as the motorcycle

crashed through the low guard rail and soared up, up, up into the glare of the setting sun, Allie stood up, her arms spread out wide, and laughed as the wind caught her behind the knees and just below the shoulders, wafting her even higher into the sky. Below her, the motorcycle was executing somersaults in exact synchronization with the body turning and twisting in the air just above it. Man and machine hung, seemingly suspended, while the golden light of late afternoon expanded and deepened until the whole world was bathed in it. Then suddenly it faded; Mike and the machine began twisting and tumbling again, plummeting faster and faster towards the valley floor, while she was carried ever higher in the arms of the wind.

Like milkweed, she was carried over the horizon and out of knowledge.

Later, they found the motorcycle, and they found Mike LaStrange, but they never found Allie Woodie.

Chapter

15

The funeral was not until Thursday.

Wednesday morning, Emily woke early. She was in the small attic bedroom of the main farmhouse. Light trickled in, skim-milk blue, through thickly frosted glass, forming a pool at the foot of the bed; she wondered if it was snowing again.

She lay on her back, her hands behind her head, and welcomed the chill air against her bare arms, a reminder she was still alive. At times she had woken during the night and thought for a moment the weight of the blankets was Daniel's arm or leg against her own; other times, she'd been sure she was dead, too, packed in satin cushioning.

She wriggled further out of the blankets and let frigid air prick at her throat and chest. A door opened and shut quietly below. That made her throw back the covers, swing her legs out from the nest of blankets, and reach for her clothes. She had someplace she wanted to go that morning, and she wanted to go before people were up and about.

In her stocking feet she crept down the back stairs (the same stairs Davy had thrown himself down, more than forty years before) into the kitchen. It was bathed in a chill, gray light; the dishes on the drainboard, canisters filled with flour, sugar, and rolled oats in the cupboard, a dishtowel draped across the back of a chair, all looked as though they had been in motion, then frozen, and now awaited some burst of light or warmth to bring them back to life. She crossed into the living room; on the far side was the door to the parlor. Gently she turned the knob and pushed it open just enough to put her head through.

Buddy was lying motionless on the bed, his wide, blue eyes fixed on the light that hung from the middle of the ceiling. His face was round, babyish, in spite of the rough stubble of untended beard on his cheeks and chin.

"Hi, Buddy," she whispered. He didn't even turn his head to look at her. For a moment she stood in the doorway, undecided whether she wanted to go in or not.

Each time she saw him, she was surprised again by the strength of her fascination. She couldn't bear to look at him sometimes: his smooth corpse-flesh, his loose wet lips, the round baby face perched grotesquely on an adult man's body. Yet, she couldn't resist squeezing his pudgy wrists either, to see the perfect red imprints of her fingers against his skin.

She hesitated in the doorway until footsteps upstairs sent her hurrying towards the mudroom. She struggled into Daniel's plaid wool jacket and her own Sorrel boots, then let herself out the back door and slid down the steps, boot laces still flapping. It had snowed again during the night, enough to make walking tricky where old, packed-down snow was slick beneath its fresh cover.

Emily skidded down the drive onto the East-West Road. She pulled a wool stocking cap out of a jacket pocket and wondered how long ago Daniel had stuffed it there. She pulled it down over her forehead and ears, wishing he'd left a pair of gloves in the coat as well. It was about three miles into town, and another couple of miles beyond that to the quarry. She wasn't sure why she was making this trip, on this morning before the funeral, in this weather; it would be the first time in fifteen years she'd been there. She stood at the bottom of the drive wavering between the ribbon of cold, white road before her, the house behind. Once, she turned and looked back; smoke was coming from the chimney, so she knew someone was up and starting the woodstove. Independent of the rest of her, her feet started back up the drive. With a force of will she turned them around again, jammed her fists deep into her pockets, and started down the road towards town and the quarry beyond.

In her mind she could see the place she was going to: a narrow ravine a few hundred yards from the quarry. She pictured it as she had last seen it, on a midsummer's afternoon fifteen years before, coarse brush creeping up over the lip of the ravine, thick, lush vegetation tumbling down from above to conceal it. She wondered if she'd be able to find the place again, so many years later in the naked winter, and decided she would, if it took her all day.

Emily flagged down a car at the intersection of the East-West Road and Clark Hill Road that took her into Esperance center. The car had out-of-state plates, the only reason she'd put her thumb out; she didn't feel like talking to anyone who knew Daniel or her.

The car dropped her off in front of the general store.

There were lights on inside; for a moment she considered going in and getting some coffee. She imagined the warm smell of coffee and sweet rolls rising from the counter at the back, the warmth of a mug between her hands, the disembodied reflection of her own face in the red Formica counter. She pictured herself looking Dolly Devereaux, who ran the fountain in the mornings, straight in the eye and saying:

"Danny thought he killed a man up at the quarry, fifteen years ago, and now I'm going to see if he's still there."

The road to the quarry looked different in winter.

Emily trudged the side of the road leading towards Bennington, stepping carefully on the thin crust of packed snow covering the shoulder. Occasionally a car passed and she would step from the road entirely and stand with one leg planted, at times almost to her hip in the bank the snowplow had thrown up.

Bare trees and the blanket of snow lent uniformity to a scene Emily remembered as infinitely varied. In the years when she and Daniel were children, they'd followed this route a thousand times; in dreams, she still did. She felt she knew each bend in the road, each individual maple along the way. She could visualize exactly the shallow brook running parallel to the road about twenty-five feet away; how it looked in August, a thin, brownish trickle blocked with leaves and dead brush. She knew exactly where the lightning–blasted birch tree stood in relation to the turnabout, fifty yards or so before where the path to the quarry ran down the steep bank, cutting through a tangle of black raspberry bushes, to meet the road.

It was February now; one place looked much like another. She wondered if the path might be completely covered, the raspberry bushes buried under the snowbanks. If the turnabout was plowed, it would serve as some warning the path was coming up, but she could not be sure that it had been. She couldn't even be sure how far she had come; the sun was still low in the trees and she doubted it was much past seven o'clock.

She heard a truck behind her and floundered up the side of a snowbank, balanced precariously until the vehicle went by, showering her in a spray of rock salt and wet slush. She stood sunk in snow up to her knees and asked herself just what she expected to find in midwinter, without even a shovel to help her look.

The road stretched before her, white and anonymous. A hopeless pilgrimage, she thought. Her body turned to go back, and there, directly behind her, was the birch tree. She was standing where the turnabout should be. She turned her head, squinting against the glaring snow. Yes, the stark tangle of bushes was visible up ahead—a wiry mass of cordlike branches hanging down like snarled black hair against the smooth white shoulders of the snowbank. Emily sighed; she would have to go on now.

It was a little difficult getting over the bank; ignoring the pricks and scratches from invisible raspberry spines, she grabbed the bushes and pulled herself up. Once through the tangle, the path ran easily over a small rise, then gently down between the trees for a hundred yards or so until it stopped at the edge of the quarry. The winter was mild; the January thaw had lasted almost two weeks, and there hadn't been much snow since then. Before her, the sheer cliff face rose steeply for 150 feet or so; at the top, she could see the edge of the flat boulder where she and Daniel had whiled away their summer days. It jutted out a few feet over the water. She had proposed to him up there, the summer she turned fifteen, the last day of her summer vacation and also the last day they would spend together at the quarry, though she didn't know it at the time; the following year, Daniel had refused to come to the quarry anymore.

She hadn't understood it then, but now she supposed it was on account of the dead man in the ravine.

If there was a dead man.

Brian Bishop had been dead a year when his daughter Emily came to Esperance for the first time. The first summer after Major Bishop was shot down, they didn't go anywhere; Emily's mother stayed in Elmira and had the baby that had been started just before Emily's father shipped out, while Emily stayed with her grandparents in Albany.

In the summer of 1969, the tenth summer Bobby Dufore and his family spent underground, the third summer since Mike LaStrange's death and Allie Woodie's mysterious disappearance, they went to Vermont.

"How come your sister has that big scar?" Emily asked Daniel one afternoon during that first summer.

"She's a twin," he said. "The other one used to be attached right to her, but when they got cut apart, one of 'em died."

"Wow."

They were sitting at the kitchen table in the house Emily's mother had rented. It was a week since they'd first met on the basketball court; almost two weeks since the LaStrange dog was killed.

"Do you think she'd let me touch it?" Emily asked. She'd seen Joelle at the quarry a couple of days before, swimming in just her underpants.

Daniel shrugged.

They'd only known each other for a week, but already Emily knew many things about Daniel. She knew he shrugged when he didn't want to talk about something and that he thought she was pretty weird, but nice. She knew he only gave her about half his attention and that she was going to marry him as soon as she was old enough.

She sat across from him at the scratched Formica-topped table staring with absolute adoration at the top of his head. They'd been making their own science fiction magazine, cutting pictures out of newspapers, *Redbook,* and *Life,* then pasting them onto typing paper and writing their stories around the pictures. Cutouts and scraps of paper fluttered around the table legs and under the chairs; Magic Markers were scattered across the Formica. Opposite her, Daniel sat, his head bent over the page he was working on so she could see the whorls in his thick, coarse black hair, and the fringe of stiff black lashes against his pale skin. She willed him to look up; when he did she looked away.

There wasn't much snow in the quarry. The sun had melted it and the high cliff walls protected it from drifts. It wasn't too difficult climbing the path that cut up through thick brush to the cliff top and the flat overhanging boulder there. Emily climbed bent almost double, grabbing the naked brambles to help pull herself up, jamming her feet through crusted snow as though she were planting posts. When she reached the top, she stopped and turned to look back down the way she'd come; a staggered march of holes at regular intervals marked the smooth surface of the snow. The air felt cold and clean against her cheeks, but the rest of her was warm; suddenly she realized she hadn't thought about Daniel's funeral since she'd left the house that morning.

The ravine was only fifty feet or so away, but she was reluctant, now, to approach it. Instead she slid carefully along the edge of the cliff to where the big rock jutted out over the water. With one foot she kicked free the snow blanketing it, then gingerly sat down, her legs dangling over the edge. Frozen granite bit through her jeans, but it didn't matter; as long as she stayed right here, on this rock, she was out of time. The funeral could not take place because Daniel was not dead, had not, in fact ever existed.

Nor had she, really.

She sat, her legs swinging out over a seventy-five-foot drop, her buttocks growing numb from the rock, and gave herself up to the relief of being outside of grief, of love, of being.

The next time they went to the quarry, Emily asked Joelle if she could touch the scar.

"No," Joelle said, wrapping her arms tightly around her chest. She didn't like this big, skinny red-haired girl; she never left them, Joelle and Daniel, alone.

"C'mon, Joelle," Daniel pleaded, but not even for him would she let the red-haired girl touch her scar. It was not very often Joelle had something older and bigger kids wanted.

"Baby!" Daniel sneered. He knew that would get her pretty hot. He felt sort of responsible for disappointing Emily and searched his mind for something he could offer her instead of Joelle's scar. There wasn't much in Esperance that could rival it, he knew—he'd already shown her Uncle Bobby's bomb shelter, had pounded on the manhole cover to show her how they knew everyone was still okay down there. She'd been impressed when the muffled thumps from under the ground had come soon after in response. There was Ab's Leap, of course, but that was just a tree standing on a cliff over Crockett's Brook, and he doubted she'd believe the story. She'd already experienced firsthand the phenomenon of the barking turkeys.

Finally, he said: "You wanna see a wtich?"

"A real one?" Emily asked skeptically.

He nodded, and she shrugged noncommittally.

"C'mon," he said, starting up the steep path from the water to the cliff above.

"What about them?" Emily asked, jerking her head towards where Joelle sat with her back turned towards them and, just beyond her, pulled into the shade of a tree, Buddy in his wagon.

"They'll be okay."

They hadn't got more than halfway up the cliff before Joelle shouted after them: "Where you goin'?"

"Never mind, baby!" Daniel called back.

"I wanna come!" she yelled.

"Babies can't come," he yelled back.

She was on her feet now, her face almost as red as her scar. Her legs were planted far apart, her arms crossed over her chest. From halfway up the cliff, she looked very small to Daniel.

"I'm *not* a baby!" she shrieked. "I'm *not!* I'm *not!*"

He didn't say anything, just kept climbing. Behind he could hear her loud, gulping sobs.

"Oh, let her come, Dan," Emily said. "She's so little."

He shrugged, then yelled down: "Okay, brat, you can come."

Joelle wandered towards the foot of the cliff and started up slowly, her climb punctuated by frequent hiccups of grief. By the time she caught up with them, the redness had faded from her cheeks; what Daniel saw was an enormous, moon-shaped face, desolation etched in the tracks of dirty tear stains. He felt sorry and tender then.

"You sure are some baby," he remarked, but affectionately, so she wouldn't mind. Harmony restored, Daniel took Joelle's hand and held it all the way to Aimee Bouchard's house.

Ernest was in his pen beside the house when they arrived.

There was no sign of Aimee. They squatted down behind some bushes to the side of the narrow drive up to the house and surveyed the scene.

"That's the pig that broke into Ren Fortesque's shed," Daniel whispered to Emily. His mouth was up close to her ear, almost like a kiss. She turned her head so her mouth was next to his ear and whispered:

"How do you know she's a witch?"

He shrugged.

"Everybody knows," he said. "You just gotta look at her to know."

He sensed she was skeptical, so put his mouth even closer, whispering so soft she could barely hear. "She's the one who gave Joelle that scar. People say a doctor in a hospital couldn't have done it so neat."

"So she must not be a bad witch," Emily said. "She must practice white magic."

Daniel had never heard of magic being colored.

"She's okay," he said.

"Danny," Joelle whispered, "I gotta *pee.*"

"So pee," he told her.

"I don't wanna go in the woods," she said.

"Well, you're gonna have to," he said.

"Danny . . ." Joelle's voice began to rise. "I don't *wanna!*"

"Then you're gonna have to wait."

"I *can't!*"

The screen door of the house banged open. Aimee stood in the doorway.

"Who's there!" she called. Her voice, shrill with age and the onset of deafness, did not waver or break as some old people's do. "You kids! You come out of there!"

Sheepishly they stood up and came out from the bushes. Joelle had started crying again; there was a large, wet, warm stain on the back of her dress and streaks of urine down the insides of her legs.

"Daniel Dufore, what do you mean by hiding yourself in my bushes!" Aimee demanded.

"And what in blazes have you got to be crying about?" she asked Joelle.

"She wet herself," Daniel explained.

"What, a big girl like you?" Aimee snorted. "Best come in then, and get cleaned up."

She opened the door a bit wider. Daniel led his howling sister up the drive, up the porch steps, and into the house, Emily trailing a little reluctantly behind. As she came up the steps, she raised her head and saw sharp amusement in the old woman's eyes, as if Aimee could read her mind exactly.

Inside the house it was cool, dark, cluttered, smelling slightly of mildew and herbs. Aimee went through the kitchen into a room off the back and returned with a coarse white towel.

"Here," she said to Daniel. "Wrap her in this and give me her clothes."

Daniel did as he was told and Aimee disappeared once more into the room off the kitchen.

"You kids thirsty?" she yelled out to them. "There's some lemonade in the icebox."

They hesitated.

"You can pour me some, too," she called, so Daniel led them silently into the kitchen and settled Joelle into a chair in the corner while he hunted for glasses. He found two glasses, a jam jar, and a chipped coffee mug in the cupboard over the sink. He got the jug of lemonade out of the icebox, poured equal amounts into each glass.

"It's warm," Joelle whispered after she'd taken one sip, "and there's hardly any sugar in it!"

"Shut up!" Daniel hissed back.

They heard a door slam off to the back, then slam again a few moments later. Aimee came through into the kitchen.

"I put your stuff out on the line," she said. "In this heat it oughta dry pretty damn quick."

She picked up her glass of lemonade and took a deep swig, smacking her lips as she set it back down on the table.

This is what Emily saw: a tiny woman, hardly bigger than a child herself and older than Emily thought a human being could possibly be; face nut-brown from too many years in the sun, and lines like they'd been carved there with a chisel. Emily was certain her skin would feel hard as granite; she had to fight an impulse to raise her hand, touch one of those cratered cheeks. Aimee's hair was thin, a dirty grayish-white color. She wore it in a braid down her back but there was always a halo of short, unruly strands that escaped from the braid and stood up all around her head. Her eyes were almost black; though she looked old as the hills, she stood straight as Emily did and her hands were strong.

Aimee drained her glass, then picked up the jug and re-filled all of them.

"Hungry?" she asked, pulling out a tin of hard and dusty gingersnaps before they could answer. Daniel and Emily each took one. Joelle shook her head.

"They're *old,*" she said, then yelped when Daniel kicked her savagely under the table.

Aimee sniffed.

"Suit yourself," she said, taking one out of the tin and biting into it.

There was a lengthy and frigid silence in the kitchen. Aimee continued taking large bites out of the gingersnap; they could hear her teeth grind as she doggedly chewed the rocklike pieces till they were soft enough to swallow. Daniel took a small bite himself and wondered if his teeth would stand up under the strain. He noticed Emily was nibbling the edges of the cookie without actually eating any of it and he started doing the same.

"Delicious!" Aimee said firmly, when she'd swallowed the last of the gingersnap.

Daniel saw Emily surreptitiously drop her cookie into the breast pocket of her overalls and wished he were not wearing a T-shirt and shorts.

"Come see my pig," Aimee said.

They trailed out behind her and stood in a line outside Ernest's pen. At first the pig ignored them, then the thought of handouts came into his cunning brain; he sidled over and leaned suggestively against the rails of the sty. The space between the second and third rails was just the right height and width for him to get his snout through, right up to his eyes. His keen nose picked up the alluring odor of the gingersnap Daniel still clutched in his fist. He made a sudden dart for it but only succeeded in butting Joelle, who was next to her brother, standing close to the pen, hard in the stomach.

"That pig could eat you up!" Aimee told her maliciously.

Furtively, Daniel dropped the gingersnap just inside the pen and realized as soon as he'd done it Aimee had seen. She didn't say anything about it, though, just nodded towards the clothesline and said:

"Yer stuff's prob'ly dry now, or near enough as makes no difference."

Inside, she watched Joelle raise her arms to let Daniel drop the sundress over her head. The towel fell in a heap around her feet and for a moment the scar was exposed.

"I gave you that," Aimee told her, pointing at her stomach. "With yer Mama's great big kitchen knife!"

She came up close, bent over with her hands on her knees so she was eye to eye with Joelle.

"In all my years of midwifin', I only seen something like come along once before, and they was dead. But I slapped life into both of you, then I took that big knife of your mama's and split you apart neat as melon."

Her voice had changed, almost as if she were singing. Her eyes never left Joelle's, never blinked, yet Emily, mesmerized by the rhythm of her voice, could not be sure Aimee was even seeing the little girl in front of her.

"And make no mistake, child," she said, "there weren't no particle of difference a'tween you; not one speck. I just scooped them innards off the table and sewed 'em up pretty well inside you, and never cared one way or t'other which one of you it was."

Her eyes grew sharp and focused again, her voice became normal.

"Don't care now," she told Joelle sternly, running one gnarled, bony finger down the front of her dress, exactly where the scar was. "But you owe me."

Emily sat on the flat rock until she was numb from buttocks to knee. She wondered if she would get frostbite on her ass if she sat there long enough and, if so, what kind of treatment was prescribed for such a condition. She wondered if she could be frozen solid as quarry water if she sat there long enough: cold creeping up through her body by inches, stopping the blood in her veins, petrifying her bones, causing every organ to suspend activity until finally she was stiff and hard and cold as a marble statue, preserved in a perfect state of immobility until spring came.

In the hope and warmth of spring, perhaps she would be able to face the end of Daniel better.

At the thought of him her mind shied away again; she wondered suddenly, irrelevantly, if old Aimee Bouchard was still alive. For a moment she considered climbing further up into the woods behind her, up to the tumbledown house she'd visited once, years before, with Daniel and Joelle. Surely the woman must be dead by now, she thought; she'd been ancient enough almost twenty years before, when Emily had first seen her.

Emily got up stiffly and stood for a moment pounding her feet against the rock as she tried to restore some feeling to her legs. She had no idea how long she'd been sitting there; she wondered if she had managed to sit through the funeral. Perhaps she'd mixed the days up or maybe she'd sat through the night without noticing.

Her mind was playing tricks on her. Sudden death could do that, she knew. Ever since Sunday evening when she'd come home to find Daniel spattered across the garage walls, she could no longer entirely trust what her mind told her. The only thing she knew absolutely anymore was Daniel was dead, and even that truth could be betrayed in dreams and in the first few moments after waking.

She sighed and stepped off the rock onto the frozen crust of snow. She crunched fifty yards or so to the lip of the ravine, stood for a moment looking down its steep shoulders to the brush-covered bottom.

What was the point, she asked herself, her eyes scanning the unbroken carpet of snow covering the ravine. Even supposing there was a dead man, even supposing that he, or any remnant of him, had managed to lie here undiscovered for fifteen years, what hope had she of finding anything now when the world was safely hidden under snow? Even supposing she did go down and look around, even supposing she found anything, would she be able to get up again?

She hesitated at the edge of the ravine until it occurred to her the only alternative to going down was returning to the farm and sitting with Daniel's coffin.

She'd get back up somehow, she decided, and started down the steep bank.

At the end of August 1969, Emily and Daniel went to the quarry, cut their thumbs with Daniel's slightly dull jack-knife, and mixed their blood together. They did this the day before Emily was leaving for Elmira. Afterwards, they lay on their backs on the sunbaked boulder, watching clouds that billowed like ship sails as they blew across an electric-blue sky.

They'd left Buddy and Joelle behind, for once; in the part of her brain that was waiting for her to grow up and want the knowledge already stored there, Emily knew he had done for her something he would do for no one else. She felt deeply satisfied. Even the coming year back home, in a house strangely silent, back at school where the other children made fun of her awkward body and carroty hair, back in Elmira where there was no Daniel, seemed survivable now she knew she was special to him.

"I'll write to you," she said.

"Yeah?" Daniel had never received a letter in his life.

She sure was a weird kid, he thought as they lay there on the rock side by side. Out of the corner of his eye he could see her chest slightly rise and fall; she was still pretty flat, but he thought he could detect the faint beginnings of tits under the T-shirt. He wondered if she'd have big ones by next summer.

Yeah, she was weird, always wanting to pretend something and play stuff where you had to imagine you were on another planet, or lived in a cave in prehistoric times, and she got mad at him when he forgot her make-believe names when they were playing. He liked her, though. He even liked playing her games, because they were even stranger than the stories he made up in his own head and wrote down for Buddy. He was really going to miss Emily.

"You're coming back next summer, aren't you?" he asked.

She caught the note of worry in his voice, and the glow of satisfaction inside her deepened.

"Maybe," she said.

After almost an hour of scraping around at the bottom of the ravine, Emily finally admitted defeat.

The snow was deeper there. Snowfall upon snowfall had piled up and no sunlight had penetrated to melt it. In places it was almost up to her waist; she began to fear she might flounder into a deep drift and be unable to pull herself out. She'd been stupid to even think she might find anything here in February; a fresh corpse could lie safely hidden until spring, let alone what might remain of a fifteen-year-old one!

I'll come back in the spring, she told herself, scrabbling up the side of the ravine. I'll come back some weekend and stay in a hotel in Bennington and not tell anyone I'm here. I'll come out to the quarry really early in the morning and I'll go over this ravine from one end to the other. If there's anything to be found, I'll find it.

No you won't she answered. You'll go back to Boston and try to raise the kids Daniel left you with as best you can. You'll call Dennis and Jeanette now and then, just to say hello, and you'll send birthday cards and Christmas cards every year, but just signed with your name and the girls'. When they're older, you'll probably send them to Esperance for a couple of weeks every summer. But you won't come back here again. Not ever. Not after this.

The ravine was steeper than she'd realized; the sloping sides were slick with frozen snow. She managed to break through the crust with her hands and knees, climbing up on all fours, catching hold of the occasional exposed branch or root of some buried shrub. Her gloveless hands were almost frozen; once or twice she thought she would not make it. She imagined sliding slowly back down into the ravine and dying of exposure there, no one knowing what had become of her until spring when some child in search of birds' eggs would find her there.

And then she was over the side and climbing shakily to her feet, taking great, gasping gulps of air into her heaving lungs while she swayed wearily on the edge of the ravine. She felt tears roll hotly down her cheeks, felt a sense of shame that the nearness of her own death could make her cry when she had not yet shed a tear for Daniel.

Her hands were white, bloodless, practically frostbitten. She shoved them into her armpits and lurched on rubber legs away from the ravine, back to the boulder. The tears were coming faster and hotter now, streaming down her face, dribbling over her jaw and down the sides of her neck. She was furious with herself because they were tears of rage and not grief.

She was mad, mad, *mad* at Daniel. Because he'd told her there was a dead man in the ravine, and there wasn't. Because he'd married her, then deliberately gone forever where she could not follow. Because he'd left her to take care of the mess—the debts, the kids, the blood on the garage wall.

And because, after all he'd done, she couldn't even cry for him.

She stood there on the big flat rock that jutted out over the quarry and bawled, her mouth wide open, the harsh, ugly sounds of her angry crying echoing off rocks and trees and cliff walls of the quarry.

She knew, all at once, someone else was in the quarry, and her sobs stopped as though they had never been.

Twenty yards away, at the edge of the woods, Aimee

Bouchard stood watching her from beneath several pounds of wool mufflers.

Even through eighteen years and six scarves, Emily knew her. She wondered how long Aimee had been watching and, at the same time, why she didn't feel in the least bit embarrassed about being caught crying like a madwoman.

They looked at each other for a moment, then Aimee took a step or two forward, out of the trees. She said, as though finishing a conversation they had started the day before:

"You were looking for the dead man, weren't you?"

Chapter

16

The dream was always the same:

It is quiet in the quarry. She sits on the ground, her legs splayed out in front of her, the soles of her feet pressed firmly against the soles of Desiree's. She rolls her favorite cat's-eye marble, nicks the creamy one the color of a robin's egg. She scoops up her prize and and drops it into the big, square pocket of her sundress.

She doesn't hear him come up behind her. She doesn't know anyone is there until a shadow falls across her legs and she looks up. His face is filthy, hidden beneath a knotted, savage growth of beard, yet his eyes are strangely gentle; they look down on her as though they didn't see her at all, as though they saw someone quite different, someone standing far away, on the edge of time and memory.

Obviously, he has come looking for Desiree. He's one of De-

siree's friends, one of the many who keep her company during the long nights when they are separated by hours of sleep. He stands there, looking at Joelle but seeing Desiree. Joelle isn't afraid; he's a friend of Desiree's.

He stoops down so his face is close to hers.

"Nettie," he says softly, just one word exhaled on a breath that fans her cheek, hot and sour, smelling faintly of blood and rotted teeth.

He touches the hem of her dress, his eyes still gentle, and she knows he is a friend of Desiree's anyway, so she isn't afraid.

She doesn't feel afraid at all until Buddy screams and Daniel comes.

After so many years of dreaming it, Joelle almost never needed to wake up from it anymore. There had been a time, though, when she'd wake up crying and only Daniel could comfort her.

"It's okay, Joli," he'd whisper. "It's only a dream."

She'd dreamed it every night for a while; for several weeks she refused to sleep, and Dennis and Jeanette began worrying she'd end up like Gran Marie, then entering her fiftieth year of wakefulness. Night after night Joelle would sit up in a chair downstairs by the woodstove, waiting for the rest of the world to wake up. She stayed awake for almost a month and might have continued that way indefinitely except the dream began following her into waking hours. He's appear suddenly in the kitchen doorway; his hand would reach out from behind the stovepipe to pluck at the collar of her nightgown.

Somehow it seemed more frightening to see him when she was awake, so she eventually went back to bed. By the following summer, she'd hardly dreamed of him at all, anymore. . . .

Had hardly thought of him for years until a few days

earlier, when footsteps had come up the stairs, and her mother had stood in the doorway with a queer, frozen look on her face.

"Danny's dead," Jeanette had said.

And now, two nights before Daniel's funeral, she'd had the dream again.

It was nearly ten o'clock. She'd been awake since five, but Joelle didn't want to get out of bed.

Not yet.

Getting out of bed meant accepting once and for all it had happened.

Yesterday, the day before, she could get up and still pretend it was a day like all other days; pretend her mother's silence, the way her father's flesh had seemed to melt away from the bones in his face overnight, were normal; pretend she would put on her dance clothes in a little while, dance till she was exhausted, then borrow the truck, drive into town, and go to work. She could get up and pretend because there was nothing real to spoil the dream.

But Emily had come last night, bringing a body in a coffin with her, and Joelle knew she would see them in her parents' eyes, as soon as she went downstairs. She'd see where the coffin had lain outlined by snow in the back of the pickup truck; she would see it, black and dull, in the sitting room of the main house. Even if she tried pretending it wasn't Daniel inside, she would see it was in Emily's face. I won't get up, she thought. I won't believe it yet.

Daniel's sister, Joelle, had a long red scar that ran from breastbone to pelvis, dividing her torso neatly in half. When she and her twin, Desiree, were born, they'd shared but one heart and liver between them. So old Aimee Bouchard, who'd been midwifing in and around Esperance for longer than anyone could remember and who had, some said, made an agreement with the devil when he'd passed through Esperance many years before, took up a great sharp knife and split them neatly apart. The heart and liver fell right out on the dressing table, so she just shoved them both into the baby on the left, tied off the blood vessels leading into the baby on the right, then sewed up the incision neat as a Thanksgiving turkey.

There were those in Esperance who considered the fact only one of the babies died proof that Aimee was indeed possessed of unnatural powers. That she had performed the operation immediately after taking the babies from Jeanette Dufore's body, without waiting until a priest could be found to baptize them, was conclusive, damning evidence.

"Hell!" Aimee scoffed. "T'weren't no more'n cutting an extra finger off; I done that hundreds o' times and no one the worse for it, don't ya know, and no one accusing me of having truck with the devil."

When she was very young, Joelle had an imaginary friend named Karen. They were exactly the same age and size, but Karen had straight blond hair and blue eyes; her stomach and chest were smooth and white, unmarked by the touch of a kitchen knife. Karen was Joelle's willing slave; she made Joelle's bed in the morning, and ate her lima beans at dinnertime. When they played together, Joelle made up the games.

Joelle didn't know about Desiree, then.

Daniel's bedroom was in the attic, too. When Joelle was four, old enough to move from the crib in her parents' room, Dennis built a partition dividing the attic into two halves separated by a narrow walkway. The rooms were both small, each with a big octagonal window at one end. From Joelle's room, you could see the main farmhouse where her grandparents and great-grandmother lived; from Daniel's, the trees marched down the far side of the ridge, then up a higher mountain beyond.

Daniel was ten; for the first few nights of her exile in the attic, Joelle had found comfort in his bed. He didn't seem to mind when she padded silently across the pine floors and crawled under the covers with him; indeed, he seemed happy, almost relieved, to have her there. He didn't mind her cold feet pressing against his bare shins as she curled her back into the comforting hollow created especially for her by the curve of his stomach and knees. Within the safe circle of his arm, she listened with drowsy pleasure as he talked, sometimes through the night.

One night, she felt the slight pressure of his thumb moving down along the scar on her chest. He traced it from top to bottom, then again from bottom to top.

"That's where the other one was," he whispered in her ear.

The other what, she wondered. She rolled over so they lay face to face in the darkness. She could see Daniel's eyes glittering in the moonlight, and his face on the pillow, just a few inches from her own, seemed serious.

"They buried the other one in the graveyard," he said. "She's there right now, under the ground, all alone.

"She's *dead*," he said.

"Who's dead, Danny?" she whispered.

"The other baby, just like you," he told her. He ran his thumb down the scar again. "The one that was here.

"I worry about her a lot, Joli," he told her, while she stared, mesmerized, into his eyes and drowned in the pools of worry she saw reflected there.

"She's all alone. And nobody knows which one she was!"

He rolled suddenly onto his back, and she felt as if the world's warmth had been taken away from her. She huddled down miserably under the blankets, but little drafts snaked in between the covers, chilling the length of her body that Daniel's arms and stomach and legs had once kept warm.

Another baby, just like her; no one had ever told her. Why had the other baby died, she wondered; why hadn't she? Danny knew everything, but he didn't know which baby was in the ground, all alone in the dark under the ground.

What if somebody found out the wrong baby had been put there? Would she, Joelle, have to go into the graveyard in its place, while the other one took her bed, her brother, her parents, her sunlight and safety and air?

She closed her eyes and thought about the kitten she'd helped Daniel bury the week before. They'd put it in a shoe box and he'd let her wrap it carefully in Kleenex, to keep it warm. Then they'd put it in a hole under the maple tree, marking the grave with a cross made from Popsicle sticks.

She thought of the dead pigeon she'd found in the road last summer, its head crushed by a car, its body crawling with beetles and ants, flies and little white worms.

She imagined a baby wrapped in Kleenex, ants and beetles crawling across her body.

Did she, Joelle, belong there?

The cold was creeping in from places where the blankets had pulled out from under the mattress. It tickled her ankles and crept up her legs. She lay in wakeful misery, feeling the cold inch up under her nightdress and trace its icy fingers from pelvis to breastbone, all along the length of her scar.

Karen went away one day and never came back.

In her place was Desiree.

Desiree didn't have a name, at first; Joelle just called her "Baby," or "You," and sometimes "We." She didn't get a name until almost three years later, after Joelle learned to read and found her christening name engraved on the little

stone in the cemetery on Clark Hill Road. By then, however, it didn't seem very important.

Joelle lay in the bed where she had slept for twenty-four
years. A narrow bed, its iron bedstead was painted white and
pushed under the slope of the eaves. It was instinct now to sit
up slowly, stopping just short of the low ceiling. There was
a large octagonal window behind her head, and a view of
the fields at the bottom of the ridge, the main farmhouse
beyond. She flopped onto her stomach, pulled the blankets
up over her head like a monk's cowl, and rested her chin
against the low iron bed frame.

Outside her window, the whole world was black-and-
white. Naked trees stood stark against the carpet of snow
that ran down the flank of the ridge. Their glistening black
branches thrust upward, twigs splayed like begging fingers.
Unclothed, raped by the season, they stood as silent remind-
ers that winter was a mortal season and February a hell of a
month to die in.

Far down the hill, she could just make out a smudge of
red against the whiteness surrounding the farmhouse. It
moved slowly across the yard and disappeared over the crest
of the drive.

She wriggled further down into the warmth of her bed
and rolled onto her back, the covers tucked up under her
chin, and allowed herself to think about Daniel. He'd been
dead for four days now. She hadn't permitted herself to
really think about it yet, hadn't allowed herself to imagine
what Emily must have found, or think about a lifetime
without Daniel in it. She closed her eyes and tried to picture
the body inside the coffin.

He'd shot himself in the head, she knew; not even the
most skilled undertaker could have repaired that damage.
She tried picturing him faceless in the coffin, but found

instead the dream-man's features superimposing themselves, and she greeted him almost with relief.

I'll think about Daniel later, she promised herself. I'll imagine him dead tomorrow, at the funeral. That'll be the right time for it.

This was Joelle's compromise: she'd get up, but she would not go downstairs. Not yet.

In her room she did her exercises, using the iron footrest of her bed for a barre. She was naked, and could see herself from the waist up in the mirror on her dresser.

"Pas de chat . . . pas de chat . . . glissade and *pas* de chat . . ."

Joelle talked to herself when she danced. When she was learning a new combination, she recited the names of the steps. It was the only French she knew, and she wished she knew more, because it sounded like it might be a pretty language.

When she knew the steps, and could perform them automatically, she talked, instead, to Desiree. The talk was always inside her head, of course; if she spoke the words out loud, Desiree wouldn't answer.

"Head *up,* Joelle!" she reminded herself. She imagined a string running through the center of her body, right up to the ceiling.

She pulled up a bit and realigned her body.

"Brosse and demi-plié and *up* into pirouette . . ."

She marked a spot on the far wall and began ten rapid turns.

"Arms *up,* Joelle!" Desiree whispered, just behind her.

She spun round and round, her head turning to mark the spot on the wall until the last moment, when it snapped around to follow her body, then found the mark again. She turned with power, spinning between invisible hands; Desiree stood directly behind her, she knew.

They'd been together for a long time, she and Desiree, as long as Joelle could remember. They shared everything; they'd gone to school together, sat at the same desk, shared the same schoolbooks, tormented the same little boys. Joelle had started dancing because Desiree wanted her to.

She dropped again into a demi-plié, then rose into an arabesque. In the mirror she saw herself extended fully, the line of her outstretched arm and raised leg creating an almost perfect bow. Her body glistened with sweat. Demi-plié . . . her breasts seemed to rest on the edge of the mirror frame. Grand plié . . . she disappeared completely from view. She leaned into an arabesque and smiled as her leg and foot seemed to grow out of her head and her breasts wobbled ridiculously, suspended like giant raindrops from her chest. She straightened up again, brought her foot into third position, then dropped forward, sweeping her arm forward so her fingers almost brushed the floor, then rising up again, back straight, arm an extension of her body's line and continuing through, till her back was arched and she was looking over her right shoulder at the floor behind her.

She turned and repeated the entire sequence on the other side. Desiree stood, just out of sight, as always, in one corner of the room humming the appropriate music.

"Jumps?" she asked Desiree.

Desiree shook her head; jumps would shake the house, let Jeanette and Dennis know she was awake now. There'd be no excuse to stay up here then.

She turned to look at herself in the mirror again. Straight, thick black hair, straight black brows with Daniel's eyes beneath them. They had both favored their mother in most things, except the eyes. Those were strictly Dufore.

The scar seemed very pronounced to her today, redder than usual against her matte ivory skin. Desiree had a scar like this, too, though Joelle had never actually seen it. De-

siree was shy, even with her, and could only be looked at
out of one's peripheral vision, glimpsed briefly in the corner
of a mirror, or caught unexpectedly in the aftermath of a
sneeze. Most times, she stayed behind Joelle, just out of
sight.

She dropped to the floor and began to stretch. Through
the closed door of her bedroom, she could hear the faint
jingle of the telephone.

She moved to the dresser, swung her leg effortlessly up,
her heel against the cool wood, and stretched her torso flat so
the scar was aligned with her thigh. She gripped the arch of
her foot between both hands and massaged gently, her forehead resting lightly against her knee.

Every morning before she went down to the beauty salon
in Esperance, and every evening when she came back, she
danced here, in her room.

She dropped her leg and sank to the floor, the soles of her
feet pressed together, and gave herself up completely to
sweat and tired muscles while her mind emptied.

She traced the line of the scar from the spot between her
breasts where it began, down to where it disappeared into
the curly mass of black hair between her legs.

For the first time in a long time, she thought about Agnes
LaStrange. An almost forgotten warmth flooded her stomach and spread through her loins. Desiree's jealousy slapped
her hard between the shoulder blades; Desiree had been jeal-
ous of Agnes. Joelle was beginning to suspect Desiree hated
Daniel, too.

Joelle felt a hand brush her shoulder as she sat straddle-
legged on the floor of her room, her torso stretched the
length of her right leg. For a crazy minute, she thought it
was Daniel.

"He's *dead*," Desiree whispered from somewhere just
beyond her field of vision. "He's *dead*."

Chapter
17

The funeral was tomorrow.

Jeanette stood in the living room, a can of furniture polish in one hand, a rag in the other, and wondered what she had planned to do with them. Through the frost on the window she could see a break in the clouds, a sliver of blue peering through the lowering gray of the February sky. What a hell of a month to die in, she thought.

Dennis was in the kitchen. She couldn't bear to look at him; she'd grabbed the polish and rag out from under the sink and escaped to this room. Whenever she looked at him, she saw Daniel's eyes looking back, and then she felt terribly, terribly afraid: for her son's soul, of course; for the long years ahead she would have to face without him, but most of all, for the uncertainty of how much pain could fill a man's eyes before he could no longer bear to live with it.

There was an empty place, just below Jeanette's heart; today, just now, it felt emptier than ever. It hadn't always been empty; it had expanded to hold first Dennis, then Daniel there, as well. The space had stretched again when she was pregnant with twins; for nine months, she had carried them there, close to her heart, then one of them had died.

That baby's death had left a hole, a small, black, empty space that could never be filled. Now Daniel, too, was gone, and Jeanette began to feel she was balancing between two extremes, as though she was exactly half full, half empty, and even the tiniest thing could tip the balance irrevocably one way or the other.

She was afraid to move, afraid to think or feel for fear of upsetting that balance. A phone call from her daughter-in-law on Sunday had jeopardized everything. Now she moved through her days stolidly, outwardly composed, performing necessary tasks, only her husband noting her grief in the set of her shoulders and the dead look in her eyes.

She dealt with the arrangements competently, calmly, but she could not pick up the telephone when it rang.

Footsteps climbed the front steps, and a moment later there was a heavy knock on the door. She stood three feet away, the can of furniture polish raised before her like a talisman, unable to open it. The knock came again.

"Dennis," she whispered, and he was there, opening the door.

Don Sumner, from the post office, was on the porch, a telegram in his hand.

"We usually just phone these things up," he said, "but under the circumstances . . . well . . ."

The telegram said:

"Sorry to hear the news about Daniel stop all my sympathy stop still no sign of her stop still looking stop Max."

When Joelle finally came downstairs, her parents were in the kitchen, a telegram in their hands.

"Your Uncle Max sends his sympathy," Jeanette told her, laying the telegram down on the scrubbed oak table for her to look at if she cared to. She brushed the back of her hand gently across her daughter's cheek.

"You slept late today," she said.

"Mama," Joelle said, "I'm gonna go in to work for a little while."

"There's a lot to be done before tomorrow," Jeanette said.

"I know."

As long as I don't see the coffin, she thought, it hasn't happened. As long as I keep this day normal, it hasn't happened. She looked up and caught her father looking at her, understanding in his eyes.

"I'll be back soon," Joelle said. "I'll help tonight; I swear I will."

"Want a ride into town?" her father asked, and she nodded, grateful to him for making it so easy.

They got in the pickup, Joelle sitting closer to her father than was strictly necessary because Desiree preferred sitting next to the window. Shirley wouldn't be expecting her for another week, at least, and had either canceled or rescheduled all her appointments, but even if there weren't any customers Joelle figured she'd find something to do around the salon.

They were almost to the end of the East-West Road when Dennis said:

"Doesn't seem quite real, does it."

"Maybe it isn't real, Daddy," she said. "Maybe it doesn't have to be."

He didn't take his eyes off the road as he reached one hand over, covering her knee with his strong, warm fingers, and squeezing gently.

"How do you figure that, Joelle?"

His hand still rested on her knee; she closed her eyes and imagined it was Daniel driving the truck, Daniel's hand on her leg. That's how, she wanted to say; if we all believe together, it will just have to be true. You thought Desiree was dead too, she wanted to tell him, but she's not. I brought her back! She's right here!

Out of the corner of her eye she could see Desiree's head turned towards her, wearing an expression of—what?—jealousy, anger? But how could we have grieved so much for you, Joelle asked her; we never even knew you.

"Dunno," she mumbled.

They reached the intersection of Clark Hill Road and the East-West Road. Dennis slowed to a stop, looked both ways, then let the truck idle motionless while he sat, his right hand on his daughter's leg, his left on the wheel. He looked out in front of him, across Clark Hill Road to the wide expanse of meadow on the other side. Barbed wire had been run along the perimeters of the field, but the posts were old, bleached by summer sun, splintered with age. Snow had piled up around them so only the tips and the top strand of wire were visible. Beyond them snow stretched a quarter of a mile, dotted here and there with bushes or rotted logs exposed by the thaw and never covered up again. The school was up the road a piece; he supposed his son had cut through that field on his way to the schoolyard, just as he had himself when he was a boy.

"That telegram from your uncle, for instance," he said, as though they were in the middle of a conversation. "He's been traveling around the country for twenty years now, looking for Allie, and what's he got to show for it? What reason does he even have for doin' it?"

"They never found her," Joelle said in a soft voice.

Dennis nodded.

"You're right," he said, "they never did. But so what? She's just as dead to Max, either way; he'd have found her by now if she wanted to be found."

They sat close together in the pickup listening to the engine rumble and cough, thinking their separate thoughts. At last Dennis jerked the truck into gear; as they headed down the Clark Hill Road into town he said:

"He ought to have let her go."

He dropped her off in front of the general store, and Joelle crossed over Main Street, then climbed the steep, narrow stairs to the salon over Ernie's Tavern. Even from the doorway, cold February wind in her face, she could smell creme rinse and perm solution. The odors were permanent, she thought; the faded woodwork and worn stair runner were drenched in them; even if the salon disappeared tomorrow, the smells would remain behind forever.

At the top of the stairs a frosted glass door had "Shirley's Salon" etched in blue cursive across it. A bell tinkled shrilly when she pushed the door open, and Shirley yelled out from the other room:

"Be right there!"

"It's me, Shirl," Joelle called back.

Shirley appeared almost immediately. She was wearing clear plastic gloves covered with muck the color of old blood; Meredith Parrish must be getting her hair dyed, Joelle thought.

"What in hell's name are you doing here, hon?" Shirley asked.

"I thought you might need some help."

"On a Wednesday? Joelle, you go home. You shouldn't be here."

"I'll straighten up the back room," Joelle said, as if Shirley hadn't spoken, "and vacuum out here."

She started straightening the stack of old magazines that sat on a low table between two chairs.

"This *McCall's* is four years old," she said. "We oughta get newer issues."

She picked up a copy of *Hollywood Screen* and flipped through the pages idly. Something caught her eye, and she turned back a page or two. Yes, that woman in the background, standing between two famous movie actors, did look a little like her Aunt Allie. She dropped the magazine back onto the stack.

Shirley stood with her hands held up in front of her like a surgeon, the blood-red dye running off the plastic gloves onto her forearms. "I gotta get back," she said at last, with a bewildered look at Joelle. "If you need anything . . ."

Joelle was behind the reception desk, straightening the drawer that held pencils and paper clips. She nodded but did not look up.

Shirley went back into the other room. Joelle finished straightening up the desk and went into the storage room for the watering can. She came back and sprinkled the sad-looking diefenbachia gracing the windowsill, then the wandering Jew that spilled from a hanging pot over her head. She eyed the spider plant in the other window with distaste; she hated spider plants and had been waging a secret war against this one for a long time. She simply never watered it. The plant got browner and scragglier, but it never completely died out. Joelle suspected Shirley probably watered it from time to time, when its desperation became apparent even to her.

Today, however, Joelle knew a sudden impulse to relent. It took real force of mind not to take the watering can over there and pour mercy over its drying leaves. Nothing about today could be different, though; if she changed anything, if she showed a scrap of remorse, grief, or pity out of the ordinary, the magic she was making would not work.

She put the can back in the storage room without watering the spider plant.

She heard the front door open and close. Footsteps came up the stairs, slow and heavy, weighted down by snowboots and heavy clothes. She looked in the appointment book, but no name was written down. The footsteps stopped just outside the frosted-glass door. The door opened and a woman with fox-colored hair and wolf-pale eyes came through.

It was Agnes.

Agnes LaStrange sat in the back of the classroom.

All the LaStrange children sat at the back. Starting with the first day of school in the first grade and continuing on through sixth or seventh, when most LaStranges stopped coming entirely, the back row was left empty by the other children. That there would be at least one LaStrange, and possibly more, per class was a given; that they would beat up any child who sat in the back row without being invited was part of Esperance oral tradition.

From Joelle's first day of school onward, Agnes La-Strange occupied the third seat from the left in the last row. Joelle sat in the second row from the front, fourth seat from the left. When the teacher handed out worksheets, they were passed back from the first child in each row to the last; whenever Joelle twisted around to hand the papers to Lennie Devereaux, who sat directly behind her (and was secretly sweet on her from first grade on, though no one had ever suspected it), she saw Agnes in the back row, making terrible faces at her.

As far as Joelle could tell, Agnes never made faces at anyone else, just her. At first, Joelle assumed she was being threatened. For several days she hung around the school grounds waiting for Daniel in order to walk home with him. After a week or so, however, she realized Agnes La-Strange took absolutely no notice of her outside the class-room, and she stopped worrying.

So it went through first grade and second, through third, fourth, and fifth, Joelle always in the second row and Agnes in the last. They never spoke to each other; Agnes had innu-merable brothers and sisters in school, and during recesses she generally disappeared into a frenzy of recreating La-Stranges in one corner of the schoolyard. Joelle was com-pletely absorbed in Desiree, and Desiree did not care to play with other children, so they stayed mostly to themselves.

Joelle walked past the LaStrange trailer often, and often saw Agnes out front with the other children, engaged in their never-ending games. Once or twice, when she was still in first grade, Joelle had waved when she passed, but Agnes never gave any sign of recognizing her, so after a while Joelle stopped waving. The next day in school, though, she would turn around and Agnes would grimace and contort her face once again.

Gradually, she came to think of Agnes as a friend, of sorts. She missed her during the summers when school was not in session, and was always anxious the first day of school, won-dering if Agnes would be in the same class again, or if by some horrible mischance she had been spirited away, out of the school, out of Esperance, out of Joelle's life.

But Agnes was always there.

"I hate her!" Desiree whispered in Joelle's ear the first day of school, every year. "She's dirty and strange. Don't talk to her!"

So Joelle didn't.

Agnes unwound the scarf from around her mouth and neck, then from around her jaw, ears, and the crown of her head. It had been a white scarf once, made from some kind of synthetic knit, but it was grayish yellow now. Once completely unwound, the scarf dropped limply across her shoulders, revealing springy, reddish hair that stood out like an aura all around Agnes's head.

"You think you could fit me in?" she asked. "I got kind of a special occasion this evening and I want to look my best."

Joelle hesitated. She didn't want to do Agnes's hair, and she supposed Shirley wouldn't have anything better to do once she'd finished Meredith Parrish's dye job. On the other hand, Joelle was running out reasons to keep her at the salon.

"I suppose I could do it," she said finally. "If that's okay with you."

Agnes nodded and started unbuttoning her coat. It was an old khaki-green overcoat that had belonged to her Uncle Pete. When he died, two years before, it had come to her.

"I was sorry to hear about your brother," Agnes said, but Joelle was already asking her to hold up her hair in back so she could clip the apron round her neck.

"Right over here," Joelle said, pointing to the washing sink in the styling room. Meredith Parrish was sitting under the dryer with her head wrapped in a plastic cap; blood-colored dye smeared the edge of her hairline. She looked up as Joelle shepherded Agnes through the door.

"Look here!" she said, waving *Hollywood Screen* at Joelle. "Ain't that woman there the spittin' image of your Aunt Allie?"

Joelle nodded without looking and adjusted the taps until the strength and warmth of the gushing water were just right. Agnes was lying back in the chair, her head hanging over the sink and her pale eyes fixed on a point just over Joelle's shoulder. Her thick fox-colored hair sprang out from her skull; not even wetting it could subdue the strength in it.

It felt strange to stand like this, Joelle thought, her hands sunk deep into Agnes's hair: surprisingly soft, looking like steel wool; she remembered the feel of it, though, from many years before. Their faces were just a foot or so apart. She massaged the shampoo into Agnes's scalp as she had done for a thousand other shampoos, yet this felt different. Her hands moved caressingly through Agnes's hair, like a lover's might, investing the act with deeper, more intimate meaning. She felt embarrassed by the tenderness in her hands and tried adopting a brisker, more businesslike manner.

Agnes's eyes flickered up at her as Joelle's hands rubbed harder at her scalp, then returned to the spot on the ceiling.

"Creme rinse?" Joelle asked. Agnes nodded. Joelle squirted a glob of thick, white, apple-scented conditioner into the palm of her hand and rubbed it through the thick red hair. She turned the hose back on and began rinsing, running her fingers through Agnes's hair from forehead to the nape of her neck while the water streamed over her hand, through strands of hair that had turned a deeper, burnished orange from the wetting.

When the creme rinse was completely out, Joelle wrapped a rough white towel around Agnes's head and gently patted the hair dry.

"Over there," she said, jerking her head towards one of the two styling chairs near the dryer.

Agnes got up with heavy grace and moved silently towards the chair. She was a big woman, tall, big-boned; when she walked, she reminded Joelle of a thoroughbred draft horse, of an elk or one of those Spanish bulls, she moved with such grace, power, and deliberation.

Agnes sank into the chair. Her eyes met Joelle's for the first time in the mirror.

"Tomorrow is Valentine's Day," she said. "I want to look special."

On Valentine's Day, the year she turned twelve, Joelle received two valentines: one from Lennie Devereaux, though she never knew it was him, since he was too shy to sign it, and one from Agnes LaStrange. The first was store-bought: heart-shaped with lace all around the edges and a message written in curly writing inside. The sender had marked it only with three X's (written with his left hand, if she only knew it, to keep her from recognizing his writing).

The other was cut out from a piece of red construction paper and had "Be Mine" inexpertly traced in Elmer's Glue and glitter across the center of the slightly lopsided heart. This one was also unsigned, but Joelle knew immediately who'd sent it; everything about it screamed "LaStrange!" She was not surprised Agnes had sent her a valentine; she was absurdly happy Agnes obviously felt the same tenuous bond of friendship Joelle had come to believe in over the years.

The valentine had been pushed into her desk at school, the pointed tip of the heart poking out from beneath the desktop. Desiree had seen it first, guessing as quick as Joelle who'd sent it.

"Throw it out!" she whispered in Joelle's ear during attendence. "We don't want her!"

But Joelle wouldn't. Instead, she took it home and put it in the corner of her mirror, where it remained for many months. That afternoon, Agnes was loitering in the hallway outside the lunchroom door when Joelle came out.

"Hey, Joelle," Agnes said.

"Hey, Agnes."

They didn't speak again until after Easter vacation.

Agnes wanted a permanent.

"Not real tight curls," she told Joelle. "Just wavy-like."

Joelle was using the biggest curlers. She started at the top of Agnes's head, carefully separated a hank of hair from the rest, slipped the tissue round it, and began rolling it expertly—not too tight, but tight enough to ensure a good curl—to the crown of her head, where she snapped the pin into place. The roller hung there, baby-blue, wrapped in wet burnished-orange hair, like a pig-in-a-blanket. Another one rolled up to join it, then another, until Agnes had a row of fat, sausage-shaped rollers running across the top of her head from one ear to the other. Joelle chose slightly smaller ones for the back and separated the remaining hair into three equal sections.

Neither of them had spoken through most of the operation, but now Agnes said:

"You remember that carnival come through here last summer?"

Around the Fourth of July a troupe of jugglers and acrobats down from Boston had set up in the parking lot behind the Bucket o' Bubbles laundromat for a few days. A bunch of youngish kids, she remembered, with funny, spiky haircuts and glitzy costumes, who juggled flaming torches and swords, Indian clubs and balls. They'd had a contortionist, too, who bent himself into fantastic positions and played piccolo at the same time. After each performance, they'd passed a hat around. People in Esperance had been glad enough to watch, but were less forthcoming with their money, probably why the troupe had left after only a few days.

Daniel and Emily had been up while the troupe was in

town; she remembered Emily saying she'd seen them before in Harvard Square.

"They go to Florida in the winters," she'd said. "Or maybe it's California."

"Yeah, I remember," Joelle said as she finished setting the first section of hair.

"Remember the guy with the long hair and the tattoo on his back? Remember?"

Joelle didn't but she nodded anyway.

"He's here again," Agnes told her. "I'm goin' away with him tonight."

Joelle raised her eyes, looked at Agnes in the mirror. Agnes's reflection smiled at her, and Joelle knew Agnes had come to the salon on purpose that day, had come with the intention of getting her hair done by Joelle, had come especially to tell her this piece of news.

"Hollywood?" Joelle asked, even though she knew the answer.

Agnes nodded, the smile widening a fraction of an inch. Joelle caught a sharp, angry movement out of the corner of her eye, in the place just out of sight where she knew Desiree was standing. For a moment, she thought Desiree was going to pick up the metal tray of curlers and bring it crashing down on Agnes's head.

Agnes had not forgotten the plan they'd made eleven years ago; apparently, Desiree hadn't either.

"Wow," Joelle said, and began rolling another lock of wet hair between her fingers.

When they got back to school after the week-long break at Easter, Agnes invited Joelle to sit in the back row with her. The significance was not lost on anyone in the sixth-grade class. Joelle was now Agnes's property, deserving of the rights and privileges that went with that position. She became an accepted member of the group of LaStrange children patrolling their territory at one end of the schoolyard; any remarks made in the locker room before or after gym concerning the livid scar that ran the length of her body were swiftly and painfully dealt with by Agnes herself, while any attempt to win her away from the LaStrange camp was met with immediate retribution by the entire clan.

"I hate her, I hate her!" Desiree whispered constantly in Joelle's ear. In those days, Desiree still stood face to face with Joelle, so she could see the hate in her eyes as well as hear it in her voice.

"We don't need her," Desiree whispered. "I hate her!"

"Give her a chance," Joelle pleaded. "She likes us."

"Dirty, dirty dirty!" Desiree hissed, but Joelle didn't listen.

She was in love. In love the way only twelve-year-old girls can love. She loved Agnes's bushy red hair and would have exchanged her own black eyes for Agnes's in a moment. She wanted desperately to live in a silver trailer as Agnes did, bring money to school and buy Hostess Ring-Dings for lunch as Agnes did, have sisters and brothers beyond count to fight like rats with, as Agnes did. Everything about her own life paled in comparison with Agnes's.

Her parents' reactions were mixed. Jeanette accepted the friendship philosophically; she, better than most, could understand the strange fascination that family could have for other people. Dennis was appalled. Even twenty years later, he still avoided going past the LaStrange place when he could. The sight of that silver trailer perched precariously on its cinder-block foundation reminded him of the fire, of Maury LaStrange facedown in a pile of rotting cabbage leaves, of Mike LaStrange's shattered body entwined around the twisted metal of his motorcycle. Every time he went by, he smelled the LaStrange odor in his nostrils again, and remembered it clinging to Jeanette's skin. He began to imagine it on Joelle, as well.

But love made her reckless and defiant. She ignored Desiree's whispered venom, her mother's silence, and her father's revulsion whenever Agnes's name came up. They walked to and from school together, spent every afternoon and every weekend night at the LaStrange trailer. Joelle was never sure exactly which of the several adults permanently positioned around the table in the kitchen playing cards and drinking Budweiser were Agnes's parents, and Agnes never enlightened her. Likewise, she never sorted out cousins from siblings in the whooping tribe of LaStrange children in the front yard. It didn't matter, though; they accepted her and her adoration of Agnes was unhindered, unobstructed, unquestioned by any of them.

Joelle loved sleeping over at Agnes's. At night, the trailer underwent an amazing transformation as unremarkable fixtures ceased their daytime functions and became instead places to sleep. The kitchen table sank down to meet the cushioned benches flanking it and metamorphosed into a double bed where six LaStrange children could fit snugly, if not comfortably. Another trundle bed slid out from beneath that one, sleeping an additional four people. The kitchen counters, a love seat in the living room, a fold-out couch, and a second trundle bed under the one in the bedroom accommodated nearly everyone who lived in the trailer; sleeping bags on the floor took care of any overflow. Joelle loved the companionship, the security of bodies wedged against her own, the warm, fetid smell of shared bedding. It reminded her a little of when she'd been small and crept into Daniel's bed.

The nicest part about sleeping over, Joelle thought, was the time after the lights were out when she and Agnes lay rolled against each other, the comforting sound of other people breathing all around them filling the darkness. Desiree hated the closeness and refused to lie in the bed next to Joelle and Agnes; she prowled, instead, outside the trailer. Occasionally Joelle heard her whispering through the windows: "I hate her! I hate her!"

But Agnes's voice was louder. Agnes's mouth was right up close to her ear, and it was easy to ignore Desiree, listen to Agnes instead. In the dark, in the LaStrange trailer, Agnes first told Joelle about her secret plans to go west, to Hollywood.

"My grandpa Maury nearly made it once," she told Joelle one night, her mouth so close Joelle could feel Agnes's breath condense in a cool vapor along the shell of her ear.

"He was gonna go out there an' buy some land and start another dump. He was gonna call it 'Garbage of the Stars.' He figured he'd make a bundle."

"How?" Joelle asked, fascinated by this original entrepreneurial move on the part of the now legendary Maury LaStrange.

"He was gonna sell stuff to tourists. Stuff like John Wayne's tuna cans and Shirley MacLaine's frozen-fish-sticks containers. He was gonna have special trucks divided so the stars' garbage wouldn't get all mixed up. My grandpa wanted everything to be genuine, authentic star trash."

"How come he didn't go?" Joelle asked.

She could feel Agnes shrug in the darkness.

"Dunno," she said. "I'm sure gonna go, though."

"D'you want to collect Garbage of the Stars?" Joelle asked.

"Nope," Agnes said. "I'm gonna be an extra."

"Extra what?"

"A movie extra, dummy! One of those people in crowd scenes."

They lay together after that, neither one wanting to sleep,

neither having anything in particular to say. They just lay
there, enjoying being awake when others were asleep.

Finally Agnes whispered, "This'll be my last year at
school, most likely."

"Why?" Joelle asked, despair gripping her heart. "Don't
you want to graduate?"

"What for?" Agnes demanded. "You don't need anything they teach past sixth grade."

Agnes's hand crept out from beneath the covers and
groped across the space between them until she found Joelle's. She squeezed her fingers affectionately.

"I'm tired," she said, rolling over so her arm lay lightly
across Joelle's chest and her body was pressed all along Joelle's.

"Don't worry," she whispered. "I'll still be around. For a
little while, anyway."

When Joelle combed out Agnes's hair, it swooped and
spiraled from the crown of her head to her shoulder in
elegant waves, its natural, springy frizziness ruthlessly op-
pressed by chemicals. Joelle met Agnes's eyes in the mirror
and saw satisfaction there.

"I've been saving my money for almost seven years,"
Agnes whispered.

Seven years of working at the True Value hardware store
weekdays, behind the bar at Ernie's Tavern on Saturday
nights. Seven years to tame her wild hair, picturing in her
mind, time and again, how it would be when she left Esperance forever.

"You wanted to come with me, once," Agnes reminded
Joelle. "You remember that?"

Of course she remembered. For almost the whole summer
between grammar school and junior high, she and Agnes had
plotted their escape from Esperance, their future success in

Hollywood. Then they'd had their unfortunate falling-out and the dream, as well as the friendship, had been broken. She wrapped a lock of fox-red hair around her forefinger and twisted it into place behind Agnes's ear.

"You still can," Agnes said. "If you want, you can still come with me."

Behind them, Joelle heard Desiree exhale sharply, as though she'd been punched in the stomach, as though she could make her breath sharp as a scissor blade, aim it at both her and Agnes, stab them with the force of her exhalation.

Agnes was still watching her in the mirror.

"You worried about her?" Agnes asked. "Don't worry about that. If you want to come, we can take care of her."

Agnes's eyes weren't on Joelle anymore; she was staring straight at Desiree, instead, and she was smiling.

Agnes was the only person Joelle ever told about Desiree. She told her one night as they lay comfortingly crushed between the bodies of various LaStrange children in the silver trailer. She told her, her mouth up close against Agnes's ear, darkness muffling the sound of her voice so Desiree herself, just outside the window jealously straining to hear every word, could not catch what she said.

When she had finished her whispered confession, Agnes said:

"She must get awful cold standing outside on nights like this. Why don't you just tell her to come in?"

"She won't," Joelle said. "She doesn't like you."

"Well, I don't like her, either," Agnes said. "Let me feel your scar."

Agnes's hand snaked up under Joelle's T-shirt, palm against her collarbone. Slowly, the hand moved down between her small breasts and across her stomach until it stopped at the elastic waistband of her underpants. It hesitated there for a second, then dipped just beneath the elastic to find the end of the scar at the top of her pubic bone. Where Agnes's hand passed Joelle felt a warm glow. It rested, tucked confidingly beneath the waistband of her underpants; Joelle felt a twinge that faded when Agnes took her hand back.

"You're my friend, now," Agnes said. "You tell her that. If she doesn't like it, she can leave us alone."

But she wouldn't leave them alone. She was always there, always spying on them, whispering hateful things in Joelle's ear. It was that summer, the last summer of the friendship with Agnes, that Desiree started standing just behind Joelle, just out of sight.

Agnes couldn't see her, but she knew she was there. She woke up often enough in the night with a bloody nose from the slap of an invisible hand. She had red pinch marks on her upper arms, bruises from vicious, unseen kicks on her legs; she knew well enough who had given them to her. Finally, Agnes demanded Joelle choose between them. It was then that Desiree played her card.

"I'll tell about the dead man," she threatened. "They'll put Daniel in jail forever if I tell."

After that, there really wasn't any choice to be made. Joelle and Agnes didn't speak for eleven years.

After Agnes left, Joelle put the rollers and pins back into their tray slowly, one by one, stacking them carefully one row on top of another, making sure the rollers were all exactly even at the ends. There was a pile of crumpled papers on the counter. She scooped those up in her hand and crushed them before tossing them into the waste can.

When she and Agnes met by accident, in the general store or on the street, they looked at each other with strangers' eyes, passing without a word. Over the years, Joelle had forgotten the feel of Agnes's hair, the coarse, large-pored texture of her skin, the hoarse timbre of her voice. Agnes LaStrange became just another of the tawny-haired, pale-eyed tribe occupying the silver trailer on the East-West Road.

Touching her brought Agnes back to life for her. She had twined the thick burnt-orange hair around her fingers, and suddenly love was in her hands again. She had brushed the hair up off of Agnes's neck, aware as she did so how much she had missed her.

They had gone everywhere hand in hand, arm in arm; they had slept with their bodies wound tightly around each other; it was the smell of Agnes's skin, the feel of that hair against her cheek or shoulder, Joelle had woken up to more often than not during that year. Just one touch and Joelle was twelve again; watching Agnes walk out of the shop, the sound of her boots on the stairs, the door creaking shut behind her, was a parting as painful as the first.

She'd said, "You can come with me if you want."

Joelle sorted carefully through the perm rollers as though the fate of the world depended on each roller being placed end to end exactly with other rollers of the same size and color: medium pink with medium pink, small mauve with small mauve—careful! A medium pink crept in with a large pink; the world trembled on the brink of disaster.

"You can come with me."

She could feel Desiree's breath on the back of her neck and her hands, delicate as moth wings, hovering over her shoulders.

"What about me?" Desiree whispered.

Chapter

18

T he funeral was tomorrow, but Buddy couldn't know that.

He lay on the daybed in the parlor while the world re-formed itself with every blink of his eyes. The room was cold, but he felt warm enough under the blankets. The room was dark at first, gradually becoming lighter as the sun rose and the day wore on. Shapes and shadows that had filled the room at dawn in subtle shades of gray emerged out of the gloom and became themselves. While Buddy looked on, each object was created anew, and lived the span of its entire life between blinks of his eyes. Ghosts crowded round him; a man tumbled, tumbled head over heels, the sun glinting in fox-red hair.

Buddy blinked. He looked into the ghost eyes of the man in khaki, saw the yellow-dress-girl sprawled in the dust,

heard the man's voice whisper, "Nettie, Nettie," saw the
rock coming down to smash his face. Buddy blinked. The
baby at the foot of his bed whispered, "I'm cold, I'm cold."

The morning before the funeral passed; the afternoon
wound down into evening; night swallowed up the last
threads of daylight while Buddy lay calm at the center of
things.

Jeanette went down to the main house after Dennis and
Joelle left. It hadn't snowed much since the thaw, but it had
been cold; the path down the face of the ridge, across the
apple orchard, was pocked with boot prints, iced over and
preserved in the snow like fossils.

She chose her footing carefully; she was nearly fifty now,
fifty come August, but her hair was still blue-black as when
she was eighteen, her skin still smooth and wheat-colored.
She had thrown on an old jacket of Dennis's and wrapped a
wool muffler around her head; she looked Biblical, coming
slowly down the ridge path.

As she walked, she thought about the apple trees in the
orchard below; their branches were naked now, but in a few
months the green shoots would appear, then the blossoms,
then the apples. Twelve years ago, Jeanette had started making cider from those apples and selling it locally. It had
proved so popular she was soon selling it in Bennington and
Brattleboro, as well.

She thought about the meadow she was passing through,
how dead and forlorn it looked beneath its patchy cover of
crusted snow, broken skeletal bones of shrubs and deadwood
thrusting through here and there; a forgotten graveyard. For
a few weeks in April, she thought, this will be a sea of mud.
Then it will suddenly dry and blossom; by July Rich will be
out here with his mower cutting hay.

She thought about the maple trees dotting the ridge,

climbing up the back of the mountain behind her house. It was almost time to tap them, she thought. Soon buckets would hang from them and every few days they'd go out to collect the sap. Dennis would take it down to the sugarhouse behind the barn and the smell of boiling sugar would hang in the air for days.

She thought about the hot summer coming up, the blazing foliage after it setting the mountains aflame with changing leaves. She imagined the smell of woodsmoke, the crack of rifles as hunting season progressed. She thought about another winter when the land lay deathlike beneath its cold shroud.

Finally, she thought about Daniel. He'd been born at the beginning of summer and died in the deadest part of winter.

Jeanette didn't think she believed in God. When her brother Tommy had been reported MIA in Korea, when the baby lying in the Dufore plot had died, when her father fell into a vat at the paper mill and died two years after she was married, when her mother succumbed to the tumor grown unchecked in her womb, and now, when her only son lay dead in the parlor of the main house, Jeanette took no comfort from promises of God-love or eternal life for any of them.

She found peace, instead, in absolute certainty that apple trees would blossom again in the spring, that there would always be hay in the fields, that maple trees would go from green to gold to bare branches and back to green again. Surely, she thought, there must be a place in all that for us.

Surely we are a part of it, too.

Gran Marie was in the sitting room when Jeanette got there. Flowers were everywhere: huge bouquets and wreaths of lilies filled the room with the sick-sweet smell of death. Daylight at last. Gran Marie stretched in her chair; no need to sit with the dead during the day, only at night, when they became lonely and required company from the living. She rose stiffly to her feet. The light through the window had settled itself comfortable as an old cat on top of the coffin; the oak glowed richly, and Gran Marie thought what a lovely piece of furniture that wood might have made.

She stood, palms flat against the lid of the coffin, and shifted her weight so she was leaning against it. Anne came in, followed by Jeanette with a bowl in her hand.

"Macaroni salad," she said.

"I was just thinking what a good table this could've made," Gran Marie said.

"Maybe we should just lay out the buffet on the coffin," Jeanette said, setting the bowl down in the exact center. They stood back, admiring the effect of the white ceramic bowl, its glistening mound of shell-shaped macaroni and diced celery coated with mayonnaise, against the dark glow of wood. The sight was so exquisitely funny, so absurdly solemn and shrinelike, they laughed, and, having started, couldn't stop until tears poured down their faces.

Finally Anne Dufore managed to get hold of herself and the laughter died out; the three women stood wiping their streaming eyes, embarrassed, unsure of what to say next.

"Where's Mary?" Jeanette asked at last.

"Upstairs, same as usual," Anne told her. "I made her promise she'd come to the wake, but you know Mary."

Mary Dufore, Ab's widow, had not aged well.

She'd been a fair, pretty woman when Ab married her, full-figured and inclined to put on weight. While Ab lived, she had tried first one diet, then another: nothing but carrots and grapefruit for several weeks one time, another time a mysterious greenish powder that she dissolved in water and drank. After Ab died, Mary gave in to her inclinations; now, almost thirty years after her husband leaped to his death from the cliff behind the paper mill, Mary was quite fat and content to remain so.

She had stayed up at the cabin on the ridge for a while after Ab died, but when Dennis announced he and Jeanette were marrying, it was Mary's idea to give up the cabin to them, and Anne's idea she move into the farmhouse.

She occupied Dennis's old room, filling it with objects that reminded her of the days when she was a wife, not a widow. She had brought Ab's favorite lounge chair down to the big house with her. It sat in the room, which was too small for it, next to the window; sometimes when the afternoon light shone through Mary imagined she could see faint grease marks where Ab's head had rested against the back every night of their life together. Next to it was a small gate-legged table with a large photograph of the two of them, taken in front of the motel in Burlington where they'd spent their honeymoon. It wasn't a very good photograph, really; they'd asked the desk clerk to take it, and he'd managed to cut off the top of Ab's head. It was a little blurred, too, but it was the only one she had.

Ab had not written any letters, during or after their courtship; there'd been no need, since they'd lived less than three miles apart. Sometimes Mary wished Ab had gone to war after all; then there would have been some reason for him to write and leave her something more to remember him by.

For a few weeks after the funeral, it was the lack of letters that kept Mary going. She was so damned angry with Ab for *not* joining the army, getting sent overseas, and writing tender love letters to her before he was killed in action. When the anger wilted, only regret was left; an overstuffed chair, a blurred photograph, and his clothes were all she had of him.

She wished she'd saved the two toes he'd shot off his left foot, so shortly before he climbed the tree overlooking Crockett's Brook. She could have put them in a mayonnaise jar filled with rubbing alcohol and kept them on the mantelpiece next to the photograph. You just never know, she thought, what's really important.

Eventually, she'd written a few letters herself, the kind of letters Ab might have written if there'd been any reason to. For almost a year, she spent every Sunday night in the bedroom they'd shared writing herself a letter which she then signed, "Your loving husband, Abner."

By the time she moved into the big house, towards the middle of 1957, she had quite a stack of them, neatly bound in red ribbon.

The day before her great-nephew Daniel was to be buried, Mary Dufore sat in her room, the pile of love letters in her massive lap, and read through them, one by one. It was almost thirty years since the last one was written; over time Mary had come to believe Ab really had sent them himself.

"Dear Mary," one said.

"How are you? I'm pretty fit. I had a dream about you last night. You were wearing that real pretty blue dress that I liked so much last Fourth of July, and your hair was all piled up on top of your head. You looked real pretty and I asked you to dance and we did. It was a nice dream.

"I sure feel lucky you married me. . . ."

The clock in the sitting room downstairs chimed the quarter hour. Mary put the letter down and sighed. It was almost time to go down.

She put Ab's letter back into its yellowed envelope, then swept all the envelopes in her lap into a neat pile, tamping them all around till they were even before she slipped the ribbon around them. She placed the stack carefully on the gate-legged table, then pulled herself out of the rocking chair, pushing up hard with both arms as she rocked forward and propelled her massive bulk out of the chair. Even with the forward motion of the chair to help her, it took two or three tries before the chair had sufficient force behind it to throw her out. Finally, she felt her buttocks leave the seat; with a grunt she thrust up and out with her arms and staggered to her feet, with short, drunken steps. She came to a full stop a few feet from the wildly rocking chair, and stood with her palms pressed flat on the top of the bureau as she leaned heavily against it and struggled to catch her breath.

Her enormous body nearly filled the large mirror that hung between two posts on the back of the dresser. When her breathing became steadier, she straightened a little and automatically patted her hair as she caught sight of herself in the glass. She saw a big woman there, a strong woman, capable of accomplishing anything. Her fair hair had faded to a whitish yellow, which her great-niece Joelle had arranged in neat permed waves, cresting back from her forehead and rolling serenely down the back of her head. A good girl, Joelle, Mary thought; she came down to the big house once a week and did her great-aunt's hair right here in this very bedroom. She patted at an unruly lock of hair again, smiled at her reflection. Then she thought of Daniel, and tears welled up in her eyes. So sad, she told herself, so sad and so unnecessary. And his poor little wife—what was her name? Had he written her any letters? she wondered. Left anything behind to be of comfort to her?

Mary shook her head sadly and turned to the business of heating tea water on the hot plate in her room. She pulled a box of vanilla wafers (her favorites) out of the bookshelf and put two handfuls of the pale yellow cookies on a plate. Then she set out her cup and filled her silver tea ball with the spice tea she liked so well. When everything was ready, she stood in front of the window drinking tea and nibbling cookies; she wouldn't sit down, since it only meant getting up again to go downstairs.

She wondered what kind of food they'd have at the wake.

In the kitchen, Dennis sat quietly at the table, remembering. He felt the light, warm pressure of Jeanette's hand on his shoulder. His own hand fumbled to cover hers. His hands seemed less sure of themselves these days—was he getting old? He hadn't thought so until just a few days ago. His fingers closed quickly, a little desperately, around hers. He felt the wedding ring on her third finger and rubbed it gently under his thumb.

"I was thinking about deer season," he told her.

Remembering the year they'd gone up the ridge behind the cabin, Dennis with a rifle and Daniel, who was eight, carrying a sack containing a box of cartridges, some sandwiches, and a thermos of hot, sweet, milky coffee. It was near the end of the season; the first, vibrant blaze of fall color was subsiding; trees dropped their leaves and covered the plain brown earth in temporary glory. They scuffed through sheaves of gold and red, almost as brilliant themselves in their orange vests and caps.

("The deer'll see us, Pop," Daniel had complained.)

"When are we gonna shoot a deer, Pop?"

They'd been climbing the ridge for an hour or more when Daniel asked; it felt like all day, to him.

"Gotta find one first," Dennis said, wondering again if the weight of the cartridges and thermos was enough to keep the boy anchored (he was counting on the trees to act as a windbreak) or if he should give Daniel one of the rocks in his own pocket, as well.

The sun was beginning to dip just below the crest of the mountains at their backs. Dusk was the best time to find deer; the time they felt safest, hungriest. Gradually, the shadows lengthened under the trees, the leaves gave up their glowing fire. The woods became muted and the sound of their feet was loud in their ears. Dennis loved the woods at this time of day, in this season: the faint smell of smoke and evergreen, air so crisp and thin it stung your lungs a little when you breathed. He liked the crunch of drying leaves under his boots, the pleasant tiredness in his legs as he climbed. He and Jeanette had come up here often, in the beginning, to make love or just be together.

He began to feel glad they had come; he was almost sure they would find no deer. In a half an hour or so, they could admit defeat with honor and return home after a pleasant walk together in the woods in autumn.

Then Daniel said, "Deer!"

There were three of them, up ahead. A buck and two does emerged from the shadow of the trees into a tiny clearing, upwind from the man and boy.

"Shoot him, Pop!" Daniel breathed.

Dennis didn't like hunting. There had been yearly expeditions when he'd been a boy: Ab and Rich, Dennis, Bobby, and sometimes the Woodie men. They went out at dawn, hunting until it became too dark to see. The year Ab died, the hunting parties stopped, and Dennis had been secretly relieved.

"Pop!" Daniel whispered, a little louder. "They're gonna get away!"

Reluctantly, Dennis raised the gun to his shoulder and looked down the sight. He had no stomach for this kind of killing. Slaughtering a pig he'd raised from a suckling was one thing; the pig had been bred and reared for that sole purpose, and perhaps both of them knew that. When the time came, he slaughtered it without compunction but also without pleasure in the act.

Now, he was about to end this deer's life, not because he

wanted its meat (though, of course, they would eat venison for weeks to come) but for the pleasure of killing it.

Daniel was becoming frantic.

"Shoot it, Pop! Shoot it now!"

This was his first hunting trip. He'd been after Dennis to take him since the beginning of the season, when Paul Devereaux's boy had come to school with a deer's tail and a proud story about watching his dad shoot it on the first day.

Dennis drew careful aim at the buck's chest and slowly began squeezing the trigger, all the while praying a sudden change in the wind, some unexpected sound, would frighten the trio off.

The three continued to graze in peace. *"Kill it,* Pop!"

The buck looked up just as Dennis squeezed the trigger. For a millisecond before the bullet exploded inside its chest, the two looked at each other. The crack of the shot was followed by a burst of motion: the buck dropping gracelessly to the ground, the does sending up a frantic spray of leaves as they shot back into shadow, a blur of panicked birds darting en masse from tree to tree. Then, silence.

"You *got* him, Pop!" Daniel exulted.

"C'mon," Dennis said. "Take a look at him."

The deer's eyes were still open, but the warmth and sweetness had gone out of them; the soft, ridiculously long fringe of dark lashes made their blank stare grotesque. Its white chest was torn and blood matted the soft fur.

Daniel stopped about ten feet from the body.

"C'mon, Danny," Dennis said. "Come and look at it now."

Daniel came closer. Almost any day during the year you could see a deer standing by the side of the road, or crossing the yard at the back of your house. He'd seen them in fields as he walked down the East-West Road, surprised them on the path as he cut through the apple orchard on his way to the main house. Ever since he could remember, he'd wanted to touch one.

He put his hand out and touched the deer's head. There was a trickle of blood at the corners of its mouth, and his hand came away red.

"Help me get a rope round its legs, Dan," Dennis said. "We'll hang it in a tree until we can get some help bringing it down the ridge."

It was horrible, lifting the hind legs so his father could get the loop of rope round them. It was horrible, watching the body drag across the ground as his father strained to hoist it up; once he lost his grip and the deer's body fell against the earth with a dull thud.

When it was finally done, Daniel's eyes were burning, his sight so blurred it seemed the path of flattened leaves where the deer's body had traveled were stained red; by blood or the season, he was never sure.

In the kitchen, Dennis held his wife's hand tight, stroking, stroking the band of gold around her finger.

"I never would've figured he'd use a gun," he said.

She squeezed her fingers around his, stood very still, very quiet, for a long, long moment. Then she said:

"Almost five o'clock. Joelle should be coming home soon."

"I'll get her," he said.

Dennis got into the pickup truck and headed back to Esperance. He'd expected Joelle to call, but she hadn't. It was a bitter night, and he didn't like to think of her coming along the unlit East-West Road in the dark; he remembered how close he'd come to being run over there by a fire truck late one summer's night many years before.

He drove slowly over the Crockett's Brook bridge past the LaStrange property. He didn't see his daughter; she had

drawn back into the shadow of bushes and rusted car bodies
that lined the road at the bottom of the knoll where the
trailer perched. His headlights swept the ground four feet
from where she stood and continued on down the road
towards Clark Hill.

When he got to the main road he turned towards town,
slowing down every time he passed a pedestrian coming up
the hill—not often, given the weather—until he reached the
town common and saw the darkened, staring windows of
the salon over Ernie's Tavern.

He let the truck idle while he stared unseeingly through
the frosted windshield and wondered where his daughter
might have got to.

Almost anything might have happened to her. She could
have been hit by a car as she walked up the Clark Hill Road
in the dark, kidnapped by some sex-crazed pervert from out
of state. She might have had a brain seizure and dropped
down dead in the snow; a good, sharp wind might have
lifted her right off the ground, dashing her against a tree
trunk or the mountain face.

When his children were small, Dennis had sewn rocks
into the lining of their jackets, put bricks into their book
bags, insisted they wear sturdy shoes and wind-resistant
clothing. He'd made sure they came home before dark,
warned them against diving into water they'd never swum
in before, and taught them never, never to play with
matches. In spite of it all, Daniel was dead.

For no reason in particular, Dennis put the truck in gear
and drove down the road until he reached his cousin
Bobby's old house. He pulled into the driveway, overgrown
and rutted in the summer, unplowed in the winter. He shut
the engine off and sat there in the cab of his pickup truck,
warmth gradually seeping out and cold creeping in, sliding
itself up between the layers of his clothing to lay itself flat

against his skin. He sat staring at the spot where the bomb shelter had been, thought about Daniel and Joelle, his wife Jeanette and Maury LaStrange, his sister and his brother-in-law and his idiot nephew Buddy. He thought about Bobby Dufore and the bomb shelter. He sat there for a long time thinking, until the windows were iced over with his breath and the cold February night had chilled his bones.

Chapter
19

In the fall of 1959, ten years before Emily's mother rented a house in Esperance for the summer, Bobby Dufore finished the bomb shelter in his backyard. Then he, Alice, their three children, and Bobby's mother disappeared down into it once and for all.

"Don't know how long we'll be," Bobby told his cousin Rich on his last day above ground. "I expect that meteor'll strike most anytime now, so it mightn't be long at all."

He shook his cousin's hand and said, "Take care of the house for me."

Then he led his unhappy family down the rickety ladder into the cellar and dragged the lead-reinforced manhole cover over the opening behind them.

For a while, people talked about Bobby and his bomb shelter. There were reports of lights going on late at night in the back of the house, the shadow of a man's body against the curtains. Folks swore they heard arguing voices rising up from the earth as they passed the Dufore house. For weeks after Bobby took his family into the shelter, betting was heavy on the probable date of their return; as the weeks turned into months, however, betting dropped off.

"This kind of craziness is to be expected from one of them Dufores," Arlene Devereaux said to her friend Babe Prescott, at the post office, one Saturday morning. "But why Alice Dufore doesn't take those children and leave, I'll never understand!"

"I hear he won't let her," Babe said. "Arnie says he got a shotgun and won't let none of 'em near the stairs. When he comes up at night, he locks the door behind him!"

Meanwhile, the house stood empty for a year, a year and a half, two years. Rich stopped by, now and then, to check the locks and cut the grass. Dennis reshingled the roof one spring. From time to time, one or the other would pound on the lead-reinforced manhole cover with a sturdy pipe, receiving a muffled thump in response, so they knew Bobby and his family were still alive down there.

Time passed, and there was still no sign of the meteor.

Time passed. Eventually people in Esperance almost forgot that Bob Dufore and his family were even there. The house stood empty—Bobby didn't want to rent it, in case the meteor should strike, accidentally killing innocent people. After a while Dennis came less and less often to mow the lawn, though he kept the roof in good repair.

Now and again, in later years, people thought they saw lights in the house late at night, as though someone were going through it with a flashlight. Indeed it was Bobby, who had laid in some additional supplies in the kitchen pantry against the off chance the meteor might take longer to find him than he had anticipated. His trips were infrequent, quick, always in the dead of night.

Then one day, the creamed corn ran out.

There was none left in the bomb shelter; when Bobby made an evening foray into the house, there was none there, either. Hash and creamed corn was a Tuesday-night ritual, like macaroni and cheese on Saturdays, for as long as he and Alice had been married. Now there was only one can of hash left, and the creamed corn was completely out.

Kids! Bobby thought, standing in the empty pantry, a sack drooping from his hand and the flashlight playing over dusty, empty shelves. Kids must have been getting in somehow, maybe through the windows in the cellar, and stealing the food. Probably fornicating on the beds as well, he thought, drinking hard liquor and smoking behind their parents' backs. But even as he thought it, he knew it wasn't true; the house had the abandoned, unused look of a museum display. Not a stick of furniture was out of place, and there were no footsteps in the grit coating the floor except his own.

He went out the way he'd come and climbed back down the steps into the shelter. Alice met him at the bottom of the ladder, the last can of hash in her hand.

"Where's the corn?" she asked.

A pale woman to start, Alice had, over the years, become even more pale, her skin taking on the translucent quality of pearl or abalone so she seemed to glow whitely in the dark. Her hair had thinned; her eyes seemed sunk into her skull and wider, as though lack of light in the bomb shelter had forced them to grow larger and larger in order to see.

They all had that quality, in fact. The boys were grown now—the eldest in his thirties while the youngest had just turned eighteen. They, too, had glistening, fish-belly skin and saucer eyes. Bobby looked at them as they gathered around him, their huge eyes fixed on the empty sack, their white, flabby arms dangling limp as string at their sides.

"All out," he said.

"Can't have hash without creamed corn, Bobby," Alice said. That, and cling peaches in heavy syrup, had been Tuesday supper for fifteen years. To have one without the other was unthinkable.

"Why don't we have macaroni and cheese, Alice," Bobby said.

"That's Saturday's dinner!" Alice said, scandalized.

"Well then, why don't we have the hash by itself," he said. "Just for tonight. We got cling peaches for dessert, and Dennis or Rich oughta be stoppin' by in a day or so—"

"Can't have hash without creamed corn," Alice insisted. Her lips were thin, her voice implacable.

"But Alice," Bobby pleaded.

She slammed the opened can of hash down on the counter and went to sit in the chair next to old Mrs. Dufore, who had become so white, with eyes so large, she had begun to resemble some monstrous blind larva curled by age and despair, living her last years underground in a corner of the room.

"I'm hungry, Pa," Marty, the eldest, said.

"Me too," the other boys whined.

Alice sat silent and thin-lipped in the chair. Old Mrs. Dufore also said nothing, but that was not unusual, for she had stopped talking entirely a year or two after they had begun living in the bomb shelter. Only cling peaches in heavy syrup got any kind of reaction from her—a faint smacking of the lips that let the rest of her family know she was still capable of appreciating the finer things.

The silence was considerable.

"All right," Bobby said finally. "I'll get some creamed corn."

He turned and started slowly back up the steps, his shoulders sagging a little at the thought of walking through the exposed streets of Esperance to the general store. It was not just the meteor that frightened him: he'd spent most of the fifteen years underground playing pinochle with his sons and listening to the radio; he'd heard about the sexual revolution and the drug problem. He'd heard about growing poverty, loss of faith, and violence in the streets. In fifteen years he had not gone further from this safe little cave than the back door of his own house, ten yards away; he wondered if there would be violence in Esperance's streets now.

At the top of the ladder, he pushed back the heavy manhole cover and climbed out, then shoved the lid back into place. For a moment he stood sniffing the night air and getting his bearings. It was a quiet early-autumn evening; the street seemed deserted. With short, hesitant steps he started down the driveway now foreign to him as the moon, and stopped again when he reached the shoulder of the road. Fearfully he looked up and down; no sign of youth gangs. The general store was a quarter of a mile; he hadn't walked a quarter of a mile in fifteen years, he realized. Pins and needles shot through his legs, making them weak and rubbery.

His heart pounded uncomfortably in his chest; for a moment he thought he might have a heart attack, right there and then, and drop dead by the side of the road. Someone would find him, maybe, but would anyone recognize him after so much time? They'd take him to the hospital in Bennington, but no one there would know him, and he wasn't carrying any identification. He'd be buried in an unmarked grave while his family waited in the bomb shelter, staring at the lone can of hash, getting thinner and thinner, weaker and weaker.

The weakness passed off.

"Can't have hash without creamed corn," Bobby told himself, and started walking.

Paul Delagarde's youngest daughter, Cher, was working the cash register when Bobby reached the general store. It wa seven minutes to nine when he walked through the door, and she was ready to close out the register. She'd made plans to meet Jimmy Boyd at Ernie's when he got off at the paper mill at nine; now it looked like she'd be late. When Bobby asked if they had any creamed corn, she hunched one shoulder and pretended not to hear.

She didn't recognize him, of course; she'd only been a baby when he'd taken his family out of town life and didn't remember the only time she'd ever met him, a Labor Day picnic sixteen years before when Bobby had found her and his youngest boy examining each other's naked body under one of the picnic tables. He'd whacked them both once across the bottom and scrambled them back into their clothes. A year after that he took Alice, the boys, and his old mother down into the bomb shelter and never came up again.

"Got any creamed corn?" he asked her. "Del Monte creamed corn?"

She turned the radio up a little louder and looked very busy counting out the cash.

The lights in the store were very bright. Bobby had not seen such bright light for years. It hurt his eyes and confused him a little. He couldn't remember where old Paul Delagarde had kept things fifteen years before. He went hesitantly down one aisle and up the next, fingering half-forgotten products (marshmallow creme . . . blueberry jam . . . bottled salad dressing . . .), his eyes blinking rapidly in the blaze of fluorescent light, the riot of multicolored packaging, his finger blazing a trail over unfamiliar territory (sanitary minipads . . . disposable diapers . . . gourmet pop-corn . . .).

He got lost in the coffee and tea section, took a wrong turn at pet food, and found himself ascending a flight of stairs into a welter of dish detergents, floor waxes, and scrubbing brushes. It was a little after nine o'clock when he finally ran creamed corn to earth next to breakfast cereals, and picked up six cans. That would hold them till the next time Rich or Dennis stopped by and he could place a whole-sale order for a dozen cases or more.

He brought the six cans over to the register and set them down. He eyed the girl behind the counter with some un-easiness; she was a hard-eyed little thing, he thought, proba-bly one of them kids that hung around on corners and waited for trouble to find them. Probably a member of a gang.

"That'll be four seventy-six," the girl told him.

He flinched back a little from her hard, unfriendly eyes, stood blinking stupidly in the glare of fluorescent lights and the girl's impatient eyes, and wondered what to do.

"Four seventy-six," the girl repeated; he thought he heard violence in her voice.

"I'm afraid I don't have any money," he said. "I mean, I forgot it. At home."

The girl behind the counter just looked at him.

"Maybe you could wait and I'll run home and get some?" he asked. He thought he remembered where he'd put his old checkbook; he'd have Dennis or Rich make good on the check later.

"It's almost quarter past nine," the girl said. "I was sup-posed to close up fifteen minutes ago."

"It's not far," he pleaded. Under no circumstances could he return without that creamed corn.

Desperation inspired him.

"Maybe you could start a tab for me," he said. "The name's Dufore. Bob Dufore."

Her expression changed.

"You're kidding," she said. "You the guy that lives in the hole in the ground?"

"My cousin Rich Dufore will make sure you get the money," Bobby said.

"Wow," Cher said. "I've heard about you! So, what's it like? Don't you get bored down there?"

"I know Paul Delagarde," Bobby told her. "He still owns this store, doesn't he?"

"Sure," Cher said. "He's my pop. So, do you really eat worms and bugs and stuff like that?"

"Look," Bobby said, sweat breaking out on his forehead. "I gotta get back. Will you start a tab for me or not?"

"You really Bobby Dufore?" Cher demanded. When he nodded, she said:

"It's on me," and started loading the cans into a paper bag. "Wait'll I tell Jimmy about this!"

He could feel her eyes boring into his back as he stumbled out the screen door and down the steps of the general store. He felt her burning holes through his jacket and shirt with her bright, hard eyes, doing violence to him with her avid stare; he clumped thankfully down the wooden steps, out of the too-bright light, into the welcome black night. It was almost nine-thirty. They must be starving, he thought, clutching the paper sack full of canned corn to his chest like a trophy.

Just as his foot touched down on the bottom step, there was a brilliant flash in the sky, and for a moment Esperance was lit up as if by some giant strobe light. For a moment the whole of Main Street was picked out in high relief, houses, trees, and cars a weird, bluish white against the black night, all color washed out completely. Then something at the very heart of the flash seemed to plunge through the star-spattered sky; the next moment there was a resounding explosion and the earth rocked.

Time seemed to stand still for an eternity after the explosion. Bobby stood rooted to the steps of the general store while echoes of the blast reverberated in his ears and black spots swam across his eyeballs from the glare. Every door and window in the whole town seemed to open at the same time; people were coming out of their houses, sticking their heads out of windows, shouting questions about the explosion, about the light.

At last! Bobby thought, and started to walk very fast, the bag still clutched to his chest.

"Oh merciful God, at last!" he whispered, breaking into a shambling jog, the cans knocking back and forth against his breastbone as he ran.

A crowd had gathered on the sidewalk outside Ernie's Tavern; the guys at the paper mill were all standing around outside; Cher Delagarde had run out onto the porch. Everyone in town was watching an old gray-haired man still clutching half a dozen cans of creamed corn to his stomach run down the road.

At last. At last. At last. At last. He chanted in time to his pounding feet and the clinking cans. As he ran he planned the repairs he'd have to make on the house, assuming any of it was left. Even if there was nothing, he thought, even if the meteor had completely razed the building, it was worth it. He could build another house. He could build a house right over the bomb shelter; poverty and violence in the streets could never touch them. He'd keep them safe forever, he thought. He'd build a big, safe house right over the bomb shelter; any time the world looked like it might be getting too unsafe, they'd all go back down into their cozy cellar and pull the lid over behind them.

The cans of creamed corn knocking against his ribs reminded him of the secret war he and Alice had been fighting for fifteen years, what this trip had been all about; Alice had never accepted their subterranean exile and she'd found little ways to remind him of it, like refusing to eat hash without creamed corn. She'd have to admit he was right now. The cans banged hard against his chest and bruised him as he ran, victorious, through the night.

Things happen.

Sitting in his cold pickup truck on the bitter February night before his son was to be buried, Dennis stared out at the abandoned house and remembered how it had looked when he and Rich had driven down a little after ten o'clock (having received a phone call from Bill Prescott at the sheriff's office) and found a crowd of people blocking the driveway. Standing apart from them was a frail, gray-haired man, a bag clutched to his chest. At his feet, where the bomb shelter should have been, was a huge, black, steaming crater.

Chapter

20

You can come with me.

Agnes's words ran round and round in Joelle's brain as she wrapped the flannel scarf around her head, tucking the ends carefully into her coat. It was beginning to get dark out; it would be like pitch by the time she got home. Daddy expected her to call for a ride, but she wouldn't do that. She'd walk instead, up the Clark Hill Road, along the East-West Road to the bridge over Crockett's Brook, opposite the LaStrange place. Maybe she'd stand there at the bottom of the LaStrange driveway and stare up at the silver trailer for a while; maybe she'd catch a glimpse of Agnes through the window.

When was Agnes leaving? How would she go? Would she tell the family she was going down to the general store for cigarettes, then never come back? Or wait until everyone was asleep, then creep silently out of the trailer, down the East–West Road? Where would she meet the juggler, and where would they go that first night?

You can come with me.

Joelle locked the shop door behind her and clumped down the steps in her awkward, heavy boots. Outside, long slanting bars of blue-gray light were falling across the snowdrifts as the sun dipped below the horizon and was extinguished like a cigarette dropped into a wet ashtray.

You can come with me.

She could hear Desiree walking just behind her. Unlike her own feet, solidly encased in thick leather-and-rubber boots, Desiree's made no sound and left no prints in the snow. She was barefoot, as always, wearing the same plain white nightgown she'd been buried in. She was the same age and size as Joelle now, but the gown had grown with her, still covering her from her chin to her feet. It was made of thin material, though; Joelle knew Desiree felt bitter cold during the winter months.

Back before Agnes, back when she and Desiree had still been bound more by love than guilt and talked to one another face to face, she had tried to warm her sister's icy body against her own warm flesh. She'd put Desiree's cold hands in her armpits and laid her icy feet against the inside of her thighs. Desiree had felt no warmer, though; not even the heat of summer could touch her.

"I'm cold," she whimpered, over and over. "I'm so cold."

She'd draw closer to Joelle then, wrap her legs around Joelle's body and press against her, breast to breast, so the matching scars were perfectly aligned.

"I'm so cold," she whispered, her grave-scented breath

cold against Joelle's cheek, the chill from her body seeping through her sister's flesh into her bones until there was no warmth left in either of them.

"So cold," she sighed now, trailing Joelle up the steep, slippery shoulder of the Clark Hill Road, her voice thin and chill as the wind coming down off the snow-capped ridge.

When they got to the turnoff for the East-West Road, Joelle felt Desiree's fingers clutch at the cuff of her jacket.

"Wait," she whispered. "Why walk so far in the cold? Daddy will come. Just wait."

She wouldn't, though. The road was nigh pitch-black, only the faintest glimmer of distant starlight against the snow, but she kept walking, walking, with the sound of the wind keening, the rustle of night creatures off among the trees, her sister's whispered pleadings soft in her ears. She kept going until she came to the LaStrange place, then stopped.

"Let's go! Let's go!" Desiree shrilled.

But she wouldn't. Joelle stood in the dark at the bottom of the LaStrange driveway for a long time. She stood in the shadow of rusted cars and unpruned bushes, her eyes fixed on the lighted windows of the trailer, and waited. Out of the corner of her eye she could see Desiree fluttering agitatedly at the side of the road.

"I'm cold! I'm cold!" she whined. "Let's *go!*"

But Joelle paid her no mind and stayed there in the shadows, waiting.

She had no idea what exactly she was waiting for— whether she would be content with a last glimpse of Agnes before she left Esperance forever or whether she intended more, Joelle didn't know. Her father drove by and she pulled back further into the darkness. Desiree rushed out into the road waving her arms frantically in the glare of the headlights; all Dennis saw, though, was a ribbon of mist threading through the beams of his lights, and he kept going.

"You have to go back," Desiree said. "It's his funeral tomorrow. You have to go back."

"Nobody can see you, Desiree," Joelle said. "Nobody at all, except me."

Time crawled by. Bitter cold crept into Joelle's bones, yet she found the sensation strangely pleasant, something close to immortality, standing there in the dark. She felt exhilarated there at the bottom of Agnes's driveway, cloaked by the evening, everything frozen in time and darkness. As long as she remained out here in the night, no one would ever die, nothing would ever change. Cold as she was standing there in the dark outside Agnes's trailer, Joelle had never felt happier, a happiness so huge it swelled within her, threatened to burst her loud as an exploded paper bag. I am alive, she thought, and everyone I love is alive so long as I stay out here.

There were footsteps coming down the road; she drew back further into the shadows. The footsteps grew louder, crunching briskly along the thin patina of snow-dusted ice, as though the walker were trying to stamp his footprint into the road with every step. Joelle held her breath and waited motionlessly for the walker to pass.

The footsteps stopped.

"Waiting for me?"

Joelle peered out at the shadow in the road. Desiree was nowhere to be seen.

"Come out, come out, wherever you are," the walker whispered.

She stepped into the road. He stood there, slapping his arms and stamping his feet, his breath wreathed around his nose and mouth in puffs of fine white mist. The exhilaration inside her grew, spurted suddenly, like a geyser. The man laughed, put a cigarette in his mouth, and lit it. In the brief flare and glow of the match, Joelle thought she saw her brother Daniel standing alive as could be in front of her; after he'd blown out the flame she realized it was the juggler.

"So, are you coming with us?" he asked.

He sounded like Daniel now. In the dark, he could almost be Daniel.

"I'll show you my tattoos," he said, and she could hear the smile that lifted the corners of his mouth in his voice.

"You can dance for me, Joelle."

She wondered how he knew her name.

"I know all about you," he said.

At least three feet of the East-West Road separated them, yet she felt something like a finger tracing across the lines of her cheekbone and jaw.

"You worried about her?" the juggler asked. "Don't be. You know what to do."

Yes, she knew. She'd known what to do about Desiree for years, ever since that day at Aimee Bouchard's house. She'd known all the years she'd secretly cared for Aimee's pig— the price of Aimee's silence. Was that Desiree she saw out of the corner of her eye, trembling in the bushes on the opposite side of the road?

The juggler finished his cigarette and dropped the butt onto the road, grinding it beneath his heel.

"We'll wait for you," he said. "For a little while."

At the beginning of summer the year Daniel turned fifteen and Emily proposed to him on the flat boulder overlooking the quarry, people started noticing something a little strange going on in the woods: small wild animals, badly mauled and torn in ways that did not suggest the usual predators. Folks were puzzled, but not unduly concerned until Emma Pettigrew's cat, Jubal, was found ripped to pieces in a hedge not far from her house. Not long after that, several of Bernie Oliver's chickens were slaughtered, not a hundred yards from Bernie's house. More cats, a dog, and finally one of the Bruxelles' lambs were found savaged in the woods.

At the end of that summer, Daniel killed a strange man who was attacking his sister and rolled his body down the steep shoulder of the ravine on the hill behind the quarry.

A few weeks later, Joelle found herself standing, almost against her will, on the very spot where it had happened. There was no sign now of the circle she'd drawn in the dust for the marbles game, the patch of rust-brown sand where the man's head had rested after Daniel hit him with the rock. She herself had erased the trail left by the man's feet when Daniel dragged him to the edge of the ravine; there was no reason to be suspicious of the broken branches and flattened vegetation along the slope unless you had seen, with your own eyes, a limp, ragged body rolling and sliding down it. A couple of times the body had snagged on something and Daniel had had to go down after it, unhook it, then push it off again.

"Crows are eating his eyes," Desiree whispered in the dark, that night. "Flies and ants are crawling into his nose and mouth. I watched them."

Joelle couldn't sleep after that.

She lay awake in her narrow bed imagining once again how it felt to be dead. Something tickled her ankles under the blanket, spread up her legs and over her thighs to her stomach. It felt like flies or ants crawling over her flesh; she flung the thin flannel cover off her body and rolled over violently.

She felt Desiree's light touch on her back.

"Never leave me," Desiree said, and her breath, cold on

Joelle's cheek, smelled of new-turned earth.

The next morning, Daniel went down to the big house. From her window a while later, Joelle could see a speck that was Daniel and another that must have been Gran Marie, so slowly did it move, come down the back porch steps and climb into Grampa Rich's pickup. She heard the faint, pro-testing snarl of the engine starting up, then the old truck bumped slowly down the driveway to the East-West Road, where it was instantly swallowed in a cloud of thick dust that dragged behind it like a parachute. She waited for him all morning. When he came back, he was even quieter than usual and spent most of the day in his room, writing furi-ously. She could hear the paper crackle and the pencil sharp-ener grind from time to time; once she knocked on his door, but he didn't even bother to tell her to go away. He didn't speak to her at all that day, but that night, when she woke up screaming from the nightmare that would recur again and again over the next few years, he was beside her, cra-dling her in his arms and whispering:

"Shush now, Joli, it's only a dream."

That's what had brought her to the edge of the ravine again. Daniel said it was a dream, but Desiree insisted she'd seen crows perched on the dead man's shoulders, pulling away blood-stiff hanks of hair with little shreds of scalp attached. She'd watched the flies buzz and swarm around his eyes, crawl in and out of his half-open mouth.

Finally, Joelle came to see for herself, but there was noth-ing there. Maybe Daniel was right, she thought; if someone had found the body, they would have heard by now.

"Crows were eating his eyes," Desiree insisted, gripping Joelle's arm tightly with her death-cold hands. "Let's go down and look closer."

There was still nothing at the bottom of the ravine. No trace of flesh or blood, no crushed vegetation; Joelle felt her heart lighten. She wanted to climb back out of the ravine and go home, secure it had all been a dream after all, but Desiree was still holding her arm. "Look," Desiree said, pointing at broken branches and torn grass where something had forced a path through the brambles and bushes clothing the ravine bottom.

Desiree's cold fingers bit into her upper arm and dragged her unwilling into the bushes. Thorns caught at her clothing, left long, stinging welts on the bare flesh of her legs, though Desiree passed through untouched. Someone had passed this way recently; in places the long, tough grass had been torn out of the earth, crumbling lumps of dirt still caught in its roots. Branches hung at crazy angles, the lower twigs and leaves crushed underfoot. Desiree dragged her along this rough path, twigs snapping across Joelle's face, stinging her arms and legs, until they emerged suddenly at a clearer space where there was a shallow mound of freshly turned brown earth.

They stood together, hand in hand, and looked down on the new, unmarked grave. Joelle did not doubt for a minute it was a grave, or that the man Daniel had killed was in it. For a crazy moment she thought about plunging her hands into that crumbling brown dirt, bringing up fistful after fistful until finally she would brush away a last film of earth and see the dead man's face revealed. She would see for herself where the crows had eaten his eyes, know, at last, what it was to lie beneath the ground.

She fell to her knees at one end of the grave, took a handful of dirt, felt the moistness of it as she kneaded it in her closed fist and let it drop in clumps onto the grass beside her. She had even burrowed her other hand into the mound up to her wrist, imagining the feel of the dead man's mouth beneath her fingers, when she heard a shout. A hail of pebbles rained down over her head and shoulders.

Aimee Bouchard was standing on the lip of the ravine. "What the hell are you doing?" she asked.

Aimee made them come back to her house with her.

They walked in heavy silence, Aimee a little in front, she and Desiree behind, up the slope of the mountain. She could feel Aimee looking at her from time to time, but she kept her eyes on the ground in front of her. She was busy making up a story to explain the grave and why she was there. She wondered how much Aimee knew about the body in the ravine, or if indeed she knew anything at all.

A faint pungent odor was in Joelle's nostrils as they trudged up the narrow track to Aimee's ramshackle house. It seemed to waft up from Aimee, a familiar, insistent smell that tickled the edges of her memory until it occurred to Joelle she'd been smelling pig ever since Aimee had found her digging up the grave in the ravine and ordered her to climb out.

She could see the peak of Aimee's roof poking out from behind the fringe of bushes crowning the top of the hill where the house sat. A moment later they were trudging up the narrow track, the house and yard before them. The pigpen was just as Joelle remembered it from years before: a run-down, piecemeal affair of corrugated tin and pine two-by-fours nailed to ancient, listing posts. The pen was empty, of course; Aimee had reported her runaway pig to the police several weeks before, but so far there had been no sign of him. The strong smell of pig clinging to Aimee was unmistakable, however.

When Joelle glanced at Desiree, she saw fear in her sister's face.

"Let's go, let's go!" Desiree whispered in her cold, desperate voice as they reached the bottom step of the back porch.

"You march right up them steps, missy," Aimee said at almost the same moment. "I want to talk to you."

Joelle hesitated on the bottom step. She could feel Desiree's icy hand on her elbow, tugging at her arm. Joelle would've rather been almost anywhere else; she knew she could easily outrun old Aimee. A gnarled and knobby hand prodded her in the small of her back.

"Get up there, now," Aimee said, and she found herself climbing the steps.

At the door, Aimee suddenly turned to Desiree and said:

"There's no place for you here. Be off with you."

She shoved Joelle into the house and shut the door right in Desiree's face. She turned then, looking Joelle over slowly, from head to foot. Finally she said:

"How's that brother of yours?"

Joelle stared mutely, wondering if she could get past quick enough to get through the door without Aimee catching hold of her.

"You still wet yourself when you get scared?" Aimee asked, and laughed like a madwoman when Joelle blushed dark red.

"Thought I'd forgotten, didn't you?" she snorted. "Not me. I never forget anything. C'mon."

She moved away from the door into the kitchen. Desiree's fingers were scratching at the closed door, and Joelle's hand was reaching out to grasp the knob when Aimee called out:

"Leave her! I want to talk to you alone."

Reluctantly Joelle followed her into the kitchen. Aimee was standing in front of the larder door with a tin in her hand. She took a chipped green earthenware plate down from the cupboard, then pulled a handful of hard brown cookies out of the tin and dropped them onto the plate. They looked like the same ones she'd offered Joelle, Daniel, and Emily three years earlier.

"Want one?" Aimee asked, her voice rich with malice.

Joelle shook her head and settled gingerly on the edge of one of the kitchen chairs.

Aimee shrugged and picked up one of the cookies.

"Suit yourself," she said, biting into it fiercely. The cookie shattered under the assault of Aimee's teeth. One half dropped to the floor, where it broke again into three smaller chunks; Joelle could hear the other half grinding between Aimee's molars.

Aimee finished her cookie, picked up another one, then another. She poured herself a glass of milk and washed down a fourth cookie while Joelle sat a little further back in her chair and began to relax a little. "You know who's buried in that grave?" Aimee asked suddenly.

Joelle shook her head, and Aimee laughed.

"No, of course you don't," she said, and laughed some more. "Of course you don't, and like as not it's better that way."

She picked up another cookie and dug her teeth into it.

"Know who killed him?" she asked through the pebble-like crumbs filling her mouth. When Joelle shook her head again, she said:

"Yes, you do. So do I. Rolled the poor fella over the edge of that ravine like a basket of dirty laundry."

She swallowed the last bite of cookie whole and took another swig of milk.

"Who do you s'pose buried the poor bastard?"

"You?" Joelle whispered.

"Me," Aimee said and nodded vigorously. "It weren't

easy, mind you. I'm an old woman and it weren't easy to dig the grave, let alone put him in it. Took me a good part of that afternoon and then some!"

She leaned forward and looked into Joelle's terrified face.

"Don't worry," Aimee said, "I won't tell no one. That's our little secret, just yours an' mine."

There was a rattling at the kitchen window, and Desiree's face appeared. She stood with her bloodless white face framed by the palms of her two hands pressed flat on either side of the glass. Aimee didn't even turn around.

"Leave her," she said, and took the last cookie from the plate.

When she'd finished it, she stood up.

"I got something for you in the other room."

Joelle followed her out of the kitchen into the dim, musty washhouse built onto the back. There was a sink and a hand wringer set up back there, with a clothesline stretched from one end of the room to the other; a worn gray union suit hung forlornly in the far corner, looking as if its owner had vacated it so recently it had not had time to lose its human contours. There was a shelf over the sink, a jumble of cans and bottles lining it. Joelle's eyes wandered over rusted tins of varnish and paint, a rusted, unopened can of putty, and a collection of ammonia bottles until they came to rest on the big pickle jar at the end.

The jar was filled with dark-colored fluid; within it something floated. She felt a spark of recognition, a fleeting millisecond when she knew exactly what was in the jar, and why it was there and what she would one day come to want with it. Then the moment passed.

The old woman jerked her head towards the pickle jar.

"That's for you," she said. "You'll want it one day, I think. Go on, girl! Take a closer look!"

Slowly Joelle moved closer to the shelf until she stood,

with her eyes level with the bottom of the jar. She pulled herself up onto the sink, balanced with her knees on the stone rim, her hands clutching the edge of the shelf. She looked at the mass that hung motionless, suspended in the amber liquid.

There were two things, actually; suddenly Joelle knew what they were.

"Got 'em from him," Aimee said. "Thought of you at the time, and Lord knows he won't need 'em no more, poor bastard."

Joelle couldn't take her eyes from the pickle jar. She felt hypnotized by its contents, as though she would be obliged to spend the rest of her life balancing on the rim of Aimee Bouchard's stone sink, the sharp, cold rim biting into her knees and her fingers aching from having to grip the wooden shelf so hard. Meanwhile, the dead man's heart and liver floated peacefully in a gallon of hard cider.

"I'll keep 'em right here for you, just as long as you want," Aimee said. "It'll be our little secret. There's just one thing you gotta do for me, in exchange."

Behind them, Desiree began to pound a little desperately on the washroom door.

It seemed like days had passed since she'd come to stand at the bottom of Agnes's driveway. The cold crept up through the soles of her boots and into her feet, up through her ankles to her legs, thighs, and stomach, straight through her heart to her brain, until she felt like an ice sculpture standing frozen for all eternity in Agnes LaStrange's driveway.

At last the lights went out in the trailer. Joelle felt her breath quicken a little, the blood stir in her veins again. Something would happen for sure now, she thought.

Time passed, then she heard the snick of a latch being released, caught the gleam of starlight on the metal storm-door as it swung gently open and released a black, shadowed figure.

Agnes came slowly down the driveway until she was exactly abreast of the place where Joelle stood hidden. "I knew you'd come," Agnes said, reaching out both her hands to draw Joelle into her warm and human embrace, kissing her full on the mouth.

Now, where she had felt so cold and frozen before, great waves of heat surged and lapped through her body until she felt she glowed orange as the coils on an electric stove beneath her clothes.

"C'mon," Agnes said, putting her arm around Joelle's shoulders in just the way she had when they were twelve. "We're going to Hollywood."

Joelle hung back.

"I got to do something about her, first," she said. Desiree was, she knew, peering out at them from the trees across the road.

"We'll go together," Agnes told her, and planted another soft, warm kiss on her mouth.

They went down the driveway together, arms tight around each other's waist, and started along the East-West Road, so lost in love Joelle barely heard the soft padding of her sister's dead feet in the snow behind her, or the plaintive cries of "I'm cold! I'm cold!" that followed them all the way into town.

Chapter
21

><

O n his way back up Clark Hill, Dennis saw a figure
trudging along the side of the road. He slowed
down, hoping it was Joelle, but discovered, instead,
his daughter-in-law; he hadn't seen her all day. He pulled
the truck over to the side of the road and waited for her to
catch up.

Emily's face appeared in the passenger-side window, then
the door opened and she slid into the still-cold cab without a
word. Her breath steamed white in the darkness; the climb
uphill had winded her.

"Where you been?" Dennis asked as he pulled slowly out
into the road again.

"The quarry."

It seemed an odd place to go in February; the day before
her husband's funeral, too. But Emily Bishop had always

been a strange girl. He stole a sidelong glance at her profile, saw, as he always did when he looked at her, the unfinished twelve-year-old she'd been when they first met. He remembered well the wiry red hair she'd kept imprisoned in a braid down her back; angular, bony elbows and knees that always seemed to have scabs or ingrained dirt on them; the fierce scowl on the thin, freckled face.

It must be hard for her, he thought. Here, among his family, no one to be on her side. Does she wonder if we blame her? Does she blame herself?

"You mustn't blame yourself, Emmy," Dennis said.

Emily looked out the front of the truck at the sweep of headlights across white banks of snow lining the shoulder of the road. She hadn't eaten anything all day; she was cold, a bleak, nibbling cold that had nothing to do with the weather. No amount of blankets or hot tea or water bottles would make it go off. Just inches away, her father-in-law's breath ballooned out, a white mist that fogged the windshield, crystallized where the air from the heater did not directly blast it. She thought she saw faces in that mist; eyes, a black hole for the mouth. . . . Her own breath spread across the windshield, lending the face in the glass a cloud of white hair.

Blame herself? She realized all at once that she hadn't even been thinking of Daniel, hadn't thought of him, in fact, since she'd left the quarry that morning with Aimee Bouchard.

Aimee Bouchard lived in a ramshackle house up in the woods beyond the quarry. No one in Esperance could remember a time when Aimee hadn't lived there; she and the town might have come into existence simultaneously for all anyone could recall a time before Aimee.

She had always been old, too. Even Gran Marie, who was

over ninety, could not remember Aimee ever being young. She'd been a wrinkled old woman back when Marie's babies were born, when her grandchildren or great-grandchildren needed help into the world, too.

Her nearest neighbor was Ren Fortesque, a good mile away, further down the mountain where the road widened, approximating something a car might have a chance of getting up; by the time it reached Aimee's place, it was little more than a rough cow path.

Relations between Aimee and the Fortesques had never been warm, but they managed to rub along as neighbors tolerably well for the years they'd lived near each other. Aimee had, in fact, delivered Ren ("A breech birth he was," she started telling anyone who would listen, once the pig war had escalated, "and near enough to killing his own mother as made no difference!"), and Ren's father before him. In winter, Ren stopped by every two weeks or so to see she was all right and cut firewood if she needed any. If she needed any repairs done, which was seldom, since Aimee was not what you might call house-proud, Ren came round and did them.

Then, in spring of the year Daniel turned fifteen, Aimee's pig broke into Ren's shed, doing him out of at least thirty-five dollars' worth of chicken feed and new eggs, and all that changed.

People will tell you pigs are smart animals. More intelligent than dogs, certainly brighter than cats; almost human, pig lovers will say.

Aimee Bouchard only had the one pig.

There'd been others, once, years before when old Matthieu, who may or may not have been Aimee's legally wedded husband, was still alive. When he died, though, Aimee sold all but one male pig; that one she named Ernest, and she loved him like a child. There was no smarter, sweeter, handsomer pig in all of Vermont; she'd even taken him to the Townshend Farm Day one year to prove it. The judges had been blind, halt, and half demented, for they'd only awarded Ernest an honorable mention; Aimee never went to another Farm Day thereafter.

"Corruption!" Aimee hissed, anytime the Townshend Farm Day was mentioned in her hearing. "Bribery! Shenanigans!"

So when Ren Fortesque came to her one evening complaining Ernest had raided his shed, Aimee was a little cool.

"Don't know how you can be so sure it was my pig," she said.

"Damn it, Aimee," Ren said, "you got the only pig for miles around here!"

"So, maybe it weren't a pig a'tall."

"I know pig tracks when I see 'em," Ren said, a little grimly. It was common knowledge that Aimee was pretty tight with her cash, but the pig had done considerable damage in the shed, besides eating almost two weeks' worth of feed and three dozen eggs he'd been planning to sell at market.

"You got proof it was *my* pig?" Aimee asked. "You seen him? You got a picture of him breaking into your shed?"

She cackled and added, "Maybe you got one of them hidden cameras like they got in banks out in your chicken coop. You got one o' them, Ren?" she asked, roaring at her own wit.

She was still chuckling when he left a few minutes later, red-faced and frustrated.

"God *damn* that old witch!" he hollered when he got back home, and slammed the screen door behind him.

Marguerite popped out of the kitchen, a pained expression on her face, as though she was suffering from gas. Ever since she'd joined those Evangelicals, he imagined she spent entire days just behind the kitchen door with her ear pressed to the wall, waiting to hear him blaspheme. Then out she'd jump like pop goes the weasel. She didn't say a word now, never did, but he could feel waves of silent reproach breaking against him; he'd taken the Lord's name in vain, again.

"Sorry," he muttered, "but I swear, Marguerite, that woman is the very devil! She won't pay me the thirty-five dollars I asked her for. She says it wasn't her pig."

He dropped into the armchair, sank comfortably into its sagging springs.

"Of course it was her pig!" Marguerite said. "Who else's pig could it be? You oughta call the sheriff, Ren."

"Yeah, maybe," he said, leaning his head against the chair back. He would have liked a beer, but Marguerite wouldn't allow it in the house.

"I wouldn't be surprised if there was more to this than meets the eye," said Marguerite, going back to the kitchen.

Ren remained where he was, longing for beer. Idly, he wondered what his wife meant about there being more to Aimee Bouchard—or did she mean her pig?—than met the eye.

He'd give it a day or two, he decided, then talk to her again. If she still wouldn't see reason, well . . . time enough for the sheriff then. Ren sighed deeply, wriggled his butt further into the sagging seat cushion and closed his eyes.

He was sure everything would work out fine.

The next time Ren went by Aimee's place to talk about restitution, she accused him of trying to sharp an old woman out of what little money she had.

"Some skunk or fox prob'ly done your damage for you," she said, "and now you come sniffin' around here trying to get me to pay for it."

So Ren went and swore out a complaint against her with the sheriff. When Bill Prescott, who had married Jeanette's sister Maude some twenty years earlier, came out to serve the summons, he nearly took the whole exhaust system out of the bottom of his cruiser. The road was so rutted and rock-strewn he'd finally pulled over a quarter of a mile from her house and walked the rest of the way.

The pig was there in the yard when he arrived. Ernest was mottled pink and brown, weighing near two hundred pounds. He moved with the assurance only a pig that has never smelled the blood of its own kind can have. He was wallowing in porcine ecstasy in a dust bath when Bill came up the last bit of road; he rose to meet him, presenting a shoulder for scratching.

"Aimee!" Bill called from the bottom of the back porch.

"Aimee Bouchard!" he yelled again, when there was no answer. "It's Bill Prescott from the sheriff's department. I got a summons for you I got to deliver."

He waited again, while Ernest rooted around behind him, gently nudging the backs of his knees with his snout, testing how much pressure it would take to make him fold. A trickle of sweat ran down between his shoulder blades; he took his hat off once or twice to wipe the perspiration from his forehead. It was a scorching day and he was tempted to go up on the porch, out of the sun, but was deeply conscious of his presence there in an official capacity; taking shelter from the heat on somebody's porch was something a neighbor, not a policeman, might do. She finally came after he'd called her a third time.

"What d'you want?" she asked, a little fretfully. "I was taking a nap."

He knew very well she hadn't been; he'd seen her peering out an upstairs window when he'd come up the road.

"Got a summons to appear in court on the twenty-sixth

of next month," Bill told her. "Matter of Ren Fortesque's shed."

"Had nothin' to do with that, and so I told him," Aimee snapped.

"I don't know nothin' about that," Bill told her. "All I know's you got to appear in the county court in Bennington next month, and here's your summons."

He handed her the paper and started back down the steps. At the bottom he paused and turned. Aimee was still standing in the door, the summons pinched between her thumb and forefinger. She'd delivered him, he thought. She'd taken him form his mother's body and slapped the breath into him; she'd wiped the birth blood from him, cut the cord, and given him his first bath. She'd done the same for Maudie when Bert was born, and he supposed she'd be there when Bert's children came—it was impossible to imagine Aimee could ever end.

He took his hat off, ran the back of his hand across his forehead, and said: "If I was you, Aimee, I'd pay Ren the thirty-five dollars and have done with it. No good can come of going to court."

Aimee made a harsh, derisive sound in her throat. "In a pig's eye!" she said.

The road, more than anything else, accounted for the relative ease with which Aimee managed to bamboozle the sheriff and Ren when the second order concerning her pig came.

When the 26th of July came and there was no sign of Aimee at the county courthouse in Bennington, Bill Prescott drove the cruiser up as far as Ren Fortesque's place, then walked the rest of the way up to her house. There he found Aimee laid on a bed of sickness, complaining of chest pains and dizziness.

When he came through the door into the sitting room, she half sat up from the daybed where she was lying and said:

"So, take me down to the courthouse! It'll kill me, most likely, but mebbe that's what yer hopin' for, you and Ren Fortesque and that dried-up sack of guts he married!"

Even lying down flat in a nightgown, Aimee knew how to get the advantage.

It was convenient, he had to admit, but there was no way he could prove she didn't have pain or dizziness. A crafty thought came into his head.

"I think I'd better take you to the hospital down in Bennington, Aimee," he said. "They can give you a real thorough going-over in no time!"

She didn't even hesitate.

"I didn't like to ask, Bill," she said, "but since you offered, I'd be real glad of the ride. Yer car's right outside, I s'pose?"

She had him, and they both knew it. There was no way he could ask her to walk a mile down the road to his cruiser in the condition she appeared to be in. He considered offering to carry her down but discarded the thought immediately; he was damned if he'd be made a monkey of twice by the old woman. Even if he carried her all the way to the car and got her to the hospital, he wasn't sure she wouldn't be able to bamboozle the doctors there anyway.

"No?" she sighed, drooping back against the cushions. "Well, that's all right," she said in a weak voice. "I s'pose I'll be fine in a day or two, if the good Lord wills it."

He left in a rage; he'd been taken and he knew it. What was worse, old Aimee Bouchard knew he knew and was probably howling in her pillow even as he stumbled back down over the rutted, miserable track that led eventually to the road and his car. Even his parting shot had landed wide of the mark.

"I'll be up to check on you in a day or so," he'd told her, "when I come to deliver the new court date."

"I'll look forward to it," she'd said graciously, holding out her hand.

But the next time Bill came up to the house, the pig was gone.

The day had turned bitter, and a sharp wind was blowing down off the mountain as Aimee and Emily trudged up the narrow track to the house.

"Drink this," Aimee said when she and Emily had rid themselves of their coats. She poured a glass of maple beer and set it down on the table in front of Emily. She had opened the vents on the woodstove as soon as they'd come through the door; now she opened the top and wedged another log into the stove's belly. Warmth began radiating through the room, even touching Emily's frozen feet through her Sorrel boots and two pairs of socks.

"Take your boots off," Aimee said. "You'll warm up faster."

Emily did as she was told, sitting in an old rocker, its back slats bound to the side poles with chickenwire and duct tape. The maple beer had an odd, sweet taste; warmth spread quickly through her veins.

When the stove was going to Aimee's satisfaction, she came to sit in a straight-backed wrought-iron chair that looked as though it had come from an ice cream parlor (as indeed it had) opposite Emily.

"You're Daniel Dufore's bride," she said. "You growed up better'n I remember you."

"I'm surprised you remember me," Emily said. "It was a long time ago. I was twelve."

"You haven't changed overmuch," Aimee told her. "A little taller, a little broader 'cross the beam. Hair's the same, though; prob'ly still all knees and elbows underneath them sweaters."

Silence spun out between them; Emily began imagining the two of them trapped until Judgment Day in a fine web of unasked questions and untold explanations, neither willing to begin the conversation they both knew they'd come here to have.

"You still talk to yourself?" Aimee asked suddenly.

"I beg your pardon?"

"Lord, I remember you walkin' down the road by yerself, talking a mile a minute to all sorts of invisible folks," Aimee said. "You thought there wasn't nobody around to hear you, but you never saw me."

Emily shifted uncomfortably in her chair.

"Every kid plays games," she said.

Emily concentrated fiercely on her glass of maple beer while Aimee kept her eyes unswervingly on Emily's face. The old woman leaned forward in her chair and asked:

"D'you remember my pig Ernest?"

"Sure."

Aimee nodded and leaned back. "Hell of a pig, wasn't he?"

Emily nodded politely.

"Did you ever find him?" she asked.

"Never lost him," Aimee said and made a peculiar sound that might have been a snort or a chuckle. "Kep' him hid in the woods out back beyond the quarry, all those years."

Emily stared at her, unable to think of anything to say. On the day before her husband's funeral, when she had come so far to discover the truth about a man he said he had killed fifteen years before, it seemed ludicrous to be talking about a long-forgotten pig.

"Ernest never done half the things he was accused of," Aimee said. "It weren't him that tore up old Emma Pettigrew's cat. He was ever a peace-loving pig, and mostly vegetarian at that, 'cept when he was especially hungry."

She looked at Emily with eyes extra-bright and knife-sharp.

"I have a story might interest you," she said. "The time Ernest ate meat. Yes, that might interest you considerably."

Emily slid her coat sleeve up off her wrist and glanced at her watch; The wake was at seven o'clock. She looked up to find Aimee smiling maliciously.

"Don't you worry now," she said. "I won't let you miss your own husband's wake. I delivered that boy, remember, and I know what's due him. I know what we owe the dead—better'n most, I can tell you. Better than Daniel Dufore did, that's for sure."

She stood up and moved to a trunk that stood against the far wall. It was old, black, with brass studs that had glowed bright many years before when Aimee was young and concerned with such things. Now it stood neglected, covered with a film of dust that was interrupted only rarely when Aimee needed one of the seldom-used objects she stored inside.

She opened it now, rooted down to the bottom until her fingers found what she was looking for, and she drew up an old khaki-colored jacket, like soldiers wore.

"Belonged to him," Aimee said, and Emily knew she was talking about the dead man.

She sat down in the wrought-iron chair, the jacket laid across her lap. The material was old, moldy, and it had come apart in several places along the seams.

"I took it off him when I found him in the ravine that day."

The stranger showed up one morning shortly after Bill Prescott came to take the pig Ernest into custody and found him gone.

Aimee heard something rattling in the trash bin outside her back door, went to chase off whatever animal was rooting through her garbage, but found a man there, instead. He didn't even look up when she opened the back door, just kept clawing through the trash and stuffing edibles—corn cobs, cabbage leaves, a spoonful of baked beans—into his mouth and the pockets of his worn Army jacket.

"What the hell you doin'?" Aimee asked. She was startled to find a man eating out of her trash can; angry too because she'd been separating her garbage into two containers mentally labeled "fit-for-a-pig" and "other." The man was rapidly depleting the former.

"Get out of that garbage, man!" she yelled when he did not answer her question.

The man paused to brush coffee grounds from a slightly molded bread heel, then crammed it whole into his mouth and continued mulling through Aimee's garbage, chewing on the bread, mouth wide open.

"That food ain't fit for humans," she told him, one worried eye on the fast-emptying bin. "You put that stuff back and come inside. I'll give you a real good meal."

The stranger looked up then, and Aimee, who never forgot a face she'd brought into the world, suffered a shock.

"I thought you was dead," she said, and the man smiled. His mouth stretched wider and wider, revealing teeth that were yellow and brown around the gums. Little gobs of bread still clung to his tongue, and Aimee wondered how his teeth had managed to stand up to the stale crust.

"Best come in, then," she said, standing back to let him pass. He smelled bad—like old blood and mildew, cellar rot and sour milk. He didn't look like he'd bathed in years, and his hair was long and greasy. It had been black when he was younger, she could see, but was salt-and-pepper, now.

She settled him at the table, heated up some baked beans

from the night before, and sliced the rest of the loaf into three thick pieces, which she buttered sparingly and set on the same chipped blue plate as the beans. While he ate she sat across from him, sipping hard cider and considering. Finally she said:

"You plannin' on stayin' around here for long?"

The stranger shrugged.

"You can sleep here, if you like," Aimee said. "You can sleep on the back porch and eat your meals here with me. All I ask is you do one little thing for me."

The stranger said nothing, just picked up the last piece of buttered bread and ran it around the rim of the plate to catch the last of the molasses and brown sugar from the beans. Aimee took that to mean he agreed.

"Good," she said. "You finish up your breakfast and then I'll show you what you have to do."

It had been a good arrangement, all in all; better than she'd expected. It was hard work hauling the bucket of leavings down to the place where she'd hidden Ernest, not too far from the quarry. She wasn't getting any younger, and a two-hundred-pound pig takes considerable feeding.

Now the man was taking care of that, she could stop worrying. In the last few days before the man had come, Aimee had begun imagining Bill Prescott had staked out her house and was watching her, hoping she would lead him to the pig. So convinced of it was she that one day she didn't go down to Ernest at all, but got up at two o'clock in the morning instead and staggered all the way to the hiding place with a double load of slops in the pitch dark, for fear a flashlight might give her away.

For several days after that, she'd taken long, circuitous routes through the woods, approaching Ernest's hiding place from the north, from the east, dragging the bin of slops over rough, broken ground and through thick brush. Sometimes she went in the mornings and sometimes in the evenings; between worry and the weight of the bin, she was on the road to collapsing from sheer exhaustion. Then the man came.

They'd gone down to Ernest's pen after that first meal, and he'd seemed taken with the pig. The first week or so, she'd gone down from time to time to make sure the water was fresh and the food tub full; they always were, so after a time she stopped checking up on the man.

She kind of liked having him around. Not that he talked much; in fact, he barely spoke at all, but that was all right, too, because Aimee had plenty to say. It wasn't long before they fell into a comfortable routine, parting after breakfast to go about their separate lives, coming together again over supper to share a little bit of the evening. Aside from caring for Ernest, Aimee had no idea what the man did with his days; she knew who he was, though, and he knew she knew. After supper, they sometimes shared a smoke and a glass of cider. Then the man went to the back porch, where she'd made him up a bed of sorts, and she retired to the daybed in the parlor.

It was a good arrangement; comfortable, and convenient for both parties. Aimee hoped it would last for a long time.

Then one evening, the man didn't come. It was towards the end of summer, a hot August night, and she'd waited a long time, potato salad and cornbread laid out on the table, cider sparkling in the glasses. She waited until the mosquitoes drove her from the front porch; finally she sat down to supper by herself and found she had no appetite for it after all. So she went to bed, telling herself he'd be there in the morning.

But he wasn't.

"He was takin' care of Ernest for me," Aimee said, stroking the jacket lightly with her gnarled, bony fingers. Aimee looked up with her dagger eyes. "You know who he was? Got any idea?"

When Emily shook her head, Aimee said: "Never mind. Let the dead lie, I always say. Anyway. He was here maybe five, six weeks. I knew who he was; I never forget one as I've delivered, but it weren't none of my business if he didn't want no one to know he was back. He took care of the pig and he didn't get in my way, so I never said nothin'. Then one night, he didn't come back."

She poured more maple beer into her own glass, then took a long pull off it. Emily could see the dark ring on the pinewood floor where the glass had rested. Aimee smacked her lips and set the glass down again; a second ring intersected the first.

"I didn't worry much that first night, but when he didn't come back the next day, I started wondering if Ernest was okay, so I went down that afternoon to check up on him."

She was leaning forward in the chair, her hands lightly clasped and dangling between her old, skinny legs, encased in red wool men's pants.

"He'd busted clean out of his pen, poor bastard, but I followed the tracks, and where, missy, do you suppose I found him?"

"At the quarry?" Emily whispered.

"Yep," Aimee said. "In the ravine. The poor feller was hungry, not havin' been fed for three days or so. Can't blame him for eatin' whatever he could find, now could you?"

In her bones she'd known that first night he didn't come home that he would never come again. In her bones she'd known what she would find when she went looking for him.

Which is why she put off going till two days had passed without any sign of him.

It was the juggler appearing suddenly, swinging up the hill under an Indian-summer sky, whistling, happy to see her after several years' absence, that forced her to leave her house and walk down the path towards the quarry at last. Aimee sat on her porch rocker watching him come, thinking about all the other times he'd passed through Esperance over all the years she'd lived here.

He didn't stop to talk as he sometimes did, just kept walking on up the hill past her house and disappeared into the woods. He waved as he went by, though, letting her know he hadn't forgot her, and she knew then something new was afoot.

If the man was indeed gone, the pig would need feeding. Strangers may come and go, bringing some scrap of comfort to our lives, Aimee thought, taking down her stout walking stick and pulling the thick wool cap she wore summer and winter over her wispy white hair, but pigs are eternal.

The pen was empty when she got there. For one bitter moment she wondered if the stranger had stolen Ernest, perhaps sold him to some slaughterhouse or turned him in to Bill Prescott for a reward. Then she saw how the wire fence at one corner had been beaten down and trampled over— the work of a runaway pig.

She was still afraid for him; how long had he been loose, she wondered? What direction had he gone in, and why hadn't he simply gone home?

There were still faint traces of pig spoor on the ground around the pen. She found one clear imprint in the dirt almost fifty feet further down the hill, leading to the quarry. The pig would be thirsty after three days without water.

She was still a hundred yards from the quarry when she heard the unmistakable sounds of a pig in bliss. Grunts, smacking, sucking, gulping sounds were coming from the ravine that ran up from the quarry for several hundred feet like a wound across the face of the slope. Aimee groaned. If Ernest had got himself down there, it would be the devil's own work to get him out again.

From the steep north shoulder of the ravine Aimee had a clear view of her pig at the bottom. Ernest was plainly visible, and so was what remained of the man. After two nights with the crows and the ants, not to mention Ernest, there wasn't a whole lot left; Aimee was deeply thankful what there was lay sprawled on its face.

Her first thought was, I am too old for this.

Her second was she had to do something about the dead man before someone else found the body and the police started snooping around for evidence. They'd be sure to discover Ernest then.

So she went slowly back up the slope to fetch a shovel from her shed in order to bury the dead man, then spent the afternoon digging a shallow grave in a barren spot in the ravine. Somehow she managed to drag what was left of him a hundred yards through brambles and coarse grass by herself and roll him into the hole. She went back over her tracks, scooping up anything that got left behind—the crows had pulled his entrails out to almost their full length, festooning the bushes with them like party bunting. She used his jacket to gather his innards, then dumped them into the grave with the rest of him. His heart and liver, though, she kept out to lure Ernest up the steep slope of the ravine and back to his secret pen when she was done.

The sun was high overhead, now. She swept the wool cap from her head and used it to mop her face and the back of her neck. Flies were beginning to congregate in the dead man's matted hair. Aimee swore, swatted at them with her hat, then jammed it back on her head and took up the shovel again. Slowly she began covering the body.

It was not until later on the evening of that memorable day when she looked at the two plates laid out on the table waiting for supper to be served that she really understood he was dead.

"Course I felt bad about the feller an' all," Aimee said. "But hell! He was dead an' there weren't much I could do to help him by then, an' there was Ernest to think about. So, I buried him and never told no one."

There isn't much you can say after that, Emily thought. The old woman sitting across from her pulled a rumpled pack of Camel cigarettes out of the pocket of her red wool pants and offered her one. She took it, felt the smoke burn the back of her throat like brandy.

Suppose the man had family, she wanted to ask. Suppose somewhere a woman is waiting—has been waiting for the past fifteen years—for news about her man. Knowing Daniel was dead, finding him in the garage like that, was horrible, but at least she knew. Aimee had said she'd recognized him. If that was so, she'd know his family. She'd never told them.

Well, now she knew: there really had been a dead man in the ravine, and Danny, her Danny, had killed him.

"So now you know," Aimee said, eerily echoing her own thoughts. "Don't change anything, though, now does it?"

Bumping down the East-West Road in her father-in-law's pickup, Emily thought about old Aimee Bouchard living all alone in her little house on the hill behind the quarry. Ernest was dead now, and Aimee was alone. Daniel had told her once that Aimee Bouchard trafficked with the devil. That was why she'd been able to save Joelle, he explained. He thought she had to be at least two hundred years old; Emily wondered if it might be true.

A malicious little wind whistled through a gap in the window, drummed its icy fingers against her exposed cheeks, up the sleeves of the old jacket she wore, and down her collar, winding itself around her neck and shoulders.

So the dead man was real. She wondered now how much of everything else Daniel had written over the years was real, too.

She thought about the last time she'd seen Daniel alive, when they'd lain tumbled across the bed straining together towards a moment outside themselves. She'd opened her eyes, seen his face just inches from her own, black hair fanned across white pillow, his eyes open, too, fixed on her face but as though it were not her he was seeing. She'd watched the change come over him as the wrenching power of sex rushed through his body into hers and she recognized the words he'd been whispering over and over in her ear:

"Buddy please oh please oh Buddy please please please..."

An hour later, he was dead.

Chapter

22

O n the last day of his life, Daniel did something
    unusual. He left his typewriter, stopped writing
    altogether, and made love to his wife.

This was unusual, because Daniel hardly ever stopped
writing. He wrote from the moment he woke till the moment he dropped into exhausted sleep; even in his dreams
words and images, stories and visions ran through his head in
a riot of unformed confusion. Voices shouted in his ear,
whispered from across the room; over and over a man bursts
into flames, plunges into water. A machine tumbles end over
end entwined with its rider. Fish with human faces swim
across his quivering eyelids; he sees himself smash a stranger's
head with a rock, while overhead the bright, metallic shapes
of cats and ducks revolve slowly, slowly. Often he woke in
the middle of the night, such a backlog of stories clamoring

to be told he returned to the typewriter and remained there until he was too tired to go on.

The closet in his workroom overflowed with pages of manuscripts, finished ones neatly bound and neatly stacked on the floor, those still in progress or abandoned altogether stuffed into shoe boxes on top. And still there was a legion of other stories, begging, pleading, commanding to be told. His head filled with them; some had been waiting for years. Once it had been enough to whisper them in Buddy's ear, but now they all wanted to be committed to paper. Once it had been enough to tell their stories one time to have them fade from his mind; now they demanded sequels, trilogies, fourth editions, and miniseries. They crowded his brain, made his skull ache from expanding so much to hold them. The voices of the dead and the not yet born were burying him.

So, on the last day of his life, Daniel turned to Emily, sought a moment's peace in passion-soaked sheets, felt her living flesh against his own, remembered the days when her stories could make him forget his own, thought perhaps this was salvation after all, saw instead the revolving metal ducks in red, cats in blue, and fish in green and yellow.

When she left to pick up the girls, he went down into the basement and found Ab's old hunting rifle. He'd discovered it, half-buried, apparently forgotten, in a corner of the cellar in the old farmhouse, and he took it with him when he married Emily and left Esperance, not knowing then why he'd done so, but knowing now.

He went out to the garage, with its aluminum walls and concrete floor, and squatted there, the rifle barrel pressed against the roof of his mouth. Even then, the ghosts would not leave him alone; ducks and fish turned in lazy, eternal circles, pigs squealed, and he wondered again which pig he had touched that day. A little girl whispered, "I'm cold," and he wondered again which baby lay in the Esperance graveyard. He saw himself, arms raised over his head, a rock in his hands, reflected in the hollow eyes of a wretched madman and wondered again who he'd killed that day at the quarry, whose stories he'd been telling all those years.

His final thoughts were of Buddy.

"Please, Buddy, just leave me alone."

Chapter
23

Nobody had paid much attention to Buddy since Emily brought Daniel's body home. He lay by himself in the back parlor, smoky eyes fixed on the mobile over his bed, recreating the world with every blink of his eyes.

The only person who had much to do with him these days was his grandmother Anne, who, in spite of tragedy and upheaval in the family's life, still remembered to wash him every morning, feed him three times a day, and change the bedpan regularly. Emily came in once or twice; she'd spoken to him that very morning and touched him, but of course he didn't remember, since he had no memory at all. Gran Marie had come in during the night to check him, and his grandfather Rich and Uncle Dennis had passed back and forth through the room, moving chairs out of the parlor into the living room for the wake.

None of them had really looked at Buddy, though; none of them noticed his flesh seemed tauter, shinier, stretched almost, as though he were expanding from within, being blown up like a balloon.

Everything he saw or heard, all the hopes and fears and unspoken dreams of the people around him, the voices of all the dead and the yet unborn, poured into Buddy's receptive brain and wrote themselves on the blank slate of his mind in the millisecond before they were washed away, unremembered, by the relentless onslaught of minutes and hours.

Time was when they had washed out of Buddy's mind into his cousin Daniel's, but that time had passed. Now they eddied and whirled in space, then slopped back into Buddy, causing him to bloat from the backwash of untold stories that had nowhere else to go.

He didn't realize it, of course, but Buddy was in imminent danger of exploding.

Before Aimee left her solitary house to go to Daniel Dufore's wake that evening, these are the preparations she made:

She got out her best plate, a piece of blue bone china with a willow pattern on it she'd bought many years before at a tag sale, and washed it lovingly in warm, soapy water. (Aimee rarely used soap to wash her dishes, preferring instead to simply run them under the tap.) Then she dried it with a clean towel and carefully arranged several of her rocklike homemade gingersnaps in a pleasing pattern of rings within rings within rings, each snap, chosen especially for the uniformity of its size and shape, laid edge to edge.

Next, she straightened up the daybed in the living room. Aimee seldom made her bed, since she knew she'd be getting into it again before long; the evening of Daniel Dufore's wake, however, she not only made the bed, but straightened the doilies on the arms of her horsehair easy chair and even swept up the pile of twigs and cinders that had collected under and around the woodstove.

Last, she wiped off the scarred oak kitchen table with a damp cloth before placing the large pickle jar containing the last mortal remains of the dead man preserved in hard cider in the middle.

She turned the gas lights down low when she left, but not completely out, because she was expecting company to come by while she was gone.

The juggler had told her so.

The table in the Dufore living room was laden with cakes, casseroles, and salads of all descriptions. Each neighbor had brought a covered dish, which was placed on the gleaming walnut table. Green Jell-O with marshmallows, meat loaf, tuna surprise, coffee cake . . . the variety was tremendous.

The room filled with Prescotts, Delagardes, and Devereaux; Angel LaFleur Smith had come down from St. Johnsbury, where she'd moved with her husband some years before, and Maryellen was there from Springfield with both her boys. There were Legeres, Duplessises, Morgans, and Petersons. Ron and Jack Woodie stood at the corner of the room furthest from the parlor where Max's Buddy lay, oblivious to the event beyond his bedroom door.

In one corner Bobby Dufore, who now occupied the basement of the farmhouse, huddled, scrubbed and dressed for the occasion, clutching a plate of creamed corn and hash—the only food he ate, anymore—between his trembling white hands.

Everyone in Esperance, it seemed, had come to Daniel's

wake. They stood about in their church clothes talking in hushed voices, helping themselves to little portions of the food and larger portions of the drink. Emily drifted, soulless, through knots of people she barely knew; Jeanette moved stolidly from kitchen to living room and back, plates and bottles in her hands and November in her face; Dennis stood with his head bent towards whoever was speaking to him at the moment while his heart bled in his eyes.

There was no sign of Joelle.

The only people who did not speak in lowered voices or avoid looking at Daniel's family were Ab's widow, Mary, and Gran Marie. Mary, indeed, was quite cheerful, standing by the table loading her plate with green Jell-O and meat loaf time and time again. She imagined Daniel meeting Ab, his great-grandfather Davy, his cousin Alice, and her boys, bringing them the latest news of the living. She saw Emily across the room, considered going over and telling her that, but then Marguerite Fortesque came in with an angel food cake and Mary forgot about her great-nephew's wife.

Gran Marie sat in her chair at the head of the coffin, hardly aware of the crowd of people in her living room. She was busy rearranging history in her head, groping for some elusive event that might have changed everything, and she had no time for Jell-O or tuna casserole.

Aimee Bouchard came in with a plate of stale gingersnaps. A cold, musty wind seemed to follow Aimee through the doorway, a desolate odor of freshly turned earth and corrupting flesh that filled Marie's nostrils, telling her Aimee had come even before she looked up and saw that wizened old figure in the red wool hunting pants and checked lumberjack coat.

"Well, Marie," Aimee said, taking the seat beside Gran Marie.

Aimee was probably the only person in Esperance older

than Marie, though they were the only ones who remembered it. They sat side by side in silence until at last Aimee sighed deeply and said:

"Who'd have thought it would come to this."

At the end of August, that memorable year Aimee Bouchard's pig disappeared, the thirteenth year of Bobby Dufore's subterranean existence, the year Emily started writing love letters and Rich Dufore had an apocalyptic dream about his grandson Daniel that caused him to take his brother's old rifle out of the locked gun case and hide it in the cellar, the year two sets of two-headed lambs were born, the sky was unusually full of shooting stars and the inhabitants of southern Vermont were treated to an unprecedented three-night show of the northern lights, that summer, Daniel came to his grandmother Marie telling her he'd killed a crazy man at the quarry two days before, then rolled his body into the ravine in a panic.

She went there with him; as they approached the lip of the ravine, Daniel hung back a little and Gran Marie remembered how ever since the day his father shot the deer, Daniel had been unable to look at dead things.

"Stay here and keep a lookout," she told him. She sat herself down on the edge of the ravine, skidded down the steep shoulder, and landed (though she didn't know it) on the exact spot where the crazy man's body had come to a final stop two days before. There was no sign anything had ever rested there. She looked the way she had come, was about to shout up to Daniel to come down and help her out, since the way was far too steep for a woman of nearly eighty to negotiate alone, when she heard the faint and subtle sound of a shovel biting into earth not too far away.

"You find him, Gran?" Daniel called down to her in a tight, childish voice.

"Bide there," she called back, and started to force her way through the tangle of brambles that caught at her polyester pants and twisted themselves around her ankles. I'm too old for this, she thought, remembered suddenly the times she'd made her way down to the pond on just such hot August afternoons, hand in hand with Davy, in the days of her youth.

The sound of heavy breathing accompanied the steady thud of metal against earth; she was through the thickets, confronted by the vision of Aimee Bouchard shoveling dirt over the back of a man's head and shoulders.

The heat was considerable; Aimee had stripped off her shirt and stood clad in stretch pants and a brassiere, the wool cap she wore summer and winter pulled firmly over her ears. Sweat poured down her red face, leaving streaks in the dust that coated her bare arms and chest. Her body was shriveled, emaciated by age, each rib standing out individually beneath the band of her bra, her collarbones clearly visible beneath the thin stretch of dirty, liver-spotted skin. She was breathing heavily and swearing steadily as she lifted shovelful after shovelful of dirt and dumped it onto the rapidly disappearing body of the dead man.

"Damn." Thump.

"Damn." Thump.

"Damn." Thump.

Oaths and falling dirt alternated in a steady rhythm.

She stopped when Gran Marie came through the bushes. The two old women confronted each other across the sprawling grave, the crow-picked body of the dead man. A few feet behind Aimee the pig Ernest nuzzled a rolled-up khaki-green jacket.

"Afternoon, Marie," Aimee said, then turned and swatted Ernest with the handle of the shovel as he seized the jacket in his mouth and began to unroll it.

"Git away from there! Git!" she hissed, and he moved away, grumbling.

"Afternoon," Marie returned. "What you got there?"

"Pretty obvious, ain't it?"

Gran Marie moved a little closer, until she stood with the toes of her black lace-up shoes protruding slightly over the edge of the grave.

"Know who he was?" she asked.

"Maybe," Aimee said. "What're you doin' here?"

"My great-grandson says he killed someone here, a couple of days ago. Most likely this is him."

The two of them stood ruminating over this turn of events for several moments. Then Aimee said:

"Well, what you gonna do about it?"

"I thought your pig had gone missing," Gran Marie said, irrelevantly.

"Found him again," Aimee told her. "You gonna call the police?"

"Reckon it's best," Gran Marie said.

She didn't need to ask why Aimee hadn't done so herself. The presence of the pig, combined with certain signs about his forelegs and snout indicating pretty clearly what he'd been doing with himself in the ravine, gave Marie explanation enough for Aimee's unusual afternoon activity.

"I'm not so sure it is," Aimee told her, a trace of malice in her voice. She jerked her head down at the half-buried body between them.

"You know who he was?" she asked.

She reached down suddenly, grabbed the dead man by the hair, and yanked up with such unexpected strength in a woman so old that the corpse's shoulders and chest were lifted off the ground as well.

"Recognize him?"

Gran Marie looked down at the heat-bloated face. The

left side of his head had been seriously dented by the rock
Daniel had wielded, and insects and vermin had done a
creditable job of wrecking whatever was left of an already
unlovely face. Nevertheless, something in the bones, the
way the thick black hair grew and fell, reminded Marie of
someone. She no longer noticed the ants tracking across his
flesh, or the wounds left by feeding crows, concentrating
instead on trying to reconstruct what had been there before
death. It came to her, all at once.

"I thought he was killed in Korea," Gran Marie said.

Aimee let the body drop back into the grave. "Still want
to call the police?" Aimee asked her.

Gran Marie looked down at the body of Tommy La-
Fleur.

"S'pose not," she said, and left Aimee to finish filling in
the grave.

She beat her way back through coarse grass and thick
overgrowth, calling for Daniel to come down and help her
back up the bank of the ravine.

"Nothing here," she said, when he arrived in a small
landslide of pebbles and dirt. "Mebbe he come to and went
away. Mebbe you just imagined it."

They never spoke of it again.

The wake was over, a success, so far as those things go.
Gran Marie sat in her rocker staring at the bouquet of flowers that had arrived that afternoon, FTD, without any card
to signify who had sent them. Allie, she supposed. She
looked at the coffin beside her, saw her own face reflected in
the sheen of the oak finish. She looked over at the table still
laden with leftovers from Daniel's funeral feast, then at
Daniel's widow, hunch-shouldered at the piano opposite the
casket. Gran Marie looked at her carefully, thinking about
what Aimee Bouchard had said earlier.

"Increasing," she'd said. "A boy, most likely; I know the signs better'n anyone."

Was she? Gran Marie wondered. Did she know? I wonder where she went today and what she found there. Another boy to carry on the Dufore name. She supposed she ought to feel happy, but she only felt tired. How else was she expected to feel at the end of a long and trying day when she hadn't slept in nearly seventy years, anyway?

How could Aimee be so sure?

"Where's Joelle?" Emily asked, when Jeanette and Dennis came in to say good night. They'd never been close, she and Daniel's sister, but they'd both loved Daniel.

"Prob'ly home," Dennis said. "I expect she just couldn't face it."

Once past the Fortesque place, the road leading up to Aimee Bouchard's house was slick with ice. It took Joelle and Agnes the better part of forty minutes groping and skidding over slippery ruts and crusted drifts till they eventually found themselves climbing the lopsided steps leading to Aimee's front door.

"Doesn't look like anybody's home," Joelle whispered after they had knocked and waited, then knocked and waited again.

"Must be," Agnes said. "Lights are on."

They stood at the door awhile longer, shifting from one cold foot to the other. Finally, Agnes stepped over to the front window and peered through.

"Don't see anyone," she said. "Try the door."

"We can't just walk in," Joelle said.

"What else are we gonna do if she isn't here?" Agnes asked. "You do want to go with me, don't you?"

"Yes," Joelle said.

"Then we gotta take care of her, first. Try the door."

Joelle turned the knob, and the door swung soundlessly open. She stood hesitating in the doorway, Agnes whispering "Go on in" in one ear, Desiree sighing "Come home, please" in the other. She felt a firm, flesh-and-bone hand in the small of her back; the next instant Agnes had pushed her over the threshold and the door had swung shut behind both of them.

"Aimee Bouchard?" Joelle called softly. "Are you home?"

But the house had felt empty to her the moment she'd opened the door, and she did not wait for an answer. There was a dim light burning in the gas lamp on the living-room wall, another in the kitchen. Agnes had gone on ahead of her, and she could hear her moving around the other room now.

"Is this it?" Agnes called from the kitchen, and appeared in the doorway with the big pickle jar in her arms.

Joelle nodded. Beyond Agnes's shoulder Joelle could see Aimee's kitchen window and the desperate face of her sister Desiree framed there, palms pressed against the frosted window, and her frantic mouth crying out, just as she had appeared so many years before, the summer Daniel killed the crazy man and the dreams had begun.

"Let's go then," Agnes said.

At the entrance to the graveyard, Joelle suddenly stopped and said:

"The ground will be frozen, and we have no shovel. Even if we did, how could we dig in this?" She kicked at the unresponsive earth with the toe of her boot, a hard knot of frustration in her throat.

They looked at each other while the hope drained out of their eyes; the pickle jar Joelle held in her arms was suddenly weighed down with their own foolish plans.

"I don't care!" Agnes said. "We've come this far. We'll

leave the damned thing on top of the grave if we have to, but we're not giving up now."

She took the jar out of Joelle's arms and started into the graveyard.

"Where is she?" she asked.

"Over there," Joelle said, pointing to a place further up the hill, under a stand of maple trees. "It won't work, though, Agnes, you know it won't."

Agnes didn't say anything, just marched up the hill with the jar clutched to her breast with one arm, Joelle dragging from the other. When they reached the crest of the hill and stood beneath the maple trees, the thin beam of their flashlight shining down onto the grave of Desiree Dufore, they found the grave open and the tiny coffin exposed. Shock rooted them to the ground and fogged their senses so much Joelle barely heard Desiree's thin wail of despair from somewhere behind her; neither of them noticed the juggler standing not too far away, behind the tomb of Obediah Wills.

"Come on," Agnes whispered. She set the jar down and lowered herself gingerly into the grave.

"We've got to get the lid up," she said.

It was a small grave, and cramped when Joelle slid in to squat beside her. Their fingers scrabbled to find the lip of the coffin lid and gain enough of a hold to lift it up.

"There," Agnes said. "Now lift!"

They pulled up hard, but there was no need. After nearly twenty-five years the wood was rotten. The coffin splintered under the assault of their hands and broke apart, exposing a collection of tiny bones, more birdlike than human. A yellowed, moldering substance that might once have been cloth clung to the skeleton—Desiree's burial robe.

Agnes pulled herself out of the grave and held the jar down to Joelle.

"Go on," she said.

She took it into her arms, cradled it like a newborn. The glass felt smooth and cold under her hands; she could hear the gentle slap of cider beneath her palms. Suddenly, she knew an impulse to take the contents of the jar into her hands, hold them for an instant before she placed them amongst the heap of chicken bones at the bottom of the grave.

She unscrewed the cap. An odor of fermented apples rose up from the jar, filling her nostrils and bringing memories of crisp October days and her mother's cider press.

"You can't!" Desiree pleaded in her ear. "I gave my life for you!"

Joelle reached her hand into the icy liquid and felt something solid and heavy knock against her knuckles.

"We've been together so long," Desiree whispered form where she crouched just behind her.

Joelle drew out the fleshy heart, laid it carefully in her lap. A dark stain of cider spread out from under it, penetrating her coat, her clothing, soaked right through to the skin on her thighs and left a cider-colored mark there that no amount of washing would ever cleanse away.

"Please, no," Desiree said. "Things will be different, I promise."

Joelle lifted the liver, cupped it in both hands, so slippery and malleable it was.

"Nobody can love you as I do," Desiree said.

Joelle hesitated, while the liquid from the liver stained her palms the same faint amber color the heart had left on her thighs. In years to come Agnes would often kiss those stains, finding there the taste of love and revenge.

"Hurry up, Joelle," Agnes said from the edge of the grave, and Joelle remembered the heat of Agnes's lips against her own, the dead chill of Desiree which no amount of chafing or holding could ever warm.

She stood up suddenly. The organs in her lap tumbled down into the coffin, landed in the middle of the tiny skeleton, crushing the rib cage with the force of their fall and knocking the baby skull askew so it seemed to watch them, its head cocked in puzzlement.

Agnes reached a hand down and pulled her out of the grave into her human arms.

"That was easy, wasn't it?" she said.

Chapter

24

I n spite of his wife's sour looks, Ren Fortesque offered
Aimee a ride back to her house, and she accepted it,
more out of a desire to spite Marguerite than to avoid
the six-mile walk.

She got out at the Fortesque place and walked the remaining mile to her house, following faint footprints, visible only to her knowing eye, left earlier by Daniel Dufore's
sister and Agnes LaStrange.

Aimee could also see the places where Desiree had skit-
tered over the ice on her cold, dead feet, for Aimee had
delivered that child, too.

They had been uncommonly neat—she approved when
she got home and found nothing disturbed in the house,
only the pickle jar gone from the table where she'd left it. In
a way she'd miss that jar; those few weeks so many years

before, when the man had come to her and they'd eaten supper together every night on the back porch, had been pleasant; the contents of that jar were all she'd had of him in the years since.

I'm old, she thought, conjuring up a bit of pain in her lower back and a pinch of self-pity. She shuffled over to her horsehair easy chair and lowered herself gingerly onto its lumpy, shapeless cushion. Hot tears stung her eyes and she felt strangely pleasured by thoughts of age and a lonely death. She concentrated on the twinges in her lower back until she'd convinced herself she was practically paralyzed by the pain.

Old and alone, she told herself with perverse enjoyment. Nobody cares.

She stayed in the chair for some time, nursing the pain and sadness, until she remembered her favorite blue china plate was still wrapped in her muffler, crumbs clinging to its border. She got up immediately, carried the plate into the kitchen, and washed it again in warm soapy water, then climbed from a chair onto the counter and put it back on the top shelf of her cupboard.

When that was done, she felt much better and went to bed.

Just before she nodded off that night Aimee let her thoughts rest just briefly on the juggler. He'd only passed through Esperance a handful of times since the first time she'd seen him, back in the half-forgotten mists of her girlhood, but she was always prepared for the next visit, no matter how infrequent. She thought about Joelle Dufore and wondered sleepily when the juggler would come again.

Stumbling down the road, gasping for breath, skidding almost out of control, their feet independent of the rest of their clumsy, laboring bodies. Half sobbing from excitement, cold, and terrible,

terrible guilt possessing one and gradually infecting the other.
Taking turns clutching the big glass jar to their chests, its contents
sloshing crazily in a sea of hard cider, beating like waves against
the shore. Laughing in relief and horror when one nearly slips
and drops the jar onto the frozen road. Running, pursued by
ghosts, running down the main road until finally they reach the
place they're going to. . . .

Buddy lay on his daybed in the parlor while the images
flowed through his mind, starting a hundred smiles of wonder on his lips that faded even as the images faded, unmarked
and unremembered. With nowhere to go, they simply settled in his own brain, gathered and rose, the flotsam and
jetsam of other people's lives, while Buddy's head expanded
imperceptibly and what little brain he had began leaking out
his ears onto the pillow.

Emily woke from an uneasy sleep and lay in the tumble
of blankets, her arms supporting her head, eyes fixed on the
dim silhouette of the window.

She'd dreamed again of Daniel, floating in a viscous sea,
curled on his side, one hand tucked beneath his cheek as she'd
often seen him sleep in life. She rolled over onto her side,
felt just the tiniest stirring in her belly, and suddenly wondered if she might be pregnant.

All around her the house creaked and groaned, its old
bones settling and shifting slightly as age and the elements
wore it away bit by bit. This house had stood for nearly two
hundred years, built by Dufores and inhabited by them
down through the generations in spite of hangings, drown-
ings, sudden leaps, and meteors. They'd all thought the name
had finally come to an end with Daniel; Bobby's boys were
dead, and Daniel had fathered only girls.

I expect I am pregnant, Emily decided. In light of all this

house has seen, it would be presumptuous to think one man could end it all by his own hand.

Her hand slid down to her stomach and lay slightly cupped over where the newest Dufore, barely more than a cluster of cells, was setting out in blissful, biological ignorance on its journey towards Esperance and life.

I'll take you away from here, she told the tiny smear of cells in her body. I'll take you to Boston, or Elmira, and raise you there. I'll change your name and keep you safe from meteors, the wind, and the voices of the dead and not yet born. I'll keep you safe; you'll grow up, grow old, and die in your sleep, in your bed, and not in February, she promised, even as the cells in her body divided again, weaving together spontaneous combustion, second sight, and how to breathe under water along with black hair, green eyes, and a host of the other qualities locked in the genetic code Daniel had passed on.

February wind keened through the bare branches of the trees lining the driveway and the East-West Road. The old farmhouse shifted and creaked in response.

Downstairs, in the belly of the house, Bobby Dufore slept curled on his bed of old newspapers, dreaming of Alice and fire in the sky.

Downstairs, in the parlor, Buddy lay staring at the newest ghost who squatted on the floor, a rifle barrel in his mouth, while the voices of the dead and the living and the not yet born filled his head and his brain continued to expand until his skull began to crack under the strain.

Mary Dufore lay smiling in her sleep while Ab came to her in peaceful dreams and made love to her in the full light of a heated afternoon; down the hall, Rich, an old man now, nearly at the end of his life, lay in the grip of uneasy, prophetic dreams, and Anne, still awake, held him in her gentle grasp, tenderly stroking the rough scar on his wrist.

In the cabin on the ridge, Dennis and Jeanette slept the sleep of grief and exhaustion, yet unaware that their one remaining child was, even then, nestled in the front seat of a black station wagon, her head laid against the fox-colored head of Agnes LaStrange, the hand of the tattooed juggler gently stroking her cider-stained thigh as they headed west, to Hollywood at last.

Gran Marie sat, ever vigilant, in the living room of the old house and listened to the wind moan, the house settle around her. She had stayed awake for nearly seventy years; in spite of her care, husbands had died, sons had died, meteors had struck, grandchildren had disappeared.

In spite of her vigilance, the last male in the Dufore line had taken his own life, yet, if Aimee were to be believed, his life would continue, the line would continue for at least another generation.

It don't seem to matter what you do, Marie thought, playing through the various permutations of her life one more time, changing this detail or that one, following these new threads to their hypothetical conclusions. Life just seems to lead you where it wants you to go, by whatever route. She looked at her great-grandson's coffin and laughed. Apparently I stayed awake for seventy years just to see you in your grave, she told the body in the casket.

In the parlor, she heard a faint pop, as though someone had pricked a water balloon with a pin. She considered going in to check up on her other great-grandson, then decided whatever it was could wait until morning, could wait for someone else to discover it; she didn't want to know.

God, I'm tired, she thought.

Marie laid one hand on the brass handle of the gleaming oak casket beside her, laid her head against the high, cushioned back of the rocking chair.

The wind dropped off a little; familiar sounds of shifting beams, stonework settling, the gentle rattle of glass, were loud in Marie's ears.

The sounds of life, she thought, smiling a little as finally, thankfully, Gran Marie closed her eyes.